THE CATHERINE HOWARD CONSPIRACY

The Marquess House Saga
Book One

Alexandra Walsh

SAPERE
BOOKS

THE CATHERINE
HOWARD
CONSPIRACY

Published by Sapere Books.

20 Windermere Drive, Leeds, England, LS17 7UZ,
United Kingdom

saperebooks.com

ISBN: 978-1-913028-25-1

To Mum, Dad, Unc and Freda
Thank you for everything

DRAMATIS PERSONAE

Marquess House

The Woodville Rivers Family:

Dr Perdita Elizabeth Woodville Rivers — Unexpected heiress to a vast fortune

Piper Eleanor Davidson *née* **Woodville Rivers** — Perdita's twin sister, who inherits equally with Perdita

Jeremy Davidson — Piper's husband

Warren Dexter — Perdita's fiancé

Mary Fitzroy — Grandmother of Perdita and Piper. (Deceased)

Louisa Woodville — Daughter of Mary Fitzroy. Mother of Perdita and Piper. (Deceased)

James Rivers — Husband of Louisa. Father of Perdita and Piper. (Deceased)

Cecily Fitzroy — Mary's sister, mother of Randolph Connors

Lettice Hawkland — Ancestor of Perdita and Piper

Bethan Bridges — Childhood friend of Mary Fitzroy. Mother of Sarah Eve. Grandmother of Larry and Billy Eve and Briony and Mark Llewellyn. (Deceased)

The Mackensie Family:

Dr Christopher 'Kit' Mackensie — Works for his family's company, Jerusalem. Lives at Marquess House

Alistair Mackensie — Father of Kit, Stuart and Megan. Husband of Susan. Owner of Jerusalem and integral to the running of Marquess House

Susan Mackensie — Mother of Kit, Stuart and Megan. Wife of Alistair. Integral to the running of Marquess House

Stuart Mackensie — Middle Mackensie child. Works for Jerusalem. Lives in New York

Megan Mackensie — Eldest Mackensie child. Runs Jerusalem from the family home in Andorra

Pablo De León — Megan's fiancé. Works for the Andorran government

Lydia Brooks — Kit's girlfriend

The Dig:

Dr Olaf Dade — Colleague of Perdita's

Professor Maggie Cartwright — Running the archaeological dig where Perdita is working

The Marquess House Team:

Jenny Procter — Chief Librarian and Archivist at Marquess House. Distant cousin of Alistair

Izabel Barnes — Jenny's granddaughter and her assistant

Sarah Eve — Head of Catering and Events at Marquess House. Godmother of Perdita and Piper

Alan Eve — Sarah's husband. Former Head of Security, now semi-retired

Billy Eve — Eldest son of Sarah and Alan. In charge of building maintenance and architecture at Marquess House. Cousin of Mark and Briony Llewellyn

Larry Eve — Younger son of Sarah and Alan. Head of Security, referring to his father while he learns the job. Cousin of Mark and Briony Llewellyn

Mark Llewellyn — Works at The Dairy. Engaged to Izabel Barnes. Elder brother of Briony. Cousin to Billy and Larry Eve

Briony Llewellyn — runs the Louisa Woodville Trust, the animal sanctuary based at Home Farm, the childhood home of Perdita and Piper. Cousin to Billy and Larry Eve

Elliot Black — Eldest son of Deborah Black. Pilot of the Jerusalem planes

Samantha Carver (Sam) — Wife of Elliot Black. Pilot of the Jerusalem planes

The Connors Family:

Randolph Connors — Son of Mary Fitzroy's sister, Cecily Connors, and father of Xavier Connors

Lady Marianne Connors *née* **O'Rourke** — Estranged wife of Randolph Connors and mother of Xavier Connors

Xavier Connors — Son of Randolph and Marianne Connors. Second cousin to Perdita and Piper. Father of Ruby and Pearl Connors

Amber Connors *née* **Prust** — Xavier's wife. Mother of Ruby and Pearl Connors

Ruby Connors — Elder twin. Daughter of Xavier and Amber Connors

Pearl Connors — Younger twin by half an hour. Daughter of Xavier and Amber Connors

Other Characters:

Kirstin Chaplin — Girlfriend of Jeremy Davidson

Stephen Haberfield — A Watcher

Morton Keller — A former Watcher

Inigo Westbury — Head of MI1 Elite

Rory Hughes — Perdita's ex-fiancé

Jason — Friend of Kit

Nathan — Friend of Kit

The Tudor Court

Henry VIII — King. Famous for his tangled love life

Anne of Cleves — Fourth wife of Henry VIII. A foreign princess

Catherine Howard — Fifth wife of Henry VIII. A scared teenager

Katheryn Parr — Sixth wife of Henry VIII. A respectable widow

Princess Mary — Daughter of Henry VIII and Katherine of Aragon

Princess Elizabeth — Daughter of Henry VIII and Anne Boleyn

Prince Edward — Son of Henry VIII and Jane Seymour

Lady Margaret Douglas — Niece of Henry VIII. Daughter of his elder sister, Margaret Tudor

Catherine Howard's Family:

Lord Edmund Howard — Catherine's father. (Deceased)

Jocasta Culpepper — Catherine's mother. (Deceased)

Thomas Howard, Duke of Norfolk — Catherine's uncle

Lady Isabel Baynton — Catherine's half-sister. Wife of Sir Edward Baynton

Sir Edward Baynton — married to Isabel. Vice-chamberlain to Anne of Cleves

Charles Howard — Catherine's brother

George Howard — Catherine's brother

Lady Margaret Arundell, *née* Howard — Catherine's sister

Lord William Howard — Catherine's uncle. Scottish envoy for Henry VIII

Agnes Tilney, dowager Duchess of Norfolk — Catherine's step-grandmother

Catherine Howard's Court:

Kathryn Carey — Daughter of Mary Boleyn. Wife of Sir Francis Knollys

Sir Francis Knollys — Husband of Kathryn Carey

Jane (Parker) Boleyn, Viscountess Rochford — Widow of George Boleyn

Thomas Culpepper — Catherine Howard's cousin

Katherine Tilney — Lady-in-waiting to Catherine Howard. A distant cousin

Joan Bulmer — Lady-in-waiting to Catherine Howard

Katherine Willoughby, Duchess of Suffolk — Married to Charles Brandon. Lady-in-waiting to Catherine Howard

Eleanor Paston, countess of Rutland — Lady-in-waiting to Catherine Howard

Francis Dereham — Catherine Howard's secretary

Courtiers and Other Characters:

Mother Superior — Llyn Cel convent

Charles Brandon, Duke of Suffolk — Widower of Mary Tudor, Henry's sister. Best friend of the king. Married to Katherine Willoughby, Duchess of Suffolk

Thomas Cromwell, Earl of Essex — Right-hand man of Henry VIII

Thomas Cranmer, Archbishop of Canterbury — Protestant cleric who helped Henry solve his marriage problems

William Fitzwilliam, Earl of Southampton — Lord Privy Seal, replaced Thomas Cromwell

Elizabeth Seymour — Daughter of John and Margery Seymour. Married three times: Sir Anthony Ughtred, Gregory Cromwell, 1st Baron Cromwell and John Paulet, 2nd Marquess of Winchester

Gregory Cromwell — Son of Thomas Cromwell. Husband of Elizabeth (Bess) Seymour

Brunhilde — Lady-in-waiting to Anne of Cleves

Edward Seymour, Earl of Hertford — Brother of Jane Seymour, Henry's third wife. Uncle of Prince Edward

Edward Bonner, the bishop of London — Officiates at the wedding of Catherine Howard and Henry VIII

Maud Page — A young girl eager to meet the king

Helen Page of Lyndesey — Maud's mother

Joshua Page of Lyndesey — Maud's father

Prologue: Pembrokeshire, 1542

"Is there news?" asked the man as the shadowy figure of the Abbess appeared in the doorway.

"She bleeds heavily. We may not be able to save her."

"And the child?"

"You must pray, sir, pray as you have never prayed before."

The man bowed as the elderly nun glided from the room on silent feet. It had been this way for hours. He did not see how she could continue: his beloved niece, the culmination of his family's hopes and dreams, whom he had betrayed, selling her into a cursed marriage as though she were horseflesh.

How, he thought as the hours passed and self-pity, fear and weariness overwhelmed him, has it come to this? Waiting in such a godforsaken place while she fights for her life in childbirth. He swore vehemently to himself, staring out of the window as another bleak, cold day dawned. The sky was heavy and bloated with the threat of more snow; the frost glistened like poison on the rutted track leading away from the tiny priory. Then he heard a step behind him.

A tall, imposing young man wrapped in a travelling cloak, entered the room. His presence filled the gloomy space with an intense glamour. Even though his cloak had been designed to disguise his status, it was still made from a thick, sumptuous wool and his boots glistened oxblood red. To his side was a sword and in his belt a sheathed dagger. Incongruously, he cradled a newborn baby in his arms, his serious expression softening as his tiny charge gurgled.

"Well?" demanded the older man.

"A girl," replied the younger, handing his small charge into his companion's arms, *"and a boy. Twins."*

"Twins?" the older man exclaimed. *"And…?"*

He could not bear to say his niece's name.

"Weak but alive, as is the boy-child. This little one, though, she's a fighter," he said, a boyish grin lighting his handsome features.

"Charles, you mustn't become attached to the child," said the older man. "We have no choice but to see this through. If we don't, you know the consequences."

Charles nodded, even though it was clear from his expression that he was apprehensive about their plans.

The baby gurgled and the older man looked down at his great-niece. His breath caught in his throat as her brilliant blue eyes, still unable to focus, glanced towards him. Her tiny hand came free from its wrapping and waved towards his face. Instinctively, he reached out and her minute, perfect fingers gripped his thumb. She stared at him for a fraction of a moment and as his heart contracted with love, a name floated unbidden to his lips.

"Elizabeth," he whispered, and then in a tender voice, almost unrecognisable as his own, "you have your mother's hair."

A sharp knock on the door caused all three to start. Covering the space in two strides, Charles threw it open to reveal a slender young woman. Stepping back to admit her, she gave him a small smile then hurried forward, bobbing to the older man.

"She is comfortable, as is the boy. If they make it through this day, then there is a chance." Her voice was low, determined. "Mother Abbess has informed me that the horses and the litter are ready, sir."

The older man nodded.

"Take her, Charles," he said, thrusting the baby back into the arms of his conspirator. "Take her and flee. The future of our very nation relies upon her safe passage."

Charles gathered the baby into his cloak.

"Until we meet again, sir," he said. The men clasped hands.

"Until that day, Charles, may God's grace go with you."

PART ONE: Pembrokeshire, 2018

Chapter One

Sunlight glinted on the waves as Dr Perdita Rivers perched on the edge of the dinghy.

"Ready?" shouted one of her two companions. She gave him a thumbs up. "Go!"

Tipping gracefully backwards, Perdita disappeared into the shimmering depths of the Welsh sea. Spreading out below the dinghy lay one of the dig sites she was exploring. It was part of an extensive archaeological investigation taking place along the Pembrokeshire coastline.

As she swam down, she saw other divers picking over the remains of a recently discovered Tudor shipwreck. A storm and unusual spring tides had uncovered it and the team was trying to establish whether the boat had been part of the Spanish Armada; blown off course and lost in a storm on the Pembrokeshire coast hundreds of years ago. On land, a hoard of coins, weapons and jewellery had been discovered, and it was hoped the two would prove to be connected.

Kicking hard, Perdita swam towards the gathered archaeologists and glided to a stop beside the underwater team leader, Dr Olaf Dade, a man she had worked with many times. He gave her the thumbs up sign, then pointed to the section they were trying to excavate. If she had not been wearing breathing apparatus, she would have laughed. The box they were painstakingly extricating looked like a miniature treasure chest, the kind beloved of pirate films and adventure stories where X always marks the spot. *Too perfect*, she thought, *a romantic Tudor shipwreck complete with buried treasure.*

She returned the thumbs up sign and swam nearer. Perdita specialised in jewellery and its symbolism. Her preferred area of expertise was the Mediaeval period, but she had written papers covering the topic up until the Restoration in the 1660s. While underwater digs were not her usual way of working, she understood why Olaf had asked her to join them: seeing the discovery in situ would be invaluable when she began analysing whatever might be inside.

The panels of broken up wood around the box suggested this would have been the captain's cabin, with the small chest secreted in a cupboard. Perdita also mentally noted the rotted remains of another, less robust, wooden container nearby. Then something glinted, a chink of gold caught by one of the underwater lights.

Touching Dr Dade's arm, she pointed towards the glimmer. He shone a powerful beam towards it and the treasure shimmered once more. Perdita hung back, allowing her colleague to investigate. After a few moments of careful digging, she saw him pull something from the swirling sand and rotting wood. He rubbed it clean then swam towards her, his excitement palpable, and shoved the golden coin into her hand. Turning it over, Perdita grinned — nestled in her gloved palm was a Spanish doubloon. She handed the coin back to Olaf before giving him a double thumbs up. Finding the coin did not mean the ship was Spanish — it could have been an English ship with a pirate haul on board — but at least it gave them dateable evidence. Coupled with whatever was in the treasure chest, if there was anything, this could prove they had discovered an important new site.

Perdita felt a buzz on her wrist. The timer on her watch, she had to surface. Giving a final thumbs up to Olaf, she rose slowly, her head gently breaking through the rippling waves, already working out what she would record in the report of her dive. If this was a lost ship from the Spanish Armada, it could give them information on what had happened to the fleet when it fled, their battle lost, their only wish to find a way home. It could, perhaps, even answer the question as to whether any survivors found their way ashore. The hoard on land suggested this was certainly a hypothesis that had to be more thoroughly explored.

She yelled to the dive boat and swam towards the ladder at the back, hauling herself onto the small rear platform, allowing the team to unbuckle her breathing equipment before freeing herself from her wetsuit hood. It was only as she finished shaking her head to free her cloud of dark, shining hair, that she realised there was another boat moored alongside. Climbing up to the main deck, she started in surprise. Her fiancé, Warren Dexter, was talking earnestly to Maggie Cartwright, the other dig leader.

"Warren!" exclaimed Perdita, walking towards him and slipping her wetsuit from her shoulders as she went. "What's happened? What are you doing here?"

She felt cold fear flood through her. Warren should have been in Peterborough giving a lecture. If he was here, it had to be an emergency.

"Is it Piper?" she asked, feeling sick at the thought. "Has something happened to my sister?"

"No, darling, no," said Warren, hurrying to her side and throwing a towel around her shoulders. "Piper's fine. We can tell her when she wakes up, the time difference…"

"Tell her what?" interrupted Perdita. "Warren, what's happened?"

Aware she was overreacting, Perdita took a deep breath, trying to calm her nerves. Her father's recent death from a rare form of cancer called soft tissue sarcoma was still fresh in her mind. Despite the best care, he had deteriorated quickly, dying only months after his diagnosis. Now she was braced for more terrible news.

"It's Mary," said Warren, "Mary Fitzroy, your grandmother." Perdita guessed what was coming next. "She died last night. Her housekeeper found her body this morning. I'm so sorry, Perdita."

"How did she die? Does anyone know?"

Warren shook his head. "There's going to be a post-mortem, but she was eighty-six…"

Perdita turned away, tears welling unexpectedly in her unusual storm-coloured eyes, as she felt despair wash through her and she mourned another loss.

The next morning, Perdita lay cocooned in her warm sheets. She had been at the dig for a week and was scheduled to stay for two more. Until now, she had been alone in her hotel room, but a smile crept over her face as she listened to the shower gushing over Warren's body in the en suite bathroom. For a moment, her mind wandered to her fiancé: tall, athletic, tanned and, despite her shock and grief, she felt a flutter of lust. However, it quickly sparked and fizzled away as the death of her grandmother, Mary Fitzroy, once more clouded her thoughts. Part of her wondered why she felt such bleak, dark grief at the loss of someone whom she had only ever known from afar. Yet, she was astute enough to understand it was not only the demise of the woman she was grieving, but also the end of a dream.

Rolling over, she pondered the situation. After the death of her mother, Louisa, the only daughter of Mary Fitzroy, her grandmother had disappeared from their lives. Perdita and her twin sister, Piper, had been seven years old and, from then on, had been brought up by their father, the respected artist, James Rivers. When they were old enough to ask for more details, James had dropped hints at a family argument, Mary's stubbornness and her refusal to back down. On what point she would not be budged, James had never illuminated his daughters. He became so angry whenever they asked. Eventually, they admitted defeat, instead trawling the internet and reading their illustrious grandmother's books as a way to try to bring her into their lives.

Over the years, the twins had discussed their grandmother, desperate to remember anything about their lives before their mother died. Now, Perdita screwed her eyes tight shut, searching her memories. Their father had once let slip the name of the village where they had lived, St Ishmaels, and the twins had taken this hidden treasure and stored it in their hearts. Apart from that, all she and Piper had ever been able to recall was the name of their old home, Air House, which was a farmhouse in the Pembrokeshire countryside.

Perdita knew it must have been near her grandmother's home, but she could not recall the house clearly. She remembered visiting a stately home with Mary on what must have been a day trip, but the images were fleeting and vague. All she had ever been able to glean from her research was that her grandmother had still lived in Pembrokeshire, as they had once.

Sitting up, Perdita reached for her laptop and tapped her grandmother's name into the search engine, suddenly wanting to see a photograph of the woman who had hovered beyond her reach and was now lost to her forever. A black and white image from the inside cover of her last book popped up and Perdita felt a wrench somewhere in the region of her solar plexus, then she noticed a link to an obituary and, taking a deep breath, she clicked on it and began to read:

Eminent historian Mary Fitzroy died at her home last night, aged 86, wife to businessman Hector Woodville (deceased) and mother to Louisa (deceased). The eldest daughter of David and Eleanor Fitzroy and sister to Cecily (deceased), Fitzroy was known for her championing of women's rights and of bringing women's roles in history to the fore. Her first book The History and Symbolism of Names *was published in 1955. It received praise but it was not until 1958 when she wrote* The Scottish Link: A Study of the Trade and Personal Links between the Tudor and Stuart Courts *that she was recognised as a fresh, new historical voice with some gravitas. From then on, her work focused on the women connected with the Tudor and Stuart dynasties:* The Winter Queen: Elizabeth of Bohemia — The Forgotten Stuart Princess *(1963);* Women in Power: The Degradation of Female Autonomy from the Time of the Conquest to the Tudor Court *(1966);* Catherine de Valois: Tudor Matriarch *(1972) and* The Anne Boleyn Question *(1985).*

However, after the publication of her controversial book The Missing Heirs of Henry VIII, *discussing not only his many illegitimate offspring, but also the many legitimate pregnancies and the few children who died shortly after their births, notably Anne Boleyn's pregnancies, her only child, Louisa Woodville, died, aged 34, and the pen of Mary Fitzroy was silenced for many years. She was not to publish again until 1999, when her area of focus had shifted from the tumultuous courts of the Tudors and Stuarts to pre- and post-Conquest royal women. Her most notable work was a biography of Alfred the Great's daughter* Aethelflaed, Lady of the Mercian's: Warrior Queen *(1999), which was followed in 2010 by* Edith Swanneck: Wife or Concubine? A Study of King Harold's Handfasted Bride *and, earlier this year, with the groundbreaking biography of King Harold and*

Edith's daughters — Gunhild and Gytha of Wessex: Royal Sisters.

Mary Fitzroy was also known for her philanthropy and...

Perdita scanned to the end of the obituary where it listed the many charities Mary had helped, the scholarships she had created and the work she and her late husband, Hector, had done with an historical trust called Jerusalem, but there was no mention of either her or Piper.

"It's as if we don't exist," murmured Perdita.

Even in death, she and Piper remained unacknowledged in their grandmother's life. Sighing, she shut the laptop. Had she really expected their names to be mentioned? Very few people knew they were related to Mary Fitzroy.

She kicked off the covers, pulled on a robe and, walking over to the dressing table, began to brush out her thick, glossy hair. Although she had not discussed it with anyone, not even Piper, she had been formulating a plan to visit her grandmother. When she had been invited to take part in the dig in Dale, only a few miles from where she hoped her grandmother still lived in St Ishmaels, she had felt the Fates were guiding her and, somehow, whether contrived or by the strange powers of coincidence, she and her grandmother would finally be happily reunited. Mary's death meant this daydream would never be fulfilled.

The bathroom door clicked open and Warren emerged, a towel around his hips, rubbing his blonde hair dry with another. He dropped a kiss on the top of Perdita's head as he passed her. She smiled. "It's all yours," he said. "I'll wander down and grab a newspaper when I'm dressed. Meet you downstairs for breakfast."

"OK," said Perdita as she walked into the bathroom.

Forty minutes later, Perdita slid into the seat opposite Warren.

"Anything interesting?" she asked, nodding to the broadsheet neatly folded in front of him so he could fill in the crossword on the back.

"Not much," he said. "Although, there is an obituary of your grandmother."

Perdita felt her heart contract and said lightly, trying to mask any disappointment: "Does it mention Piper and me?"

Warren reached across the table and squeezed her hand.

"I'm sorry, darling, no," he said, his voice gentle. "Would you like to read it?"

Perdita shook her head. "No, I read an obituary earlier, they're probably all the same."

Ignoring both the proffered newspaper and Warren's curious look, she pulled the menu towards her, dropping her head so he could not see the tears filling her eyes.

She found it difficult to explain her emotions to Warren. The obituary would, no doubt, eulogise Mary Fitzroy's brilliance and her outstanding work as an historian, presenting her life as a list of scholarly achievements, interspersed with some personal details to give readers a sense of the woman behind the achievements. Yet, these comments about Mary's family represented the most painful parts of Perdita's life. Reading one obituary had been enough, she did not want to read any more.

Blinking away her tears, she scolded herself: *pull yourself together*, she thought, *Mary showed no interest in you while she was alive, why would you or Piper be mentioned in her obituary?*

She had finished eating and was pouring coffee when the manager interrupted them. He seemed agitated as he handed her a thick cream envelope.

"Dr Rivers, a message has arrived for you," he said. "A courier is waiting if you wish to send a reply. I'll be happy to relay any answer."

"Er — thank you," said Perdita, surprised. "I'll let you know if there's a response."

The manager nodded and retreated. Perdita turned to Warren, her eyebrows raised in confusion. "What the…?"

"Open it," urged Warren, who seemed suddenly nervous. "It's probably from the University asking if they need to send a replacement."

"Unlikely," said Perdita. "No one I work with knows about my connections to Mary Fitzroy. Anyway, they'd have emailed, not gone to the expense of a courier."

She slit open the envelope and unfolded an expensive, heavyweight sheet of headed writing paper. In one corner was a small and unusual emblem of a portcullis surrounded by a repeating pattern of tiny swords, interwoven with a plant Perdita did not recognise. The motto underneath was in Latin: *Ecce signum!* and across the top, the word *Jerusalem*.

"Behold the proof!" she murmured, translating the motto. Across the table, Warren stiffened slightly, waiting while Perdita read the letter. White-faced she looked up from the short note and handed it to him.

"Read it," she said, her voice hoarse.

"Tell me first, what's happened?"

"It's from Mary Fitzroy's solicitor, he's requested a meeting of the utmost urgency and has suggested today at 11 a.m."

"What?" said Warren. "Where?"

"Marquess House, Mary's estate in Pembrokeshire. It's not far from here," she replied.

He looked at her in confusion. "This morning…?"

Perdita nodded. "Am I being paranoid?" she whispered. "Or is there something strange happening?"

"What do you mean?"

"I live in London and, in theory, have no connection to Mary," she said. "How do they know about me and, more importantly, how the hell do they know I'm here?"

Warren squeezed her hand.

"There are lots of ways they could know you're here," he said calmly.

"How?"

"The news of the dig has been in the local paper," he continued. "As one of the more senior members of the team and a known expert in the symbolism of jewellery, your name was mentioned…"

"But why have her solicitors been keeping tabs on me?"

Warren took the letter from her and smoothed it out on the table. "Do you see this?" He pointed to the emblem in the corner and Perdita nodded. "Jerusalem is a historical trust that funds archaeological digs, particularly in this area. Perhaps they were financing yours and, if your grandmother's solicitors are affiliated to them, it's likely your grandmother was aware of which projects they were involved with this summer. It could have been your grandmother who was keeping an eye on you, not the legal firm, and now with her sudden death, you are fortuitously in the right place for the solicitors to contact you quickly." Perdita was unconvinced and beginning to marshal counterarguments, when he added with a final flourish: "It's a village, Perds, it isn't London, people know each other's business."

Looking into his calm, grey eyes, she sighed. She knew he was trying to offer a rational explanation and, now he had put it so bluntly, she agreed with the assessment of how the solicitors knew her whereabouts. It did not stop the powerful sense of pain that had shot through her at the thought that her grandmother might have been monitoring her. Mary may have been aware of her proximity, but she had still made no attempt to contact her. This was why she was reacting so skittishly to the letter: after a lifetime of being ignored by Mary Fitzroy, it felt strangely sinister to be contacted by her solicitor the moment her grandmother had died. It was unlikely she and Piper had been remembered in her will, so for what possible reason had she been summoned to Marquess House?

"Will you go?" Warren's voice floated across her teeming brain, bringing her back to the present and the sunny dining room.

"Yes," said Perdita, tight-lipped but determined. She glanced at her watch, then pushed away her unfinished cup of coffee. "I'll tell the manager to let them know we're coming."

In a swift, elegant movement, she stood and walked from the room. The manager was hovering behind the reception desk.

"Ah, Dr Rivers…"

"Tell them, I'll be there at 11 a.m.," she said, then ran up the stairs to her room. Piper was in Austin, Texas, so she was six hours behind them and still asleep. Taking a deep breath, Perdita walked to the window and looked out over the landscaped gardens, breathing deeply to steady her nerves. When the door clicked open, she did not turn, knowing Warren would come to her and encircle her in his arms as he had done so many times before when the strangeness of her family situation had shaken her to the core.

"Whatever they say, whatever they do, you don't have to stay or listen to anything that might upset you," he said, his arms around her waist, his head resting next to hers.

"I know," she said, her voice hoarse with tears. "But you understand, don't you? I have to know, to see…"

She felt rather than saw him nod. "Of course," he said. "I'll drive us there."

Perdita stared out of the car window, barely noticing the beauty of the Pembrokeshire countryside as it moved into the full bloom of summer. Hedgerows billowed in the breeze, the grass and flowers brushing against Warren's Audi as he weaved them down the winding lanes.

"Do you remember it? Your old home in Pembrokeshire?" asked Warren.

Perdita shrugged. "Bits," she said. "Our home was called Air House. There were stables, I think, and chickens. We had a dog called Copper. She came with us to Chiswick."

"And your grandmother's house? Was it nearby?"

"I don't recall," she murmured. Her eyes once more drifted to the scenery as she contemplated this unexpected summons to confront her past.

From hints her father had dropped, she knew her grandmother was wealthy, but she assumed this had come from her writing and from her grandfather, Hector Woodville, who had been a businessman and had died before she and Piper were born.

Perhaps, she thought, as they turned off down even narrower lanes, *her grandmother had left her and Piper something that had once belonged to their mother.* A book; a piece of jewellery? Or, a small voice said, perhaps they are warning you off and making it clear you have no claim on the estate, despite the fact you and Piper are Mary's only living relatives. *That's more likely*, she thought.

"Not far now," said Warren. Perdita glanced at the satnav screen that indicated they were only three minutes away. "You OK?"

"No," said Perdita and managed a rueful laugh. "I might be sick."

"It would certainly be a memorable entrance," he replied.

"Definitely."

They took a tight left turn and the satnav announced they had reached their destination. Warren raised his eyebrows and crept slowly down the tiny lane. It curled around to the right and a pair of magnificent wrought iron gates that were fastened open greeted them. On one of the posts was a polished slate plaque that read: *Marquess House*. Perdita stifled a giggle.

"How many miles to get up the drive to the front door?" she grinned.

"Ten, at least!"

Her laughter was a mixture of wonder and hysteria. *Get it together*, she told herself, gripping the door handle until her knuckles were white. Then they rounded the corner and Perdita gasped.

Marquess House was magnificent. The endless windows glittered like diamonds in the early summer sunshine. At the heart was an old square castle tower from which the rest of the house had flowered. The majority of the building was Tudor with a timbered central structure and winding red brick chimneys reaching endlessly towards the sky. The crenellations that topped the house mirrored the old tower. Down the east side was what appeared to be a Jacobean wing and glimmering to the west was a Victorian addition with dramatic gothic arches. Marquess House stood huge and imposing on a slope, the vast mullioned windows facing a lake that spread away from the house towards the sea.

"Oh my goodness..." whispered Perdita.

"What?" asked Warren.

"The only clear memory Piper and I have of Mary is being taken by her to a stately home," she said. "I thought she'd taken us on a day out, but this was the place, I'm sure of it." Fishing her phone from her pocket, she took a rapid succession of shots. "Piper is never going to believe this! It was her home."

Warren gazed at her. "Are you sure you want to do this?"

"Yes, and having you here makes it easier." She smiled at him. "You really are remarkable, dropping everything to drive down here to support me."

"I love you," he said. "Your happiness and well-being are more important to me than my own."

She reached up to kiss him as a small ripple of happiness ran through her, giving her confidence. Until she had met Warren, she had never understood what it was like to feel unconditional love. Her ex-fiancé had been a kind man, but Warren had swept into her life like a chivalric knight of old and she had not needed much persuasion to end her engagement to placid, safe Rory.

"I love you too," she said. "Now, let's go and see what this man —" she checked the name on the bottom of the letter — "Alistair Mackensie wants."

Perdita climbed out of the car and stared at the building in awe. She had expected her grandmother's house to be large, but not a full-blown stately home.

"She can't have made this much money from selling books," said Perdita. "This is old money."

"Do you think you're about to inherit a title?"

"Don't be ridiculous! If anything, I'm probably being told never to darken their doorstep again."

"I wouldn't be so sure," replied Warren. "If that was the case, they would have sent you a snotty letter full of threatening legalese. You might be Lady Perdita Elizabeth Woodville-Rivers."

She shook her head. It was hard enough processing the shock of seeing her grandmother's home, Marquess House, and the realisation there was a great deal more to her grandmother and, therefore, her mother's family, than she had ever suspected. It made her nervous. What else was she about to discover? Despite the warm weather, she shivered.

"Come on," she said through white lips, "let's get this over with."

Squaring her shoulders, she strode towards the large, studded, Gothic wooden front doors with their metal bell-pull. Quashing the nerves fluttering in her stomach, Perdita grasped the handle and yanked with all her might. Somewhere in the depths of the house there was a resonant clang, then a few moments later, footsteps hurrying across the hall.

"Do you think the butler will answer?" murmured Warren. Despite herself, Perdita giggled.

"I'd be very excited if he did. I hope he's in full livery."

A moment later, the door was flung open by a tall, dark-haired man in his late twenties. His piercing blue eyes were hooded and wary, and his full, generous mouth was set in a fierce line. He appeared to be about to shout something, before checking himself and pausing, his face relaxing very slightly.

"Dr Perdita Rivers?" he asked, his voice deep and resonant.

"Yes," she replied, taken aback by the oddly aggressive greeting.

"Sorry," he said, his entire demeanour softening. "We've had some press door-stepping; I thought you were them coming back. I'm Kit Mackensie. You obviously received my father's letter? Please come in, come in."

He ushered them into the double-height entrance hall. A huge, ornately carved wooden staircase swept upwards, dividing at the first floor and disappearing to the west and east of the building. Above the ancient front doors was a vast rose window beaming coloured rays onto the wall opposite. Here, the intricate designs on the window were echoed in a delicately carved wooden frieze surrounded by a minstrel's gallery. Underneath this was a separate pane that seemed to balance above the door. Etched into the glass was a coat of arms bearing the motto: *Fide sed cui vide*. Perdita's eyes slid across it, "Trust but be careful in whom," she translated and, unbidden, a shudder ran down her spine.

Panelling covered most of the walls, giving way occasionally to sections of silk wallpaper, leaving Perdita to wonder whether the swirling patterns could be original William Morris designs. Paintings adorned the walls and she noticed several suits of armour. Glancing down, she gasped. The floor was a masterpiece of design; hand-painted quarry tiles of flowers and intricate patterns in pale greens and golds mixed with garnet reds and brilliant peacock blues surged in front of her like an ancient meadow. An enormous rug woven to replicate the pattern underneath, covered the bulk of the tiles.

"This floor," said Perdita. Unable to resist, she lifted the edge of the carpet to look more closely at the tiles. "Surely this isn't original Tudor?"

"Perdita!" admonished Warren, but Kit grinned.

"A lot of it is," he said. "Although, it's been heavily restored. A few tiles around the edge are as they were. Mary had them

31

covered in Perspex so they could be left in view. She commissioned the carpet to protect, but not hide, the beauty of the tiles."

Perdita jolted slightly at the easy way he referred to her grandmother.

"It's incredible, I've never seen one like it. Are there others, or is this the only one in the house?"

"There are a few other original sections and the ceiling in the chapel is thought to have some images dating from approximately 1530. You're welcome to have a look at it, but perhaps we should see my father first."

"Of course," replied Perdita, brought back to reality.

"He would have greeted you himself but an urgent call came through," Kit explained as he led them through the hall towards the west of the house. "He's in his office."

"His office?" asked Warren.

"Yes, my father and Mary worked together on various charitable and funding projects. As our business headquarters are in Andorra, Mary let him set up an office here. She and my father are old friends and she enjoyed the company. My brother, sister and I practically grew up here."

Perdita knew Kit was merely imparting information, but each casually flung out mention of her grandmother was akin to tiny knives piercing her heart and soul. *There was no need for my grandmother to have been lonely*, she wanted to scream — *she had us; she had me and Piper, and Dad before he died*. We could have kept her company — but she did not speak and merely took Warren's hand for comfort.

"Kit, is that you?" called a voice as they walked down a less ornate corridor leading towards the back of the house. "Was that the press back or is it…?"

A man appeared in a doorway. He was in his mid-sixties, tall and elegantly dressed in a grey suit with a black tie to indicate he was in mourning. His hair was silver, brushed back from his forehead and, like his son, he had piercing blue eyes. Although his were surrounded by fine laughter lines.

"My dear," he said as he saw Perdita, "how wonderful to meet you at last." He clasped her hand in both of his and, to her amazement, Perdita saw his eyes fill with tears. "If only things had been different," he said. Then, before Perdita could ask what he meant, he turned to Warren. "And you must be Warren Dexter, Perdita's fiancé. Good to meet you. I understand you had an exemplary military career until the bullet you took in your shoulder meant you were invalided out."

Perdita's eyes were wide, and even Warren looked unnerved. Few people knew the reason he had left his military career.

"You're very well informed, sir," said Warren coldly.

"Yes," replied Mackensie with a smile that seemed to welcome Perdita and freeze Warren. "Now, please, come in." Gesturing them forward, he led the way into his office.

It was a large room. An antique desk dominated one side, behind which were floor to ceiling bookshelves, laden with heavy law books. A vast fireplace was the other focal point, carved to match the endless swags of flowers that Perdita had seen throughout the house. Above this hung a portrait of a woman with long red hair. Her style of dress placed her in the Victorian era and this time it was Warren who exclaimed.

"Is that a John Singer Sargent?" he asked, stepping forward to examine the painting more closely.

"Yes," replied Mackensie senior. "It's a portrait of Lettice Lakeby, née Hawkland, your great-great-great grandmother, Perdita."

Perdita turned to look at the picture. It was unnerving; it reminded her too vividly of her twin sister, Piper. Although her and Piper's faces and build were almost identical, their colouring was vastly different. Perdita had a wild cloud of dark hair and haunting, grey-green eyes that held lights of gold, while Piper had a mane of ferocious red waves and curls with brilliant green eyes. Perdita spun on her heels and faced Alistair Mackensie, her nerves at breaking point.

"What's going on?" she asked bluntly. "I receive a strange letter from you this morning concerning the grandmother who cut me and my sister out of her life, and now you're talking me through family history as though we're old friends."

"I'm so sorry, my dear," said Alistair. "Seeing you at last quite overwhelmed me. Please, let's sit and I'll get to the point." He steered Perdita towards a large wooden carver opposite his desk. Warren followed, seating himself in a smaller, less grand chair that had been positioned next to Perdita's.

Kit nodded to his father. "I'll leave you," he said. "Good to meet you, Dr Rivers, Mr Dexter. I'll have Mum organise some refreshments."

"Thank you, son," Mackensie said as the door closed on Kit, then turned back to Perdita. "We're something of a family business, my wife often acts as my assistant."

Perdita did not reply. Her nerves were so taut, she felt she would soon reach screaming pitch if this man did not start to explain himself. The solicitor unlocked his top drawer and pulled out a brown paper folder. *Very hi-tech*, she thought sarcastically and shot Warren a conspiratorial glance. He, however, was rigid, watching Mackensie, and missed her look.

"Dr Rivers, I apologise for the speed in calling you here, but as you were in the vicinity, it seemed the safest option," he began.

"Safest?" queried Perdita. It seemed an odd choice of words.

"Yes, my dear, safest," he said with a gentle smile. "In time, of course, we will have a full reading of the will, but it is very long and detailed. So, would you mind if I summed up the salient points?"

Perdita nodded, alert now. Had their grandmother acknowledged them in death? If so, why?

"Your grandmother was an extremely wealthy woman and, with the exception of approximately twenty personal bequests and some trust funds for charitable organisations, you and your twin sister, Piper, are her main beneficiaries."

"Which means, what?" asked Perdita, hardly able to believe what she was hearing.

"You inherit Marquess House and its contents, your grandmother's personal and professional assets, including the copyright to all her work, published and unpublished, several large trust funds set up for you by both your mother and grandmother, a number of other properties worldwide, your grandmother's art and jewellery collections, the Louisa Woodville Trust, the research centre which is in the grounds, your grandmother's horses, in fact, more or less everything, to be divided equally between you both. Approximate worth, after inheritance tax, give or take, is £150 million each."

Perdita laughed.

Mackensie smiled. "It is faintly ludicrous, isn't it? When read out as a list of bald facts."

Perdita dropped her head in her hands, allowing her long dark hair to cover her face, grasping for a moment of composure. Then, with a well-practised sweep of her hand, she flicked her hair back into place and stared calmly at the solicitor. This news was so unexpected. It seemed her grandmother had known about her and Piper all along, and cared enough to leave them her estate, making them incredibly wealthy women. So, why had she ignored them in life?

"I don't understand," she said. "We've heard nothing from our grandmother since we were seven years old, yet we're the main beneficiaries of her will. You knew her, Mr Mackensie, why would she behave so irrationally?"

Alistair met Perdita's fierce gaze.

"That's a question I'm afraid I can't answer," he replied. "Old friend of Mary I may have been, but in matters of her will, I was merely her solicitor."

Staring into Mackensie's blue eyes, Perdita was convinced he was lying, but she was equally as sure this was not the moment to press him. She decided to change tack.

"Could you give me the details of my grandmother's death?" she asked.

Alistair nodded.

"Our housekeeper, Sarah Eve, was concerned when your grandmother didn't come down for breakfast at her usual time. After ringing Mary's room and getting no response, she and her husband Alan went to investigate. Using her passkey, Sarah let herself in and discovered your grandmother sitting in an armchair by the fireplace. She had been dead for some hours. The attending doctor has suggested her heart may have given out, but a post-mortem will confirm the cause of her death."

Perdita allowed these words to wash over her, each one slowly sinking in to her teeming mind.

"Your grandmother's body is currently with the undertaker's in town, if you would care to see her. I can make arrangements," Alistair continued. "Her funeral will be here in our private chapel, as she requested in her will, obviously at a date that suits you and Mrs Davidson." He was watching Perdita closely, her ashen face, the sadness in her eyes. "This must be a terrible shock for you, my dear, Mary's death, your inheritance..." His voice tailed off as he looked at her with concern.

Perdita knew he had seen the tears welling in her eyes and was angry with herself for losing control in front of this man, this stranger who was treating her like a long-lost daughter. After a long pause, she spoke, her voice tight with emotion, "What if we don't want it?" she snapped, hurt and anger mingling. "What if Piper and I don't want Mary's money? She didn't want us, why would we want anything from her?"

Beside her, she felt Warren stiffen. He reached for her cold, rigid hand, but she moved it away.

"Well," said Mackensie calmly, "the money will be held in trust until you either decide to claim it for yourself or give it away. The house will continue to be run under the terms of various charters created by your ancestor Lettice Hawkland, and if you or your sister have any children, it can be passed to them. Unfortunately, it would be a lengthy legal process if you wished to sell the estate as there are various long-term covenants and protection orders on the building, particularly the library and the tower on the island in the lake, all of which are recognised as having important historical value."

Certain words dropped through Perdita's shock: library, important historical value, lake... "There's a library?"

Mackensie nodded. "It is of huge historical importance as it contains some Tudor graffiti, as well as a vast collection of books and manuscripts. There's also a dedicated research centre that Mary had built in the barn complex. The more delicate documents are housed here, where the atmosphere can be controlled to protect them."

"And there's a chapel?"

"Yes, it's Tudor. I'm sure Kit must have mentioned it, it's his favourite part of the building."

Perdita nodded, hardly hearing Alistair's last comment. Now the shock was receding slightly, excitement was building inside her. This house belonged to her and Piper! The stately home she had thought they had visited as children was actually their family residence. Not only that, their grandmother had left them a fortune, as well as a vast collection of historical documents and their own research centre. It was the last thing she had expected. She had hoped for something small, maybe a book or a piece of jewellery that had once belonged to her mother, Louisa. She had not anticipated the size of the bequest, but then, she had not known the estate existed until an hour ago.

Before she could say any more, there was a knock on the door.

"Come in," called Mackensie, rising to open it, but Warren beat him to it. An attractive woman in her early sixties pushed a laden trolley into the room.

"Ah, thank you," said Mackensie. "Perdita, this is my wife, Susan."

Susan Mackensie was a petite woman with dark hair that fell in soft curls to her shoulders. She smiled at Perdita, extending her hand. Perdita took it but quickly dropped it when she saw tears well in Susan's soft brown eyes.

"Leave the trolley, I'll sort everyone out," her husband said in a gentle voice. After staring at Perdita with an intensity that left her unnerved, Susan Mackensie walked swiftly from the room.

"Just like her mother…" Perdita heard as the door closed behind Susan.

Suddenly, anger flared inside her again. Their behaviour was making her feel like an exhibit in a zoo.

"Is anyone else going to come in and stare at me?" she asked coldly as Mackensie handed her a cup of coffee.

"No, my dear," he said in an avuncular manner. "Everyone here is very excited to finally meet you, that's all. Now," he continued before Perdita could ask why, "this must all be something of a surprise, and I imagine you'd like to discuss things with your sister, Mrs Piper Davidson. If you're in agreement, I can email you both with more details of your inheritance, then, when you're ready, you can instruct me of your wishes. In the meantime, perhaps you would like to see the house and estate?"

Perdita placed her cup on the edge of Mackensie's desk and looked at Warren who was white-faced and appeared angry.

"No," she replied, surprising both men with her answer. "You seem to think that, now we've inherited Mrs Fitzroy's estate, everything is forgiven and I can wander around as though nothing has ever happened. My grandmother cut us from her life. Of course, I'm grateful for what she's left us, but why didn't she invite us here when she could have shown us around herself?"

Perdita could feel her control slipping again. She needed air, a chance to think and to talk to her sister.

"If you could email those details to Piper and myself, we'll discuss them and I'll contact you when we've made a decision. Do you have a card?"

"Of course," he said, handing her his business card, which she slid into her handbag.

"One last thing, Mr Mackensie, how did you know I was at The Orwell Hotel?"

Alistair Mackensie reached for a file on his desk and opened it. Perdita looked at the list of names, hers was near the top.

"Jerusalem and Marquess House have been funding your dig in Dale," he said. "Mary knew you were here too. I think she was hoping to visit the site, maybe see you, but…"

He let the sentence hang. Perdita's eyes filled with tears as she turned away.

"Let me show you out," said Mackensie, and led them back to the front door.

"Get me out of here," Perdita muttered as soon as they were in the car. Gunning the engine, Warren roared down the drive, leaving an impressive shower of gravel in their wake.

"Are you OK?" he asked as they turned out of the gates and back into the lane. "Did you know about her estate?"

Perdita shook her head. "I'm stunned," she replied. "I had no idea she was so rich. Where did all the money come from?"

"It wouldn't take long to do a genealogical sweep, you might have had some rich ancestors. Money like this is usually inherited not earned," he mused. "The basics of your family tree will be in the censuses but I have a friend who could look into it for you. It might offer a few clues as to where it all came from. You might still find your title!"

Somewhat reluctantly, Perdita smiled. "Interesting idea," she said. "There might be a family tree in the library…" She broke off, staring out of the car window at the sun-dappled Pembrokeshire coastline as the reality of the situation filtered through her numb brain. "Oh my God, Warren," she whispered. "It's got a library! Piper and I own a house with a Tudor library."

"You do," he said, relieved Perdita was sounding more like herself again. "Why didn't you want to look around? I was itching to nose about."

"I need to talk to Piper first," she said with an apologetic shrug. "She's my twin sister, we've always done everything together — I can't start exploring the house until she knows about it. Anyway, she has a right to say what she wants to do with the inheritance too. It isn't only mine."

Back at the hotel, Perdita walked across the bedroom, flinging off her clothes as she went, and dragged out her shorts, a T-shirt, sweatshirt and her boots from the wardrobe.

"What are you doing?" asked Warren, watching her from his vantage point, leaning on the closed door.

"Going to the dig," she replied. "I need to do something normal while I try to make sense of this and wait until a decent hour to ring Pipes."

"OK," he said. "I get that…"

"And, much as I hate to say it," said Perdita, walking to Warren and putting her arms around him, "you, my darling, need to go home. You're supposed to be in France in three days' time on a research and lecture tour."

"Perds, you've had a huge shock…" he began.

"Yes," she interrupted, "but I'm also a grown up and able to look after myself."

"You're right," he said, then unable to contain himself: "Are you going to accept the legacy?"

"Of course I'm going to accept it!" she said, laughing as she disentangled herself from their embrace, before finishing getting changed.

"What if Piper doesn't want it?" he continued.

"She will. Anyway, we'd be mad not to grab it with both hands. How many people are ever offered the opportunity to

41

own a property like Marquess House? Practically no one! Imagine what's in its archive, the scope for research is incredible."

"Perhaps your grandmother has already exhausted the Tudor papers," he said. "After all, she switched eras to pre-Conquest women."

"Maybe she did, but I might spot something she missed." She scrutinised his face. "Is that relief in your eyes, Professor Dexter, Mediaeval weapons expert?"

"Absolutely, did you see the armour in the entrance hall, and the swords? Some of them were definitely Mediaeval. One could have been a fourteenth century French estoc, if it's original — and if the John Singer Sargent portrait of your ancestor is anything to go by, it could be — it might be one of the few surviving examples. Not only that, imagine the art collection…"

"Indeed! Imagine the art collection and the research centre and her horses? What's that all about? Did she own racehorses or something?"

"Who knows?"

Perdita picked up the smart handbag she had taken with her to the meeting and began decanting things back into the battered leather rucksack she used on digs. Picking up her car keys, she slung the bag over her shoulder and headed to the bedroom door. When she reached it, she turned to Warren and said, almost as a peace offering, "You could come down later. Olaf is convinced the ship is part of the Armada. He might like your opinion on the ordnance they've found inside. Personally, I think it's a bit later, possibly Jacobean. Anyway, there don't seem to be enough cannons on board for it to be a warship."

Warren walked across the room loosening his tie. "I'd be happy to take a look, as long as I'm not stepping on any toes," he said. "And, if you're sure dealing with this alone is what you want, then I'll stay tonight and go home tomorrow."

Perdita nodded, her hand already twisting the door handle, such was her eagerness to be out in the sunshine and back to her normal life for a while.

"See you this afternoon," she said and blew a kiss as she darted out.

The main reason Perdita wanted to call her sister from the dig was that she wanted complete privacy. Much as she loved Warren, she did not want him pacing about in the background while she spoke to Piper. The two had never got on and she could do without his tutting. The computer buzzed. Perdita pressed accept and her sister's face appeared on the screen.

"Piper!"

"Hey, big sis!" replied her twin, who was younger by fifteen minutes. "Is this real?" She waved a few sheets of paper at Perdita. "I printed out the email like you suggested. This is a joke, right?"

"No joke! Did you see the pictures of the house?"

"Yes, it's the one, isn't it? The one she took us to when we were kids. Although, she didn't take us anywhere, did she? We were visiting Granny at home!" Perdita nodded, allowing her sister to babble. "Perds, this is madness. The woman never spoke to us, why would she leave us her estate?"

"I've been thinking about it and I wondered whether it was some kind of primogeniture thing, only through the female line, rather than the male, giving her no choice but to leave it to us. When I asked the solicitor, Mr Mackensie, what would happen if we were to refuse the estate..."

"What?" she yelped.

"I had to ask, he was so pleased with himself, I wanted to ruffle his feathers," continued Perdita, and Piper grinned, understanding Perdita's motives. "He said the estate would continue to be run under various covenants and trusts that were put in place by our great-great-great grandmother, Lettice Hawkland, so perhaps Mary had to leave it to us."

"It's possible, but equally, we were estranged from Mary and she had plenty of time to change the covenants and trusts. She also had enough money to ensure they were acted upon once she was dead, but she didn't. From what you've said, and from what Mackensie wrote in his email, she left a detailed will which made it absolutely clear we were to get everything and it was signed on our eighteenth birthday."

"But why?"

Piper shrugged. "It is peculiar. By the way, Lettice? What a great name! And, what's this about horses?"

"No idea," grinned Perdita. "Maybe we own a string of racehorses too!"

They looked at each other and burst out laughing.

"This is crazy!" exclaimed Piper. "What are we going to do? Accept it, obviously?"

"Of course! Pipes, you should see the place, it's incredible, and it has a library and a research centre and a lake with an island…"

"We must have loved it when we were young," said Piper. "Before she walked out on us, of course, and Dad stopped talking about her."

The words cut through their excitement and for a moment they were little girls again, flinching as their father berated them for asking about their maternal grandmother, forbidding them to raise the subject or mention her name.

"There's something else too," said Perdita, her voice hesitant.

"What?"

"Have you looked at the list of properties we now own?"

"Not closely no, why?"

"Dad's house, our home in London, it's on the list. It belonged to Mary."

"No way?" said Piper, running her eyes down the list until she found it. "We moved there after Mum died and I assumed Dad rented because he didn't want to tie himself to anywhere permanently. You know what he was like."

"It would also explain why, after he died, the letting agency told us the rent was paid until the end of the year so there was no need to worry about clearing it. We could take as long as we needed. It belonged to our grandmother. She'd given us a beautiful home and never taken any credit."

"It does explain things, Perds. I always wondered how Dad afforded the rent on a five bedroom house in Chiswick on the money he earned from selling his paintings."

"It makes me feel a bit queasy, though. Mary gave us somewhere to live, perhaps paid our bills, maybe even supported Dad financially — but she didn't come near us. Why?"

"I suppose the only way to find out is to ask Mackensie, but I suspect he won't tell us…"

"Or, I could move into Marquess House and see if Mary left an explanation somewhere for us to find," suggested Perdita.

"Do you want to?" asked Piper in surprise. "Aren't you going to France with Warren?"

"Yes, but that isn't for another month and only for a two-week holiday at the end of his tour. The dig finishes next

Friday and term doesn't start at the university until September, that's if I go back."

"But you love your job!"

"Yes and no," said Perdita. "I spend most of my time chasing sponsors and funding. It'll be even worse this year as they're discussing reducing the staff in my department. Mary's inheritance gives us both the opportunity to follow our dreams. For me, that means I can do my own research rather than having to crowbar it into something deemed useful by the university, and for you, well, you can finally set up your own studio. We might even be able to sponsor other people too."

"But Perds…" Piper interrupted.

Perdita shook her head and kept going. She was concerned that, if she stopped, she might change her mind. "Let me finish. I've been thinking about it since I left Marquess House this morning. You're in America for at least another eight months, maybe longer. Warren will be back in Bristol, there's no need for me to go back to Dad's, especially as it's our house anyway."

"What about your flat?"

"Rory has finally bought me out," she said, referring to her former fiancé. "So, apart from collecting my things, which are minimal, a few books and clothes, I have no reason to go back to London. Anyway, if I'm at Marquess House, I can sort out all the paperwork, explore the house and…"

"Maybe understand our grandmother's motives," finished Piper.

"Yes."

Perdita lifted her hand to touch the screen and Piper did the same. More than anything, they both knew they were looking for any trace of their mother, Louisa, in their grandmother's life.

They continued to talk, catching up on each other's lives. Piper was in America with her husband, Jeremy Davidson, a computer analyst who was on secondment with the US arm of the large blue-chip company he worked for in London. Piper was a talented artist, specialising in sculpture, but to earn a living, she used her other talent, IT, working at the Tate Modern helping to curate exhibitions. She had been given a year's sabbatical to accompany her husband to Austin, Texas, and had been gone three months; it was the longest the twins had ever been apart.

"Will you come back for the funeral?" asked Perdita.

"Yes, I think so. You said it wouldn't be for another week or so, which gives me time to sort a few things out here."

"What things?" Perdita noticed a dip in her sister's tone.

"Oh, you know, things," sighed Piper, then her smile faltered and she took a deep breath. "Jeremy and I are finding America difficult."

"Meaning?" said Perdita, alarmed.

"I'm sure it's nothing, just pressure of work. I'll tell you when I see you," said Piper, not quite meeting Perdita's eye.

"If things aren't going well with you two, do you really want to come all this way? Wouldn't you rather stay there and sort things out?"

"Honestly, Perds, he's being so horrible, I could do with a break. Anyway, I'd like to see the house, meet everyone, speak to the horses…"

Perdita managed a smile, despite her concern.

"So, what's your next move, Perds?" asked Piper, changing the subject.

"I'll call Mackensie, tell him that we, of course, graciously accept our inheritance and that I'll be moving in next week. Once I'm there, I can go through the will properly and try to find out what happened between Granny Mary and Dad to cause such a devastating fracture in their relationship."

A shadow passed over both their faces.

"We haven't called her that for years," said Piper.

"Not since Mum died," replied Perdita, her voice tight with unshed tears. "I wish you were here, this is so — unbelievable."

"I'll be home in a week, you won't have to hold the fort for long."

Perdita nodded. In the background behind Piper, she heard a door slam and Jeremy's voice.

"OK, Perds, I'd better go, keep me posted," said Piper, her face tense. "Maybe Mackensie could book me some first class tickets home."

"Of course," replied Perdita. "Love you, sis."

"Love you more," said Piper and, with a brief touch of the screen from them both, Perdita watched her sister's face disappear.

Chapter Two

For some time after she had spoken to her sister, Perdita gazed out of the window, watching the land-based part of proceedings. Although her eyes slid over the activity, she took very little in; her mind was on the strange events of the day. There was a tentative tap on the door and Olaf peeped in.

"All OK?" he asked.

"Yes, yes, come in," replied Perdita, jumping to her feet. "Sorry, I didn't mean to commandeer your office."

"It isn't only mine," he replied. "Was Piper OK?"

She and Olaf had been work colleagues and friends for years. She knew he would never pry, but she felt she owed him an explanation.

"Piper is fine," she said. "I wanted to talk to her about our inheritance."

Olaf sat at another desk and placed a cardboard box on the table.

"Inheritance?" he asked in surprise. "I thought you'd dealt with all your dad's things. Has something else been found?"

"Not Dad, my grandmother."

"Your grandmother?"

"Mary Fitzroy, the eminent historian, was our estranged grandmother, and she's left Piper and me her estate."

"She was ... what? Your grandmother? You've never said."

"We haven't seen her since we were children. Mentioning our connection seemed irrelevant," she replied, glancing at the box.

He followed her look but to Perdita's irritation, refused to take the hint and change the subject. Instead, he continued on the more fascinating topic of her unexpected inheritance. "What do you mean by estate?"

"A massive manor called Marquess House with its own library, chapel and lake with an island, a research centre, houses all around the world, oh and horses. And lots and lots of money."

"My God, Perdita, that's unbelievable!"

Perdita bit her lip and nodded, saying it aloud to Olaf made it more real.

"I have to ring the solicitor and tell him we accept, then I suppose there will be endless paperwork, inheritance tax and stuff to sort out. We've barely finished dealing with Dad's estate and that was tiny in comparison with what Mary's left us."

She turned away, gazing out of the window, lost in thought.

"I'm not sure if this is appropriate," said Olaf tentatively after a few moments of silence, "but would you like to see what was in the treasure chest?"

"What?" She spun around in surprise. "I didn't think you'd be able to get inside it until you were back in the lab!"

"Ordinarily, we wouldn't, but the box was nearly rotten and it disintegrated once it was out of the water. It's a real shame but we managed to save a few of the pieces. On the positive side, there were still items inside."

"Items? Plural?" said Perdita in excitement.

Olaf nodded and opened the cardboard box.

"Most are too delicate to handle at present, but there is one we thought you might like to cast your expert eye over, and Maggie wondered if it would cheer you up too."

Perdita was touched by the consideration. She took the cotton gloves Olaf proffered then leaned in to look at the treasure where it nestled in layers of protective packaging.

"Oh my goodness, it's beautiful!" she exclaimed. "I'd say seventeenth century..."

"Very good, it's June 1642," interrupted Olaf.

"That's extremely precise," laughed Perdita, "is it engraved somewhere?"

"On the side."

"May I?" she asked, her hand hovering above the item. Olaf nodded.

With great care, Perdita removed the exquisite cup from the box. It was small, approximately the height of a sherry glass, but with a deeper, wider bowl and a thicker stem, giving it a slightly squat appearance. From its weight, she guessed it was made from solid gold. Around the outside of the rim was a row of tiny red gems set flush into the metal so it was still smooth to drink from, and inside, slightly lower down, was a matching row. Many were missing but there were enough left to give a hint of its former magnificence.

On one side was the date "June 1642", and on the other, the initials "PF". However, the most unusual thing about the small vessel were the engravings of mermaids. Endless numbers of the mythical creatures streamed up the short stem and around the bowl, leading to a tiny golden mermaid who sat on the inside of the bowl, poised as though ready to swim. Perdita looked at it for a few moments then carefully turned it over and inspected the base.

"What do you think?" Olaf interrupted her contemplation.

"I've never seen anything like it. It seems to have a clockwork mechanism in the stem which, I imagine, must have made the mermaid swim. Were there any keys in the chest?"

"Actually, there were three — tiny ones."

"I doubt the mechanism works anymore," said Perdita, "but we might be able to get funding to have a replica made."

As she said it, she realised she did not have to worry about such things. Depending on how the research centre worked, she might be able to provide all the necessary money to recreate this beautiful item. It was a strange and not altogether pleasant thought, although she could not explain why it made her feel so apprehensive.

"On the downside, though," she said, carefully replacing the cup, "this proves the ship wasn't from the Armada. The date on the cup is far too late to be part of the Spanish fleet."

Olaf shrugged. "I think this could be more interesting, particularly as it looks as though the ship was deliberately sunk with all its cargo but no crew."

"But why would anyone do that?" she said. "Ships were worth a fortune. If that's the case, though, it would be amazing for us. Who knows what other treasure there might be aboard?"

Her phone buzzed and, glancing down, she saw Alistair Mackensie's name on the screen.

"Sorry," she murmured, "I'd like to get this…" Olaf nodded and wandered from the office to give her some privacy. "Hello…"

"Dr Rivers, I'm sorry to bother you but…"

"No, it's fine," said Perdita. "I was about to call you. My sister and I have discussed the matter and we'd like to accept our inheritance. In fact, if it's appropriate, when this dig finishes I'd like to move into Marquess House."

"My dear, that's wonderful news," he said. "We'll have your room made ready immediately."

"Piper and I would like the date of the funeral too," added Perdita. "And perhaps we should discuss the details?"

"Mary left full instructions. She and I had often discussed her wishes. It will be a small service in the chapel here. She'll then be interred in the family vault. You will, of course, be chief mourner, at Mary's request, you understand."

"My sister will be here too, so we can both be chief mourners," announced Perdita. "Do you think it would be possible to book her some air tickets? She'd like to see the house and meet everyone, as well as pay her respects."

"Of course, my dear," replied Alistair. "We'll organise her flight immediately."

"Did you want something else?" asked Perdita. "You called me."

"No, nothing of any importance. It was merely an enquiry to see if there was anything I could help with while you made your decision," he said and for some reason Perdita sensed he was lying again. She mentally shook herself, aware she was overreacting. Out of the window she saw Warren arriving.

"I've got to go now, Mr Mackensie. I'll call you tomorrow to finalise the details."

"Of course, my dear, I'll be here all day."

Perdita clicked her phone off and hurried out to greet her fiancé.

Perdita took one last look around the hotel room, hoisted her rucksack onto her back, grasped the handle of her wheelie case and headed outside. The room had been her home for the past three weeks and her next stop was Marquess House. Now it was happening, she was strangely reluctant to be leaving the sanctuary of the hotel for this new and unexpected world, but as both Piper and Warren had pointed out, if she found Marquess House too overwhelming, she could always leave. The house in Chiswick was still there, as were the numerous other houses, flats, villas and apartments she and Piper now owned.

Checking out, she forced a smile when the receptionist said, "Good luck with everything at Marquess House, Dr Rivers."

"Thanks," she replied, trying to quash her natural nervousness at someone knowing her business, then reminded herself of what Warren had said: this was a village, not London, and it was considered normal for people to know what was going on around them. Nevertheless, she was relieved Piper would be with her the following day to share this strange adventure for a while.

A quarter of an hour later, Perdita pulled into the driveway of Marquess House. Following the winding driveway through the grounds, she slowed down enough to be able to gaze around as she drove. It was still hard to believe this was all hers and Piper's: the undulating lawns, the avenues of rhododendron, valleys of woodland and the lake glinting in the distance. *Madness*, she sighed to herself, then turned a final corner and the magnificence of Marquess House was revealed again.

Once more, the scale and grandeur took her breath away. Reaching over for her handbag, she slid out of the car and appraised her new home. Marquess House was a hotchpotch of styles, but despite the varying shades of stone and the obvious age of the tower at the centre of the house, there was a strange cohesion to the different wings. Staring at it, she could not help but like the house. It was so unusual and strangely friendly. *Stop it*, she told herself, *it's a building, it doesn't have emotions, it's stone.* Yet, by the time she rang the bell, she realised her sense of trepidation had morphed into excitement. Like a child at Christmas, she could not wait to unwrap this unexpected gift and discover what was inside.

"Perdita!" exclaimed Kit as he flung open the huge front door. "Welcome home!" He was grinning broadly and Perdita had the feeling he was going to hug her but her natural reserve made him hesitate. "I'll have someone fetch your luggage from the car once you've decided which room to have."

He took her arm and led her into the beautiful Tudor hall. Again, the intricacy in the decoration made Perdita gasp. It was even more beautiful than she remembered.

"This place is like a fairy tale," she said, her eyes taking in the sumptuousness of the handwoven carpet, the streams of coloured light flowing from the rose window and the swags and posies of flowers carved into the panelling, winding their way up the banisters like a golden rope.

Kit laughed. "Yes," he said. "And like a fairy tale, there are hidden perils, particularly with some of the plumbing. The downstairs cloakroom in the East Wing is Victorian and it's an original Thomas Crapper. Like so many other things in the house, it's listed, so Mary could never replace it. She had it refurbished, as much as she was allowed to anyway, but I'd only use it in an emergency if I were you."

Perdita grinned. "Thanks for the tip!"

Kit led the way through to the working part of the house and once more, Alistair Mackensie greeted her like a long-lost relative.

"My dear, here you are, safe and sound. Welcome home at last," he exclaimed, echoing his son. Perdita smiled in response. *Safe*, she thought, *there it is again*. "Now, what would you like to do first?"

"I'd like a tour of the house so I can get my bearings, then I'd like to see where I'm going to live and maybe meet the people who work here."

Even in the short time she had been inside she had noticed people whisking about cleaning, walking purposefully from room to room, all of whom had offered curious glances and smiles in her direction; she could also hear the purr of lawn mowers in the garden. "After that, I'm interested in my grandmother's work. Do you have her manuscripts in the library?"

"In the research centre," said Kit. "There are copies of her books in the library but if you want the originals and her research, we'd have to talk to Jenny. It might take her a few days to have it all brought out of storage."

"Who's Jenny?" asked Perdita.

"Jenny Procter, she runs the research centre and is our chief archivist and librarian," replied Alistair. "There's very little Jenny doesn't know about the house and its history. I can call her now to request she finds Mary's manuscripts, she'll be able to give us a rough idea of how long it will take."

Perdita nodded and wandered over to the large window with its cushioned seat while Alistair dialled an internal number. Kit joined her.

"How about we start with a tour of the house? If we have time, maybe some of the grounds to give you a rough idea of where everything is?" he suggested. "That'll take most of the day. You may even find you remember some of it."

Perdita gave him a cool look. "I have virtually no memories of my time living in Pembrokeshire and only one vague recollection of the exterior of this house. Nothing so far has been familiar, but thank you, a tour would be appreciated. I'd also like to see where I'll be living."

"You'll be living in all of it, it's yours."

"My room then, the place that's private," she specified. "All these rooms seem to belong to everyone but me."

"Of course."

They looked up as they heard Alistair replace the telephone.

"Jenny says she'll do her best, but the soonest she realistically thinks she'll be able to have Mary's research to you is Monday," he said.

"A week?" Perdita said. "It's only Tuesday."

"When you see the volume of paperwork in the archive, you'll understand. Mary was a great collector of documents and she also stored many things on behalf of Jerusalem, so it takes a while to access things."

"Thank you," she hesitated, then mentally bracing herself, she continued, "I'd also like to finalise the funeral arrangements for Friday and discuss what paperwork will be needed for inheritance tax, probate…"

"The paperwork is my domain," interrupted Alistair. "I have a team of people dealing with all the necessary documentation. However, we do need to have a proper meeting once Mrs Davidson arrives, so I can explain everything in detail and read the will in its entirety."

"Wow, always good to have something to look forward to," muttered Kit. Despite herself, Perdita giggled, then hastily stifled it as she did not wish to appear rude.

"Thank you, Kit," said his father mildly and Kit laughed. "As for the funeral, Mary did request that, should you or Piper attend, you would consider doing a reading. However, if you'd prefer not to, my daughter Megan will be happy to step in."

"No, we'll do it," replied Perdita. "I take it Mary specified the pieces she would like us to read?" Alistair nodded. "Do you want to go through them now?"

"You should explore the house, then perhaps we can do it later on this afternoon, or tomorrow when Mrs Davidson…"

"You can call her Piper, she won't mind," interrupted Perdita.

"Of course, when Piper is here and you've had some time to think about everything. You can change your mind about the reading at any point."

Perdita nodded: another funeral, another reading. She had read a short section of a lesser-known Bible story that was taken from the Apocrypha at her father's. He had specified it in his own funeral instructions, which he had placed in his will. The passage had been from the *History of Susanna*, a chapter completely unfamiliar to either twin. Piper had read a short passage from George Orwell's *1984* which he had often quoted to them when they were growing up. Now she would be doing it again, but this time at the request of a woman who had never spoken to her, who had shunned her in life but embraced her in death. *Mary would then be interred in the family vault*, mused Perdita, when a sharp pain of realisation went through her.

"Alistair, when we first discussed Mary's funeral, am I correct in thinking you said Mary was being buried in the family vault?" she asked, her voice becoming constricted.

"Yes, my dear," replied Alistair.

"My mother…" Perdita began, before her voice faltered. "Is she…? Was she buried there?"

"Your mother is there, as is your grandfather and your maternal great-grandparents. Perhaps Kit could take you there today."

White-faced, Perdita nodded, trying to absorb this unexpected information. Her father had never mentioned her mother's grave and, because they had not wanted to upset him, the twins had refrained from questioning him too deeply. The idea that her mother would be buried here had never occurred to her before, but now as the shock of the discovery enveloped her, she felt her anxiety levels rising.

A feeling that life was swamping her and she had no control over events, overwhelmed her. It had happened before when her father had died, but then at least they had been expecting his demise; he had been battling cancer for some months. Mary's sudden death, the inheritance and now the heartbreaking revelation that her mother's grave was within touching distance, brought panic fluttering to her chest and she desperately needed to be out of the office. Although it was a large, well-proportioned room, it was beginning to feel claustrophobic.

Kit was watching her intently. "Right, Dad, she's mine for the rest of the morning," he said stepping forward and taking her by the arm. "We'll see you for lunch. Is it on the terrace?"

"Yes," Alistair murmured, he was watching Perdita's suddenly chalk-white face with equal concern. "Have fun on your tour, children," he continued, aiming for a tone of casual nonchalance, but concern rang through his words.

Kit led Perdita from the room but rather than retracing their steps towards the entrance, he continued down the corridor until they came to a side door.

"You look as though you need some air," he said flinging it open and standing back so Perdita could walk out into a rustic cobbled courtyard.

It had once been part of the old manor and had held the workshops necessary for the running of a great house: still room, bakery, laundry and drying rooms. The barn-like buildings had now all been converted into either cottages or small studios. Perdita took deep breaths of fresh summer air as she stared around the courtyard, calmness returning now she was outside. Statues and carvings abounded and in the centre was an old water pump. Chairs and tables were dotted around but the entire place was empty, as though all the inhabitants had walked away moments before.

"Mary was very keen to help young trades and crafts people, as well as artists," Kit explained. "She let these at reasonable rates and provided accommodation."

"Why are they empty?" asked Perdita.

"They're let for three month blocks. One lot has just finished and we've held back letting them again until you and your sister have decided what you want to do with them."

"Do you have people waiting for them?"

"Yes."

"Tell them they can come as planned."

"Are you sure?"

"Of course! These are amazing, Piper is going to love them," enthused Perdita. "She emailed yesterday to say she'd like to set up her own studio at Marquess House. Maybe she could extend this area and take over part of it."

"Maybe," said Kit grinning. "I knew you'd want to continue, but Dad said we had to wait for your approval."

"Well," said Perdita with a shadow of a smile, "when we meet him for lunch on the terrace, we can tell him to reopen the studios."

"What would you like to see first?" asked Kit.

Perdita paused, glancing at Kit askance. Did he even need to ask? Now she knew it was here, her mother's grave was obviously her first priority.

"The chapel and the family vault," she said.

"I thought you would but I wanted to check," he replied. "The chapel is to the west side of the house. We need to go through the knot garden."

Perdita followed him out of the courtyard and into the beautifully landscaped grounds. Once more she was astounded by the incredible detail and the obvious love and devotion that had been lavished on the property. As they walked, Perdita drank everything in, desperate for knowledge of her mysterious grandmother, when another thought occurred to her.

"Why did your dad mention Mary's horses?" she asked.

"They were your mother's. Well, they're the descendants of the ones your mother rescued or adopted," he said. "Dad is very fond of animals and loves to ride, he was also good friends with your mother and helped her set up her animal sanctuary, The Louisa Woodville Trust."

"An animal sanctuary, I had no idea. Can we go there now? Is it on the estate?"

"It's based out at what you probably remember as Air House, but is now called Home Farm and is run by Briony Llewellyn. She's the granddaughter of Mary's best friend, Bethan Lacey, originally Bethan Bridges," he said. "We can go after you've been to the chapel if you like, it's about a twenty-minute drive."

Perdita tried to swallow her surprise. "Air House? It's part of the estate?"

Kit nodded. Perdita turned away. She had not realised the estate was so big, nor had it ever occurred to her that their old home had been within its boundaries. Suddenly, she did not want to see the animal sanctuary or the house where she had lived as a child. It was too overwhelming.

"No, I think I'd like to see the interior of Marquess House after we've been to the chapel, then settle in," she replied, fighting to keep her emotions under control. "My mother must have loved animals."

"Dad always said Louisa had a way with all animals, even the most badly behaved or stressed would calm down when they were around her."

"She didn't follow Granny into academia then?" mused Perdita, whose knowledge of her mother was sketchy as her father would never speak about her.

"Didn't you know?" Kit sounded apprehensive.

"Know what?"

"Your mother was dyslexic," he said. "She had no interest in academia at all but she was devoted to her animals, her mother, your father and the two of you. According to Dad, she was one of the kindest, funniest, most thoughtful people you could ever meet."

Perdita turned away, tears welling in her eyes. It felt wrong to be hearing this information about her mother from a stranger. He knew more about her past than she did and it hurt.

"What are the ruins on the island?" she asked, deliberately changing the subject as the lake came into view. She shaded her eyes as though wishing to see them more clearly, but really wiping away her tears.

"It was a priory," replied Kit. "Being so far away from London, it survived Henry VIII's initial dissolution of the monasteries, but was closed in 1543 after some sort of scandal. Either the prioress was pregnant or she hid a noblewoman here and helped her deliver an illegitimate baby, I forget the details. The nuns were banished and the building was left to fall into disrepair. The tower is the last of its kind, though. There's supposed to be a secret tunnel leading from the house to the island, but we never found it. My brother, sister and I spent most of our summer holidays looking for it when we were young."

His words, casually uttered and with no malice, were like knives cutting through her. She tried not to react but the force of the jealousy that engulfed her took her by surprise. *A stranger with no connection to my grandmother should not be telling me these things*, she thought. *I should have known about Mum and it should have been me and Piper spending our summers here searching for secret tunnels, having adventures and pestering Mary to tell us scary stories about the nuns on the island, not another family. If anything, the Mackensies should have been our friends, comrades-in-arms against the grown-ups as we built camps and got up to mischief. We should be sharing these memories together; he should not be telling me these things.*

Biting her lip in an attempt to stop herself saying something she knew she would regret, she finally managed to snap: "Did you grow up here?"

"Partly," admitted Kit warily. "My parents have a house in London and our family home is in Andorra but this was where we spent our summers. Dad and Mary were…"

"Yes, your father said they were good friends," she interrupted coldly.

"Perdita, I'm sorry…" he began.

"It isn't your fault," she said, once more cutting him short. "I'd like to see the chapel now."

She turned and marched away, fighting to control her temper. Kit was not to blame, it was Mary who had caused this and Perdita was determined to discover why.

Chapter Three

"I had always imagined she lived alone and embittered, in a crumbling house which she was too mean to spend any money on," said Perdita. "That she sent everyone away, had no friends and scared the local children."

"Really?" said Piper, rolling over to give her sister a concerned look.

"It was an image I persuaded myself out of as we grew up," she admitted, "but it was the only way I could explain why she abandoned us when Mum died, at the time when we needed her most. What did you think?"

"I thought she was too sad to speak to us at first, but I always expected her to turn up on the doorstep and throw her arms around us. Then, the years passed and I convinced myself she must have had a nervous breakdown and seeing us again could trigger a relapse, so she stayed away."

"That's a more realistic explanation," smiled Perdita, and the twins fell into a thoughtful silence. It was the eve of the funeral and Piper had arrived the previous day. She had been equally impressed as Perdita when confronted with Marquess House. Now they were lying on the vast, double four-poster bed that had once belonged to their grandmother. It was on the first floor of the house in the largest of the five main suites. The ones on either side of Mary's had always been known as Perdita's and Piper's rooms, something that had made Perdita shudder slightly when Alistair had told her on her first day in her new home.

"Your grandmother always hoped you would be reconciled one day," Alistair had explained. "You can, of course, choose any room, but the ones on either side of Mary's have the best views."

Perdita had considered a tower room but when Kit had shown her around the bedrooms, which were as tastefully decorated as the rest of the house, the windows were barely bigger than arrow slits and the rooms were small; ideal for a guest who was staying for a few nights, but not as a home. When he had thrown open the door to the suite her grandmother had always thought of as Perdita's, she had bitten back her gasp of surprise. If she could have chosen the décor herself, the room could not have been more to her personal taste. It reminded her of her bedroom in the house where she had grown up and the style in which she had decorated her own flat before it had been sold.

"Mary had them redecorated every year, in case you ever visited," Kit had said quietly. "There's this large living room, the bedroom is over there with an en suite and a dressing room, and through there is a small kitchen — Mary wasn't one for wandering down to the main kitchen at night. The other door leads to a small office and over there is a spare bedroom with its own en suite," he had said. "Shall I have your bags brought up?"

Perdita had nodded, wandering into the room, relaxing as she gazed upon the pale green and white colour scheme. Standing in the centre of the living room, she had turned a full circle, intrigued by the ancient details of the house that continued across the walls of these rooms too: the carved fireplace, the panelled walls and again, the decorative frieze dancing across the golden wood. Up close, she could see the shapes carved into the wood more clearly. There were flowers, a combination of lilies, daisies and roses; a strange design of what seemed to be three circles joined, but what surprised her most were the mermaids nestled in between the flowers, deeply hidden, so they were not immediately obvious.

"If you don't like the paintings, they can be changed," Kit had said, pulling her attention away from the frieze. "There are lots all over the house, as well as in storage. I'll find the catalogue so you can see what's available and what you now own."

There were three paintings on the walls: a pair of swirling abstract watercolours that reminded Perdita of being underwater, swimming through a wave as she searched for treasure; the other was a full-length oil on canvas portrait of a woman. She wore a magnificent golden dress and her cloud of dark hair surrounded her like a storm. Her unusual grey-green eyes stared out across the void of time: knowing, calm and confident. The slight up-tilt of her full lips made her look as though as she had a secret that she was longing to share. Perdita could not help but notice the similarities between herself and this woman in the Jacobean style dress.

"Who is she?" she had asked Kit, who was watching her nervously.

"We're not sure," he had replied. "Mary found the painting in the attic when she inherited the house and had it restored along with a number of others. The records say it was here when Lettice bought the house. Mary only hung it in here a few years ago. Would you like me to have it moved?"

Perdita had gazed at the woman with the uncanny likeness to herself and had found herself shaking her head. "No, leave it," she had said. "If it gets too weird, you can move it later."

Piper had been similarly entranced with her room when she had arrived the previous day. As Perdita's had followed her preferred style, Piper's reflected her love of edgy, urban design. The walls were varying shades of grey with misty purple accents, while the furniture was modern and slick. Yet it sat well in the ancient house. The layout was identical to Perdita's but above Piper's fireplace was an abstract painting of Marquess House, which on closer inspection, the twins discovered, was by their father James Rivers. Two smaller portraits hung on another wall: one of an unknown red-haired woman in Tudor dress and the other a smiling young man with the flowing locks favoured by the Cavaliers during the Civil War. Neither twin had felt the need to change anything, particularly the painting by their father.

It was Perdita who had asked Alistair for the key to Mary's room.

"Piper and I would like to spend some time in there," she had said, taking the key with a trembling hand. "To try and understand."

Now they lay staring at the oil painting of their mother, Louisa, which hung opposite the foot of Mary's bed. It had been painted on her twenty-first birthday and captured her vitality, joy and beauty. Her long dark hair, lighter than Perdita's, cascaded to her shoulders and her grey eyes sparkled. She exuded life.

"Why did Dad never tell us about Mum's dyslexia?" mused Perdita. "In fact, why didn't he talk about her? He never even told us where she was buried. At first, yes, he was grieving, but over time, wouldn't you think he'd have wanted us to know more about her?"

"Grief does odd things. Maybe he thought we'd recover more quickly not knowing. I suppose we accepted it before because we didn't want to upset Dad, but also, he was the adult and we assumed he knew best. It's only now I wonder if we shouldn't have stood our ground. She was our mother, we had a right to know, even if he did find it difficult," replied Piper.

She wiped a tear from her eye. "I'm glad we've finally seen Mum's grave, though."

"It's a shame it's too late for bluebells," said Perdita sadly.

"We have so much money now, we can build a greenhouse and pay someone to grow them all year round so Mum always has her favourite flowers," said Piper, only half joking.

Perdita laughed. "Her favourite flower was one of the few things we did know."

They both drifted into their own thoughts again, until Perdita sat up, no longer able to bear staring at her mother's portrait and its reminder of all they had lost as children.

"Come on, let's go into my room, we can finish exploring in here another time," she said.

Piper squeezed her hand and they wandered back through Mary's suite of rooms, which was slightly larger than their own and had magnificent views over the lake and out to sea, back to Perdita's. Piper settled on the sofa and Perdita emerged from the kitchen with two wine glasses and a bottle of red.

"From the cellar?" asked Piper, taking her glass.

"No, the supermarket," laughed Perdita. "Alistair hasn't mentioned a wine cellar, but I'm sure there's one somewhere."

Settling at the other end of the sofa, Perdita glanced around her living room. There were piles of boxes that Piper, after a swift visit to their old home in Chiswick, had brought with her. By coincidence, the eldest son of Sarah Eve, the housekeeper and her husband, Alan, the grounds man and head of security at Marquess House, had been in London and had been able to meet Piper at the airport, making the collection and delivery of Perdita's belongings even easier. Perdita itched to begin unpacking her books and other items, but she knew there would be time after the funeral when her sister had returned to

America. Now, she turned her thoughts to more immediate issues.

"What do you think about Mary requesting the same readings as Dad? Weird, eh?"

"Or, they meant something to Dad and Mary, which could mean the readings are somehow connected to Mum," replied Piper. "Perds, stop looking for strange coincidences that aren't there. Our situation is tough enough to get our heads around without you finding conspiracy theories at every turn."

"Have you read them both again?" she persisted, not quite prepared to let the matter drop.

Piper sipped her wine. "Yes, I know them both off by heart."

"And?"

"And what?"

"They're both about being watched, spied on, and in the case of Susanna, punished, or nearly punished for something she hadn't done…"

"Perds, I love you, but I'm exhausted and I'm going to bed," interrupted Piper in a tone of weary finality before standing up and running her hand through her abundant red hair. "You're tired, overwrought and doing what you always do when you're upset, allowing your imagination to run wild. Get some sleep. I'm going to do the same thing. It'll look less strange in the morning."

Piper hugged her sister, then walked quickly from the room, leaving Perdita feeling irritated. Perdita finished her wine while she contemplated her sister's reaction. She wondered if Piper also found the choice of readings unnerving, but was refusing to acknowledge her feelings, blocking them out until the funeral was over so she could safely put them behind her. Piper had always bottled things up, usually confiding in Perdita only when she felt more in control of her emotions. Since her arrival, she had not mentioned Jeremy or her marriage but Perdita knew it would come eventually.

Sighing, Perdita picked up their glasses and took them to the kitchen. No matter what Piper thought, she found the choice of readings eerie and a shiver ran down her spine.

The sun shone in a cerulean sky, its joyous brightness jarring with the stream of black clad people below. The procession wound its way from the entrance of Marquess House along a path to the chapel situated in the grounds. It was a short and pretty walk through an abundant flower garden where a fountain played, water gushing from the centre of a stone oval held in the delicate hands of a beautiful but sad-faced mermaid.

As Mary's granddaughters and chief mourners, Perdita and Piper walked behind the coffin as it was carried on its short, final journey. Both dressed in simple but stylish black dresses, their heels clicking on the stone path, they followed their grandmother's earthly remains through the kissing gate and into the chapel's cool interior.

Flowers covered every surface, the heady scents filling the air like a drug. Behind them walked the Mackensie family: Alistair, his wife Susan, their eldest daughter Megan and her fiancé Pablo, middle son Stuart and finally, Kit. They were all pale-faced and sad at Mary's loss.

Upon the arrival of Kit's two elder siblings a few days earlier, Perdita had been both comforted and slightly overwhelmed by the warmth with which they had absorbed her into their family group. Usually, her natural shyness acted as a barrier, keeping people at bay until she was ready to trust them, but the Mackensies had merely included her as though she were a life-long friend or even a cousin and, to her surprise, she had found herself responding. When Piper had arrived, she too, was absorbed into this happy band. As such, the twins had insisted they sit with them in the front few rows of the small chapel. Warren had offered to come back from France but Perdita had explained it was something she felt she should do with Piper and he had accepted her wishes without an argument.

Earlier that week, when Kit had taken her to the exquisite chapel, she had been surprised at its beauty. It reminded Perdita of a miniature version of the Chapel Royal at Hampton Court Palace, once the home of Henry VIII. A stunning blue and gold ceiling climbed skyward above them and stained glass windows featuring mythical creatures and various Biblical scenes filled the interior with dancing, jewel-like light. Ceiling bosses ran the length of the chapel, some decorated with flowers and, to her surprise, mermaids. Others featured delicately carved and beautifully painted faces.

"Who are they?" she had asked Kit, staring up in wonder.

"I don't know," he had replied. "There might be records in the archive but they were probably the first owners or particularly important people who have come after them."

"They're all women," she had said in surprise.

Kit had stood next to her, scrutinising the faces staring at him across time. "Do you know, I've never noticed that before."

Now Kit slid into the pew beside Perdita. She gave him a quick on-off smile, glad to have him there. The vicar stepped forward and Perdita was not surprised when Piper, crying quietly, reached for her hand. Squeezing it, trying to offer reassurance, Perdita attempted to marshal her own teeming thoughts by concentrating on the vicar's words. Then the haunting notes of Elgar's Cello Concerto rang through the chapel and the small congregation, mostly of close friends and people who worked at or were connected to Marquess House, took comfort from the flow of the soothing music. Alistair rose and read a short eulogy focusing on Mary's personal, rather than professional, achievements. Perdita found her eyes filling with tears.

She felt Kit's hand on hers and was about to snatch it away when she realised he was pushing a pristine handkerchief towards her. She smiled gratefully and took it, dabbing her eyes as Alistair regained his seat at the end of the pew across the aisle. There followed a short reading by the vicar, then they sang Mary's favourite hymn, *Morning Has Broken*, before Piper, now tear-free, walked to the front of the chapel to read the George Orwell passage from the novel *1984*, which she had read so recently at their father's funeral. It was only a few lines long and was about being watched. Perdita continued to wonder at its significance.

Piper returned to her seat and Perdita stood, walking slowly towards the pulpit. Swallowing her feeling of déjà vu, she looked down at her typewritten sheet. Susanna, verses 42-48. She cleared her throat and began to read.

These were the specific verses Mary had selected, exactly the same as her father. A short excerpt that concentrated on the point where Susanna had been falsely accused of a crime and was about to be executed, then Daniel stepped in to save her, claiming it was the people who had accused her who were guilty, not Susanna. Perdita had wondered why her father, James, had chosen this. She was even more mystified why her grandmother had too. It was yet another question she would never be able to ask. Returning to her seat, she bowed her head and after a stream of prayers, they stood for the final hymn, *Jerusalem*.

The service, while soothing, had only added to the mystery of her grandmother, and Perdita once more wiped away tears as she and Piper allowed Kit to guide them from the pew to the family vault on the edge of the small graveyard. Mary was interred between her husband, Hector Woodville, and her daughter, Louisa, and as the service ended, Perdita felt a huge sense of relief. Not because the ordeal of the service was over, but because she felt her grandmother was safe now. The world could not hurt her anymore. Piper had moved towards their mother's grave, tears streaming down her face. Perdita turned away, ready to repel anyone who might interrupt her sister. She knew Piper needed this moment of solitude.

It was as she turned away from her sister, her eyes searching the crowd for Kit or his father, that she saw two strangers by the kissing gate, watching her intently. An elderly man in a wheelchair, his suit impeccable, and what remained of his snowy white hair, brushed back in an old-fashioned style. With him was a man in his fifties. The younger man was tall, his own luxuriant hair was still reasonably dark and cut into a short, military style. Both men wore charcoal grey suits and black ties. They seemed to be observing her with interest, yet neither of them showed any inclination to come forward and speak.

Perdita turned her back on them and beckoned to Piper, feeling strangely uncomfortable. She glanced around looking for a member of the Mackensie family to ask who the men were when she saw Stuart marching towards them, his step purposeful and angry. Piper joined her and they watched as Stuart stopped by the two men and, after a short exchange, stormed away, fury on his face. It was a few moments before the men by the kissing gate turned to leave, but not before the man in the wheelchair had nodded respectfully to Perdita and

Piper, by which time Megan, Stuart and Kit had surrounded them.

"Who were those men?" Perdita asked as the Mackensie siblings guided the Rivers twins back towards Marquess House.

"People who should have known better than to come here today, where they're not welcome," said Stuart, who still seemed rattled by his confrontation.

"But who were they?" Piper insisted.

"They were from your grandmother's past," said Kit.

Megan glared at her youngest brother and continued: "And as Stuart said, they had no right to come here today, especially Morton Keller..."

"Which one was he?" said Perdita.

"The older man in the wheelchair," interrupted Kit, raising his eyebrows at his sister to indicate she should shut up. "He and your grandmother fell out years ago. I suspect he came here today looking for forgiveness."

"From whom?" asked Piper intrigued.

"From you two," said Kit.

"But why?"

"Ah, there you are!" They were interrupted by the booming voice of Alistair Mackensie. "Let's get you safely inside, Perdita, Piper," he said leading them into the house. Piper shot Perdita a bemused glance. She raised her eyebrows in response but not before she thought: *And there it is again, the word safe.* She allowed Alistair to guide them through the Tudor hall and into a large sitting room known as the Lady Isabel Room, which had magnificent French doors opening out onto the terrace where they had decided to have the reception. It was a suntrap with a long, paved platform. At one end was a pergola covered in wisteria, while numerous flights of stone steps led to the intricate Elizabethan knot garden below.

"Who is Morton Keller, Alistair?" Perdita asked as he handed her a glass of champagne, another instruction from Mary. His face went momentarily blank, then his usual avuncular smile appeared.

"He's no one you need to worry about."

"Please don't patronise us," said Piper quietly. "He wasn't in the chapel for the service but he and that other man barely took their eyes off us while we were in the graveyard. Who are they?"

For a moment, Alistair hesitated and Perdita could tell he was weighing up what he should tell them. Finally, he took a deep breath and spoke: "You are aware of how your mother died?"

The twins nodded; it was one of the few pieces of information they did have. "She was killed in a car accident," said Perdita. "She tried to stop to avoid an oncoming car which was driving too fast but her brakes failed, she swerved, lost control of the vehicle and smashed into a stone wall, then went over the edge of the cliff. She never regained consciousness."

Alistair nodded, then with great reluctance he spoke, wincing as he did so, as though each word caused him intense pain. "The man in the wheelchair, Morton Keller, was driving the other car. He was the reason your mother died."

Chapter Four

Perdita and Piper sat, pyjama-clad, clutching mugs of hot chocolate as they talked about the man in the wheelchair: Morton Keller. His name unknown until today. His condition or even his survival, never discussed. Yet, in the aftermath of their grandmother's funeral, they had been forced to confront another aspect of their turbulent past — the man who had been responsible for their mother's death when they were seven years old.

"It's all his fault," said Piper, her voice low, unforgiving, deadly. "If it hadn't been for him, we would still have Mum, we might have still had Granny. We would have had different lives…"

"Pipes, we can't think that way," said Perdita, holding back her own pain, knowing if she let go of her anger, it would be devastating. "We can't change it."

"Do you think he's in the wheelchair because of the accident?" asked Piper.

Perdita shrugged, then said: "I hope so." The bitterness in her voice was so completely out of character, it brought Piper up short.

"Do you mean that?" she asked, horrified.

Perdita's eyes welled with tears. "No," she replied. "But it seems so unfair that he survived, yet his moment of carelessness sent our lives into chaos."

The image of Morton Keller in his wheelchair and the chill stare of his companion were still making her shudder.

"If he wanted forgiveness, why did he make no attempt to speak to us?" she continued.

Neither twin spoke, the silence growing. They had no answers, only questions, which they were wise enough to realise would probably never be resolved.

After a while, Piper spoke, her voice quieter now, sad: "I think Jeremy's having an affair with a woman at work called Kirstin."

"Oh, Pipes, no," whispered Perdita, reaching out to squeeze her sister's hand. "Jeremy loves you, he wouldn't…"

The twins had grown up with Jeremy Davidson, the only son of their father's best friend since his university days. The three had been inseparable and, in their teens, when it had become apparent that Piper and Jeremy were falling in love, no one could have been more delighted than Perdita. The thought of his possible betrayal broke her heart too.

"I always thought that too, Perds, but in the past few months, he's changed."

"In what way?" asked Perdita, hoping her sister was wrong.

"I thought at first he was having a nervous breakdown, pressure of work, that kind of thing. He's become secretive, he loses his temper with me all the time — sometimes I'm scared to speak because I can't stand the shouting — and he's changed the password on both his phone and laptop. We always used the same one or variations of it, anyway: COPPER, after our old dog. He won't tell me the new one. The worst thing is that he's stopped mentioning her name."

"What do you mean?"

"When we first arrived, he was the usual Jeremy, happy, open, sharing his life and work, like we always did. Then this new woman started — she's on secondment too, but from a different office, Corby in Northamptonshire. For a few weeks, it was Kirstin this, Kirstin that. Kirstin who is supposedly married with two daughters. Then suddenly, no more mentions of Kirstin."

"Has she left?"

"No, I bumped into the wife of one of Jeremy's colleagues when I was out shopping and casually brought Kirstin's name up in conversation," she sighed. "You should have seen the look of pity she gave me, Perds. It confirmed everything I was beginning to suspect."

Perdita stared at her sister, her face mirroring the misery on Piper's. She put her empty mug on the floor and reached out to envelope her twin in a huge hug. Leaning into Perdita's shoulder, Piper began to cry.

"I didn't tell him I was coming to Granny's funeral. I went while he was at work and left him a note. Maybe me walking out will have brought him to his senses," she said, her voice muffled.

"Why don't you stay a bit longer?"

Piper wriggled out of her sister's arms and shook her head. "I can't. I have to at least try to salvage my marriage. I've loved Jeremy most of my life. What we have is worth fighting for."

"Do you want me to come? You know, moral support."

"That's so kind but no, this is something I have to do alone."

"Of course," said Perdita. "While I need to stay here and try to discover why Mary has left us everything. From what everyone says, it seems she did love us and wanted us in her life."

"And that picture," said Piper, pointing at the abstract depiction of Marquess House over her fireplace. "Do you think it's the one?"

"I've been wondering that," admitted Perdita. "The one Granny commissioned Dad to do after his final art school exhibition. What was it Dad told us — that every summer

Granny would commission a number of students after viewing their shows?"

Piper nodded.

"It was the painting that brought him here and kept him here because he took one look at Mum and fell in love with her on the spot," she finished. "But what I don't understand is, if Granny hated him so much, why didn't she destroy it? Or at least hide it away?"

"It's all a bit much, isn't it?" murmured Perdita. Piper nodded and they managed a rueful laugh.

Half an hour later, Perdita was back in her own room, her mind whirring from her conversation with Piper. But after flicking off her bedside light, thoughts of Piper and Jeremy faded as the image of Morton Keller once more swam into her mind.

Suddenly, a strange clarity came to Perdita, as clear and brilliant as a diamond and equally as hard: *Morton Keller did not want forgiveness; he was observing us as though we were rivals, challengers*, she thought. *He was sizing us up, checking how strong we would be as adversaries*. It was an odd conclusion to draw but after a few moments pondering it, trying to dismiss it as tiredness or the product of her overwrought mind, she realised the idea had become so firmly lodged in her psyche, she could not shift it. Strangely, this did not scare her. It only made her curious and, to her surprise, she also felt herself relax. Within moments, she was asleep.

Piper left the following day. Billy Eve, the younger son of Sarah and Alan, was driving her back to Heathrow Airport. It had been an emotional parting for the twins.

"Don't let him upset you any more than you can stand," Perdita had said as she hugged Piper goodbye. "I can always fly to you or you can come here."

"I'll be OK," Piper had reassured her. "You take care too. If it gets too emotional, come to me or go back to Chiswick."

"I'll be OK too," Perdita had echoed with a smile.

She had waved until Billy's car was out of sight, then returned to the house and spent the rest of the day unpacking her belongings before exploring the library and the grounds. In the early evening, she had asked Kit to drive her to the animal sanctuary her mother had loved. When they had arrived, she had taken a deep breath and walked into what had once been her family home, but to her surprise, no memories came flooding back. Instead, she met Briony Llewellyn who ran the sanctuary, and was introduced to the horses as well as an array of cats, dogs, rabbits, chickens and a pair of twin sheep.

It was now Perdita's second week at Marquess House and, as promised, Jenny Procter had gathered together Mary's research. Perdita gazed at the piles of boxes covering a series of long tables arranged end-to-end and pushed against one wall of the office that had once been Mary's.

"I can see why it took you a week to assemble it all," she said. "There's so much!"

"You're a child of the digital age, Perdita," Jenny laughed. "You've probably got a few memory sticks and a small pile of printouts. Mary was old school. Everything was on paper. A lot was handwritten, but over the years we have transcribed it. Here," she handed Perdita a small leather wallet. "All Mary's notes and research have been digitised, so you won't have to wade through boxes of dusty paper if you don't want to."

Unzipping the leather wallet, Perdita opened it like a book. Set into small compartments inside was a row of memory sticks, each with the title of one of Mary's many publications printed alongside.

"All the pages were scanned, so you can see the original then the transcription, including all of Mary's notes," said Jenny. "On the table are Mary's private copies of her own books. She left instructions that, should either you or Piper ever request to see her research, this is the set of books you were to work from. I've never looked in them, but I can only assume she may have written notes or updates which she felt were important. Anyway, have fun! Call if you need anything, I'm on extension 423. I'll have coffee sent along in an hour or so."

Petite, stylish and blonde, Jenny was in her early sixties but looked much younger. She swept out on a wave of expensive, heady perfume, giving Perdita a friendly smile.

Alone with the boxes, Perdita wondered where to begin. She sank onto one of the two large Chesterfield sofas that were situated to one side of the huge room and tried to formulate a workable plan. Mary's office took up an entire corner of the research centre, which was, in itself, huge. When she had first seen it, Perdita had thought it was a complex of offices and reading rooms fashioned into a small, unused barn. It was only when Kit and Jenny had shown her and Piper around that she had realised that, like everything else in their new world, it was not as she had imagined.

The section she had seen from the house was only the reception and visitor's area. Once inside the research centre, Perdita realised that it occupied the whole of what had once been an enormous barn complex and coach house.

"They were Victorian and quite ugly," Jenny had explained. "So Mary decided to salvage anything of historical value or beauty, but convert the rest. It was a huge project but it was worth it. The storage facility alone is invaluable. Some areas have specially designed climate control and the most advanced air filters available, but others are less complicated. Mary was a real collector and saver of documents. They fascinated her as they were such keys to the past. The building right at the back has a dedicated team of conservators. We call it The Dairy because it was built in the old…"

"Dairy?" Perdita had finished, and Jenny had laughed.

"Original stuff, eh? It's a custom-built facility that was funded by both Mary and Jerusalem. Its purpose is to restore and authenticate documents. Mary has another suite of offices near the restoration area. They're climate controlled and she used them when she was working on original documents."

Mary's office had made use of the huge coach house doors, which had been glazed and offered a clear view to the lake with its island ruins. The wooden frame was carved with a frieze identical to the design throughout the house: swags of flowers held together by mermaids who, in this incarnation, appeared to be holding ornate rings. It was a pattern that repeated endlessly.

For now, though, Perdita's mind was preoccupied with the boxes. She glanced at the memory sticks, then dismissed them. Part of the reason she had asked for the research was because she wanted to see how her grandmother had constructed her work, look at the process of discovery and how she drew the often controversial conclusions she had used in her books. No computer simulation could show her that. Only touching and reading her grandmother's notes, seeing how the handwriting changed and how the trains of thought progressed, could be done by studying the real documents.

The complete collection of Mary's published works that Jenny had mentioned were on the long, low table that was situated between the two Chesterfield sofas. Leaning over,

Perdita picked up her grandmother's first published book, *The History and Symbolism of Names*. She knew the library had pristine versions of all the first editions, many in limited edition leather bindings, which made them so valuable, but these were Mary's copies. Her grandmother had touched these, used them as reference points. Perdita opened the book and inhaled, trying to catch a hint of her grandmother's scent, but there was nothing, only the smell of an old book. This, too, was a first edition and to her surprise, the pages were covered in notes in Mary's tiny, perfectly formed handwriting.

Intrigued, Perdita began to read her grandmother's comments. They were often random and unrelated to the text: "*What a wonderful year this has been. My first book published and tomorrow, I marry Hector Woodville, the man of my dreams*", followed by the date: *4th November 1955*. Perdita had not expected to find anything so personal. She flicked a few pages on and smiled as she saw a Christmas shopping list including "*Hector — pipe*" and "*Cecily — silk scarf*". Cecily Fitzroy had been Mary's younger sister and from what Perdita had gleaned during her research, Cecily had drowned in a boating accident in Monaco in 1974.

Picking up the next book in the pile, *The Scottish Link: A Study of Trade and Personal links between the Tudor and Stuart Courts*, she was once again intrigued by the private, inconsequential notes written neatly on the white space around the printed words: "*Cecily and Albert Connors are getting married tomorrow, assuming she doesn't jilt him at the altar*" caught Perdita's eye. Then near the end: "*I am so excited to be having a baby at last, even stopping my writing doesn't seem like a sacrifice*". With a lump in her throat, Perdita realised Mary was referring to her mother, Louisa, who was born on 19 January 1959.

If her grandmother had still been alive, Perdita would have felt this was an intrusion into her privacy. But Mary was dead and these notes in her books were the first glimpse of her grandmother's true self that Perdita had ever had: it was fascinating, as well as bittersweet. What was more important was that Mary had left strict instructions for her and Piper to see these; she had wanted her granddaughters to glimpse her life. Perdita was mystified as to why her grandmother had desired that she and Piper see such intimate notes when she could have contacted them at any time over the years to tell them these details herself. She looked back at the comment and noticed that underneath, written in tiny letters, were the words: "*Cecily has a son, Randolph Connors, 30 September 1959, a cousin for Louisa*".

Her mother had a cousin? Perdita read it again, Randolph Connors. She had never heard the name mentioned. Reaching for her laptop, she keyed in his name along with his date of birth. An image of a hawk-nosed man with small dark eyes and sallow skin appeared. It was a short entry on a business website dated from ten years earlier: "*Businessman Randolph Connors donated £5,000 (sterling) to the Indian Orphanage Programme in New Delhi…*"

She continued to search but found nothing else of interest. Instead she made a note to ask Alistair what was known about this man. Had Mary cut him from her life too?

An hour later, when there was a knock on the door and Kit came in carrying a tray of coffee and pastries, she was still deeply engrossed in the books. She had found a reference to her and Piper's births, to her parents' marriage, which had followed shortly afterwards, and a reminder to order some hay for the horses. Unconscious thoughts, glimpses of her grandmother's life, an insight she had never imagined she would discover.

"How are you getting on?" he asked with his usual enthusiasm.

"Really well," she said, clearing a space so he could place the tray on the table. He dropped onto the sofa opposite her and pushed his unruly dark curls out of his eyes.

"I'm knackered," he said, and demolished half a croissant with one bite.

Perdita laughed. "What do you actually do here, Kit?" she asked as she picked up her coffee and sipped it. "Are you a solicitor like your dad?"

"Yes and no," he said, stuffing the other half of the pastry into his mouth and chewing rhythmically. "I am a solicitor but I work for our family business, Jerusalem. The legal stuff is only one side of it."

"And, apart from funding archaeological digs all around the world, what else does it do?"

"We rescue and restore important antiquities and documents. If they're of national interest, we either lend or donate the items to the government of their country of origin, depending on the political climate at the time. Megan runs the organisation from Andorra. She covers Africa and Asia. Stuart looks after the Americas, the Caribbean and a few other places. I do Europe, Scandinavia, Australia and New Zealand. I was up until 4 a.m. bidding on an item of New Zealand origin. It's very rare and extremely important. We didn't want it to be snapped up by a private collector and disappear from view forever."

"What was it?" asked Perdita, stunned by Kit's answer. With his surfer clothes, laid-back attitude and easy-going manner, the last thing she had expected him to say he did was act like some internet Indiana Jones saving rare antiquities.

"It was an ancient document of ownership of the islands going all the way back to the 1600s, and hugely predates Captain Cook who didn't discover them until April 1769," he said. "The thing is, we think it's a fake, which was why it was important we got it so we can try to verify its authenticity."

"I'm impressed," she said. He gave a mock nod of his head in thanks and helped himself to a pain au chocolat.

"How are you getting on?" he asked when he had swallowed his first enormous mouthful.

"Interesting," said Perdita. "Did you know my grandmother used her first editions as personal diaries?"

"No!"

Perdita pushed a copy of *The Anne Boleyn Question* towards Kit.

"Look at page 162."

Kit wiped his fingers on his faded cut-offs and flicked through.

"*Today I became a grandmother to two beautiful baby girls: Perdita Elizabeth and Piper Eleanor. My heart is bursting with happiness*," he read.

"If she loved us so much, why did she stop seeing us after Mum died?"

"Perdita, I don't know," he said, awkward at the personal question. "She must have had her reasons. Is there anything in the next book? *The Missing Heirs of Henry VIII*? It came out shortly before Louisa's accident." Perdita hesitated. "Would you like me to look?"

Perdita pushed the book towards him. "Yes, please," she said, then hated herself for being such a coward.

He flicked carefully through the pages but, as Perdita looked at it upside down, she realised this was the first book her grandmother had left untouched, until Kit reached the last page. He read the short inscription, then turned it to Perdita, looking puzzled.

"What does it say?" she asked, leaning forward and reading. "*It is over. They have won. Mary Fitzroy, 30 May 1993*," she read. "What does that mean?"

Perdita reached for the next book in the pile. There had been a six-year gap between the books and this was the first that moved away from Mary's study of the women of the Tudor and Stuart families. This one began her series focusing on women of importance before and after the Norman Conquest. It was about the daughter of King Alfred the Great and was entitled: *Aethelflaed, Lady of the Mercians: Warrior Queen.*

"Maybe there's something in here," she said and began flicking through, searching for her grandmother's handwriting. But to her surprise, rather than notes, there were photographs pushed so deeply into the spine they would not fall out when the book was moved.

"It's us," she said. "Me and Piper."

The first picture showed the twins aged seven, standing beside the fireplace in the house in Chiswick. What followed were identical photographs charting every birthday from then until the previous year.

"Dad took one every year," said Perdita, "then put it in a frame on the fireplace that Mum had given him. He said it was to show her how much we'd grown."

Kit said nothing but studied the pictures, putting them in chronological order so they spread across the table, then grinned. "Good look, blue lipstick," holding up a picture. "Age fourteen. Your age is written on the back."

"I loved that lipstick," she murmured, trying to hide her bewilderment. Why had her father sent these to Mary? He had flown into a rage whenever the girls mentioned her name.

"You might want to see this," said Kit, all trace of humour gone from his voice.

He handed her the most recent picture, the one taken a month before her father had died. It had been an emotional moment for them all, as they knew it was the last one he would ever take but he had insisted upon continuing their tradition. He had also taken image after image until they were both smiling.

She took the familiar picture and turned it over. On the back of the other pictures, her father had written their ages, nothing else, but on this, the final photograph, there was a short note.

"*Dearest Mary,*" Perdita read, "*the cancer is rife so this will be the last photograph of the girls I will be able to send. I have done everything we agreed upon on that terrible day and it has kept them safe. The rest is up to you. Godspeed, my old friend. Your loving son-in-law, James.*"

Perdita and Kit stared at each other in confusion.

"He wouldn't even let us mention her name, let alone ask questions about her. Why would he sign a note as 'your loving son-in-law'? How dare he?" Perdita's anger was rising, driven by confusion as she felt her world tilt. Her reality had always been that her father had loathed her grandmother, had blamed her irrationally for the death of her mother, Louisa. This hatred was then intensified by the fact that they had rowed and, afterwards, her grandmother had abandoned them. This was the world in which Perdita had grown up, this was the truth she had always known, even if she had not liked it. But now an earthquake of seismic proportions was shaking this fundamental foundation on which her family relations had been built. If this note was to be believed, her father and grandmother had remained in touch, were loyal to each other, cared deeply and yet, they had stayed apart, ensuring she and Piper were kept from anything concerning their mother and their past.

"You knew his writing," said Kit. "Do you think the note is a fake?"

"No, it's definitely Dad's writing."

Her father had terrible handwriting, messy almost illegible — there was no mistaking the note was from him. Suddenly, she turned on Kit.

"Explain this," she snapped.

"I can't!"

"Why not? You were practically brought up here. Mary was more of a grandmother to you than she was to Piper and me. You must have known what was going on. Did my father visit?"

"Yes, we were here a lot," said Kit, trying to remain calm in the face of Perdita's mounting rage, "but Mary didn't discuss anything with us, we were children. Dad might know or maybe Granddad Kenneth before he died but, Perdita, truly, I never remember your father coming to visit."

She began to pace the room, wishing Piper were here to share her confusion. Agitated, unsure how to react, she felt as though she were standing on quicksand. The past few weeks had seen her life changed beyond recognition, but this new and unexpected twist was almost more than she could bear. Her father had been in touch with her grandmother. Why? Perdita leaned over Kit to pick up the photograph. Walking away, studying the words, she re-read the note scrawled on the back.

"*Dearest Mary,*" Perdita read aloud, "*the cancer is rife so this will probably be the last photograph of the girls I will be able to send. I have done everything we agreed upon on that terrible day and it has kept them safe. The rest is up to you. Godspeed, my old friend. Your loving son-in-law, James."*

"There it is again," she snarled, glaring at Kit, knowing it was not his fault but taking her fear out on him nevertheless.

"What?" asked Kit, bemused.

"The word 'safe'. Your father keeps using it and now it's here in my father's handwriting. Safe from what? Or whom? What's going on?"

Kit stood up. At five foot seven, Perdita was tall, but at six foot four, Kit loomed over her. He took a deep breath as though it would calm her down, then placed his hands on her shoulders and gently turned her to face him, his deep blue eyes staring into hers, trying to rationalise her terror.

"I've no idea why my father keeps using the word safe or why your father wrote that note," he said, his tone gentle. "My understanding was the same as yours, that your dad and your grandmother rowed after your mother's death. I've never seen these photographs before and, as far as I'm aware, your father never visited. The only thing I knew was that the house you lived in belonged to Mary."

Perdita's worried grey-green eyes stared into his soothing blue. She believed him but it still made no sense.

"I'm sorry," she said, disentangling herself from his grip. "None of this is your fault, but something obviously happened."

Her mind was whirling as her naturally analytical brain tried to sort this new and unexpected information into a logical order. Yet, no matter how many times she rearranged the differing hypothesis, she could not resolve the information into a coherent whole. Too many pieces of the puzzle were missing. The obvious answer was to speak to Alistair but her gut instinct told her he would be reluctant to discuss the situation and, if he did, would give the accepted version of the truth as agreed by Mary and her father, rather than the real events. Still thinking hard, Perdita walked back to the boxes of research.

On first entering the office, she had not realised they had been arranged in chronological order. Now she walked the length of Mary's work, pausing first at the boxes labelled *The Anne Boleyn Question* (Published 1985), then *The Missing Heir of Henry VIII* (Published 1993), she noticed something and it momentarily distracted her.

"There are too many," she said, standing back and counting.

"What do you mean?" asked Kit who was still watching her closely.

"Over the course of her career, my grandmother published ten books, as well as articles, features, papers and inserts in other works, but there are twelve sets of research here — look at the way they're laid out, there are gaps between each set of boxes."

She and Kit moved as one to the boxes situated between *The Missing Heir of Henry VIII*, which was released shortly before Louisa's death and Mary's next publication six years later, where there were two sets of boxes, one as large as the others, the second slightly smaller, as though the research had been stopped too soon.

"*The Catherine Howard Anomaly* (Unpublished)," read Perdita from the first pile of boxes.

"*Possible working titles: The Ladies of Melusine or The Lady Pamela Letters: A Study of the Epistolary Styles of Women in the Tudor and Stuart Courts* (Early stages of research)," read Kit from the lid of the next pile.

"She wrote two other books but abandoned them," said Perdita. "I wonder why?"

"On a practical level, perhaps she felt they weren't good enough for publication," suggested Kit.

"Maybe."

"Do you have another explanation?"

"You read what Granny Mary wrote in her copy of *The Missing Heirs of Henry VIII*: '*It is over. They have won. Mary Fitzroy, 30 May 1993*'. Does that sound like someone who isn't confident of her own work? I think she deliberately pulled these books from publication."

"Why? She was a respected academic, why would she abandon perfectly acceptable books, unless it was because she deemed they weren't good enough? You're upset by what you've discovered today, you're looking for coincidences that aren't there."

His words, so similar to Piper's, made Perdita more, rather than less, determined.

"Why did she cut us from her life then leave us everything?" she snapped. "Why did Dad send her photographs of us every year? Why was he in touch with her when he wouldn't even let us mention her name? Something happened around the time of my mother's death and I'm going to find out what it was. Do you know what else I've discovered today? Piper and I have distant cousins; we're not alone in the world like we thought. If I can discover that by reading the scribbles in my grandmother's copies of her published work, what might I discover if I go through the research for books we didn't even know she'd written?"

"Perdita, please…" Kit began, but she cut across him, her voice becoming frantic, tears of anger and frustration in her eyes. "I might find answers," she said. "I might find the truth."

Chapter Five

Kit departed the following morning. He was attending the wedding of a university friend in Scotland but was travelling to London to stay with his girlfriend, Lydia Brooks, before flying to Edinburgh.

"You didn't mention you had a girlfriend," Perdita had said, surprised to find herself so irritated by this unexpected development.

"You didn't ask," he had replied with a grin. "Does that mean you won't be driving me to the station, then?"

"Don't be ridiculous," she had huffed in response, then laughed at herself. What did it matter if Kit had a girlfriend? She was engaged to Warren but, now Kit was gone, the house felt strangely empty.

Although, she told herself as she walked from the house to the research centre, enjoying the glorious summer sunshine, *it's probably a good thing he's away as he doesn't think I'll find anything other than a book that was below publication levels and a stack of research that was not strong enough to turn into a workable draft.* She was still convinced otherwise.

As always, she had confided in Piper. Initially, her sister had taken a similar sceptical line to Kit, although her motivation was because she did not want to see Perdita hurt by any possible revelations or the very real fact that there would not be any answers and Perdita's hope would be dashed. It was only after Perdita had explained all she had discovered, including all the notes in their grandmother's editions, that Piper had been persuaded.

"Keep me posted," she had said the previous evening when Perdita had explained her plan of beginning with the book entitled *The Catherine Howard Anomaly*. "I'm not doing much at the moment — except worrying obviously — email me the manuscript and I'll have a look too. We'll probably spot different things. Anyway, it'll be a good distraction."

"How are things with you and Jeremy?" Perdita had asked, concerned by her twin's white face and shadowed eyes.

"Not great," she admitted. "The shock of my walking out has receded. He was almost his normal self for a few days but now things are deteriorating again. I even confronted him about Kirstin. He told me I was being ridiculous, then two minutes later, I overheard him on the phone, saying, 'She suspects'. He's still denying he's having an affair, though. I never realised he thought I was such a fool, Perds."

The conversation had bothered Perdita all night and she had resolved that her first job this morning would be to send the manuscript to her troubled sister. She hoped it would give Piper something else to think about rather than brooding on Jeremy's behaviour.

"Morning, Jenny," said Perdita as she breezed into the research centre.

"Morning," Jenny responded. "Coffee at eleven?"

"Yes, please," Perdita replied, disappearing into the office she now considered hers.

To her delight, a pile of books, all either biographies of or relating to Catherine Howard, had been left on her desk with a note from Jenny: *These are from the main library and our archive, I'm researching and ordering other works concerning Catherine Howard. Hopefully, these will arrive tomorrow.*

Good, thought Perdita. *I'm going to need guidance while I work my way through Granny's research because this is a period of history where my knowledge is limited.*

She sat behind the desk and flipped open the wallet of USB sticks. Flicking on her laptop, she selected the one marked *The Catherine Howard Anomaly* and slotted it in. Moments later, the files appeared. Selecting the one named *Final Draft*, she opened it and read the dedication.

Oh no, she sighed to herself. *I will not cry.* It was difficult, though; the book had been dedicated to her and Piper — "*my beloved granddaughters*". Taking a deep breath, Perdita scrolled through the manuscript. It looked complete but, until she found the original, she would not know. "It'll keep Piper going for now, though," she murmured and sent it whizzing through the ether.

Standing up, she walked to the row of boxes. There was a pile of three storage boxes labelled simply as *The Catherine Howard Anomaly*, followed by a one, two and three. No dates, no indexes. Perdita picked up the first box, carried it to the desk and, taking off the lid, she stared at the contents. Everything was neatly arranged in coloured folders and, to her delight, there was a bound copy of what was obviously Mary's final draft sitting on the top. Grinning, delighted at her grandmother's organisational abilities, she lifted the manuscript out and, settling down on one of the sofas, began to read.

PART TWO: London, 1539-40

Chapter One

Catherine shivered as she waited. The corridor in Whitehall Palace was a thoroughfare bustling with people, but it was draughty and the icy wind cut across it like a shining blade. She hugged her new shawl more tightly around her, glad of its warmth. As she did, she admired the soft leather gloves her uncle had given her as a gift before she left home.

"Soft gloves to protect your soft hands," he had murmured. He had always singled her out for attention, been kinder to her than any of the other Howard girls, and he had arranged for her to be a maid to the new queen, the Lady Anne of Cleves. It was an honour but now she was here, her excitement was turning to nervousness.

She had grown up in her step-grandmother's house a few miles away in Lambeth. A ramshackle home full of orphans like her and other members of the hugely extended Howard clan. She had innocently thought that the court of King Henry VIII would be like that, only with more jewels. Now as she watched the parade of courtiers, she realised she could not have been more wrong. People hurried busily to and fro. Yeoman guards marched past in their daunting green and white Tudor uniforms, pikes aloft, metal-heeled boots ringing with a chilling authority. The women in their elaborate dresses, the men equally as ornate: it was an endless visual feast.

Court was more intense, more splendid and more glamorous than anything she had ever imagined and she was only on the edges; a mere nobody waiting with her trunk for her elder half-sister, Lady Isabel Baynton, to collect her. As she glanced up the corridor searching for a familiar face, a tall, good-looking man dressed in a sumptuous velvet cloak caught her eye and winked. Glancing over her shoulder to see if the true recipient of his intended favour was behind her, she heard the man laugh and blushed furiously as he walked by, still chuckling.

"Kitty!"

To her relief, she saw Isabel hurrying through the courtiers. Torches guttered casting shadowy light on her as she approached. It was early afternoon but the weather was cold and stormy and the sky had barely lightened all day. Taller than Catherine, with dark hair and dark eyes, Isabel was married to Sir Edward Baynton, who was to be vice-chamberlain to the new queen.

He was an important man, having worked for each of the king's wives — including Catherine's cousin, Anne Boleyn, Henry VIII's second bride. Now Edward was once again to hold this important role in the new queen's household and his stature was reflected in Isabel's dress, demeanour and, to Catherine's surprise, her spectacular jewels.

"Isabel!" exclaimed Catherine, curtseying to her half-sister as etiquette required, before being swept into a warm embrace. "Your diamonds! Did Edward give them to you?"

Isabel laughed and turned her head so the magnificent diamond drops in her ears shimmered with cold fire in the winter light.

"An early Christmas gift," she smiled. "We have a present for you to welcome you to court but we'll give it to you when you're settled. Is that yours?" She pointed to the trunk.

Catherine nodded. "Although, there isn't much in it," she admitted.

"Never mind," said Isabel. "We'll organise a new wardrobe for you. We must maintain the Howard family name. Cox, take my sister's trunk to the maids' rooms," she said to the servant standing respectfully behind her. Then, tucking her hand under Catherine's arm, she led her along the busy corridor. "What do you think of court?"

"I've been here barely half an hour but it seems, well…"

"Daunting?"

"Yes," agreed Catherine.

"Don't worry, my dear, we're all here to help you; myself and Edward, your Uncle Norfolk and, of course, our brother Charles. Although, he seems rather preoccupied at the moment."

"Is he in love again?" asked Catherine, grinning.

"Yes, but this is a little different from his usual infatuations."

"You mean the object of his affection isn't married?"

"She isn't but, well, there are other complications. However, it's never wise to discuss such things in the open court, even in jest, remember that, Kitten," said Isabel. "The court has ears everywhere and like the smiling serpent who was the undoing of Eve, there are endless charlatans lurking in unexpected places in this merry Eden."

Catherine nodded, but she was disappointed. She always enjoyed hearing about her brother's latest romantic escapades. The true chivalric and charmingly penniless knight, Charles Howard was always infatuated with someone, and Catherine suspected he was more in love with the idea of romance than the most recent recipient of his amour.

As they walked, she tried to memorise the winding route, wondering if this sprawling building would ever feel familiar. Eventually, they arrived in a quieter, but even more beautifully decorated section of the palace.

"These are the queen's new rooms," explained Isabel. "And along here are the maids' rooms. I've arranged for you to share with our cousin, Kathryn Carey. She's an old hand and will look out for you if neither Edward nor I are available to help."

"And Uncle Norfolk?" Catherine asked.

"He's a very busy man but I'm sure once he knows you're here, he'll invite you to his rooms to keep you up-to-date with family business."

Catherine laughed but she was secretly delighted.

"Hardly, Issy," she said. "I'm far too lowly for such important conversations."

"Don't underestimate your new status, Mistress Howard," said Isabel. "The position of maid of honour is not one given lightly and there were many noblemen fighting for places for their daughters. Enjoy your rise in status and use it wisely. You'll need a husband soon and being at court will improve your prospects of a lucrative match."

Catherine was relieved they were climbing a narrow flight of stairs and she did not have to respond. She knew she would be expected to make a good marriage. Her Howard blood was a catch, even if she had no dowry or inheritance. Men wanting to better themselves by winning a Howard bride had already pursued her. Her music teacher, Henry Manox, had tried to force himself upon her and another member of her step-grandmother's household had once suggested they should be married. She was relieved when that particular rogue, Francis Dereham, had attached himself to Katherine Tilney, another distant cousin of the Howards. *Thankfully*, she thought, *that is all far behind me now. This is a new adventure.*

Isabel threw open the door to Catherine's room. Two women were sitting on the deep window seat and they broke off their conversation abruptly. Kathryn Carey, the daughter of Mary Boleyn and, it was rumoured, King Henry, saw it was Isabel and relief flooded her face. The other woman also relaxed. She was breathtakingly beautiful. Her dark, auburn hair was uncovered and glinted a lustrous red in the firelight. She had pearly white skin and a heart-shaped face, highlighted by wide, brown eyes. When she stood to greet Isabel and Catherine, she was surprisingly tall and very slender. Beside her, Catherine felt like a small, rough-bred pony next to a gleaming hunter.

"Margaret," said Isabel warmly, "what a surprise. Catherine, this is Her Royal Highness, Lady Margaret Douglas, King Henry's niece."

Slightly flustered as to how she should respond, Catherine dropped a deep curtsey. She had heard about Margaret Douglas, the daughter of Henry's elder sister, Margaret Tudor. Lady Carey and Margaret Douglas laughed.

"Your royal highness…" she began.

"It's all right, Kitty, you don't have to curtsey in here," said Margaret, in a soft, melodic voice that contained the barest hint of a Scottish accent.

"You're kin, Kitty," said Lady Carey, raising Catherine up. "Possibly about to be closer kin if Charles has his way."

"That's not a wise thing to say," snapped Isabel, her voice suddenly tense.

"No one can hear us, Issy," laughed Margaret.

"People can always hear you!"

"Perhaps you're right," sighed Margaret. "Anyway, I must away. I promised Lady Rochford I'd help her arrange her new hood before banquet this evening, and we all know how exacting she can be!"

"Poor Jane," said Isabel. "She's always as sweet as can be to me."

Margaret merely raised her eyebrows, then with an expert hand, secured her own French hood and with a curtsey to the assembled ladies, swept from the room.

"That girl," sighed Isabel dropping into the seat Margaret had vacated. "Will she never learn? You'd think after her spate in the Tower she'd be more careful."

"Don't worry about Margaret," said Lady Carey. "She only pretends to be silly. She has one of the sharpest survival instincts of anyone at court."

Catherine stood in the middle of the room, agog. Only this morning she had been across the river in Lambeth, bored, lonely and eager to start life. It was hard to believe she was a party to this conversation, that she was now part of the great and glorious court of King Henry VIII.

"She's been in the Tower of London?" she gasped. "And survived?"

Isabel nodded.

"She chose unwisely in love and it upset the king, her uncle," she said. "Although, I don't imagine he'll be interested in her current infatuation with our brother Charles, he's far too lowly and unimportant."

"Spoken as a true elder sister," said Lady Carey, then she turned her critical eye to Catherine. "As for you, Kitty, we must make you presentable for the feast this evening. The new queen may not have arrived yet but it is still the role of us, her maids, to entertain with our wit, charm and beauty. We're her representatives and it's important we create a convivial atmosphere."

"Will the queen be here in time for Christmas?" asked Catherine.

"She's travelling but the weather is treacherous, as is the journey from Cleves, so we must pray to God to deliver her safely and quickly. In the meantime, we'll prepare for the Yuletide festivities in the usual way, which means tomorrow, Kitty, we must measure you for costumes for the Christmas Day masque, and teach you the dances."

Catherine grinned, excitement bubbling up inside her. Life had begun at last.

Chapter Two

"She's not in the least bit ugly," whispered Catherine to Isabel as they watched the Lady Anne of Cleves disembark from her coach. She looked a little tired, but after weeks on the road, and the terrible delays caused by harsh weather, this was unsurprising. Unconsciously, Catherine's fingers went to the beautiful silver locket hanging around her neck. Isabel and Edward had given it to her for Christmas. A delicate pattern was engraved on the front and it was set with a perfect diamond at its centre. It was the first piece of jewellery Catherine had ever owned and she was delighted with it.

"Of course, she isn't," replied Isabel. "The king can often be unkind."

"Careful, Issy," hissed a low voice. "Bess Seymour's over there. She hears everything."

Catherine and Isabel glanced around. Sure enough, Lady Elizabeth Seymour, younger sister of the former queen, Jane Seymour, and aunt to the heir to the throne, had moved within earshot of the Howard women. She nodded her greeting and turned her attention back to the events playing out before her.

"Lady Cromwell looks as though there's a bad smell under her nose," whispered Lady Rochford, the person who had first hissed the warning to Catherine and Isabel.

"Wouldn't you look like that if you were married to the grandson of a brewer?" replied Isabel tartly. The two women laughed derisively.

"I thought you said she was Lady Seymour," whispered Catherine, confused. It was one of the things she had noticed at court; people with titles seemed to have so many different variations on their names that she lost track of who was who, let alone who was married to whom or who was secretly meeting in the dark of the grounds at night.

"She married Gregory Cromwell not long ago," whispered Isabel.

"And who's he?" asked Catherine, wanting to join in the joke but finding it hard to believe the aunt to Prince Edward, the future king, had married such a lowly man.

Jane Boleyn, Lady Rochford, took Catherine's hand and nodded towards the group of men greeting the queen.

"See the tall one, quite young, good looking?" Catherine nodded; it was the man who had winked at her in the corridor on her first day at court. "That's Gregory Cromwell, son of Sir Thomas Cromwell."

"The Lord Privy Seal?" gasped Catherine.

Jane Boleyn nodded.

"Yes, the son of the man who was instrumental in having my beloved husband George beheaded, and our dear cousin accused of so many barbarous things before she, too, had her head chopped off by her insane husband." Jane's voice was low and bitter.

"Careful, Jane," warned Isabel. "The Seymours and the Cromwells are a formidable power."

Catherine stared at Lady Cromwell in wide-eyed wonder. The politics of court seemed so complex and here was a living embodiment of one of the worst times in the king's reign. It had been the moment the people around him had realised Henry was no longer the romantic, chivalric prince who had inherited the throne from his father, but that he was slowly becoming a terrifying tyrant.

"What do you think of her dress?" asked Margaret Douglas, changing the subject.

"It's — er — unusual," said Jane, trying to be polite.

"The fabric is gorgeous," sighed Catherine, "I'm sure we can help her with English styles, she's obviously not aware of our fashions."

"You're a sweet thing, Kitten," said Margaret, smiling at Catherine, who blushed. She turned back to look at the queen, wondering what it would be like to wear a dress made from sumptuous cloth of gold. Would it be heavy? After all, the cloth was made from real metal strands woven with silk. She tried to imagine how it would feel, then mentally shook herself. She was delighted to be wearing velvet and satin. What right did she have to yearn after cloth of gold? Her new wardrobe, supplied by her uncle, Thomas Howard, duke of Norfolk, and her sister and her husband, still thrilled her. Never before had she had so much choice and never had her clothes been so exquisitely made.

"Yes, Kitty, you're right," agreed Carey. "The fabric is beautiful but the style is extremely unflattering. We must try to persuade her into something more elegant."

"I suppose it must be what they wear in Cleves," said Jane.

"Yes, but she's in England now," said Margaret. "And looking like that, she's never going to win the king round, especially after their disastrous first meeting."

"What happened?" asked Jane. "No one seems to know, or if they do, no one's talking."

"The duchess of Suffolk told me," said Margaret. She dropped her voice to a whisper and the Howard girls stepped closer to listen while still half-watching the gleaming parade and displays of welcome for the Lady Anne.

"You know how obsessed the king is with the idea of chivalry and King Arthur?" she began, the others nodded. "Well, he was so in love with the Lady Anne's portrait, he decided he'd surprise her disguised as a servant, convinced true love would intercede and she would recognise him, so their first meeting would be one of love, honour and mystery."

"What happened?" gasped Catherine.

"He stormed in dressed as a servant, carrying a gift for the queen," continued Margaret. "Then, before she'd really grasped what was going on, he grabbed her and kissed her. She was horrified. She pushed him away and began shouting at him in German, ordering he be removed. He was furious. He stalked out of the room and returned in full royal purple, festooned with jewels. She was devastated and threw herself on her knees, but the damage was done. That's why he's being so rude about her — no one had told her we're all supposed to pretend he's still the handsome young prince who inherited the throne nearly thirty-one years ago."

"Margaret, be careful, that's treason," whispered Isabel, conscious of the fact Elizabeth Seymour had edged even closer.

Margaret glanced over and smiled winningly at Lady Cromwell.

"Nosy old hag," she murmured under her breath to the others. Catherine stifled a giggle.

"But what about the queen?" asked Catherine, who felt desperately sorry for the poor young woman.

"She doesn't speak English, so she didn't really understand what was going on," whispered Margaret. "Although, today I heard one of the rumours about their meeting confirmed."

"What?" asked Carey.

"Apparently, the king's doing everything he can to wriggle out of the marriage."

"No!" Catherine exclaimed, appalled. She had hoped this suggestion had merely been spiteful court gossip.

"He summoned Thomas Cromwell this morning, told him he had to make this good; find a way out for the king. Lady Cromwell might well be looking smug at the moment, but if her father-in-law can't find a loophole in the paperwork, Uncle Henry is going to be very, very cross indeed."

Catherine watched Anne as Henry, dressed in matching finery, led her from the elaborate throne where she had presided over the ceremonies. Her long, dark hair was covered in a blonde wig but underneath it was a sweet, oval face with dark eyes and delicate, pink-tinged skin. *She wasn't ugly*, thought Catherine. She was pretty in a similar way to Jane Seymour, but her colouring was different. Although she was smiling, Catherine thought the new queen looked wary and guarded. She may not speak the language, but she was an educated woman and Catherine was sure she must have picked up on the undercurrents. Perhaps she, like the king, was merely playing along and hoping that someone would rescue her before it was too late.

Isabel exchanged a glance with Katherine Willoughby, the duchess of Suffolk, who was standing to one side, ready to lead the procession, then prodded Jane and Catherine in front of her.

"Come along, girls. It's time for us to join the queen and be officially introduced," she said and began organising them. Margaret Douglas, the king's niece, led the way with Katherine Willoughby, the duchess of Suffolk. Catherine Howard moved back to stand with Lady Carey, while Jane and Isabel followed Margaret.

"We are but lowly maids," sighed Carey as they waited for the great ladies of the new queen's household to go ahead of them.

Catherine nodded, but in the midst of all the political crosscurrents, she was happy to be a lowly maid, invisible, insignificant and unimportant.

Chapter Three

"There, her." The queen pointed as her maids danced. She and the king had been married for two weeks and her English was improving each day. "The fox in the pretty gown. Who is she, Sir Edward?"

"That's Mistress Catherine Howard. We call her Kitty," he replied as Catherine's red hair gleamed in the morning light. "She's my wife's sister."

There was a small amount of pride in his voice. Catherine was an excellent dancer.

"She has hair like a fox." The queen laughed at her own joke and Edward smiled. He had never really noticed the redness of Catherine's hair; a hood usually covered it. But here in the queen's chambers, it was loose while she danced and it was a deep, luxuriant auburn. "You call her Kitty, like a cat?"

"It's a familiar name for Catherine," he explained. "With so many Catherines, it makes it easier to distinguish her."

The queen smiled. "You ask your Kitty to teach me to dance," she said. "Maybe the king, he like it."

A shadow drifted across her face, which was quickly replaced by her ever-ready serene and enigmatic smile. Edward beckoned to Isabel and after a brief, whispered conversation, she bobbed a curtsey and retreated.

"My wife will arrange for you and Kitty to dance together every afternoon so she can teach you the steps," Edward said.

"Good, she has pretty ways, like a fox," sighed the queen.

When Isabel told her about the dance classes, Catherine was appalled.

"I can't spend my afternoons alone with the queen!" she exclaimed.

"Why? Do you have something better to do?" asked Margaret Douglas, looking up from the intricate embroidery she held in her hands. She smiled lewdly. "Or is it someone? Do you have a secret lover, Kitty-Kat?"

Catherine blushed. "Of course not!" she retorted. "But I've never been alone with someone royal before. What if I offend her?"

"You won't," said Isabel. "And anyway, you won't be alone. Edward will be there and probably the duchess of Suffolk or the marchioness of Dorset, perhaps the duchess of Richmond."

Catherine went even paler. "Why not invite the Privy Seal and be done with it," she said faintly.

"I'll do it if it gets me out of this wretched sewing," interrupted Lady Carey as she bit through a piece of cotton with her neat, white teeth.

"You go then," said Catherine, only half joking. "I'll do your sewing for you!"

The others laughed, but Catherine remained apprehensive until the following afternoon when Isabel led her into the queen's inner chamber. To her surprise and horror, the queen was alone, except for her interpreter. She had removed the long, blonde wig she often used for ceremonial and court appearances, and her dark hair hung loose around her shoulders. It curled slightly, framing her face and accentuating her deep, green eyes. She smiled shyly as Catherine curtseyed.

"Your grace, may I present my younger sister, Mistress Catherine Howard," said Isabel, also curtseying.

The queen indicated for them both to rise.

"You're lucky to be together," she said via her interpreter. "I miss my sisters, Sybille and Amalia. Yet, Lady Isabel, you were Lady Leigh, were you not?"

"We are half-sisters, your grace," Isabel explained. "We have the same mother, Jocasta Culpepper, but my father was Sir Ralph Leigh, while Catherine's was Lord Edmund Howard."

The queen nodded as though she understood, but Catherine noticed her interpreter discreetly translating.

"Ah, so this is why," said the queen after a few moments. "I was a little confused. Did your mother teach you to dance? You are both very good."

Catherine looked at Isabel, who nodded for her to respond to the queen.

"Our mother has been dead for some years now," said Catherine. "As are both our fathers. We are orphans."

The queen looked startled when the interpreter explained this.

"Then you must both be under my care, as I am mother to this realm. I will be mother to you both," she said. It did not matter that she was younger than Isabel and only a few years older than Catherine. It was a gesture of friendship and Catherine smiled.

"Thank you, your grace," she said, dropping her eyes demurely.

"And now, we dance," said the queen. She clapped her hands and the musicians who were waiting on the gallery above, struck a chord. "What shall we learn first?"

Anne was on her feet, eager to begin.

"We could start with the pavane," suggested Catherine, thinking this ceremonial dance that was rather like a procession, would give the queen the basic grounding she needed, particularly as most of the other dances used the pavane between breaks. "Then once you've mastered that, we can move onto the faster dances like the gavotte, the almain, the volte, the galliard, maybe the saltarello."

"And you know all these dances?" the queen asked, astonished.

Catherine thought back to the nights of dancing at her step-grandmother's house.

"Oh yes," she said. "I know all these and more."

"Then let us begin," said Anne, indicating for Catherine to take to the floor with her. Catherine shot a nervous glance at Isabel, then joined the queen.

Now, several weeks later, Catherine looked forward to her afternoons spent with Queen Anne. Although Anne was not a natural dancer, she was eager to learn and Catherine was a patient teacher. It amused her when, during other court duties or under the table during banquet in the Great Hall, she often noticed the queen practising her dance steps surreptitiously when she was seated, thinking no one would see her feet moving under her capacious skirts. However, despite Anne's efforts to win the king around, the rumours of the growing discontent of Henry with his new bride were becoming more and more pronounced.

"Do you think they've consummated the marriage yet?" mused Margaret Douglas one grey morning as the queen's ladies trooped into Mass.

"Douglas, are you mad?" whispered Kathryn Carey.

"No, but the rumours say she's as much a maid now as she was the day she arrived," Margaret replied. "If there's no consummation, then Cromwell will have an easier time of annulling it."

"Cromwell doesn't want to annul it," Catherine murmured.

"What?"

"Yesterday, when I was leaving the queen's chambers I overheard him speaking to Thomas Cranmer, the Archbishop of Canterbury," she said. "Cromwell thinks it's important the king has an alliance with Cleves and remains part of the Schmalkaldic League of Protestants to protect the country. Apparently, the king no longer believes this is necessary because the treaty between France and Spain has collapsed, so he can once more woo them as his allies. Not only that, Cromwell said the king had told him he wants rid of the queen no matter what the political cost."

Margaret and Lady Carey stared at Catherine in surprise.

"What's the Schmalkaldic League?" asked Lady Carey.

"It's a defensive alliance of Lutheran princes," replied Catherine. "Their aim is to challenge the dominance of the Holy Roman Empire."

Carey and Margaret Douglas exchanged a glance of surprise.

"You've become quite the politician!" said Margaret. Then her voice dropped and she said with none of her usual wryness: "Be careful though, Kitty. Getting involved in politics is a dangerous game, even discussing it can be hazardous. Why do you think I always play so dumb? Be pretty and empty-headed with all men and those women you don't trust, but be wise with your friends and yourself."

Catherine looked at her in surprise but nodded, understanding the wisdom of Margaret's words. She wished she had not boasted but it was pleasant for once to know something the others did not. It made her feel as though she really belonged at court.

"How's the dancing coming along?" asked Jane Boleyn to break the silence.

"Very well," replied Catherine, relieved to be back on a safe topic. "I'm teaching the queen the gavotte this afternoon."

"Perhaps she should dance it for the king, get him excited," quipped Margaret, as they filed into the chapel, only to be heavily shushed by Katherine Willoughby, the duchess of Suffolk.

They danced face-to-face. One taller, dark curls flying, the other smaller, auburn hair glowing like fire, calling instructions as she took the lead. Neither were aware they were being watched.

"The girl with the red hair," the king whispered. "Who is she?"

"She is one of the queen's maids, your majesty," his servant, Thomas Culpepper replied. "Her name is Catherine Howard, the niece of the duke of Norfolk."

"How long has she been teaching the queen to dance?"

"Some weeks now, sire."

"She is beautiful," he sighed. "So pure, so innocent, yet the way she dances shows she is ripe for a husband. Is she betrothed?"

"Not that I'm aware, your majesty."

The king watched, leaning forward, his eye pressed eagerly against the spy hole. He often sat on the hidden balcony watching the ladies practise their dancing. Now, he followed Catherine's every move, leering as she whirled across the brightly tiled floor, her cheeks flushed, her hair flying as she and the queen danced, laughing, unaware anyone could see them.

"Summon her uncle to me immediately, I wish to send Mistress Howard a gift," said the king. "He can tell me whether there is an annoying betrothal in the balance. If not, then I will dine with Mistress Howard tomorrow."

"And the queen, sire?"

"What of the queen?" snapped Henry. "We are illegally married. She was betrothed to another and it was never annulled, as such God in his infinite mercy and wisdom has seen me impotent with her. However, God has pointed me towards a more suitable match and, even now, is proving my impotence is with the queen alone."

Culpepper averted his eyes as Henry's hand slid inside his clothing, his face growing redder as his excitement increased. Down below, the dance reached a crescendo, as did the king. As the queen forgot all etiquette and hugged Catherine, Henry groaned.

"Oh yes," he sighed. "God has shown me the way and she will be mine."

The king nodded for Culpepper to open the door of the hidey-hole. As they walked into the king's privy chamber, Henry turned to him.

"Send for a whore with red hair, small, but not a child," the king breathed. "One that is clean but won't be missed if I become careless."

With a sinking heart, Culpepper nodded. This was not the first time the king had made such a request, and Culpepper knew it would not be the last.

Chapter Four

Catherine had been waiting for a summons from her uncle, Thomas Howard, the duke of Norfolk, for some time. Although he had greeted her when she had first arrived at court the previous year, he had since been occupied with matters of state, namely, the issue of ridding the king of yet another wife who displeased him. The duke was one of the great men in Henry VIII's court: powerful, cunning and, when necessary, ruthless. Yet, to Catherine, he had always been kind. In a life of being shoved from home to home, always the penniless relative living on the charity of others, his small crumbs of solicitude had been enough to earn her loyalty and affection. Now, as she approached his door, she felt a small thrill of excitement at seeing him again.

A tall man in Howard livery guarded the entrance. She bobbed a curtsey, then waited for the herald to announce her arrival.

"Mistress Catherine Howard," his voice rang out and she walked into the luxurious rooms that befitted her uncle's standing at court.

"Come in, my dear," he called.

"Thank you, Uncle," she said, dropping into a curtsey. She waited, aware he was watching her, but did not move until he bade her rise. He was the head of their family and therefore certain etiquette had to be observed.

A fire roared in the grate and piles of paperwork were stacked on his desk. Nearer the fire on a smaller table rested a jug and two wine goblets; it was towards this that Thomas

Howard ushered his niece. She settled into one of the chairs and watched as he poured her wine.

"No servant, Uncle?" she asked.

"It may surprise you to hear, Catherine, that occasionally even I, the great duke of Norfolk, am capable of pouring my own drink."

"How very modern of you," she teased, her fingers unconsciously going to the beautiful silver locket around her neck, sliding it backwards and forwards along its chain. He smiled as he handed her the goblet.

"That's very pretty."

"It was a gift from Isabel and Edward," she replied, sipping the goblet of rich, sweet wine. "Would you like to hear about my dancing lessons with the queen?"

"At some point, yes, but there are other, more important things to discuss first," the duke replied, and Catherine was surprised to see the sudden bleakness in his expression.

"Uncle, has something happened?" she asked, fixing him with a stare of such intensity, he nearly flinched. No one else at court would have dared to challenge the terrifying duke of Norfolk in such a way, yet Catherine knew she was on safe ground. He had always singled her out for special attention: nothing untoward, she had always felt he had her best interests at heart.

"Yes, my dear, something quite unanticipated," he sighed, finishing his wine and pouring himself a second. The grey pallor of his face caused Catherine to pause, her voice took on a nervous timbre.

"Has something happened to my Howard brothers, Henry, Charles or Edward? Or my sisters, Margaret and Mary? Or my Leigh half-brothers and sisters?"

"No, they are quite well. In fact, Charles will be delighted with the news," he sighed, draining his second goblet of wine before continuing in a low, tense voice: "Tomorrow evening, I am to take you to Bishop Gardiner's house on the other side of the river and you are to dine…"

"What?" she exclaimed. Bishop Gardiner's house was notorious for the group of prostitutes he maintained there, known as his geese.

"If you would let me finish," he thundered, fear and disgust at what he was about to say making him angry. Catherine cowered back into her chair. "I am to take you there to dine with the king!"

"Why would the king wish to dine with me?" she gasped. "How does he even know who I am?"

Her voice faltered as her heart raced. This must be a mistake. She was nobody, Kitty Howard, a penniless orphan, an unimportant member of an admittedly important family, but she was not someone who was summoned to dine with the king.

"He is very aware of who you are. He has watched you dancing with the queen and was most struck by your beauty and your grace," replied Norfolk. "In fact, shortly after he watched you, he summoned me to his chambers and gave me a gift to prove his intentions are honourable."

Thomas Howard closed his eyes as though trying to protect both himself and Catherine from the memory of his recent interview with the king. The monarch had been in a state of high excitement when he had asked whether Catherine was betrothed. When the duke had assured the monarch Catherine was tied to no such contract, the forty-nine-year-old king had shouted in glee. The conversation that followed had startled even Thomas Howard as the king explained he wanted to marry Catherine immediately. As far as he was concerned, his marriage to Anne was a mere inconvenience and he boasted how, only that afternoon, he had proved that his impotence was caused by Queen Anne by bedding a prostitute who looked like Catherine.

"But not so sweet as your niece will be," he had snarled. "This one was a common dog who deserved all I gave her and more."

Thomas Howard had found his eyes drawn to the bloodstain on the floor, which the king's gentleman of the privy chamber, Thomas Culpepper, was scrubbing hard to remove. The duke had heard rumours about the king's growing violence, but he had chosen not to believe them; now, with the evidence before his eyes, even he, a man not unused to the barbarity of the court, could not bring himself to ask whether the girl had left the king's chamber alive. The thought that this man, who had already executed one of his nieces, now wanted to marry another Howard girl, made even the battle-hardened duke want to weep. Worse, he wanted to marry Catherine, the duke's favourite niece.

"No," exclaimed Catherine. "The queen is my friend. She's trying so hard to please the king. This would be a complete betrayal of her trust."

"And the king is your sovereign lord, your duty is to do as he commands, as I am head of your family and must be obeyed," he snapped. He placed his goblet on the table, then rose from his chair and stalked across the room. From his desk, he took a small velvet pouch and a scroll of parchment sealed with the king's private crest. "If you don't want the king to think you're a whore, you must refuse both," he said, handing them to Catherine.

"You don't need to tell me that. I may only be fifteen years old, but I'm not a fool," she replied, equally as tense and snappy. "And when he's bored with me? What then — another pair of boots for the executioner? Or are you going to promise to protect me, as you once did my cousin, Anne Boleyn, before sentencing her to death?"

The fury on her uncle's face matched her own and, knowing his history of violence towards his wife, Elizabeth, the duchess of Norfolk, she braced herself, expecting him to strike her. Instead, he recoiled as though she had struck him. She was shaking as the horror and revulsion at what she was being told to do was sinking in. The king was old enough to be her father, her grandfather even, and she found him repulsive. The romantic prince who had inherited the throne was now a corpulent and terrifying tyrant. She had watched him from afar, revelling in her anonymity as she observed this larger-than-life king who held all their lives in the balance.

With each passing day, she had pitied the new queen more intensely. Shuddered at the thought of the sweet Lady Anne having to share a bed with the rotting, pus-filled monster that was the king. No wonder Anne had been so horrified at that first fateful meeting. Yet, Catherine had come to admire Anne too. Despite the unhappiness of her marriage and the dislike she felt for her husband, Anne knew her duty was to be a good queen.

Catherine had been impressed with Anne's ability to put aside her own feelings in order to fulfil her royal demands: her determination to learn English, her obvious care for the motherless prince and the two princesses, her good-natured tolerance of the rumours that abounded concerning the state of her virginity. No matter what she encountered, she rose above it all with dignity and yet now, she, Catherine, the queen's friend, was being asked to betray her. She could not believe it.

"Send the jewel, or whatever it is, back with the letter, unopened," she said turning away from her uncle. "Give him my thanks but say as I am unwed, and as a member of the queen's court, it would be unseemly of me to accept them, generous though his majesty has been."

"You will not be expected to bed the king tomorrow," her uncle said coldly.

"Good!" retorted Catherine.

"It will be a small affair. I will be there, as will your sister Isabel and her husband, Edward, your brother Charles and the king's niece, Lady Margaret Douglas."

Unsure whether she was pleased to have her family and her friend witness her humiliation, Catherine spoke her next words with deliberate intent.

"And where is your hand in all this, Uncle?" she asked. "Did you offer me up as bait? Is that the real reason you brought me here, to flaunt me before the king? Am I to follow in the footsteps of Mary and Anne? One bore him bastards; the other lost her beautifully crowned head. Which is to be my fate — Mary's or Anne's? After all, it was you and their father, Thomas Boleyn, who arranged those matches."

She was deliberately goading him. In her fear, she wanted him to lose control too, to lash out so she could retaliate, vent her growing panic and hysteria on him.

"You have neither Mary's sweetness of nature nor Anne's intelligence and wit. You will dance your way into the king's heart and give him the reason to push through the divorce to the queen. Do you honestly think she'll mind, Kitty? She hates him probably more than he despises her. It's nothing personal, they are incompatible. If he were not king, they would do their duty, have a child and then live separately…"

"Like you and my aunt of Norfolk?" Catherine interrupted spitefully. "How is your concubine, Lady Elizabeth Holland?"

"Yes," he seethed, "like me and my wife. We do our duty, then we leave each other alone and enjoy other distractions. However, it's not so easy when you're king and queen. He needs another heir. He will never have one with Anne. He wants to have one with you."

"The heir to the throne?"

"If you are queen, your children will carry royal Tudor blood. There will be no question about their legitimacy, they will outrank the princesses Mary and Elizabeth, both of whom are now declared bastards. If you have a son, he will be the duke of York, the spare to the Seymour brat. If young prince Edward were to die, your son, a Howard prince, would be king of England."

"And what, my lord, if the king is incapable of getting a baby on me?" she said. "He is old, infirm and his body does not work well. What if he is the problem and not his blameless wives? Like my cousin, Anne Boleyn, will I end my days on the block on trumped-up charges of witchcraft and adultery?"

When her uncle struck her, Catherine was not surprised. She knew what she said was treason but she could not help herself. She did not want to die because a vain old man was no longer capable of having children. She would rather take a beating from her uncle and be sent from court in disgrace than succumb to the king's decaying flesh. She waited for the next blow but it never came. Instead, her uncle pulled her into his arms, holding her tight, tears streaming down his face.

"I give you my word," he gasped, finally releasing her. "I will protect you with my life. If I could take you away from court and keep you safe, I would, but the king has fallen in love with you and nothing will stop him marrying you. I'm so sorry, Kitten, there's nothing we can do to stop this."

She stared at him for a long moment, then turned and walked from the room, leaving him ashen-faced and ashamed.

Catherine stormed down the corridor, fear and fury making her fly. She could feel the curious glances like knives in her back and wondered: *do they know? Were they eyeing her as a potential queen or were there already plots afoot to discredit and remove her from the king's affection?* She shuddered at the thought. She may only have been at court a few months but she had observed the endlessly shifting factions as families jostled for power and position, switching allegiances and enemies as often as the sun rose in the east and set in west.

She was desperate to reach the safety of her room and slam the door firmly shut before the bitter ache in her throat and the tears that threatened to well from it became too hard to resist. Such was her intent upon her destination that, as she entered the corridor to the queen's court, she was almost upon the kissing couple hidden in the shadows before she realised they were there.

"Charles, what are you doing?" she exclaimed as her elder brother hastily disentangled himself from the embrace.

"Oh, bugger off, Kitty," he snapped. The woman in the shadows giggled and Catherine's eyes widened.

"Margaret Douglas? Are you insane? Why would you want to kiss my brother?"

"Because he's very pretty and extremely good with a lance," laughed Margaret. "Now, run along, Kitty, there's a precious little chicken."

"Yes, leave us to get on with grown up things while you go back to your dolls and your sewing," smirked Charles.

Catherine, however, was near breaking point.

"Don't you dare speak to me that way," she shouted, the tears she had been fighting finally breaking free. "You have no idea what you're doing…" The rest of the sentence was lost as she choked trying to hold back her terror.

"Kitten, what's the matter?" Charles said, sounding genuinely distressed that he might have upset his sister so much. "I was only teasing."

"Don't be ridiculous, Charles," said Margaret. "This isn't because of us. What's happened, Kitty?"

"Uncle Norfolk…" she began but now the tears had started she could not stop them or speak through their ferocity.

"We'll take her to Isabel and Edward," said Margaret, her pretty face full of concern. "They'll know what to do," and walking either side of her, they escorted Catherine along the corridor.

Charles had barely knocked when Isabel flung open the door and hauled them into the room before slamming the door behind them and turning the key in the lock. Catherine, Margaret and Charles looked at her ashen face.

"Uncle Howard has sent word, Kitty," Isabel said, steering her sister to a chair by the fire. "Edward, fetch Catherine a brandy," she added to her husband. "This is an unexpected turn of events."

"Will someone please explain what has happened?" said Charles, bemused at the seriousness of the expressions on Isabel and Edward's faces. "Has somebody died?"

"No, worse," said Isabel, passing a drink to Catherine before accepting her own glass of brandy from her husband. "The king wishes to dine with Kitty tomorrow. We are all invited, along with Uncle Norfolk."

"What?" Margaret Douglas gasped. "How does he even know Kitty?"

"He saw her teaching the queen to dance and has fallen in love with her," replied Isabel.

"No, he can't love me," choked Catherine. "He can't!"

There was an ominous silence, then Isabel's husband Edward took charge, his years at Henry's court and his great experience as a courtier coming into play. He had been vice-chamberlain to Katherine of Aragon and Anne Boleyn, and Jane Seymour's Master of the Horse. He held the post of vice-chamberlain again now and, having survived the turbulent court for many years, he was a skilled diplomat.

"The most important thing to do now is to stick together and work out a way to keep Kitty safe," he said in a low, serious voice.

"And how are we supposed to do that?" asked Isabel. "Look what happened to the Boleyns: Mary banished, Anne and George executed. If the king has one of his sudden changes of heart — that could be us!"

"No!" exclaimed Charles as the full impact of events hit him.

"There's no reason why any of us should be executed," snapped Edward. "We need to learn from past mistakes. Anne upset too many people along the way, Catherine, thankfully hasn't been at court long enough to make any enemies. We're used to dealing with our old ones, the Seymours. However, now they have joined forces with the Cromwells, it is them we need to watch closely. Thomas Cromwell, the Lord Privy Seal, holds the king in his pocket." He glanced over at Catherine who was on the point of collapse. "But for now," he said, "we must look after Kitty. Margaret, is Lady Carey in her room?"

"I think she was dining with Sir Francis Knollys, but she should have returned by now," replied Margaret.

Edward nodded, then turned to Charles. "Charles, accompany your sister to her room but leave her on the threshold. From now on, no man must enter Kitty's room," he said.

"Why not?" asked Charles. "I'm her brother!"

"Have you forgotten about George Boleyn? Executed for the monstrous crime of incest with his sister Anne?" roared Edward. "We all know it was a lie but use your head, Charles. From now on, Kitty must be as pure as the Virgin Mother herself so our enemies can start no rumours. No male, not even close family like yourself or any other of your brothers or half-brothers must ever be alone with Catherine."

Charles shook his head in disbelief.

"And don't forget the more recent rumours about the Seymours that spread through the inner sanctum of the queen's court while she was lying in with the young prince," said Edward.

"But they were surely rumours, they disappeared after Jane died," said Margaret. "I know it was suggested that Jane's father had an affair with his first daughter-in-law but you're not going to credit the whispers about Jane and her eldest brother, the earl of Hertford?"

"All I will say," continued Edward, "is that it was probably fortuitous that Jane Seymour produced a boy then had the decency to die, or there could have been an even bigger scandal than when Cromwell released the lies and the trumped-up charges about cousin Anne."

Charles and Margaret stared at Edward in awe, but Isabel turned away as though she could not stand to hear the words spoken again.

"Now you understand why your sister has to be as pure as the down on a swan's back," said Edward.

Nobody spoke. Instead they all looked at Catherine, who had gathered herself a little.

"Issy?" Catherine whispered, desperately. "Please, this can't be necessary…"

Isabel walked over to Catherine and hugged her.

"My dear, Edward is right," she said, her brown eyes swimming with tears. "We've seen this with other queens, you must be careful. Word will no doubt already be spreading that the king has requested you dine with him. The court has been waiting to see which lady would catch his eye from the moment he returned from his first unfortunate meeting with the queen. You will no longer be safe alone. I'm sorry, my dear, we'll have to organise a proper guard for you tomorrow. This is out of all our hands now."

Catherine was so horrified, she could not even summon words to reply.

"Come on, Kitten, let's get you to bed," said Margaret. "I'll stay with you and Carey tonight. We need to make sure there can be no vile rumours spread about you. If I'm there, or Carey, no one will dare question you."

"Why you? Or Kath Carey for that matter?" asked Charles.

"Because Charles, I'm the king's niece and Carey's his daughter," snapped Margaret. "If Kitty has two royal women with her, there can be no doubting her virtue."

Chapter Five

"Her, the short one next to Lady Douglas!"

As the court awoke to the news that the king had chosen his fifth queen, Catherine found it impossible to escape the whispers and stares. They followed her along the corridors into church, into the Great Hall, everywhere she went, always accompanied by a female member of the Howard family. At first, Catherine had bowed her head, trying to avoid the obvious looks and overloud comments, but as the morning had worn on, her anger had risen and she had begun staring people down when they looked too long or threw a barbed comment in her direction. This was not of her making and she was going to show people they could not intimidate her.

"Will the queen still want me to teach her dancing today?" asked Catherine, as she and Isabel returned from a walk around the rose garden. Until yesterday, her hour spent dancing with Anne had been the high spot of her day. The two had become friends and enjoyed each other's company. But in the space of one night, everything had changed and Catherine was now in the position of rival.

Isabel nodded. "Yes, everything must continue as normal for now," she said as they made their way to Anne's chambers.

"Do you think she'll be angry?" Catherine asked as they arrived at the now familiar doorway.

"Who knows, Kitten?" sighed Isabel, hugging her tightly. "I'll be waiting for you out here. If it's too upsetting for you both, then leave."

Catherine nodded, then indicated for the guard on the door to allow her into the queen's chamber.

Anne was staring out of the window, her back to Catherine when she entered and curtseyed. As soon as she heard the door click shut, Anne spun around, her face white and pinched with worry.

"Oh, my Kitty, what is to become of you?" exclaimed Anne, hurrying towards Catherine and lifting her from her low curtsey into a sisterly embrace. "You are my friend, yet, he takes even this from me. Sweet child, what will those awful men make you do?"

It was the last thing Catherine had expected: anger, a sense of betrayal, even pleading to leave the king be, yes, but not sympathy and concern for her safety.

"I will do all in my power to keep you safe," said Anne. "My brother has much influence, he will protect us both, yes?"

"My lady, you're too kind, but I worry for you," replied Catherine as Anne led her to the window seat. "You're here alone, a princess in a foreign land with no champion. I have my huge family forming a wall around me."

"Very true, my dear, but my protection is my royal blood," said Anne, with some help from her interpreter. "Extensive though your family is, a precedent has been set with your cousin. You must be careful."

Catherine felt her stomach tighten in fear; a chill ran down her spine. Surely, it could not happen again? Henry had already killed one Howard wife; it would be truly terrible for the family if he did it again, did it to her. Even the thought made her tremble. She looked up into Anne's concerned face and said what had been playing on her mind all night.

"But you're my friend and I've betrayed you," whispered Catherine, tears beginning to fall down her pale cheeks. "Why would you care about what happens to me? If the king goes ahead with this, you'll no longer be queen."

"You have not betrayed me," said Anne. "We have no choice in these matters, which is why we must try to protect each other." She gently wiped away Catherine's tears. "You are correct, though, I will no longer be queen and this does make me sad…"

"I'm so sorry…" Catherine interrupted, but Anne held up her hand to silence her.

"You, my dear, do not need to be sorry. My only sadness is that I will no longer be able to continue with my plan to reunite Henry's poor motherless children and make them into a proper family."

"Even now you only think of others," whispered Catherine in awe. "If things continue as they are, if I am forced to marry the king, I'll try to do as you wished, bring Henry's children to court, reunite them. I'll do my best to keep you safe too, my lady."

Anne smiled.

"We will save each other," she said, then she stood and straightened her skirts. "Now, shall we dance? It may be the last time we are together and it will cheer us both…"

There was a fanfare outside and both Catherine and Anne jumped.

"His Lord, the Privy Seal," announced a herald, and with much scurrying and, to Catherine what sounded like very voluble protestations from Isabel, the door was flung open and Thomas Cromwell oozed into the room.

"Your Majesty, I apologise most humbly for the intrusion," he began, bowing deeply. Anne turned to her interpreter speaking in rapid German. The woman nodded and hurried from the room.

"It is indeed an intrusion," retorted Anne. "It is my request you leave immediately."

She glared at him imperiously, but Thomas Cromwell merely smiled and turned his back on the queen. Catherine watched his smirking face with horror. Overnight, the established order at court had changed. Previously, Cromwell would never have dared to enter the queen's chambers in such a brusque manner or treat her with such disdain. Yet now, he dismissed her as though she were a servant.

A small knot of anger lodged in Catherine's solar plexus. Until yesterday, Cromwell had continued to champion Anne's marriage to Henry, now he was ready to disregard her entirely: his only concern was how to further himself and his own ambition, no one else mattered. Fury began to build in Catherine as Cromwell threw Anne a contemptuous look before his beady eyes settled on her. They were like cold, dark pools and she felt as though she were looking into the soul of the devil himself, but she drew herself up, standing tall, her shoulders thrown back, and met his soulless gaze.

"It is Mistress Howard with whom I have urgent business, your grace," he said smoothly and dismissively. "If you will permit her to accompany me, then I will gladly leave and ask forgiveness for this unseemly interruption."

"No!" barked Anne. "She stays here with me."

"With my most humble apologies, my lady, it was not really a request," he said, his eyes glinting coldly. "Mistress Howard will accompany me or I'll return with a warrant for her arrest, or maybe yours, your majesty."

"On what grounds?" spluttered Catherine.

"I'm sure I'll think of something," he replied.

Catherine looked from the queen to Cromwell. She did not want Anne to take risks with the king's chief courtier. He was a ruthless man and he would do anything to stay in favour with the king. The most important person in Cromwell's considerations was always Cromwell and, whether a royal princess or queen, if a woman became troublesome, he would find a way to dispose of her. Cromwell had created the Cleves marriage in order to further his own political ambition; it was within his power to destroy it, particularly if it meant saving his own life over that of the queen. Catherine knew this precarious situation placed Anne in enough danger. The queen was her friend and she would do what little she could to safeguard her.

"Very well," Catherine said, her voice suddenly crisp and authoritative. "I will accompany you, my lord, but only to my uncle of Norfolk's chambers and with my sister as a chaperone. Anything else would be unseemly, particularly at present."

"Indeed?" said Cromwell, his eyebrow raised quizzically.

"Indeed," retorted Catherine. She nodded to Anne, trying to tell her with her eyes she was sorry, then gathering her skirts, she swept past Cromwell as though the decision to leave the room was hers and not a direct order from the Privy Seal. To her relief, Isabel was waiting, accompanied by Lady Rochford; they immediately fell into step behind her as she strode along the busy corridor. Cromwell stalked after her, quickening his pace until they were level, then he walked so closely at her side, he was almost stepping on the hem of her dress.

"Do not try to outwit me, child," he hissed in her ear, pulling her to a standstill so that Isabel and Jane nearly cannoned into them. He ignored the other women, unconcerned by their presence. "Wiser men and women than you have tried and failed to better me," he continued. "Remember the fate of your cousin, and she was a far greater thinker than you."

"I will never forget or forgive you for what you did to Anne Boleyn," replied Catherine. "You're hardly better than a murderer and I won't allow you to harm this queen. She is innocent of anything apart from having clear sight when it comes to the king."

Cromwell laughed mirthlessly.

"Why, Mistress Catherine, you do indeed have the Howard spirit buried in that pretty bosom," he said. "Try not to let it lead you into danger. You may have the eye of the king today but women are silly creatures, easily discarded. There is always another one available to satisfy a man's urges, so tomorrow he may have changed his mind. If that's the case, my dear, you will reap the harvest from all the bad seeds you have sown."

She glared at him. "Is this the urgent business you wished to discuss?" she asked. "A warning to be a good girl and do as I'm told?"

"Partly," he nodded. "Although, your family will probably have already issued a similar command. No, my business is this: while Henry has you in his heart, you will begin to feel you can do anything, ask him any favour and do as you please. Be careful, Mistress Howard, the king has a mercurial temper and a suspicious mind. He is easily led into believing lies. Your uncle will have plans to control the king through you, possibly to do me damage too. Warn him it would be most unwise. Tell tales about me to the king, my dear, and you will find greater mischief spread about you than any member of your vain and arrogant family could even begin to imagine."

He patted her cheek in a patronising manner.

"You'll do for now," he whispered into her ear, "but don't get comfortable or begin to think you will be queen for long. I have other plans for Henry and this realm."

With a self-satisfied chuckle, he moved away down the corridor, leaving Catherine cold with fear.

Chapter Six

My heart is sore with weeping, but it will not change my predicament and I must shed no more tears of blood... Catherine dipped her pen into the ornate crystal inkwell and continued: *...the court is shifting its allegiance from the sweet Lady Anne but, at present, only a few are taking the Howard side. In the seething nest of vipers that is the Privy Council, these self-serving creatures know from bitter experience that, while the king may currently be enamoured with me, his favouritism can alter in a heartbeat. They have witnessed the king's mood changing as swiftly as the wind blowing the weathervane from north to south: he is either as stubborn as a bull or as easily led as the meekest of lambs and, in this, they sense opportunity. Even now, the Cromwells and the Seymours dance their pretty girls in front of him, trying to turn his heart away from me. Despite what my uncle thinks, my position is far from secure. In fact, I feel that I am in more danger than ever...*

The door to Catherine's new and spacious rooms crashed open, making her jump away from the desk in fear. Expecting to see the king's guard come to arrest her on some trumped-up charge created by Thomas Cromwell, she was relieved to see her uncle, Thomas Howard, her brother Charles, her brother-in-law Edward Baynton and, to her surprise, Charles Brandon, the duke of Suffolk and best friend since boyhood of the king. Yet, they wore grim expressions and her momentary relief evaporated.

"This is an insult directed at the Howard family, at me and, most particularly, at you," snarled the duke of Norfolk, throwing a roll of parchment down onto the desk in front of her. Bemused, Catherine picked up the document that held the ornate Privy Seal, a device that made it legal and binding.

"At me?" queried Catherine. "What has happened?"

"Cromwell has given the order to dissolve Thetford Priory," said the duke of Suffolk.

Despite her growing relationship with the king, Catherine had not yet been formally introduced to the duke of Suffolk. Charles Brandon had once been married to the king's youngest sister, Princess Mary, but since her death he had remarried. His current wife, his fourth spouse, was Katherine Willoughby, a woman who had been his ward and the intended betrothed of his son, until Charles had married her when she was only fourteen years old. Yet, despite the age gap, rumoured to be as great as thirty-five years, the marriage appeared to be successful. Brandon was still a good-looking man. He had once been said to be the mirror image of the king. But now, with the king bloated and unhealthy, Brandon looked like his younger, fitter brother.

"By dissolving Thetford Priory, where the Howard family has buried their dead for centuries, he is forcing us to exhume their remains and move them to the chapel at my seat in Framlington," her uncle said furiously. "By doing this, Cromwell is demonstrating his power. He is showing us that, while the Howard family may once again be enjoying the king's favour, it could be taken away at any moment, as it is really he, Thomas Cromwell, who rules through the king and we would be wise to remember it!"

"This is on Cromwell's orders?" gasped Catherine.

Edward nodded. "After his meeting with you last week, the Lord Privy Seal is demonstrating how he still holds power over us all."

"The question is this, though," said Brandon, "are you prepared to accept this insult from the upstart brewer's boy?"

Catherine turned to her uncle. She knew what was expected of her, both as a member of the Howard family and a future queen consort, yet to utter such words would make her complicit with their plans, an idea that scared her more than anything else she had so far experienced during her time at court.

"Uncle, I do not understand…" she began.

"Will you allow Cromwell to insult you?" repeated the duke of Norfolk, his eyes glinting with fury.

Suddenly, she realised the true helplessness of her situation. Although her betrothment to the king had elevated her status at the court, to her family and, most particularly, her uncle who was the head of the Howards, she remained a puppet to be used in order to help him achieve his own plans and ambitions. Her blue eyes rose to meet his and she shot him a look of desperation, he raised his eyebrows questioningly.

"Well, Kitten?" he persisted. "You are to be queen, your words hold power. Will you allow Cromwell to torment us in this manner? Or will you act and put a stop to his machinations?"

Turning away from him, her response ringing with reluctance, Catherine spoke the words expected of her.

"No, Uncle," she whispered. "I am not prepared to accept Cromwell's insult."

Charles dropped his eyes, staring at his boots, and Edward stifled a groan of despair. Her uncle, however, nodded his approval. A shiver ran down her spine and she reached into the neck of her gown, touching the locket Isabel had given her as though it were a protective talisman.

"Cromwell may think he has power, he may be able to decree that we move our dead," the duke of Norfolk snarled, pacing the room. "He may stalk the corridors as though he is the power in this kingdom. He may have had your cousin Anne's head, but, in revenge, I will have his."

"Your grace, have a care!" gasped Edward. "How would you even begin to plan such an act?"

Norfolk shot Catherine a triumphant look. He had not needed her words to set this plan in motion, but she was fully aware that, should this scheme backfire on her uncle, now she had given her approval, he would not hesitate to ensure she was his scapegoat.

The fire crackled, keeping off the afternoon chill. Then, from the shadows beside the hearth, the duke of Suffolk spoke in his smooth, rich voice.

"Perhaps Catherine could ask for Cromwell's head as a wedding present."

Edward and Charles baulked at this unexpected pronouncement and Catherine, horrified, stumbled back into the chair behind her. *Is he bewitched?* she thought. She stared at Suffolk, conscious of his incredible good looks and easy charm, yet she shuddered. His smile may be that of a god but his heart beat with an evil as potent as that running through the veins of Cromwell and the king. *He is as tainted by power as the rest of the court*, she thought. Glancing over at her uncle, she noted that his expression had not altered. This suggestion was no surprise to Norfolk and she wondered how long the two dukes had been hatching this terrible plot.

"When are you next seeing the king, Kitty?" continued Brandon, who seemed not to have noticed the thickening silence that had followed his words.

"Tonight, after banquet," she replied. "He has asked me to join him for cakes and wine before he retires this evening."

"Then while you are with him, Kitty dear, you must sweetly explain to the king what Cromwell plans. Tell him he forced you out of the Lady Anne's presence in order to threaten you, and cry about the fact you're worried about the spirits of your ancestors," he said. "You must pretend to be reluctant to confide in him and you must play down the fact you want anything to happen to Cromwell. Tell the king he scares you. At this stage, it will be enough." Brandon paused as though thinking things through. "Then dance for him."

"Your grace, are you sure this is the best solution?" asked Edward Baynton, shuddering.

"Yes," replied Brandon. "If Kitty says dancing makes her happy, the king will encourage her, and as she twirls, he will become aroused and excited. When this happens, he'll want to do something to make Kitty smile again. He knows he can't bed her yet, this will frustrate him and he will take this frustration out on Cromwell who hasn't yet had his marriage to Queen Anne annulled. After that, Norfolk, you and I must lead the king into thinking it was his decision to rid himself of Cromwell."

Another long silence stretched between them, as deep and as black as a curse. Finally, Catherine spoke, "You wish me to dance a man to death, sir?"

Her words dropped like pebbles into a millpond, each one flowing outwards, before vanishing into the minds of the gathered men.

"Yes," came the short, dark reply.

"I will not," she gasped, but her words were lost to the firelight as her uncle took her hand and raised her from her seated position. He twirled her around like a doll and a cruel smile spread across his long, thin face. Catherine felt her stomach churn.

"Kitty is an excellent dancer. Show the duke how well you move, my dear."

He stood back, smiling, as though encouraging a child to perform a party piece to impress the visiting adults. Catherine felt hot tears of humiliation rising. All her life she had been the poor but pretty relation, passed around when her dancing and dimples were required, but otherwise shoved to one side as unimportant, a burden on the rest of the family.

Her brother Charles opened his mouth to speak in her defence but the duke of Suffolk cut across him.

"Do not embarrass her, Thomas," he said his tone clipped. "There is no need for her to dance for us like a tuppenny whore."

Thomas Howard scowled but before he could respond, Suffolk turned from him and focused on Catherine.

"It's a dangerous game, Kitty, but you are more than capable of persuading His Majesty that this would be beneficial to us all," he said. "Cromwell has committed many heinous acts, not only against your family, but against many noble houses. He manipulates the king, plays with him as though he were a toy. It was Cromwell who disposed of Anne Boleyn because her influence over the king was becoming too powerful. As far as Cromwell was concerned, she had forgotten her place, so he punished her in the cruellest possible way. If he continues as Privy Seal, he could do the same to you or someone you love. Do you not see, sweet Catherine, if you are brave enough to rise against this monstrous insult, you will rid England of the worst kind of parasite. We will be free from this upstart and the country will be happier because of it. Not only that, you will have avenged your cousins Anne and George Boleyn."

She stared at the duke, horrified at the way she was being manipulated. Her heart had been broken upon the demise of her cousin Anne. Catherine had always looked up to her and her sister Mary, thinking them sophisticated and charming, envying them their protective parents and their effortless swathe through the courts of England and France. Anne's downfall had been a devastating blow to the young Catherine, yet she had never sought to avenge her cousin's dreadful death.

Swallowing hard, trying to control her mounting terror, she balled her hands into fists and stared into the fire, her eyes following its hypnotic, pulsing heart. She was not worldly-wise like Anne or vivacious like Mary, she was the child who had been left to her own devices, who had scurried through life, learning the etiquette of court as best she could from observing others. She was not equipped to seduce a man as experienced as the king, and persuade him to execute his most trusted advisor.

She turned to her uncle, the one person whom she had always thought would protect her. But his fierce expression told her she would receive no compassion or support from him. Charles was as white-faced and horrified as she imagined she must look, and Edward, his face ringed with resignation and sorrow, could only give a small, sad smile. She realised this was the most comfort she would be offered, it also confirmed that she had no choice but to succumb to the wishes of her family, whether she agreed with their plans or not. Taking a deep breath, she gave Charles Brandon a small, sharp nod.

"Good, then that is settled," he said. "Tonight, after banquet, dance for Henry and ask for Cromwell's head." He bowed to Catherine, who bobbed a curtsey. "You are doing the country a great service," he said, then swept from the room, leaving Catherine to gulp back her sobs.

Chapter Seven

The sky was black. They were in the dark of the moon. *The witches' moon*, thought Catherine. *Will I be met by witch-light this evening after I dance a man to his death?* She shuddered, desperate to write her feelings down, to try and resolve them by committing them to paper as she had done all her life, but she feared their discovery.

"Oh, Kitten, you look beautiful," said Isabel. Catherine forced a smile to her lips, bringing her attention back to her sister.

Isabel, Kathryn Carey and Jane Rochford had stepped away from their final titivations of Catherine's hair and dress and were now admiring their handiwork. Isabel hugged her tightly.

"You look beautiful, Kitten," she sighed. "If only our mother could see you now, see that her daughter is going to be queen."

Catherine smiled and allowed Isabel to propel her forward to the expensive Venetian looking glass Henry had given her as a gift.

"Oh, my word," she exclaimed when she saw her reflection. "You are witches to have transformed me so."

The women all instinctively placed their thumbs through their fingers to make the symbol of the cross, the sign to protect them against evil wishing and witchcraft.

"Take that back, Kitty," snapped Kathryn Carey. "You should never say such things, even as a joke."

"I'm sorry. I take it back," she murmured, still stunned by her appearance.

"Spit on the fire," insisted Jane Rochford. "It stops the curse."

Catherine did as she was asked.

"How have you transformed me?" she said, smiling, trying to lighten the mood her ill-advised comment had soured.

She could hardly take her eyes off her image. The new Tudor-green dress — another gift from the king — suited her pale colouring and, now it had been loosened slightly to reveal glimpses of the deep cream linen underneath. Her skin glowed a rosy pink. She had added the decorative embroidery herself using thread that shone when it caught the light, so the underdress seemed to have been woven from moonbeams.

Her hair had been let down, a sign of her virginity, and brushed until it shone. Isabel had then rubbed it with red silk to bring out the highlights. Her eyes had been dabbed with kohl to make them appear bigger and her lips stained with a tint made by Isabel from flower petals. Delicate perfumed oils had been applied to her skin, so she smelled mysterious and irresistible.

"Thank you," she whispered to her friends and her sister. "You've made me beautiful."

"Sweet, Kitten, you've always been beautiful," said Isabel, hugging her in a maternal way.

A knock at the door interrupted them. It was Charles Howard.

"The king's waiting," he said. "I'm to accompany you and so is Jane."

"Jane?" said Kathryn Carey. "Why?"

Charles shrugged. "Uncle Norfolk's orders. He said you had things to explain to Kitty and me before we arrived at the King's chambers."

Isabel took Catherine's hand and spoke. "Kitty, remember Charles will be outside the door if you need him. Just call his name and no matter what the king says, do not bed him tonight."

"You have my word," said Catherine, shuddering at the very thought. Then, taking a deep breath, she smiled at Isabel and Lady Carey, before following Jane and Charles from the room.

As the door shut on her sister and cousin, she heard Isabel whisper, "May God help her this night," and Kathryn Carey stifled a sob.

Catherine, however, was no longer scared; like a soldier going into battle she had prayed to her saints and asked for help to do what was righteous and good. This had offered her solace and resolve: her dress was now her armour, her hair was her shield and her face was her weapon. Tonight, she would fight to protect those she loved from a terrifying enemy, whether this was Cromwell, the king or her uncle, she was unsure.

Charles took her arm and she allowed herself to be led along the corridor towards the king's private chambers. The three of them walked in silence, until Jane beckoned them into a small alcove.

"Charles will not be the only person waiting outside the door this evening," she whispered. "My betrothed, Thomas Culpepper, an honoured member of Henry's privy chamber, will also be waiting in case the king has need of help."

Catherine was startled by news of Jane's betrothal. Thomas Culpepper was a distant cousin on her mother's side, and held an important position in Henry's household. At one point, it had been mooted that he might be a suitable match for Catherine herself but the suggestion had been put aside. Now Catherine understood why: he had become involved with Jane instead. Despite the fear in her heart, she was momentarily distracted by Jane's news and sent a quick prayer that, this time, Jane would finally find the happiness she so deserved.

"What help might the king need?" Charles asked warily.

Jane hesitated then, clearly agitated, said in a low voice: "He sometimes has fits of melancholy. If he seems to change suddenly, as though he no longer recognises you, then you must excuse yourself. Call for Charles immediately. If this isn't possible, if you need to find a more subtle way of absenting yourself, call Thomas, requesting small ale. This will be the signal that something is amiss and he will come to your aid."

Catherine and Charles exchanged an apprehensive look.

"Very well, Jane," said Catherine, her newfound confidence dented, "but let us hope it doesn't come to that."

"Dear God, Kitty, let us hope it doesn't," agreed Jane fervently.

They stepped once more into the corridor and sooner than Catherine expected, they arrived outside the impressive oak doors that led to Henry's inner sanctum. The herald, rather than announcing them, slipped discreetly inside, before beckoning for the three of them to follow. Jane hovered in the antechamber, nodding to Thomas Culpepper. Charles took Catherine by the hand and led her through to Henry's private rooms.

The king was sitting by the fire, his finery from the evening removed. He was now dressed in a loose white chemise with an ornately decorated red and golden robe over it. On his head was a silk hat with an extravagant tassel, but his magnificent jewels were gone. He looked old, tired and bloated. His greyhounds, stretched out beside him on their soft cushions, were dozing. One raised a head as Catherine and Charles entered, the other thumped its tail, but neither roused themselves.

Charles hugged Catherine, then backed silently from the room.

As the door clicked shut behind him, Henry, without looking up from his contemplation of the fire, stretched out a hand to Catherine. Swallowing her revulsion at the overwhelming stench of rotten meat emanating from the king's ulcerated leg, she took his hand and allowed him to lead her around until she was standing in front of him, their knees touching. She was so small she was barely taller than the seated king. His raddled face was level with her chest and, to her horror, Henry leant forward, resting his head on her spilling cleavage.

"I had hoped," he sighed, "you'd have removed your finery and be dressed in a less formal manner, as I am myself."

Catherine hesitated, unsure what to do. Henry seemed to be trying to burrow further into her breasts. His touch made her feel sick. "There will be time enough, my lord, for you to see me without my formal attire when we are married," she whispered in a strangled voice.

"Is that all you want from me? A marriage vow?" His voice was low, almost a growl as he looked up and his rheumy brown eyes locked with the clear crystal blue of her own.

"No, my lord, I want nothing except to make you happy."

"You wish only to make me happy?" he snorted derisively. "No one ever wishes to make me happy, they always want something from me."

Catherine forced a smile to her lips and, steeling herself, she ran a soft finger down his cheek, as though he were the most desirable man in the world.

"Yes, my lord, you need someone to cherish you, to care for you, to soothe away the troubles of kingship and keep you happy."

"And you will do this?"

"If you will allow me."

"And you will give me sons?"

"Yes, my lord, I will give you healthy sons."

The king smiled: "You will make the Tudor line secure, we will make my father proud."

Catherine nodded.

"This is good, this is good, my sweetheart," he whispered, closing his eyes for a moment. Then his tone changed and he sounded excited, "Will you dance for me? As you danced for me at your uncle's banquet the night we first met?"

"We have no musicians," she replied.

"Do you need music? Can you not dance to the rhythm of your heart?"

For a moment, Catherine's confidence fled. The king was a grown man; she was little more than a child and she was out of her depth. As she hesitated, the king began to clap, slowly and rhythmically, stamping his foot to add to the sensuous, pulsating beat he was creating.

"Dance, little Catherine," he said. "Dance for me, then I will make your dreams come true."

Catherine swallowed hard, fighting back the tears. Think what my cousin Anne Boleyn would have done, she ordered herself. She would have danced, then she would have destroyed the enemy of her family. Trying hard to emulate her sophisticated cousin, Catherine took a few steps away from the king and raised her arms.

"My dreams?" she whispered. "What do you know of my dreams, sire?"

She concentrated on the compulsive beat the king was creating, then allowed herself to move. It was primitive, yet irresistible. She swayed her hips; the king altered the speed of his clapping, faster, faster. Catherine whirled, her hair flying.

She moved closer to the king, her lips parted, her skin flushed, her mass of red curls tumbling over her shoulders.

"What do you know of my dreams, sire?" she whispered as she spun. "Do you know what I dream?"

The king, still clapping like an automaton, was mesmerised.

"What do you dream?" he gasped, trying to grab her as she whirled past him. "Do you dream of me?"

"Oh yes, your majesty, I dream of you. I dream of us, together…" She allowed her hair to whip within touching distance. "And I dream of our sons, strong sons…"

"What else? What else crowds your heart?"

"Fear!"

"Fear?" he replied, confused, once more altering the beat, slowing it down so she moved more slowly, swaying in front of him, her eyes bright, her cheeks flushed. "What do you fear, my sweetheart?"

"Cromwell," she whispered, as though terrified of the very name.

"Thomas Cromwell?" confirmed the king, and she nodded. He stopped clapping. "What has he said to you?"

"He threatened me and he laughed at you," she said, her voice reluctant.

The king's tiny eyes narrowed. "Laughed?" he roared. She nodded. "Would you like Cromwell's head on a platter?"

Bewildered, Catherine nodded again, managing a nervous smile. The king laughed. He hauled himself to his feet. Catching Catherine in a surprisingly strong grip, he clamped his lips on hers, his tongue forcing its way into her mouth.

"You are perfection itself," he gasped, his hands roving over her body. "You can have Cromwell's head as a wedding present, my little temptress, and then you will dance naked for me and I will sow my seed inside you, again and again and again…"

He broke away from her, grinning like a schoolboy.

"I had news today that my marriage to the Flanders' Mare will soon be over, then we can bounce together in our marriage bed."

"Anne was manipulated as you were, she is a vulnerable girl, ripped from her home and forced across the ocean to marry you, a perfect prince, but she was unhappy and homesick."

"But who would force a lady to do this?" asked Henry, completely ignoring the fact it had been on his orders she had travelled to England.

"Why, Thomas Cromwell, of course," said Catherine. "The Privy Seal. He wanted a Protestant alliance, not for your sake, but for his."

"You are not the first to suggest this to me," murmured Henry, returning to his seat by the fire and reaching to pull Catherine onto his lap. She allowed herself to be drawn forward and, gritting her teeth, settled herself. Henry groaned, her bosom was level with his face. "He took advantage of the queen, he manipulated her for his own ends, as he manipulates you. I have heard him boast that he is the true king of England, that you are his lap dog."

"He said what?"

"He scoffs that you are his pet, you do as he says and he is the power behind your throne," she whispered. "I don't believe him, you are a king of kings, a giant among men, yet he belittles you and, in doing so, he uses me too."

"How does he use you?"

"He threatened me," she whispered. "And worse, he has destroyed the ancient graves of my family."

She shifted, trying to make herself more comfortable and as she did, her gown fell forward. Henry groaned as he caught a glimpse of her pale, pink nipples. Self-consciously, she covered herself again but he stayed her hand.

"Let me see you, little Catherine. I have been so unhappy, let me see you."

He slid his hands across her shoulders, loosening her dress so it fell to her waist. He sighed heavily and, to her surprise, Catherine felt movement in his lap. *So he wasn't impotent as the cruel gossips in the court suggested*, she thought. She was surprised at the gentleness of his hands as he cupped her breasts, taking their unexpected heaviness in his palms.

"You are ripe, Mistress Howard, ready to be plucked."

Catherine braced herself as he lowered his head and took one pink nipple in his mouth, running his tongue over it until, to her disgust, she felt it hardening. He moved to the other as she sat rigid, revolted by the slurping noises coming from the king. Henry pulled her forward and buried his head in her breasts.

"I want to take you now," he whispered. Then, like a child wanting a treat, his voice took on a strange timbre. "Give me a son."

"But my lord, he would be illegitimate, and you know this would make it impossible for him to be king."

"Alas, you speak wisely," he sighed. "Even if these are not the words of desire I had hoped you would whisper."

With swift, neat movements, he pulled her dress over her shoulders and tied it demurely.

"Let us speak of other things," he said, smiling, taking her hand and kissing her fingers, one after the other. "Your words about Cromwell have not gone unheeded. He is my most trusted advisor, but he is becoming troublesome. You are not the only one he has threatened but there must be solid proof against him. My Privy Council is chasing down this necessary evidence and, if it proves true, Cromwell will learn it is not he, but I, who rules this realm."

He took her hand and indicated for her to stand, then twirled her around before standing himself. As he did, his chemise parted to reveal he was wearing nothing underneath. Catherine averted her eyes. She had never seen a grown man naked before, but it was the suppurating wound on his leg that caught her eye. She gulped and the king glanced down to see himself revealed to her.

"Do you like what you see, little Catherine?" he asked, pulling his chemise wider apart.

"My lord, you are a handsome man," she said, unsure whether to call for Charles.

The king stared at her for a few moments, then his expression changed, his face contorted as though in pain and he no longer seemed to recognise her.

"Would you like to touch me?" he snarled. "Run your hands over my naked body?" He grasped her wrist so she could not back away. "Under all your innocence, you're no better than a whore," he hissed, his face a twisted, grotesque mask of rage. "You Howard girls are all sluts in the bedroom, bouncing on me, endlessly sucking me dry, expecting me to fill you with my seed, but none of you ever gave me a son. Well, maybe one of you did, but daughters, daughters, women everywhere, grasping at me, taking from me. You expect me to believe you're different, that you want only to make me happy, that you want nothing for yourself. You're a liar, like they were liars."

The king gripped her other hand and pulled her towards him, his tongue lolling from the side of his mouth as he made jutting movements to try to kiss her. His eyes bulged and he roared in fury, throwing her violently to the floor, standing over her, his lips drawn back from his rotting teeth in a silent sneer. The door to the antechamber was flung open and Thomas Culpepper ran in, Jane Boleyn, pale-faced and frightened behind him.

"Catherine, go with Jane and wait outside," Thomas commanded. "Do not leave until we have spoken."

Jane grabbed Catherine by the hand and, helping her to her feet, dragged her from the room.

"But the king?" protested Catherine. "We must help."

"There's nothing you can do while he has one of these fits," said Jane, pulling Catherine into the antechamber and slamming the door. Catherine listened to the king bellowing.

"What's wrong with him, Jane?" gasped Catherine.

"He has these moments. When he is recovered, he remembers very little," Jane said in a quiet voice, efficiently re-lacing Catherine's bodice and tidying her hair. "Thomas says it is an illness. It comes and goes. I suggested it was from the poison in his leg, but Thomas says he thinks not as these attacks have happened for longer than the king has had the wound."

The shouting from the king's chamber had lessened and after a while, Thomas appeared.

"He's asleep," he said. "Did he hurt you, Catherine?"

"No, but he changed from being melancholic to furious. I thought he was going to force himself upon me," she said, the shock of Henry's sudden rage making her tremble.

"He would have tried, but when he is like that, thankfully, he is usually impotent or…" Thomas did not finish the sentence but merely shuddered.

"But what ails him?" asked Catherine.

"Life, illness, age, the madness of the Tudors," sighed Thomas. "The important thing is not to let anyone know."

"Why?"

"Use your head, Kitty," snapped Jane. "Imagine what would happen if people knew the king was mad? The wars would begin all over again. The Seymours would try to put their brat on the throne, the Spanish would invade, who knows which pretenders would emerge claiming they had a right to the throne of England. We would be plunged into civil war again. Do you want the Seymours to claim power?"

"No, but I don't want to marry a madman either," retorted Catherine.

"These bouts are infrequent," said Thomas. "You will be safe, but there is a risk he may not be able to perform his husbandly duty."

"And what will happen if there is no heir?"

"If he continues like this, there may not be a king," he replied. "Then his son, Edward, will be on the throne and we will have to protect ourselves from the Seymours. What has happened here this evening is known only to a trusted few and, for now, this is the way it should remain."

"Will the king remember what happened?"

"He might have snatches of it, but no," said Thomas. "Mostly, he has no recollection. When he asks me what happened this evening, I will say you were charming and you drank spiced wine, then you demurely left and he gave you this."

Thomas handed her a jewelled brooch in the shape of an arrow.

"Cupid's arrow," said Catherine.

They stared at it, then Jane spoke. "Come, Catherine, let us call Charles and get you to your rooms."

Catherine allowed herself to be led away, shocked by what she had discovered in the king's chamber, wondering how any of them would survive.

Chapter Eight

The king is mad. I am marrying a madman.

Catherine stared at the river, watching it flow ever onwards towards the sea, to magical, mystical places, lands that were not ruled by Henry and his insanity.

Perhaps this is why he killed cousin Anne, she thought. *A fit of madness overcame him and he destroyed the woman he had once adored above all others, even risking his soul by breaking with the Catholic Church to marry her. He probably would have done the same to Jane Seymour if she hadn't conveniently died in childbirth. He could kill me. He could kill the queen, although her Germanic royal blood will probably keep her safe as old Queen Katherine's Spanish royal blood saved her from the horror and humiliation of the axe…*

She pushed her frantic thoughts aside as she watched a merchant ship sailing by, its colours high, proclaiming loyalty to king and country as it headed out on an adventure. Should she flee? Board a ship and disappear abroad? Surely her family had connections elsewhere, somewhere they could hide her, keep her safe. They could tell the king she had died…

Catherine heard footsteps and saw the queen, accompanied by her translator and the duchess of Suffolk, Katherine Willoughby, approaching her.

"Good morning, my dear Kitty," said Anne, her face full of concern.

Catherine knew her red eyes gave away her misery. She was still horrified by the events of the previous night and she wondered if Anne had witnessed similar scenes. To her horror, as Anne gazed at her sympathetically, Catherine found the tears she had been struggling to keep at bay, welling up. The queen took her hand, then spoke softly in German to her translator before turning to the duchess of Suffolk.

"Your grace, would you accompany Brunhilde to my rooms to fetch my shawl, there is a chilly breeze. Catherine and I will wait in the shelter of the arbour," she said. A look of irritation flashed across Katherine Willoughby's face, but she did not question the queen. Anne took Catherine's arm and they walked to a secluded seat near the water's edge.

"We will not be disturbed here," she said, sitting on the stone bench and beckoning Catherine to join her.

"You were summoned to see the king last night," said Anne, her voice low, urgent. It was not a question, it was a statement. Catherine nodded. "You witnessed it then? The king losing his mind?"

"Yes," she whispered.

"Did he hurt you?"

"No, but only because Thomas Culpepper rescued me."

"He is a good man, he came to my aid the first time the king had one of his fits too."

"Oh, my lady, did he hurt you?"

"No, he usually collapsed before he could do me any damage," she replied. "Oh, Kitten, these men who control our lives have no idea of the horrors they put us through with their scheming and plotting."

The two women contemplated each other's misery. Both had been thrust into the path of the king by their ambitious male relatives. Both knew they were dispensable in the face of family aggrandisement.

"Has there been any word on the annulment?" asked Catherine.

"Thomas Cranmer, the Archbishop of Canterbury, has spoken to me of it," Anne sighed. "He claims I had a prior betrothal which was never legally dissolved, so the king and I are not really married."

She turned her face away so Catherine would not see her blinking back her tears. Although she knew it was against every form of court etiquette, Catherine squeezed the queen's hand. Anne clung to her as though her life depended upon it. Then, regaining her composure, she gave a watery smile.

"Will you return to Cleves?" asked Catherine.

"I'd prefer to stay here and try to retain some level of status, rather than facing the humiliation and disgrace of once more placing myself in my brother's court and under his care," she said. Then, looking at Catherine, tears brimming, she continued. "I know what the king has said about me — that I am ugly, a horse, my body is not that of a maid — would you wish to go home and have to explain why you are no longer a queen? That a man as ugly and evil as Satan has rejected you because you are not pretty enough? I would rather stay here where my humiliation is my own. At least here I have made some friends. Well, I think — I hope — I have."

"You have!" exclaimed Catherine, burning with rage and shame for the queen. "I'm your friend, so is Isabel. My influence is small, but I'll do all I can to ensure you're treated with dignity."

"We're the only two women alive who know what it's like to be married to the king and the dangers this brings. If you ever need me, I'll do all I can to help you. I still have influence outside the country and, should we need them, powerful allies at my brother's court. He and I may not be close, and I don't want to go home, but I know he would defend me."

She glanced around to check they were still alone, then drew a small, blue velvet pouch from a pocket hidden in the lining of her sleeve. After fumbling with the knot that secured the top, she pulled something out and handed it to Catherine. It was a ruby ring. The stone was oval shaped and had a subtle dark red hue. This was set in a delicately wrought filigree gold cage and attached to a golden band encrusted with tiny diamonds.

"Look," said Anne, opening her own hand, "I have one too! The only difference is that mine has an emerald on the hidden clip and yours has a sapphire."

"A hidden clip?"

"Watch," she instructed, flipping the ring over to reveal the gold base of the filigree cage. "There is a small clip here, slide it backwards and…"

Catherine's eyes were wide with wonder. If Anne had not pointed it out, she would never have noticed it. The tiny mechanism had been designed to blend into the camouflage of the delicate filigree cage, but now Anne had slid it forward, releasing it. The entire cage opened to reveal a cavity within.

"Because the rings are identical, no one will notice if we swap them over," whispered Anne excitedly. "We can pass notes to each other, to help each other, to impart news and warn each other of danger. It is clever, yes?"

"Very clever!" exclaimed Catherine, overwhelmed that Anne had gone to such trouble to forge a link between them. "Did you think of this, your grace?"

"Yes, my sisters and I had similar rings when we were growing up," she said. "Keep yours safe, Kitty, and use it if ever you need to get a message to me. If it comes with the ring, I'll know it's from you and you will always know if any message sent in my name is really from me."

"Oh, Anne, thank you," said Catherine slipping the ring on the middle finger of her right hand. Then, forgetting herself entirely, she hugged the queen. Anne was delighted and returned the embrace.

There was a discreet cough and the two women looked up to see Brunhilde holding Anne's shawl, accompanied by Isabel and Margaret Douglas.

"I'm sorry to interrupt, your grace," said Isabel curtseying, "but the king approaches."

Anne said something in German, then rose, straightening her skirts.

"If you will excuse us, ladies," she said in her soft, accented voice and, with Brunhilde behind her, she swept away.

"Unfortunately, Kitty, you have to face him," said Isabel. Catherine nodded and stood patiently while Margaret fussed around her, straightening her French hood, smoothing out her dress.

"Kitty, how did you get brambles in the hem of your skirt!" she exclaimed. "You're supposed to be practising to be a queen, not hiding in the undergrowth!"

Despite herself, Catherine laughed.

"Oh, Margaret, you who comes back with straw in your hair…"

"Once," retorted Margaret, "that happened once!"

Her eyes twinkled, then she stepped back.

"Very pretty, Mistress Howard."

"Now, Kitten, let's walk along the path and accidentally bump into the king," said Isabel. Catherine allowed her sister to lead her forward. Margaret, she noticed, quickly melted away into the shadows. She and Isabel had only taken a few steps when coming down the lime walk towards them, was Henry.

The king was accompanied by her uncle, the duke of Norfolk, Isabel's husband, Edward Baynton, Charles Brandon, the duke of Suffolk, and Edward Seymour, the earl of

Hertford, the king's former brother-in-law and uncle of the heir apparent, the young Prince Edward. A short distance behind them walked Thomas Culpepper. Before Catherine could think or even allow her fear to take hold again, the king had seen her. He shook off the other men and, grinning like a love-struck schoolboy, hurried towards her. Both she and Isabel dropped to the floor in deep curtseys.

"My dearest Catherine," he said, beaming, raising her to standing. "What a pleasure it is to see you on this bright morning. You, too, my Lady Baynton. Rise, rise, my dears and come walk with me awhile."

"But my lord…" began Edward Seymour, stopping abruptly when Henry waved a dismissive hand towards him.

"You've had my views," replied the king, "now I have other more important things to occupy my time. Culpepper, stay with us and send a boy to bring my lute, there is something I would like to play for Mistress Howard."

He dismissed the members of his Privy Council with a nod and, tucking Catherine's hand under his arm, led her away from the lime walk to one of the more secluded bowers in the garden. Isabel and Thomas kept a discreet distance. As Henry swept her around the corner Catherine caught a glimpse of her uncle's closed, expressionless face and the look of disgusted fury on Edward Seymour's.

"My dear," said Henry once they were out of earshot, "I must apologise for dozing off during our pleasant interlude. You must excuse an old man's lapse. I believe, moments before the pressures of the day overtook me, we were discussing you dancing for me."

He looked down at her, his eyes teasing. She could not understand the change in the king. Last night he had been foaming at the mouth, trying to attack her, now he was behaving as though nothing had happened. Did he really have no memory of events as Thomas Culpepper claimed? Or was he, as king, using his prerogative to insist all was well and challenging anyone to question him about his behaviour? Either way, Catherine knew her only option was to play along.

"We were indeed, sire," she agreed.

"And I believe we were also discussing Thomas Cromwell," he continued.

"Why, yes," she murmured, revulsion swooping through her. Despite the fact Cromwell was a cruel, dangerous and ruthless man, the prospect of a violent end for anyone horrified her and, the previous night, Henry had offered her his head on a platter. *Surely the angels will forgive me*, she thought.

"You must no longer worry about him, my dear," said Henry. "Men wiser than you are investigating Thomas Cromwell, the new earl of Essex, and if the rumours about him are true, then he and I will discuss the best possible outcome. However, I trust Cromwell and am sure he will be exonerated. He does ease the path of my days, even if he does occasionally take liberties. You are neither to worry nor think you are responsible. Men write their own epitaphs."

They turned into a semi-circle of box hedge, which created a private exterior room. At the centre were seats and a small fountain decorated with a chubby, naked cupid. Isabel and Thomas hovered a short distance outside the little hollow.

"We will soon have a boy like this," said Henry, "a sturdy elf to be my duke of York, to follow in Edward's footsteps should anything untoward happen. We can never be sure of God's plan. After all, was not I the second son, thought to be destined for the church until the Lord decreed I would walk a different path."

He pulled Catherine more tightly into his side. "You were most delightful last night, my dear Catherine. I can't wait to see you in such a way again. I yearn for our wedding night when I can have you all to myself."

"And when will that be, my lord?"

"Soon, then we can be together," he said eagerly.

Catherine decided now was the time to speak. "Your majesty." She hesitated. "Henry." He smiled, so she continued, "Please be kind to the queen."

"What do you mean?" he asked, but his voice was gentle.

"She's a young woman alone in a foreign land with no champion except you," Catherine said. "Imagine if it was one of your daughters, alone and scared, you'd want someone to protect them, someone to be kind."

He was listening intently and Catherine paused, unsure whether he was angry or sympathetic.

"Continue, my dear," he said, his tone soft.

"She doesn't want to return to Cleves. She'd like to remain in this country. Is there a way she can be provided for, cared for, perhaps with an establishment of her own?"

Henry was silent for a time, considering Catherine with wonder, then he nodded.

"You are a compassionate woman," he said. "Most would be eager to see their rival sent away, but not you. This is what makes you such an angel. What would you have me do?"

"Treat her kindly and with dignity. She is a royal princess and should be given such privilege, even when she is no longer your wife."

"Should I make her the same rank as my sister?" he asked. "She too is a royal princess. The terms of the annulment could make Anne my legal sister. You would still rank higher than she, but she would have the same privileges that she enjoyed in her home of Cleves."

"Oh, Henry, that would be so generous," exclaimed Catherine.

"Then this is what I will tell the Privy Council and the earl of Essex to ensure," he said. "Dignity, kindness and consideration at the behest of my beautiful English rose without a thorn."

Catherine smiled and as the page arrived and gave Thomas Culpepper the lute, which he delivered to Henry with a bow, she settled back to listen to yet another rendition of *Greensleeves*. At least she knew her impending marriage to the king had done one good thing, it had saved her friend from humiliation. Now, as the music wafted over her, she prayed for her own safe deliverance from the tyrant sitting opposite her.

Chapter Nine

Catherine closed her eyes, allowing the golden moment to envelope her. The soft, sweet-smelling air played with her flowing hair as she trotted across the meadow on her silver mare. Laughter crept around her like a lover's arms while the warmth of the summer sunshine stroked her face with a gentle caress. Surrounded by the people she loved, this was a rare escape and, for the first time since her betrothal to the king, Catherine allowed herself to bask in the purity of her happiness.

"Not far now, Kitten," called her brother, Charles. "You'll be able to see it from the top of the next hill."

She opened her eyes and smiled. "And is it really as beautiful as everyone would have me believe?"

"More than words can describe," laughed Thomas Culpepper, riding up, accompanied by a radiant Jane Boleyn.

"Is that true, Jane?"

"Oh, Kitten, it's magnificent!" she said and Catherine smiled, enjoying being with her friends.

Henry had decided it was time the court moved away from the stench of the city to enjoy the warmer weather in the countryside at his palace in Hampton. When Edward suggested that Catherine's party go separately on horseback and visit the former Queen Anne at her new palace in Richmond, Catherine had hardly dared hope Henry would grant such a wish. But, in a magnanimous mood, he had squeezed her tightly and declared, "My sweet rose without a thorn, no other woman would spare a thought for her rival and yet you wish everyone to be as happy as you are yourself. Sweetheart, it is impossible for me to refuse you anything."

To her delight, three days later, she and her sizeable entourage had set off. She rode her new silver mare, a gift from Henry, named Moonbeam, and they had spent a happy five days at Richmond Palace with Anne before riding off like a hunting party on the ten-mile journey to Hampton Court. Charles and Lady Margaret Douglas had led the way, followed by the besotted Thomas Culpepper and Jane Boleyn, and the newly married Lady Kathryn Carey and Sir Francis Knollys, while Isabel and Edward had ridden either side of her. A lavish outdoor banquet en route had made the day even more magical.

I will carry this happiness with me, she thought as she urged her mare up the hill after her brother and Margaret. *There is joy in my new life as well as fear; I must make the most of these gifts.* She glanced down at her hands and allowed herself a small secret smile when she looked at her ruby ring. This present from Anne was something that was truly hers, and not a jewel bestowed upon her by the king, one he could take back should he choose. The ruby ring and the silver locket from Isabel and Edward were her two most prized possessions and she had chosen to wear them both for her journey to Hampton Court.

"There!" called Margaret as she and Catherine crested the hill, bringing the horses to a rapid halt.

Catherine gasped in wonder. Glistening like a promise on the curve of the mighty River Thames lay the extravagant palace of Hampton Court. Spiral chimneys swirled endlessly upwards into the blue sky, mythical beasts pranced across the moat to both welcome and deter, and the glint of gold rippled through the air like fairies dancing.

Isabel came trotting towards them on her glossy chestnut mare. "Kitten, we'll have to make you look presentable again. We can't have the future queen of England trotting into Base Court looking like a wild woman."

An hour later, neatly attired and with her French hood back in place, Catherine and her party galloped towards the glittering moat with its broad drawbridge. Brilliantly painted statues greeted them: the lion and the unicorn of England, the greyhound of Richmond, the rampant red dragon of Wales, the yale of Beaufort with its portcullis flag, the white hart of York, the bull of Clarence and the falcon of the Plantagenets, each one gilded and magnificent in the summer sun, reminding visitors of the supremacy of the Tudor monarchy. The heraldic symbolism of these creatures all emphasised the Tudor's ancient links and Henry's undeniable right to the throne through both his father's Beaufort and Lancastrian blood and his mother's York blood.

As her silver mare trotted proudly under the great arch and clattered across the cobbles, Catherine wished she had another pair of eyes to take in all the detail, the hustle and bustle and the sheer spectacle of this place she would now call home. Through Base Court they went with its streams of people hurrying to and from the kitchens, through another magnificent archway to the huge cobbled expanse of Clock Court, where finally, her groom brought her to a halt beneath the magnificent astrological clock.

"This place," Catherine stammered to Isabel as her sister's horse stopped beside her, "it's magical."

Isabel laughed. Grooms hurried over and the others dismounted, merging with the crowd while Catherine remained on her mare, gazing around in awe.

"It's one of the most magnificent palaces in Europe," said Isabel. "Although, the king's new hunting lodge of Nonsuch is equally as lavish."

"How could anywhere be grander than here?" sighed Catherine, gazing around her at the impressive statues, the twinkling stained glass and the endless, brightly dressed courtiers and servants who were a living tapestry of energy and colour.

"Get used to it, my dear," said Edward Baynton, throwing his reins to his groom and dismounting in a swift, agile swoop. "This will be your home a great deal of the time once you're married to the king."

At his words, Catherine felt the usual icy gasp of fear. Events had moved quickly in the last few weeks. Anne had been removed to a residence of her own and was no longer styled as queen. True to his word, Henry had granted her the status of his royal sister. Henry and Anne's marriage was to be annulled by Archbishop Cranmer any day now, and then the date would be set for Catherine's own wedding. She pushed the thought aside.

Cromwell, too, had suffered Henry's wrath. The dukes of Norfolk and Suffolk, for once allied with the earl of Hertford, had conspired to trump up charges against the Privy Seal to remove him from power, knowing that this time, Henry would support their findings, particularly as she herself had added a claim against the former Privy Seal. On the day of Cromwell's arrest, Henry had bounded into Catherine's chambers and announced one of his wedding gifts to her would be Cromwell's head.

"Just as you asked," he had whispered. "Then we will dance."

He had chuckled, running a finger suggestively down her face, but Catherine had been horrified. She felt that her hands were stained with Cromwell's blood. While others may have pulled strings, she had a sinking feeling that it was her appeal that had finally brought Cromwell tumbling to his fate.

"But what about a trial?" she had asked.

"Do not worry yourself," Henry had laughed gleefully. "These are men's travails. You, my rose without a thorn, must practise your dance steps. We have a bargain, you and I."

He had kissed her hand, then departed, shouting for Thomas Culpepper as he strode away, for once exhibiting some of the lost vigour of his youth. It had not lasted though, and the following day he had retired to his chamber, where he remained in bed for nearly a week. It was during his illness that he had decided to move the court from the foul-smelling air of London to the sweet countryside of Hampton.

As Catherine was helped from her horse by one of the Howard grooms, she stared around, wondering at the enormity of the building.

"Your rooms are this way, Kitty," called Isabel from the grand entrance. "And later, when you are ready, the princesses will greet you."

Gathering her skirts, Catherine's first instinct was to run after Isabel as quickly as possible, but then Margaret Douglas's words of the previous day echoed in her ears.

"You're going to be queen, Kitten, make them wait for you," she had laughed when she had found Catherine dashing along a corridor in response to a summons from Edward Baynton. "It isn't very dignified to see the king's wife racing around the place like a greyhound."

Despite the teasing, Catherine had learned to listen to Margaret's advice. She was royalty. Her mother, another

Margaret, was a Tudor princess and had been queen of Scotland; her half-brother was James V, the king of Scotland. She was the niece of King Henry himself, so the trappings of state and the responsibility of her status came easily. She had been born to it. Therefore, she had never questioned it and her air of entitlement, while alienating some courtiers, gave her a confidence and sophistication Catherine admired and had decided to emulate.

She lowered her skirts again, smoothing them carefully, then did her best imitation of Margaret's long-legged, gliding walk. *Nearly*, thought Catherine, as she arrived at her sister's side. *Although, it's easier for Margaret, she's taller than me.*

"Come on then, Issy," said Catherine. "If you are now one of the Great Ladies of my court, lead the way to my rooms."

They walked along twisting corridors to the Queen's chambers. Her guard were already positioned by the door and her herald leapt forward to usher her in. The rooms were filled with dancing summer light and the sweet herbs mixed with the strewing rushes on the floor gave a delicate fragrance. Women bustled to and fro, unpacking her trunks, shaking out her gowns and arranging the lighter pieces of furniture that had been brought to the palace a few days earlier. But as she entered, they all dropped to the floor in deep curtseys, heads bowed, eyes averted. It was so unexpected, Catherine nearly laughed, particularly as one of the older women was her step-grandmother, the Dowager Duchess of Norfolk, Agnes Tilney.

"Rise, please ladies," she said, again doing her best to imitate Margaret Douglas. "Grandmamma, what a surprise," she continued, taking Agnes Tilney's hand and raising her up.

"My dear," said Agnes, smiling. "The moment your father delivered you into my care as a child, I knew we could expect great things from you."

What nonsense, thought Catherine. *You barely noticed I was alive most of the time I lived under your roof.* Yet, she smiled. This was politics. While Agnes Tilney might be family, Catherine trusted her about as much as an adder.

"Why thank you, Grandmamma," she replied, smiling so her dimples showed. "It's thanks to your education and careful nurturing that I have risen so high."

Catherine nodded a dismissal and turned to Isabel, who was watching with an amused expression on her face. Once the dowager duchess was out of earshot, Isabel murmured, "Nicely done, Kitty, you're learning the ways of court extremely quickly."

Catherine linked her arm through her sister's and walked towards the inner chambers of her court.

"It's safer that way," she replied. "Will you help me choose something suitable to wear for my audience with the king's daughters? It would be good to see Jane, Margaret and Kathy Knollys too, if the former Lady Carey can be dragged away from her new husband. I could do with the company of friends I trust before facing the court."

"Of course," said Isabel. "You rest in here, while I gather the troops."

She ushered Catherine into her bedchamber then, firmly closing the door behind her, Catherine was pleased to hear Isabel command that: "My Lady Catherine must not be disturbed" before her footsteps retreated.

Catherine waited a few moments to be sure Isabel's words had been heeded, then slid a square of parchment from her pocket. It was a letter from Anne, placed into her hand as they had left this morning.

The note was short: *My dear friend, your words last night have given me cause for concern. Keeping a journal is a dangerous pastime. It may preserve our deeds clearly and reveal our version of the truth, but it can also be used by one's enemies to discredit our behaviour. Trust no one but your sister with your true feelings and burn anything you write that you would not have used against you. These are dangerous days, my dear sweet Kitten. Remember your cousin and be wise.*

Catherine noticed that Anne was heeding her own advice and had not signed the letter. She read it over and over, fear rising once more. Like Margaret Douglas, Anne had been raised in a royal household, she knew the dangers as well as the pleasures of holding positions of power. Her instinct told her to take the former queen's advice seriously. Catherine had always kept a diary and at the end of each year, when the New Year festivities were ringing through the halls, she would take herself away and quietly burn each page, saying a small prayer of thanks or an appeal for mercy as each whisper of ash had disappeared up the chimney. Back then, she had been lowly, unimportant, and the notes she made about her everyday life had made her feel more real, more alive, as though her thoughts mattered. It had never occurred to her that now her social position had changed, her scribbled thoughts could prove to be dangerous.

The small travelling box that held her personal effects had been placed at the foot of her bed. Heeding Anne's words, she opened it and rummaged around for her journal. As of yet, there was very little of interest in the magnificent jewelled book but Catherine's plan to write her own daily version of events, keeping a log of who waited upon her and what she did, a record to prove her innocence should it ever be necessary, now no longer seemed so simple.

Will I never be safe? she thought as she scanned the room, searching for a suitable place to hide it. Although, she reasoned, if she found one, it was likely she was not the first person to have used it, so it would not be secure. Instead, she wrapped the book in an old chemise and hid it at the bottom of the trunk. She would consider whether or not to continue her journal; after all, it was not only her safety that could be compromised. There was a clatter of feet and noise outside and her sister was announced.

"Enter," called Catherine, and moments later was enveloped in a hug from Margaret Douglas, followed by Kathy Knollys. Jane Boleyn, even now she had been accepted into the inner circle of Catherine's ladies, was still shy and held back. Isabel skirted the little group, her arms full of a silver and white gown which she placed on the bed.

"This is cloth of gold," she said as she began unlacing Catherine. "Once you're in it, try not to sit down."

"Why not?" asked Catherine, who could not take her eyes off the beautiful gown.

"Cloth of gold is exactly what it says," said Jane. "Real gold is woven into the fabric. The trouble is, gold doesn't work too well in gowns. It's metal, so it can bend out of shape if you sit down for too long and it won't bend back."

"What happens?" asked Catherine, not sure if the women were teasing her.

"Nothing happens, Kitten," assured Kathy Knollys. "But it just makes the skirt a peculiar shape, that's all."

"That's ridiculous," Catherine giggled. "Although, I suppose it's no more ridiculous than me being queen."

An hour later, she was poised by the great fireplace in her rooms, as she waited for the first meeting with Henry's daughters. Lady Mary, the eldest, was now twenty-four, while Lady Elizabeth was a child of seven. It was Lady Mary who daunted Catherine the most. She was great friends with Margaret Douglas, so Catherine hoped this would soften Lady

Mary towards her. Not only was Mary some years older than Catherine, she was the daughter of Henry's first wife, Katherine of Aragon: a Spanish princess and the woman who, in many people's eyes, had always been the rightful queen. Elizabeth was the daughter of Anne Boleyn, Henry's second wife and Catherine's cousin. Although Catherine had never met her, she already felt closer to Elizabeth. They were blood family and, in Catherine's mind, this counted for a great deal.

"Issy, you and Edward were their guardians for a while, after Jane Seymour died, what are they like?"

"Elizabeth is a sweet girl," replied Isabel. "She's extremely intelligent but shy. Once you've won her trust, she's very loyal and loving. She reminds me a great deal of my eldest boy, Henry. Serious but with a huge capacity for fun."

"And Mary?"

"Kitty, you have to remember Mary has had a difficult life," said Isabel. "She was wrenched away from her mother and barred from seeing or speaking to her. Her father was less than kind in his treatment of her for a very long time. Sadly, she blames Anne Boleyn for his cruelty. But again, once you get to know her and win her trust, she can be very caring. Lady Cleves was very warm to all of Henry's children, so they'll appreciate the fact that you've helped her to retain her dignity. There are many women in your position who would have seen her banished."

"Then they are not nice women," said Catherine.

"Indeed, they aren't, Kitty, but they are often ruthless and clever, which is sometimes what you need to survive in Henry's court."

"The Lady Cleves was determined to bring the royal children together as a family," said Catherine thoughtfully. "I shall try to continue what she began. After all, we are all motherless, are we not? You and I too."

Issy nodded. "If you can achieve that, then you will have done a good thing."

"The Lady Mary and the Lady Elizabeth," the herald announced and Catherine felt her stomach churn with nerves. Surreptitiously she wiped her damp palms on the sides of her magnificent gown.

She remembered being a face in the crowd, a mere maid, watching when Anne of Cleves had been presented to Henry at Greenwich in January and envying her the beauty of her cloth of gold gown. No one had ever told her that wearing such a dress would be so uncomfortable. It was cumbersome and heavy on her hips, making her legs ache. She assumed she would eventually get used to it, like all the other trappings of being a queen.

"Remember, they will curtsey to you," whispered Margaret, who was standing beside her, excited to be seeing her friend and cousin, Lady Mary. "You only have to nod, you're going to be their mother."

The doors were flung open and Henry's daughters entered. Mary swept in first, her confidence and certainty reminding Catherine of Margaret; she sank to the floor in a low and elegant curtsey. Elizabeth followed and copied her older sister; both remained motionless with their heads bowed. Catherine remembered what she and Isabel had rehearsed while she had been getting ready. Taking a deep breath and hoping her voice would not let her down, she spoke: "My dears, what a pleasure to meet you at last, please rise and let us get to know each other properly."

Elizabeth stood at once and surveyed Catherine with huge, dark eyes that reminded her forcibly of Anne Boleyn. Her hair was a deep Tudor red and her skin pale and delicate. Mary rose more slowly and Catherine was slightly intimidated. Although they were of a similar height, Mary too had flowing auburn hair and was exquisitely pretty. Her features were dainty and her skin was slightly darker than Elizabeth's, with a faint hint of pink along her cheekbones. Her eyes were paler, somewhere between hazel and green, but it was her icy poise that unnerved Catherine.

"It's an honour to meet you too," replied Mary, but her eyes were cold as she appraised her new stepmother-to-be. They flickered away from Catherine and towards Margaret, who curtseyed then beamed at her cousin. Mary's whole expression changed as she grinned in return.

"Come, let us sit a while," said Catherine, trying to ignore the obvious dislike emanating from the two girls. She indicated the circle of chairs that had been arranged near the window and took the largest, most impressive chair in the centre. "My ladies and I have decided to create a tapestry for the Lady Anne of Cleves, to welcome her to her new home. Perhaps you would like to join us."

With great reluctance, Mary took the chair to Catherine's right. Elizabeth sat on her left. The other ladies arranged themselves on the chairs. Margaret slid in beside Mary, while Kathy Knollys and Jane Boleyn moved towards Elizabeth. Suddenly, the little girl saw Isabel and, for a moment, the seven-year-old princess forgot herself.

"Lady B!" she squealed and hurled herself into Isabel's arms. "I've missed you and Sir Edward. When can we play with Henry and Francis again?"

Isabel hugged the little girl tightly.

"We'll have to ask Lady Catherine if she can arrange for you to spend some time at court, then you can see my boys again, my lady," replied Isabel. "Do you think that would be possible, my dear?" she asked, looking at her over Elizabeth's head.

"I'll arrange it at once," replied Catherine. Elizabeth beamed and returned to her seat beside Catherine. She picked up a piece of embroidery and began sewing, humming quietly to herself. Catherine felt a small flutter of relief. She had always known Elizabeth would be easier to win over than Mary but this seemed too simple. Mary, too, had begun working on the tapestry. She also looked up and smiled at Isabel.

"It's good to see you again, Lady Baynton, I've missed our discussions," she said.

"I too," replied Isabel. "No one has your depth and understanding of the scriptures, my lady."

Mary looked delighted and blushed slightly.

"We are creating the story of Susanna," said Catherine to Mary as they began to work on the virgin linen draped before them.

"The woman who was accused by a host of men of something she didn't do and nearly paid with her life," replied Mary.

"It seemed appropriate," said Catherine. For a moment, there was a glimmer of a smile at the corner of Mary's mouth. However, she did not respond; she merely gave Catherine a quizzical look, then returned to her needlework.

Maybe this won't be so hard after all, thought Catherine, as she, too, suppressed a smile.

Chapter Ten

Catherine was in a foul mood. The heat of the July sun was making her uncomfortable and the midges by the river at Hampton Court were biting rabidly, leaving her usually soft, smooth skin covered in red marks. Worse, her fear was increasing daily as the true and terrible power of Henry's court unfolded around her. Each morning she waited, her heart pounding with dread at the prospect of her impending marriage to the king. Now things had taken another unexpected turn and she was ready to boil over.

Marching furiously into her chambers, she demanded, "Will someone please explain why I have to suffer the attentions of Katherine Tilney, Joan Bulmer and Mary Lascelles?"

Her uncle and her step-grandmother looked up from their conversation.

"Are you unhappy with your ladies-in-waiting?" asked Agnes Tilney.

"Yes!" replied Catherine. "Tilney and Bulmer are ridiculous, empty-headed fools and Lascelles is sneaky."

"You ungrateful little baggage," Agnes snarled. "Perhaps, my lady, it would befit you to remember who cared for you and created this opportunity for you to rise so high…"

"Enough, woman!" snapped Thomas Howard to his stepmother. "It was none of your doing — that is most certain."

Agnes looked as though she was about to retort then thought better of it.

"Unfortunately, Kitten, they are members of our extended family and, as such, it presents a united front to the rest of the world if they are part of your train — even if they are fools," he added. "Agnes, ensure they have minimum contact with Catherine. The same goes for Bess Seymour."

This time both women looked horrified.

"Lady Cromwell?" questioned Agnes. "That uppity madam who's married to Thomas Cromwell's son, Gregory?"

"Yes," said Thomas Howard smoothly. "She's also aunt to the future king of England, unless Prince Edward predeceases his father, so it's better to keep her close for the present. We never know when our sworn enemies may need to become our bosom friends."

Catherine turned away from them both in disgust. She had hoped the women who had plagued her life during her time with her step-grandmother were a distant memory but it seemed, once again, she was being forced into their company. She had not liked them then and there was no reason her opinion of them would have changed. It was a cruel twist of her uncle's manipulations that these women would once again haunt her days, adding to the constant nightmares she was having when she faced the prospect of spending every evening in bed succumbing to the king's passions.

Feeling sick at the prospect, she wondered how on earth she had arrived at such a position. She had hoped her marriage, when it came, would set her free. She would have a home of her own, possibly a title, definitely an income and freedom from her family. Yet, her marriage to the king seemed to tie her kin to her even more tightly as they took advantage of her elevated status.

Stalking away, craving the refuge of her private solar, she hoped for some peace before being primped, polished and powdered to be paraded before the king at dinner as his perfect, precious poppet, his sweet little plaything. Despite the jewels, the dresses and the luxury in which she now lived that far surpassed anything she had ever imagined, she was sickened by her gilded cage.

"There is one more thing, Catherine," called her uncle. "A date has been set for your wedding, the twenty-eighth of this month, July, in the year of our lord 1540. Cromwell is to be executed the same day," he added almost as an afterthought. "You will travel to Oatlands Palace in Surrey, not far from here, for the ceremony, then in August, you will return to Hampton Court where you will formally be introduced as Queen of England. I doubt Henry will arrange your coronation until you provide him with a son, so make sure you are willing once you are in his bed. We need a male Howard heir as quickly as possible."

Catherine did not turn; she merely nodded, then continued into her solar and quietly shut the door before allowing tears to engulf her. There was no chance of escape now. Nevertheless, she knelt down at her prie-dieu and began praying for a miracle.

Would poison be the answer? she wondered, but suicide was a crime against God. The thought of facing the wrath of heaven and being cast into the eternal fires of hell scared her more than the idea of bedding the king. Looking for comfort, she opened the magnificent leather-bound Bible on her lectern. It was in Latin and she enjoyed the rhythm of the words. The beautiful illuminations also gave her peace and she would often try to imagine herself lost within their vibrant colours, disappearing from the horror of her life.

It was as she carefully opened the great book that she saw it: the edge of a piece of parchment sticking out from between the pages. With careful fingers, she eased it free and, to her delight, saw it was a letter from Anne, carefully written in their

179

secret code. Hurrying to her writing desk, Catherine opened one of the drawers and slid her fingers carefully down the side until she felt the tiny mechanism that released the false bottom and removed her magnificently jewelled notebook from its silk-lined hiding place, then set to translating the note.

When Anne had first suggested the code, Catherine had thought she would never master it, but now she was becoming adept at deciphering the seemingly meaningless strings of letters. Finally, she sat back and read the note:

Sweet Kitten, by now you will know the date of your nuptials. Innocent child, may God protect and preserve you, know my home will always be your refuge. My kind friend, I have made a discovery and urge you to beware the Tilney and Bulmer women. They are traitors in your midst in the pay of the Seymours. I will implore God to deliver you from their evil ways. Good luck, my dear. Your friend, Anne.

Would these plots never end? wondered Catherine. Although a small part of her felt justified for her instinctive distrust of her former housemates. There was another question, though; when Anne referred to the Tilney women, did she include her step-grandmother, Agnes Tilney, the Dowager Duchess of Norfolk? *It wouldn't surprise me,* she thought, *I'm to be queen of England, nothing surprises me, least of all family betrayal.*

Catherine took the note to the fireplace. It might be summer but there was always a small fire burning in order to keep the chill off the rooms. She tore the parchment into tiny fragments, throwing them one by one into the flames, watching as each scrap turned to ashes and vanished, its words lost forever before she threw on the next. As the flickering flames consumed the last piece there was a tentative knock on the door.

"Kitten, may I come in? It's Issy."

"Of course, Issy!"

180

Isabel was white-faced, her brown eyes dark with worry.

"You've heard, then? I am to marry the king next week and Cromwell is to die on the same day," Catherine said.

"It's a great honour for you and our family, you'll be queen of England," Isabel managed to gulp between sobs.

The sisters stared at each other as the stark reality finally engulfed them. The shadow of Catherine's cousin, Anne Boleyn, seemed to hover at their shoulders. Despite the honours and position her marriage would bring, neither woman could find cause to rejoice.

"We must plan, Issy," said Catherine. "Good places must be found for our siblings before Uncle and Grandmamma push their Howard and Tilney relatives forward. Charles and Margaret may now be able to reveal their feelings but I suspect the king will stop short at allowing them to marry."

Isabel nodded.

"Our other Howard brothers, Henry and George, must be found good places in the king's household and, our sister, Margaret, Lady Arundell, is thankfully about to join us. We must ensure Mary does too. She is young, she can be a maid of honour." Catherine walked to her writing desk and withdrew parchment and quill, then began making notes as she spoke. "Then there are our Leigh sisters, they must join us too, both Joyce and Margaret Leigh. I will ensure I am surrounded by people I can trust, as I have already had word from a source I trust that we have spies in our midst."

"It doesn't surprise me, Kitty," sighed Isabel, drawing up a chair next to her. "Would you tell me the names of the people we are to watch?"

"Bulmer, probably Lascelles and the Tilney women, they are in the pay of the Seymours," she said in a voice barely above a whisper. Isabel's lips tightened in disapproval but she did not look surprised.

"And what of our Leigh brothers?" she asked.

"Well, John is abroad, but we must get word to him quickly. The last I heard he was in contact with Cardinal Pole. It isn't safe to fraternise with Catholics so openly, he must learn to be more subtle," Catherine said. "We should encourage him to return to court where he will be under your influence again, Issy. You were always the only one who could control him. Then there's Ralph, he too must be found a good position at court. I will try to ensure my family is protected and secure even if we cannot guarantee what will happen to me after I marry the king."

"Oh, Kitten, don't speak that way."

"We both know it's true," said Catherine, but she was calm as a sense of fatality gripped her. "With luck, the king will be able to get a child on me. If God smiles, it will be a son and we will be safe. However, if he isn't able, as I suspect is the truth, then my reign may be as short as that of Lady Cleves."

Isabel's eyes welled with tears.

"Promise me, Issy, if anything happens, if the king decides to do to me what he did to Cousin Anne, you'll stay with me until the end?"

"Oh, my darling girl, please don't speak that way…"

"Promise me," interrupted Catherine, her voice urgent. "If I know you'll always be with me, then I'll be able to face anything."

Wiping away the tears that she could not stop spilling from her eyes, Isabel nodded.

"I promise," she said in a choked voice. "I promise that whatever happens, I'll be with you until the end."

Chapter Eleven

"Do you think the king will serve Cromwell's head to Catherine on a platter, like King Herod did for Salome in the Bible?" asked Kathryn Knollys as she and Lady Margaret Douglas hurried through the corridors to Catherine's rooms in Oatlands Palace. Their arms were full of the expensive gauzy fabric that was the veil for Catherine's spectacular cloth of gold wedding gown.

"I hope not," shuddered Margaret, "but one can never be sure with Uncle Henry."

"Is it done then, do you think? Is Cromwell dead?"

"At dawn. Word has been sent that he had a good death," Margaret replied.

"And, to celebrate, the king marries our cousin," sighed Lady Knollys.

Neither woman spoke again until they arrived at Catherine's rooms. Margaret Howard, Lady Arundell, one of Catherine's sisters was waiting.

"You're to go straight in," she smiled, waving away Katherine Tilney and Joan Bulmer who hurried forward to try to relieve them of their burden. "Isabel and Jane are waiting. Now, Mrs Tilney, Mrs Bulmer, you are to accompany me back to the maids' rooms."

With a wink at Margaret and Lady Knollys, Margaret Howard ushered the other women away.

"Thank goodness we have her keeping those idiots away from Kitten," said Margaret Douglas.

"She's good at blocking Bess Seymour too, although I notice she's absent today," said Lady Knollys.

"Hardly surprising since her father-in-law was executed this morning. I imagine she's comforting that swaggering fool of a husband of hers, Gregory Cromwell. This should bring the whole family down to size again."

The page opened the door into Catherine's private inner chamber, where Isabel and Jane were dressing the ashen-faced and silent bride. The atmosphere was more akin to that of a funeral than a wedding. Catherine stood with her eyes closed, barely aware of their presence. When they had finished, Isabel touched Catherine gently on the arm.

"Kitten, would you like to see?"

Catherine opened her eyes and looked into the glass Isabel held before her.

"Thank you all for making me look so beautiful. I would never have imagined plain little Kitty Howard could one day be dressed so finely," she said. Then she squared her shoulders and a small flush of colour came to her cheeks. "Like a soldier going to war, I will walk down the aisle to my groom. For king and country. Even if it kills me."

And now, thought Catherine several hours later, *the deed is done. I am Henry's wife, I am his consort, I am queen of England. 'Til death us do part. I wonder how long that will be?*

She sat in bed, wearing an exquisitely embroidered chemise, waiting for the king. Isabel, Jane, Lady Knollys and Margaret Douglas had prepared her, anointing her with fragrant oils and loosening her hair so it fell in tumbling red curls across her shoulders. Her blue eyes were wide in her white face but even before Isabel's instructions, she bit on the inside of her lips to bring a red blush to them and pinched her cheeks to try to give herself a healthy, happy, excited glow. When the women had finished, Isabel placed a loose sheet under Catherine.

"For the blood," she said. Catherine nodded. She knew the ritual. Every noble woman in England had been trained in the mysteries of the women's quarters but she had never imagined her own marriage bed would be in such exalted surroundings. Isabel kissed her on the forehead as though Catherine were one of her three young children and she was kissing her good night.

"We will pray for you," she murmured.

"Thomas will be outside the door, he says to call for sweet wine if you have difficulties," said Jane in a low voice.

"Thank you, ladies," Catherine said. "Now, will you please send word to the king that I am ready."

Isabel nodded and ushered the others out. Then Catherine closed her eyes and prayed.

Mary, sweet mother Mary, preserve me this day and let me get with child. Mary, sweet mother Mary, preserve me this day and let me get with child. Mary, sweet mother Mary, preserve me this day and let me get with child.

Catherine heard their low voices and the stump of Henry's limp, which was more pronounced than usual today. He had obviously been in some pain as they had said their vows in front of Edward Bonner, the bishop of London, but he had been determined that nothing would stop him gracing her bed.

"You made me a promise, little girl," he had said, running his finger down her cheek. "You said you would dance for me. I have fulfilled my side of the bargain: Cromwell is dead, he will never scare you again. I would not be so crass as to bring his head to you on a platter — after all, we are not barbarians — but I am a man and my flesh aches for you."

This is the price I pay for my family's ambition, she thought, *I am their thirty pieces of silver*. My uncle of Norfolk may always have taken a special interest in me, I assumed it was because he cared about me, but he was merely breeding me as another potential bride for Henry's bed. She pushed the thought of Anne Boleyn from her mind as the king entered, resplendent in a heavily embroidered gown which was far too warm for the July weather, but was obviously a statement of his kingship. Under this he wore a white linen shift.

Dearest Mother Mary, let it be over quickly, she prayed, then smiled shyly at her husband, the king. He gazed at her, his eyes filling with tears.

"You are the most perfect woman I have ever seen," he whispered hoarsely.

Behind him, Thomas Culpepper directed two pages to place Henry's lute on a small side table, then they arranged a bowl of cakes and a jug of spiced wine before scurrying out, their eyes never rising higher than the floor.

"My lord, I will leave you now," said Culpepper and, with a swift, sad glance at Catherine, he backed out bowing from the chamber. Catherine's smile trembled as Henry sat on the bed beside her. He reached out to stroke her cheek and Catherine steeled herself not to flinch.

"You are so beautiful and you are all mine," sighed the king, burying his face in her hair. "You smell as sweet as a meadow, my darling."

Catherine hesitated, rigid with fear and revulsion, then she remembered suggestions given to her by Issy and Kathy Knollys about how to behave in the marriage bed. She raised her hand and tentatively stroked the back of the king's head. He groaned, shuddering with pleasure, then he stood, threw the covers back and helped her from the bed, leading her to the centre of the room. With a few deft movements, Henry unlaced her chemise and it fell in soft, foaming waves at her feet, leaving her naked before the king. Her hands automatically moved to cover herself.

"No," he barked. "You're mine now and I want to look upon you."

He began to circle her, like a horse breeder examining a new young filly. Catherine stood, terrified, trying not to tremble as the king completed a full circuit of her.

"You are more beautiful than I had imagined," he sighed. "You are a goddess, an angel, you are perfection and you are mine."

On his final word, he reached out and ran his hands down her face, to her shoulders, then her breasts, cupping them, his thumbs circling her pale pink nipples as he groaned in desire. Catherine stiffened but did not move. This was her duty now, her body was his, she could no longer shout for Thomas Culpepper to rescue her. She shut her eyes. The king lowered his head and was so engrossed, his tongue darting across her flesh like a strange pink fish, he did not see the tears trickling out from under her lashes. His hands slid down her back and clawed at her buttocks. One hand slid between her thighs, his fingers probing and parting her soft flesh. Catherine tried to turn her sob into a groan as the king's fingers prised into her most private places.

"You are as sweet as a peach, little girl," said the king, before pulling her into a crushing embrace and locking his lips to hers, his tongue pushing into her mouth, almost choking her. After a moment, she forced herself to respond and was horrified when he took her hand and placed it on his hard cock.

"This is a sign from God that we are supposed to make a son," he whispered. "The Lady of Cleves never made me feel like a man but I only have to look at you, little Catherine, and you raise my blood. I will own you completely. Then you will dance for me until I am ready for you again. Tonight, we will make a prince."

He pushed her down on the bed. Catherine was wide-eyed with horror as Henry dropped his chemise and stood naked before her. His once firm flesh now hung in rippling, grey folds around his enormous frame. The sore on his leg, although dressed with a fresh linen bandage, still gave off the faint smell of rotting meat. His skin was scarred and pocked from illness and a few sores wept across his stomach.

"You are mine," he declared, his tone threatening as one hand slid to her throat, holding her still on the bed, while the other forced her legs apart. Catherine thought she would suffocate as he lowered his enormous bulk on top of her. She was barely half his size and she gasped for air. Henry, his hands now either side of her head, took this to be a sign of passion and laughed. "It's good, yes?"

Catherine could do little more than whimper, such was her revulsion. She felt Henry forcing her legs further apart, then he was pushing himself inside her. Her fear was making her muscles lock and it was a struggle for him; he puffed, thrusting even harder. Sense, self-preservation and feminine instinct suddenly suffused Catherine, she could not escape this torture so she might as well help get it over with. From what she remembered from her step-grandmother's house, once the coupling had taken place, the man, after a few thrusts, usually collapsed quite quickly and it was all over.

Once Tilney had crudely described how she had helped her lover, Francis Dereham, enter her using her hand, stroking him to keep him hard. Pulling her knees as far apart as she could, Catherine slid her hand down and took the king in her hand. He gasped and she ran her hand up and down his length, feeling him harden further in her grasp, then she guided him into her, lifting her hips to accommodate him.

Henry kissed her with a frenzy and began to move above her, wheezing and gasping as his bulk pushed her further into the bed. Catherine tried to follow his rhythm. *It's like a trot*, she thought. Like being on my pony, think of my horse Moonbeam, riding her makes me feel free, when this is done I will be free. She gasped in pain as he broke her hymen, then after a few energetic thrusts, the king spasmed and groaned, collapsing on top of her.

Catherine did not dare move, even though his weight was crushing her, making it difficult to breathe. His face was turned away and she could not see if he was asleep. However, after a few moments, he roused himself, rolling off her and staring down at her prone figure.

"And now, little Salome," he said coldly, running his hand over her belly. "You will dance."

He pulled her to her feet, ignoring the blood trickling down her legs, picked up his lute and settled himself on the bed. She stood shivering and shocked before him but he laughed.

"You are mine now, little Catherine," he snarled, "and you must obey my every command. So, I say, dance. Dance, you little Howard whore. Dance until I tell you to stop."

He struck a chord and Catherine, wiping her legs with her chemise, lifted her arms and began to dance, wondering how this night would end.

Chapter Twelve

The hot August sun beat through the windows. Catherine leaned out, trying to feel the breeze from the river but to no avail. Today, after a month of torturous marriage, she had been officially presented to the court as Henry's queen consort. For hours she had sat at his side as the highest-ranking nobles in the land, along with all the foreign dignitaries, the ambassadors and the clergy, bowed and swore their allegiance. A lengthy banquet had followed but now she was back in her chambers, still dressed in her finery as she awaited a visit from her uncle, the duke of Norfolk.

Once she would have been overawed by these events but so much had happened so quickly, her feelings had become dulled and she could no longer react to anything properly. Even her beautiful dress, which would once have made her crow in delight, was another shackle binding her to the servitude of her marriage. The elaborate cloth of gold gown was so tight, immovable and hot, she felt she might faint.

Behind her, the ladies of her private chamber bustled around, tidying, exclaiming and preparing her rooms so they would be suitable for receiving honoured guests, should the necessity arise. The only bright spot on Catherine's horizon was the fact that, now her queenship had finally been acknowledged, she could secure good positions and money for her family. Her older brother George Howard was to become a gentleman of the privy chamber and work alongside Thomas Culpepper. This pleased Catherine immensely as she now had two strong men to come to her aid should the king have one of his turns.

His rages were becoming more frequent and increasingly violent.

Catherine pushed the thought from her mind, focusing instead on the other good things she had been able to bestow upon the people she loved. Charles had been appointed to the position of the king's spear and, together with George, they had been granted a license to annually import 1,000 ton of Gascon wine and Toulouse woad, something that gave them both a very healthy income. However, what had delighted her most was that her brother-in-law, Edward Baynton, had been granted the manor of Semleigh in Wiltshire, while Isabel and their children had all been granted 100 marks. A small fortune which, when she had been told, had made Isabel weep. She found it difficult to reconcile her good fortune when it came at the expense of Catherine's safety.

In the distance, Catherine heard the herald announce the arrival of yet more visitors to her chambers. People came and went all day. At first she had felt obliged to make herself available and pleasant to each one but, as so many had been people trying to win favours from the king via her intervention, her capable senior ladies now weeded out the interlopers, allowing in only the genuine members of her court.

Katherine Willoughby, the duchess of Suffolk, and Eleanor Paston, the countess of Rutland, were a formidable force and provided what Catherine thought of as her first line of defence. Isabel, Margaret, Jane and Kathryn were, in her mind, her version of Henry's Tudor guard. They stood like a protective wall around her, keeping her from as much harm as possible.

"His grace, the duke of Norfolk and the Lady Elizabeth Tudor," came the announcement. Turning from the window, Catherine caught Isabel's enquiring glance.

"Let them in here," she replied, moving back into the room and pulling her attention to the events of the day. "We can be more informal. I can't face all the bowing and scraping if we go into the main chamber, there has been more than enough of that today."

She sank onto a chair by the empty fireplace, shifting from side to side trying to find a comfortable position in her stiff, unforgiving dress. Isabel nodded to the page who opened the door to admit the duke and Henry's younger daughter. Thomas Howard gave a perfunctory bow while Elizabeth sank into a deep curtsey; her head lowered awaiting her new stepmother's blessing. Catherine smiled and gently touched her brilliant red Tudor hair.

"You can get up, Elizabeth," she said. The girl stood and smiled, then hurried over to her cousin and half-sister Kathryn Knollys, who was busy tidying away Catherine's writing paraphernalia.

"Uncle," said Catherine, "how fare you?"

"Very well, thank you, my dear," he said, taking the seat opposite Catherine. "You did well today, Kitten. It's gratifying to see that you are making friends throughout the court. All I hear from those who matter is that you are discreet, noble and approachable."

"My marriage to the king is barely one month old. It would take a particularly spiteful and careless nature to have made enemies so quickly."

"People don't become your enemy because you're spiteful," said the duke, genuinely amused. "It's for far more subtle reasons."

"Such as?"

"Your name, your religion, whether or not you support them in a petition to the king…"

"Whether or not you were instrumental in having their father executed on your wedding day?" she interrupted before she could stop herself. To her disgust, the duke merely shrugged as though Thomas Cromwell's execution had been a matter of no importance.

"Yes, Gregory Cromwell and his wife Bess Seymour are without doubt our enemies, but they were against the Howard family long before you ever became queen," he said dismissively.

"It was my fault though," whispered Catherine. "The king killed him because I asked him to; you wanted me to."

Since her marriage, she had been plagued by nightmares. Most featured Henry but, periodically, Thomas Cromwell would haunt her dreams, sometimes as he had been in life: tall, imposing, terrifying. Often, though, the dreams took the form of the spectre of Cromwell, holding his severed head towards her while tears streamed from its rotting, fly-infested eyes. Even in her waking hours, the image would sometimes flash across her mind and leave her shaking with fear.

"Kitten, what are you talking about?" asked her uncle. "Cromwell signed his own death warrant with all his double-dealing. It was only a matter of time before the king tired of his machinations. Your involvement was minimal and you bear none of the guilt. Put it from your mind, sweetling, and concentrate instead on being the bonny bride you promised in your wedding vows so you can give the king a bouncing Howard duke of York."

He threw her a quizzical glance and she raised her eyebrows.

"I'm afraid not, Uncle," she replied to his unanswered question.

"Have you made yourself available, not baulked at the king's desire? Made him happy?" the duke's usually casual, urbane manner held the mildest hint of urgency, as did his sudden grip on her forearm. Nausea rose in Catherine as she remembered all the king had forced her to do the previous evening and managed only to nod. "Good girl, no doubt you will soon be in whelp."

Horrified, she turned away. *I am a prize sow*, she thought. *My feelings, my desires, matter for nothing.* To her relief, Elizabeth appeared at her elbow holding an elaborately jewelled book.

"My lady mother," she said and curtseyed, "would you like me to tutor you in Greek this evening?"

"Unfortunately, we won't have time today, Elizabeth. Soon, we all have to go into the Great Chamber for a masque and revels."

"Very well," said the child, failing to conceal her disappointment, "perhaps tomorrow, if my lady mother has the time."

"Certainly tomorrow," promised Catherine. Her own education had been patchy and when Elizabeth had offered to teach her basic Greek, as well as brushing up her Latin, Catherine had seen it not only as an opportunity to boost her limited knowledge, but also as a way to spend time with her new stepdaughter, the daughter of her cousin, Anne Boleyn. The two had begun to form a strong bond. Catherine had promised Anne of Cleves she would continue her work in trying to bring Henry's children together as a family and with Elizabeth, she felt she had made a start.

"Is that your book, Elizabeth?" interrupted the duke, holding out his hand.

"No, sir," she replied with another bob of deference before placing it in his outstretched palm. "This belongs to my lady mother."

Throwing Catherine a curious glance, he opened the ornate cover and perused the pages inside. "Where did you get this? A book of blank parchment?"

"Henry gave it to me when I told him Elizabeth was teaching me Greek and Latin. He was highly amused but he commissioned the book as a present. It's for me to practise my letters and improve my handwriting."

The duke perused the pages. "Not only your studies. Did you draw these?" he pointed to two sketches, one of Isabel, the other of Margaret Douglas. Catherine nodded. "They're remarkably good, Kitten, and these images of birds and the patterns? Are these mermaids?"

"They're designs for embroidery," replied Catherine, wondering why she was being made to explain herself. "I draw them here first, then sketch the designs onto the cloth."

"Mermaids?" the duke snorted derisively as he continued to turn the pages.

Catherine blushed.

"And why have some pages been cut out?" He spoke across her as though her words were unimportant, his gimlet eyes suddenly furious as they bored into hers. "Have you been sending messages?"

Forcing a scornful laugh, Catherine shook her head. "I have merely removed pages where I haven't been happy with the content, mistakes in my Greek and Latin, or if they are designs. I have passed them to my ladies so they may interpret my thoughts. Look on the table, there is a new design being worked and the pattern comes from a page in this book. You may compare the two if you don't believe me, Uncle."

Rising, the duke strode over to the long table at the back of the room where Isabel was sorting the piles of linen the women used to make shirts, all of which were exquisitely embroidered. Catherine watched as Isabel produced a piece of parchment and gave it to the duke, who opened the book and studied the two documents. Elizabeth moved closer to Catherine and slid her small white hand into her stepmother's.

"I'm sorry, Lady Mother," she whispered, her bright brown eyes fraught with anxiety. "Have I made the duke angry?"

"No, child, you've done nothing wrong," she reassured her.

Moments later, the duke returned and handed the jewelled book to Elizabeth.

"I'm glad to see you're being enterprising, my dear," he said. "Now, I must return to the king. I will see you later at the masque."

He nodded then turned on his heel and left. Elizabeth trotted back to Kathryn Knollys. Moments later, Isabel slid into the seat the duke had so recently vacated.

"Well done, Kitten, you've learned to lie with the best of us," she said. "He'd be furious if he knew you were writing to the Lady Cleves."

Catherine smiled wanly. "He'd be even more furious if he knew I was writing a diary and hiding the pages in the lining of my hoods," she murmured.

Chapter Thirteen

Hurrying into her inner chamber, Catherine made straight for the roaring fire. Her cheeks were rosy, flecks of snow speckled her hood and cloak but, most unusually, she was laughing. She and her ladies had spent the morning riding through the glittering countryside on their journey back to the capital. For a few hours, she had felt free and she wanted to cherish the cheerfulness of the day.

"It's wonderful to be back at Whitehall," she sighed as she warmed her hands.

Isabel, who had followed her in, took Catherine's fur-lined cloak and shook it out, spreading it over a nearby chair to dry.

"A relief, indeed," smiled Isabel. "I'm thankful we'll be remaining here for Christmas and New Year after all the travelling of the past few months."

"Windsor, Reading, Ewelm, Rycott, Notley, Buckingham, Grafton, Ampthill and The Moor in Hertfordshire; did I forget anywhere, Issy?"

"No, Kitten, that was all of them. Now, no more progresses until next summer."

Catherine flopped into the chair nearest the fire, pulled her skirts over her soft leather boots and held her feet up to warm by the flames. She had enjoyed the tour they had taken around the country, staying in elegant houses, meeting new people. However, in her heart, the real reason she had enjoyed the progress was because it had tired the king so much that he had rarely called for her to join him at night and when he had, he had mostly wanted her to be there so he could sleep. He had barely touched her and she could feel nothing but relief.

Although, over the past few days, a rumour had reached her and she wondered if her life was about to take another turn.

"Do you think the gossip is true?" she mused, her eyes slightly unfocused as she watched the roaring fire.

"Certainly not. The king can hardly keep his eyes off you. Do you honestly think he's likely to return to Lady Cleves?"

"No," she murmured. "I suppose it's the Seymour faction again, trying to cause discontent. Anyway, I wouldn't wish that terrible fate on poor sweet Anne. She escaped from him once, what sort of a friend would I be if I threw him back to her?"

Isabel was suddenly crouched by Catherine's side, looking up at her aghast.

"Never, ever say things like that out loud," she whispered. "Even when it's only us in the room, you don't know who might be listening."

Catherine looked down at her sister, shocked to see her ashen face. "No one is listening. We're the only people in my rooms, everyone else is busy organising the baggage and furniture."

"Be careful, sweet girl, Edward is afraid the Seymours have spies in your chambers."

"We know there are spies," she laughed. "There are people everywhere, listening and reporting to either Henry or one of our many enemies. Why do you think my husband is so suspicious of his court? This is the reason he insists on his giant golden lock being taken wherever he stays, and attached to his door so no one can creep into his chamber at night and murder him in his bed. Issy, I've learned to ignore it. My aim is always to remain above the gossip and by refusing to acknowledge it, perhaps I can prevent it from tarnishing my marriage and hurting the people I love." She squeezed Isabel's shoulder. "Please don't worry. Now, where is Edward? There is business I must attend to immediately."

A few moments later, Isabel's husband Edward bustled into the room, followed by Thomas Culpepper and Jane Boleyn who had recently and secretly wed. Although they held hands, there was concern on Thomas's face.

"Catherine, we must speak to you of the people you will intercede on behalf of this evening when you attend the king," said Edward.

"Are there many?" she replied. The months since her marriage had seen Catherine develop a desire to do her best as a consort. With Edward Baynton's help, she had learned to act as a patron and was slowly beginning to understand more about finances and estate management. Her intercessions on behalf of pages and courtiers were regarded as part of her courtly duty and, as Henry was so besotted, when she asked a favour for someone, she was usually successful.

"No, but one of them is extremely important," said Culpepper. It was the seriousness of his tone that unnerved Catherine.

"What's happened?" she asked, immediately fearful for the safety of the people she loved.

"It relates to something that happened before you were queen," said Thomas. He glanced at the door and Jane hurried to close it, cutting out the hustle and bustle of the outer chambers. "Do you remember when you used to give Queen Anne dancing lessons in the Long Gallery?"

"Of course, we both used to enjoy them immensely."

"Well, so did the king," said Thomas looking faintly repulsed. "There's a secret room above the gallery where the king would sit and watch. It was how he first became aware of you and when he fell in love."

Catherine felt sick. Henry had spied on them. In those precious hours when they were as carefree as girls, he had watched and leered as they giggled and danced. The happy memories were suddenly tainted by his subterfuge.

"What has this to do with anything now?" she asked, disgusted but bemused.

"One night, after he had seen you dance, he asked me to…" Thomas paused.

"Please continue, we won't be shocked," said Catherine already prepared for the worst.

"He sent me to find a girl who looked like you," said Thomas, not meeting Catherine's eyes. "He wanted a prostitute but it was an impossible task. Then I met a girl called Maud. She was only fourteen but she was excited to meet the king." Thomas stopped as though he could not continue. Jane squeezed his hand and, with great effort, he began to speak again, his voice barely audible over the crackling fire. "Henry raped her, then beat her to death. Her murder has been on my conscience ever since."

Isabel gasped and reached out for Edward, who caught her as she staggered. Jane dropped her head, although she was less shocked — it was clear that she and Thomas had discussed the matter. Catherine felt bile welling up in her throat. Horror coursed through her.

"Kitten, we're so sorry to tell you this but it's important," Jane continued, relieving her husband of the burden of his terrible confession. "Her mother, Helen Page, is on trial for felony. After Maud was killed, Helen became unwell and stopped working as a seamstress. Her husband, Maud's father, tried to keep her in the house but she escaped one day and stole some linen. When she was arrested, she demanded to see the king, she demanded justice for her daughter. Please, Kitten, if you can help her, Thomas has arranged for Helen and her husband to be sent to one of his family's estates where they'll be cared for and kept safe. They've already lost their daughter."

Catherine rose and stood by the fire, staring into its dark shadowy heart. Each morning when she awoke, she promised herself she would try to do a good deed, as a small way to compensate for the fear and brutality her husband spread. In the few months she had been queen, she hoped she had made some difference. This, however, was the most shocking thing she had yet heard. A girl had been murdered because of her; another death on her conscience. Worse, she had known nothing about it until now.

"Of course," she said, her voice hoarse. "Of course I will. Edward, when Helen is freed, arrange for her family to be well compensated for their loss. It won't bring their daughter back but it will help to keep them safe. Thomas, have them taken to one of your properties for now but in time, she and her husband will go to one of my estates. I will take care of Maud's parents."

With her back still turned, Catherine dismissed them, explaining that she craved some peace. As the door clicked shut, she sank to the floor and tears streamed down her face. She grieved for the unknown girl, Maud, for the discarded and humiliated Anne of Cleves and out of fear for herself and what her future might hold.

Each day it gets worse, she thought. *When will this torment end?*

"Her grace, Queen Catherine," announced the herald.

Holding her head high, Catherine swept into the Great Chamber at Whitehall and approached the king. Reaching the dais where he sat on his ornate, golden throne beneath his glittering cloth of state, she sank to the floor, her head bowed. Gazing down at her, Henry licked his lips as though she were a particularly enticing piece of marchpane that he could not wait to devour.

"Your Majesty, I come to beg your favour for innocents," she said, her voice clear and bell-like in the silent court.

"Whom do you wish me to pardon?" he asked, leering down at her prone figure. The lives of those he forgave meant nothing to the king; his enjoyment came from being seen as merciful and Christ-like and, for the chance to indulge in some of the ancient pageantry that he believed reinforced his historic and legitimate right to the throne of England.

"Sir John Wallop, who has been charged with treason but begs forgiveness for his foolishness and pledges his heart and soul to Your Majesty," she said.

"He has been reckless, but for you, sweetheart, he is pardoned."

Catherine smiled. "And for Helen Page of Lyndesey who has been charged with felony but was unwell and did not know what she was doing when she caused offence. Her daughter had been murdered and it briefly disrupted the balance of her mind."

"Of course, she must be pardoned. Has the murderer been brought to justice?"

Catherine hesitated, then to her relief, saw Thomas Culpepper lean forward and whisper in the king's ear. Henry's face became impassive, then he gave a curt nod.

"Justice has been done and as a gracious monarch, I will offer this lady compensation," he announced, glancing around the assembled courtiers in anticipation of their rapturous cheering for his abundant goodness. He was not disappointed. When the applause and catcalls subsided, with the help of his men, he hauled himself to his feet and walked stiffly down the three steps to where Catherine was still prostrate on the floor. "Come, my sweet," he said raising her up. "Let us eat."

Catherine allowed Henry to lead her into the banqueting hall. At last she felt that she had done some good.

Chapter Fourteen

The king lowered himself into his enormous chair by the fire. His greyhounds, stretched out on cushions in front of the hearth, wagged their tails to show their appreciation as he threw them a handful of meaty bones. Catherine indicated to Thomas Culpepper to clear away the meal they had shared with Charles Brandon, the duke of Suffolk, then joined her husband by the fireside. After a week of storms and torrential rain, the air was cold and damp, so she was glad of the roaring flames in the king's chambers.

"So, my dear, we are once again facing a difficult decision," he sighed.

"And what is that, my lord?"

"Lady Pole, my mother's cousin," he replied. Catherine held her breath, she knew about the sixty-eight-year-old countess, Margaret Pole, formerly Margaret Plantagenet, the niece of King Richard III and a royal princess in her own right. In his continuing quest to remove anyone who might challenge his throne, Henry had executed Margaret's sons, fearing their Plantagenet blood might be enough incitement for rebels to raise an army and challenge his kingship.

"She's an old lady," murmured Catherine, indicating for the pages to bring wine and cakes and place them beside the king.

"A dangerous old woman with sons whom covet my throne," he snarled. "Her youngest son, Cardinal Pole, is still abroad spreading sedition, plotting to steal my crown. This is why I had her incarcerated without a trial, she must not be given the chance to spread more of her treasonous lies."

Catherine knew better than to try to reason with her husband. Instead, she poured him a goblet of hot spiced wine. Henry took a long deep gulp, a small droplet of the red liquid oozed from the side of his mouth and dribbled down into his beard. Hiding her revulsion, Catherine busied herself selecting his favourite sweet treats.

"Here, my love," she said. He hastily put three in his mouth in quick succession, not bothering to wipe away the flaking pastry or scattered nuts that dropped onto his beard or onto his lap.

Returning to her own chair, Catherine watched her elderly husband in disgust, sipping daintily from her own goblet. There was silence except for Henry's snuffling and gulping as he gorged himself on the huge platter of cakes. To distract herself, Catherine made a mental note to send more blankets, furs and good food to Margaret Pole, countess of Salisbury. Catherine had tried to plead for Lady Pole but to no avail.

"When will Cromwell be back?" grumbled Henry, clicking his fingers for the page to bring more cakes.

"My lord…?" asked Catherine, the unexpectedness of the question throwing her into confusion.

"Cromwell is abroad, sire," came the commanding tones of the duke of Suffolk. Like many other noblemen, he was lurking on the edges of the room, unable to leave until dismissed by the king but not welcome now that Henry was settled by the fire. It was a power game and Henry enjoyed playing it.

"So you say, Charles," growled the king, "but when will he be back?"

Catherine stared at the duke of Suffolk in horror. Cromwell was dead. Henry himself had signed the execution warrant and now he seemed to have forgotten. She looked down at her hands and saw they were shaking. Desperate to try and gain control, she took another deep gulp of her wine, then looked at Suffolk desperately.

"We're unsure, Your Majesty," the duke replied, his eyes fixed on Catherine, shaking his head, indicating for her to remain silent. "He was taken ill on a tour of Italy. It seems to be serious."

"Damn him," murmured the king. "He would know what to do. Should I behead her? That would stop her son trying to challenge me, or should I show leniency? She was my mother's favourite cousin."

Catherine dropped her eyes. She dared not say a word; it was only a few weeks since she had begged for clemency for her half-brother John Leigh after his association with the Pole family. To her relief, the king had laughed, claiming she could ask for anything and he would grant it, such was his love for her. John Leigh had been released and cleared of all charges the following day.

"More cakes, my sweet," said Henry, interrupting her thoughts. "And more wine. Come, Catherine, what's wrong with you this evening? You have been distracted since you arrived."

"I'm so sorry, my love," she replied, smiling demurely, before gathering more cakes and handing them to her husband. "It's…"

She glanced over at the men still hovering in the shadows waiting to be dismissed.

"What?" snapped the king irritably, spraying crumbs down his front. Catherine gagged.

"It's a delicate matter, sire," she whispered as she refilled his wine goblet. "Perhaps when we are alone."

His eyes, already shrunken by his bloated face, narrowed further as he glared at her, then a smile of comprehension spread across his face.

"Men, you are dismissed," he called. "Leave us for now. I'll summon you when I wish to retire."

With much bowing and scraping, Henry's men melted away.

"So, little Catherine, what is it you couldn't say before my court?" he asked, his excitement palpable.

"My lord, it's good news. I believe I'm with child."

Throwing himself from his chair, he roared in triumph, a bloated, braying colossus. Startled by the unexpected outburst, his greyhounds leapt up, barking wildly, adding to the din. Henry's roar turned to laughter, his body heaving as emotion overwhelmed him.

"You are with child!" he shouted. "I am as fertile now as when I was a young man! Who would dare to challenge me?"

Catherine said nothing. She was as frightened as the shivering greyhounds that had now crept away into the shadows.

"We are alone, child, let me bed you now. I am Mars, the god of fertility, I am all powerful," he shouted, his teeth bared.

"My ladies say it is no longer wise for me to share your bed as it may harm our child," she stammered.

"Your ladies say that, do they?" he hissed. Nodding nervously, Catherine began to edge away from the king. "And why is that? Do they think I am incapable of mounting you? They are witches sent to make mischief!"

"No, my lord, it's to protect the child," she stammered.

"The child?" he sneered, picking up a riding whip from a stand by the fire. "How do I even know it's mine, you little Howard whore?"

"Of course it's yours," gasped Catherine, her terrified eyes following the whip as he swished it through the air, testing its strength. "There has only ever been you, Henry."

"Liar!" he screamed, the sharp slicing of the whip accenting each word. "Liar, liar!"

Catherine raised her arms to protect herself, stumbling as his first blow lashed her across her face, burning like fire. She screamed for help as the whip found her breasts, then her back.

"Whore!" he shouted, his face screwed up with hatred and fury, the whip lashing her again and again until she collapsed, sobbing, begging for mercy on the floor. "WHORE!"

Outside she heard running feet but her last image was of her husband's foot flying towards her stomach before everything went black.

PART THREE: Marquess House, 2018

Chapter One

Perdita stood in the Tudor hall, listening to the silence. It was early and no one was yet stirring. Breathing in the ancient space, she smiled. This was the first time since her arrival that she had felt completely alone in Marquess House and it was glorious. There was usually someone around and the house had never fully seemed to be hers and Piper's. However, in this moment, she felt peace and ownership settling on her shoulders like a favourite scarf.

Grinning broadly, she hurried towards the enormous Gothic doors in the east wing that led into the library, her feet swift and determined. The double-height room with its elegant galleries and alcoves of endless books was Perdita's favourite part of the house. At one end was an elaborate bank of stained glass windows showing a series of women, each a mythical representation depicting a Greek goddess. Underneath was the Tudor graffiti Alistair Mackensie had mentioned on her first visit. It was covered by protective Perspex and was difficult to make out. Once more the frieze of flowers and the strange symbol, made up of three intertwined circles that dominated the rest of the house, tumbled across the walls. Mermaids and other sea creatures were interwoven with the flowers, as well as more traditional faces of Celtic Green Men.

Windows framed different aspects of the beautifully landscaped gardens like paintings: one captured the vastness of the mysterious lake Llyn Cel, another the soft rolling lawns and yet another the Tudor-inspired knot gardens that led to the huge maze formed from yew hedges, way off in the distance. Even though she had been at the house for several weeks,

Perdita still felt that she had not yet seen everything of her and Piper's inheritance. She lingered at the windows, admiring the early morning sunrise, then contemplated the task that had driven her from bed so early.

The previous evening, she had finished reading the draft of her grandmother's unpublished manuscript *The Catherine Howard Anomaly*. As usual when reading Mary's work, she had been swept along with the argument, but, to her frustration, when she had reached the end, she discovered the final chapter containing her grandmother's conclusions was missing.

While giving an outline of Catherine's life and exploring the work of the women who had surrounded her during her time as queen consort, women who were often missing from other biographies, there was also a great deal of detail about Catherine's family. Perdita had not realised Catherine had been the second youngest of ten siblings, most of whom had been with her while she was queen consort, or that she had become an orphan while still a young child.

These details, while interesting, were not what had fascinated Perdita most about her grandmother's new take on the youngest wife of the Tudor monarch. What had captured her imagination was the possibility that there was a different version of events leading up to Catherine's death. One that suggested she had not been the spoilt, promiscuous child so many biographies hypothesised but, rather like her cousin Anne Boleyn, was the innocent victim of her scheming and powerful male relatives.

The most startling change was the possibility that the affair Catherine supposedly had with one of Henry's courtiers, Thomas Culpepper, may not have happened. This was a controversial suggestion as it had been a love letter written to Culpepper from Catherine that had formed the crucial evidence against her, ultimately sending her to her death. If there had been no affair, why had she been executed on 13 February 1542 at the Tower of London?

Perdita had already requested the entire bibliography of the work from Jenny in order to check her grandmother's references. While these would be useful, her real interest was Mary's primary sources, particularly the two handwritten titles on the typed list with a note beside them reading: "*In two minds whether to include these…*"

The first was an old, privately published book called *The Llyn Cel Mermaid and Other Local Legends* by Penelope Fitzalan which, according to Mary's notes, had been written between 1640 and 1644 and was housed in the library at Marquess House. The second title intrigued Perdita even more: it was listed as *The Catherine Howard Codex*, but was given no date or location. The lack of information was particularly striking as the other notes were so detailed they were almost distracting. Yet, this major source of information, which seemed to have formed the basis of Mary's work, was hardly mentioned.

Settling herself at a desk in the library, Perdita flipped open her laptop and while she waited for the Wi-Fi to connect, she hunted for a dictionary to double check the meaning of the word 'codex'. She consulted three different publications and all agreed that a codex was "an ancient manuscript text in book form". The word originated in the late sixteenth century from the Latin *caudex*, literally meaning a 'block of wood', later denoting a block split into leaves or tablets for writing on, hence a book. Going online, one source claimed that a codex was generally made of loose leaves of vellum or parchment joined in one corner and given a cover and back of wood, making it one of the earliest forms of books.

Satisfied that her assessment of a codex had been correct, Perdita crossed this task off her list of notes and turned her attention to the two original documents. Having never heard of either source, she began by running a simple online search. Perdita tapped in the full title as listed in the primary sources: *The Catherine Howard Codex*, but received nothing useful. Scrolling swiftly down the page she saw sites about Catherine Howard and references to documents in various collections but there was no reference to the document her grandmother had cited.

She followed this foray with *The Llyn Cel Mermaid and Other Local Legends* by Penelope Fitzalan, but again, not one useful hit. There were sites about mermaids and, intriguingly, an obscure historical figure named Lady Elizabeth Fitzalan, duchess of Norfolk, who had lived from 1366 to 8 July 1425. As Perdita read the short piece, she raised her eyebrows in surprise. It transpired that through her eldest daughter, Lady Margaret Mowbray, Elizabeth Fitzalan was an ancestress of both Anne Boleyn and Catherine Howard, who had been cousins. While Perdita could not see it was particularly relevant, it was an interesting detail and she had made a note of the link.

Trying one last option, Perdita searched for the name Penelope Fitzalan but there was nothing: no historical records, no hits in the present day, nothing. No one of that name seemed to ever have existed in the seventeenth century or at any time since.

"Weird," she murmured, "that no one at any point should have had the name Penelope Fitzalan. Perhaps it's a pseudonym but that still wouldn't explain why it has never been used by anyone."

Leaving her laptop humming to itself, Perdita walked over to an alcove where a computer was positioned on an elegant occasional table. This sleek terminal stored the library's database, giving the details of every book in the collection, its age, when it was acquired or bought and whereabouts in either the library or the research centre it was situated. Perdita entered the library search code Jenny had given her and keyed in the first title, the codex, followed by the book of local legends. There was a ping: three hits. The books did exist; two were registered as: *"Marquess House, classified. J Procter authorisation code required"*. The third, a copy of *The Llyn Cel Mermaid and Other Local Legends* by Penelope Fitzalan, was listed as *"L&J copy; MH, 1990, Tudor Library"* and the code indicating its whereabouts.

Perdita pulled a face, wrinkling her nose in minor frustration. Jenny was unavailable until later in the afternoon, so she would not be able to access the two original documents until then. The delay was irritating because if what Mary had claimed in her manuscript was true, then her discovery was explosive. As an academic, Perdita knew her grandmother's theories all hung on these original documents and without authentication or corroboration it would be difficult to add gravitas to her thesis or prove its truth, which would make it little more than an interesting conspiracy theory.

Maybe that's why Mary didn't publish the book back in the early 1990s, thought Perdita. *There was no way to corroborate her evidence. Times have changed though, new information is constantly being discovered, perhaps there is something available now that I'll be able to use to prove her theories.*

It was a thought that excited her but also filled her with a strange sadness. This theory had been Mary's, as had this house and everything she and Piper now owned. How cruel of fate not to allow them to have worked together on this manuscript, their grandmother sharing her great knowledge while she used her computer research skills to help prove her hypothesis. *Between us, we could have changed history*, thought Perdita.

Shrugging off these gloomy musings, she made herself focus on the one positive hit the library computer had produced: a 1990s version of *The Llyn Cel Mermaid and Other Local Legends*. Making a note of the location code, Perdita walked up the library towards the stained glass windows before heading down one of the towering aisles of books. As she walked among the stacks, she ran her finger along the spines, shivering in anticipation at the titles, wondering what secrets were about to unfold as she explored this new text. Books had always been her comfort, her safe place and she was still stunned to be the owner of such a vast collection.

After five minutes of searching, she located the correct shelf. To her delight, it was on one of the higher locations, meaning she would have to use the old-fashioned library ladder that was attached to the shelves, enabling librarians to move from one end of a bookcase to another. After a few moments of whizzing backwards and forwards, she finally brought herself to a halt in front of the book she needed.

"Oh my goodness," sighed Perdita extracting the large hardback book. "It's beautiful."

Hurrying back down the ladder, she made for her favourite window seat and gazed down at the ornately decorated book. The illustration on the cover was of a mermaid, reminiscent of the one who swam around the walls of the house. Perdita also thought it looked vaguely familiar, not the picture itself, which she knew she had never seen before, but the artist's style. With a creeping sense of trepidation, she opened the front cover.

Such was her shock, Perdita almost dropped the book. Inside was a painting of her mother, her father and to her stunned amazement, herself and Piper as toddlers. Underneath were the words: "*For Mum, Happy Birthday. Hope and mermaids always, Louisa, James, Perdita and Piper xxx*".

On the next page, things became slightly worse because there was another family portrait, this time of the Mackensies, all five of them, with a dedication written by Alistair: "*To my best friend, Mary, on her birthday. Your favourite stories, retold by your favourite people. Ecce signum!*"

Forcing herself to turn the pages, Perdita fought the conflicting emotions that rose within her: delight at seeing her father's beautiful images, sadness at the loss of her parents and her grandmother and mounting fury that once again she and Piper had been deprived the love of their family for reasons that had still not been explained. Part of her wanted to throw the book across the room, screaming as she did, but deep down, she knew she would never be able to abuse such a beautiful book in such a terrible manner. Instead, she tried to rationalise her way through her emotions but when this proved too difficult, she reached for her usual solace at times of emotional upheaval: words.

Find the legend of the Llyn Cel mermaid, she thought. *It was the reason behind my search and reading it could offer some clues.*

Running her finger down the index, again adorned with her father's magical images, she discovered the Llyn Cel mermaid legend was exactly halfway through the book. When she found the page, she understood why. The illustration of the mermaid swimming inches below the surface of the lake, while Marquess House and the island were reflected above her, took up the centre spread of the book. It was an intricately detailed picture and Perdita studied it for some time before turning back two pages and reading the ancient legend.

From the first line, there was a familiarity to the sad tale of love, loss and despair. The delicate, aristocratic heroine who escaped from her brutal husband and gave birth to his twin children. Yet when she found a new love, he was wrenched from her and drowned in the choppy waters of Llyn Cel. Such was her despair, she threw herself into the lake and transformed into a mermaid as she searched for her lost lover. Yet, her troubled soul could not rest and on each full moon, the mermaid would regain her legs in order to walk through the village, singing her lament, searching on land for her lover too. The haunting lyricism of her song was said to bewitch any man who heard it, entrancing them into following her back into the dark waters of the lake, where they would be lost forever. At each full moon, the women of the village would leave offerings for the mermaid, hoping these kind gestures would encourage her to leave their menfolk alone.

Unexpectedly, Kit's voice floated into her mind from his tour on the day she had moved into Marquess House: "*There was a priory on the island but being so far away from London, it survived Henry VIII's initial dissolution of the monasteries. It was closed in 1543 after some sort of scandal. Either the prioress was pregnant or she hid a noblewoman here and helped her deliver an illegitimate baby…*"

And all legends have their basis in fact, she thought. *Were these two tales somehow combined?*

Her phone rang and she grinned, her spirits restored.

"Hey, gorgeous," she almost sang. "I'm so excited. In less than a week, we'll be in the south of France…"

"I'm sorry, Perdita," came Warren's strained voice, "but we can't go. I have to cancel the holiday. You must stay at Marquess House."

"What?" she replied, brought up short by his clipped tone.

"Something's come up…"

"Something's come up? What's more important than being together? Is it work?"

"No," said Warren, then added in a quiet voice, as though the softness of his tone would make it less inflammatory, "it's Jacqui."

"Your ex-wife?" Perdita's tone was calm but she was seething, her hands shaking as she tried to control her growing fury. Warren and his wife had been separated long before he had met Perdita. When Warren had explained he was divorced, Perdita did not see this as a problem, after all, everyone had baggage. However, as Warren and Jacqui had no children, Perdita had never been able to understand why they were still in touch or why Warren allowed himself to be emotionally manipulated by his ex-wife.

"It's her mother, Lillian, she's ill and Jacqui has asked me if I'll take her to hospital next week for an operation," he said, then paused waiting for Perdita to, quite rightly, explode.

"You're cancelling our two weeks in France to take Lillian to hospital?" she hissed, furious and devastated that Jacqui still took priority in Warren's life. "Where?"

"It's a specialist team in Edinburgh," he said. "It's for her back."

"Why Edinburgh? They live in Yorkshire?"

"I don't know, darling, but you know Jacqui can't drive since she had her horse riding accident…"

"So, you're dropping me, your fiancée, to run to your ex-wife's side? While it's very gallant of you, it's extremely unreasonable. Tell you what, I'll charter a plane to fly them there, pay for Jacqui to stay in a five-star hotel, hire a driver to ferry them around, then fly them home," she seethed. "Now you don't have any excuses. Unless, of course, you'd rather be with her than me?"

"Perdita, you're being ridiculous and unfair…"

"*I'm* being unfair?" Her control was fast disappearing but she fought hard to keep her voice calm, if colder than usual. Her instinct was to explode, to scream and shout then dramatically hang up; experience had taught her this would leave her feeling worse. "I've offered to fund their trip in order to leave you free to be with me. How is that unfair?"

"You're making an already difficult situation worse by being deliberately awkward," Warren shouted, unexpectedly losing control. "I can't speak to you when you're like this. The holiday is off, Perdita. Stay where you are in Pembrokeshire."

Then he hung up.

Stunned, Perdita stared at her phone. What had just happened? How could he do this to her? It had been his suggestion they spend a fortnight together at his house in the south of France, now it seemed he would prefer to ferry his ex-wife and her mother around instead. Perdita's finger was poised to return the call, then she hesitated. A feeling of sick devastation was slowly sweeping through her as a sudden, horrifying thought filled her mind. *He was trying to make another go of his marriage.* With shaking hands, Perdita placed her phone on the seat beside her and took several deep breaths.

Calm, she thought, *rationalise the situation.*

She gazed out of the window, trying to stem her welling tears and marshal her frantic thoughts. *This was a row*, she thought, *nothing more.* Yet she could not quite ignore the voice in her head that reminded her this was not the first time Warren had cancelled their plans in order to help his ex-wife. Somehow, she had always managed to justify his behaviour but this — she was not sure this was forgivable. If he had delayed the holiday a few days, she would have understood but to cancel it entirely and insist she remain in Pembrokeshire… It made her shudder.

Outside, the beautiful summer morning seemed to mock her misery. She allowed herself to be overwhelmed by her disappointment and confusion for a few moments, but then gradually, with the stubborn self-preservation instincts of one who had learned to face unexpected and debilitating loss, she pulled herself back from the brink. Warren had crossed a line and she was unsure how to react. She would not call him today. She would calm down, distract herself and keep busy until she was ready to discuss how they could overcome the recurring issue of Warren's ex-wife's interference in their lives. *And if we can't?* she thought. *Well, I'll face that if I have to.*

Clicking off her phone, she walked over to the desk where she had left her laptop and snapped it shut. Placing the ornate book next to it, she ran a hand through her hair, thinking hard. Warren, she decided, was not going to ruin her day. She had other things to occupy her mind, issues she felt were more important than allowing herself to be upset by his behaviour. She knew Jenny was busy until later in the afternoon, therefore, until she could access the other documents, she would head to the research centre with the ornate copy of *The Llyn Cel Mermaid and Other Local Legends* and see if this version had anything to offer.

If she finished studying this before Jenny arrived, she would begin checking the hundreds of references in her grandmother's manuscript in order to establish whether at least part of her argument was corroborated by other sources. It was a good plan and as she wandered into the Tudor hall, she was so lost in thought, she did not realise she had forgotten her laptop, phone and book, neither did she notice Kit until she walked into him.

220

"Morning, you're distracted," he said, putting his hands on her shoulders to steady her, then he saw her ashen face. "Hey, what's happened?"

"Nothing," she replied. Then, despite her best intentions, she wavered. "It's Warren, he's cancelled our holiday, we argued."

"Oh, Perds, no. Why?"

"His ex-wife," she managed before a sob engulfed her and she turned away, not wanting him to witness her distress. She did not see the fury that passed across Kit's face. To her surprise, he pulled her into an all-encompassing hug, her back to his chest, his head resting on hers in a gesture of comfort.

"Men are idiots," he murmured into her hair. "I bet he rings back this afternoon and apologises, then begs you to fly out to join him as planned."

"Thank you," she whispered.

"What are you up to now?" asked Kit.

"I was going to head over to the research centre to begin checking references."

"Really?"

"Yes, why?"

"Do you honestly think you'll be able to concentrate? Give it five minutes and you'll be brooding over your row."

She stared at him, aware he was correct but not wanting to admit to such shallowness.

"I'm popping out for an hour or so," continued Kit. "Errands for Dad and a few other bits and pieces. I'm heading for the Pembrokeshire Archives in Haverfordwest. They're having an exhibition and we've agreed to lend them a few pieces. Why don't you come along for the ride? It might help clear your head."

Perdita opened her mouth to refuse.

"I'll buy you lunch," said Kit as she hesitated, his blue eyes twinkling. Perdita gazed into his smiling face and suddenly nodded decisively. Perhaps it would do her good to get out of the house for a few hours.

"Let me grab my bag," she said.

Twenty minutes later, she was in the passenger seat of Kit's car as they headed towards the nearby market town but, hard as she tried not to think about it, her mind kept replaying the row with Warren. She could not quite shift the fear that he was trying to get back together with Jacqui. It was a gut instinct and, for the first time since she and Warren had become engaged, she wondered if their relationship was as strong as she had always assumed.

"Incidentally," said Kit, interrupting the string of imagined responses Perdita was running through in her mind, wishing she had flung a few of them at Warren, "I'm surprised you haven't said, 'I told you so'."

"About what?" she asked.

"Your grandmother's manuscript, *The Catherine Howard Anomaly*. You obviously think there's something worth investigating," he said, slowing down and edging into a hedge to let a tractor pass, "or you wouldn't be compiling her bibliography and checking her references."

"On any other day, I'd definitely enjoy the smug factor," she admitted. "Today, everything is slightly muted but yes, I told you so. I want to do some more research to discover the reason why she didn't go ahead and publish, because my grandmother's theories are quite extraordinary."

"In what way?"

Perdita dragged her mind away from Warren. "How much do you know about Catherine Howard?"

"Not much," he said. "She was young and I think she was beheaded. If memory serves me correctly, she's always been viewed as a bit of a foolish, good-time girl who had a number of flings. Was she Henry VIII's fourth wife?"

"Fifth," corrected Perdita. "She came after Anne of Cleves."

"And Anne was the queen Henry divorced because he didn't think she was very pretty?"

Perdita's expression darkened. "Which I always thought was a bit rich when you think what an enormous, festering tub of guts Henry was by then."

"Go on, girl, get that bitterness and fury out!" Kit laughed.

Despite herself, Perdita giggled.

"Divorced, beheaded, died, divorced, beheaded, survived," chanted Kit.

"That's right," said Perdita. "Katherine of Aragon was his first and longest-standing wife, as well as mother to the future Mary I. She was a Spanish princess and was previously married to Henry's older brother."

"Prince Arthur," agreed Kit, "and it was on the basis that their marriage was adulterous because she had been his sister-in-law, that Henry divorced her to marry Anne Boleyn."

"Gold star, go to the top of the class," said Perdita.

"I knew my history A-level would come in handy one day."

"Henry married Anne Boleyn and she gave birth to the future Elizabeth I. Things went wrong, though, when she miscarried several times and was unable to produce the male heir Henry required to continue the dynasty. So, Henry trumped-up some charges of adultery and had Anne beheaded."

"Nice guy. Jane Seymour was next, wasn't she?"

"Yes, she gave Henry his longed-for son, the future boy-king, Edward VI, but she died shortly after the birth, probably from puerperal fever but it could have been an infection due to lack of hygiene," said Perdita. Then, as Kit flew around the corner, the rugged Pembrokeshire cliffs and wild blue sea filled their view. She gasped, "Wow! Stunning!"

"Hey, it's good to see you smiling."

"Thanks, Kit," she said. He gave her a small salute then returned to the Tudors.

"Wasn't Jane Seymour supposed to be the love of his life, because it wasn't until a couple of years later that he married Anne of Cleves?"

"Well, school history lessons said so but that was the version of the past written by male, mostly Victorian, scholars."

"I take it new information has been found then?"

"It depends on your interpretation," replied Perdita. "Henry was buried next to Jane in St George's Chapel in Windsor Castle which was another reason why the myth perpetuated, but I'm not sure it was necessarily his choice."

"What do you mean?"

"When Henry died, Edward VI became king but he was only nine years old, so his uncle, Edward Seymour, became regent," she explained. "Edward Seymour was Jane's eldest brother and what better way to cement the family's power than by claiming Jane had been Henry's favourite wife? It would have reinforced what the Seymour family saw as their right to rule. I'm not saying Henry didn't care about her but that was probably because she gave him a living male heir. In reality, Jane died on 24 October 1537 and on 31 October, seven days later, Thomas Cromwell was already lining up new brides. His first two suggestions were the French king's daughter Margaret or the widowed Madame de Longueville. Margaret was the seventh child of Francis I and Queen Claude and was fourteen years old. Henry was forty-six."

"Gross," muttered Kit.

"Exactly. Madame de Longueville is probably better remembered as Mary of Guise. She refused Henry, preferring to marry his nephew, James V of Scotland."

"Wise woman."

"And she was the mother of the future Mary Queen of Scots."

"I knew I'd heard the name," said Kit. "She had a lucky escape."

"As did many other royal women and ladies of high breeding," said Perdita. "The reason there was such a long gap between Henry's third and fourth marriages was because it took that long to find someone who was willing to wed an axe-wielding maniac. Although, he had a number of mistresses in between."

"And then, after Anne of Cleves, Catherine Howard flared briefly on the pages of history."

"Yes, poor little Catherine Howard and finally Katheryn Parr."

"You said your grandmother had discovered something extraordinary?"

"If Granny was right, then what she proposes could change a lot of preconceived ideas about the Tudors, but in order to see if there's a possibility of publishing her findings, I need to do a great deal more research. I'll also have to corroborate her findings properly and authenticate the documents she used, particularly one she named *The Catherine Howard Codex* which was her main source of new information," she said. "I'd hoped you might be able to help; you must have to verify your discoveries all the time."

Kit nodded. "There is another possibility though, Perds," he said. "Please don't think I doubt you or Mary but, as she was such an experienced and gifted historian, do you think it's possible she discovered the codex was a fake and that's the reason she didn't publish?"

"I'm aware that might be the reason. The thing is, though, she must have thought there was something in it because she kept adding things to the manuscript, right up until just before she died."

"Such as?"

"New discoveries about Henry VIII, new findings on Catherine Howard, all sorts of bits and pieces, and every one of them backs up what she discovered in the codex. So, she did have some corroborative evidence, although it needs pulling together in a coherent manner. It was as though she never fully stopped building up the proof she required. Even more intriguing is that the final chapter is missing, so I wonder if she'd removed it because she wanted to rewrite it. The last update in the file was two weeks before she died. Don't you think it's at least worth investigating? And, if it turns out to be a fake, well, then you can have your 'I told you so' moment!"

"OK," he said, smiling. "Let's try. We'll speak to Jenny when we get back and take it to The Dairy for authentication."

She was still unsure whether all her grandmother had discovered was true or merely an elaborate conspiracy theory, but she had to find out. *And,* she realised, *it's made me feel calmer and more in control of my emotions about Warren. I'm sure we'll work things out.* Her mind drifted back to the day he had arrived to break the sad news about her grandmother: surely he would not have dropped everything to race to her side if he didn't love her? He did love her and she loved him, she was sure of it. *We'll find a way,* she thought, then her mind drifted back to the dig.

"By the way, who do I speak to about grants?" she asked, remembering her promise to Olaf.

"Grants? Perds, you don't need funding," laughed Kit.

"Not for me, for the dig I was on when Mary died. They invited me to take part because I specialise in jewellery and its symbolism. We found a golden cup with a clockwork mechanism inside it and I wondered if it would be possible to offer Olaf a grant to restore it and maybe commission a replica? I wondered if Piper would be able to help him find a suitable artist to take on the work."

"No problem. We part-funded that dig so I'll have all the details, I'll contact Dr Dade. And what about you? Will you be going back to your university job?"

"Not a chance," she said as they pulled into the car park of the archives. "I'm having far too much fun here. I resigned yesterday."

Chapter Two

The trip out was exactly what I needed, she thought later that afternoon as she strode across the lawn to the research centre. Warren might have dented her morale but Kit had worked hard to restore it. After making the necessary deliveries and errands, he had taken her on a whistle-stop tour of the surrounding historical monuments.

"You can't move around here without tripping over a castle or a ruined ecclesiastical building," he had said. "There's Haverfordwest Castle, which was established in Norman times, approximately 1120, then there are the ruins of Haverfordwest Priory which was a house of Augustinian Canons until Henry VIII's dissolution of the monasteries. After that, the land was bought by Roger and Thomas Barlow, who were the brothers of William Barlow, the bishop of St Davids."

"Useful contact," Perdita had laughed.

"Indeed! We'll go over to Pembroke for lunch, then you can see Pembroke Castle where Henry VII was born. Not far from there is Carew Castle which was once home to the Perrot family and between the two are the ruins of Lamphey Bishop's Palace, which was also bought after the dissolution, this time by the Devereux family. There's Picton Castle too and the ruins of Wiston Castle, not to mention St David's Cathedral itself..."

On their return, Kit had disappeared to his own office to prepare for his weekly meeting with his father and Perdita felt that at last she could begin unravelling the mystery of why her grandmother had withdrawn the manuscript from publication. As she opened the door to the research centre, her phone rang.

Fishing it out of her handbag, she saw Warren's name flashing on the screen. For a few moments, she considered her options, then rejected the call. She did not want him disrupting her mood again, she would speak to him later. As she made her way through to The Dairy, she waited for him to leave a message. When he did not, her anger surged. Pushing her phone to the bottom of her bag, she marched resolutely onwards to Jenny's office.

"Jenny!" exclaimed Perdita when she found her. "This place is amazing! Most universities would kill for this facility."

Perdita had briefly toured The Dairy before, but had not fully absorbed the scale of it. Now, as she followed Jenny through the corridors, she was awestruck by the state-of-the-art research opportunities it offered.

"I've set us up in the room Mary always used," said Jenny. "Your laptop is already there and, I hope you don't mind, I've charged it. The copy of *The Llyn Cel Mermaid and Other Legends* that you'd taken off the shelf is there too. I assumed you still needed it."

"Thanks, Jenny," said Perdita.

"I've laid out the codex," Jenny continued. "There are gloves as the paper is extremely fragile. Mary had it authenticated in the early 1990s and it has been confirmed that the parchment, the ink and the wooden covers can be dated to between 1510 and 1560…"

"So it falls in the right time frame," interrupted Perdita. "If Granny had already had it authenticated, why didn't she publish her manuscript?"

"The codex gives a unique view of Catherine Howard's reign. However, there are no recognised contemporary documents to support this version of events. Although it's dated to the correct period, it could have been a contemporary fake used to create unrest."

"But why would anyone bother? She was queen for such a short period and, if other documents are to be believed, had no influence."

They arrived at a high security door and Jenny handed Perdita a passkey.

"No one but you, Piper, me and the Mackensies are allowed to view classified documents," she said. The heavy door slid open and once through, closed silently behind them. Perdita felt a small tremor of fear at being shut in but she quashed it, focusing instead on the task in hand.

"I know your priorities are the codex and the Llyn Cel mermaid legends," said Jenny as they walked along a winding corridor, "but Alistair also suggested I include another document your grandmother had been studying shortly before she abandoned her Catherine Howard research. It's a *Book of Hours* she purchased from her old and very dear friend Lady Pamela Johnson."

"Really? A Book of Hours wasn't listed anywhere in the bibliography."

"It was a new acquisition. Mary discovered it in a batch of other documents she had bought from Lady Pamela."

"Lady Pamela?" queried Perdita, the name tugged at her memory. She had read it recently, then it came to her. "The Lady Pamela letters…"

"How do you know about the letters?" Jenny asked, startled.

"It was written on one of Granny's boxes of research. There was *The Catherine Howard Anomaly* and next to it was another partly researched manuscript with two working titles — *The Ladies of Melusine* or *The Lady Pamela Letters: A Study of the Epistolary Styles of Women in the Tudor and Stuart Courts*. Of the two, I prefer the Melusine option, although Granny would probably have used the latter. She was never known for her snappy titles."

Jenny laughed.

"You might be able to advise me, Jenny, because it's been a while since I read it, but didn't the legend of Melusine state she was the water goddess who was half woman, half fish — although I think a few versions say half serpent — and she was supposed to be an ancestress of the House of Luxembourg and the House of Lusignan?"

"Correct," said Jenny, "and through Jacquetta of Luxembourg, the mother of Elizabeth Woodville — who was the wife of Edward IV — and the maternal grandmother of Henry VIII, the Tudors were said to be distantly descended from Melusine too. After your mother died, Mary found it difficult to study anything from that period of history again. In her mind, her study of the Tudors and Stuarts had become irrevocably linked with sadness and loss."

"Poor Granny, how terrible…" murmured Perdita.

Jenny either did not hear or decided to continue her explanation regardless. Perdita was unsure but listened avidly as the librarian continued, "Her friend, Lady Pamela, was descended on one side from a cadet branch of the Fitzalan family who were related to the Howards, and on the other from the Baynton families. Whenever things became difficult financially, which they did occasionally due to the expense of running her family's enormous estates that her brother had mismanaged for years, Lady Pamela would approach Mary with papers from the family archive. Mary always paid far too much for them because she wanted to help her friend. She was studying one particular box of letters that she hoped would form the basis of a book to follow her Catherine Howard work, when she discovered an extremely ornate Book of Hours. Her rudimentary study of it suggested it might have belonged to Lady Kathryn Knollys. However, as I said, after your mother died, she abandoned both projects. We haven't translated or digitised any of this document."

"Lady Kathryn Knollys," mused Perdita. "She was the daughter of Mary Boleyn, wasn't she? Possibly Henry VIII's daughter too?"

"Correct."

"Have you dated the Book of Hours?"

For some reason, Jenny seemed reluctant to pass on the information. "Yes, and the dates are correct."

Perdita whooped. "This could be it! From what Granny said in her manuscript, Lady Kathryn Knollys was one of Catherine Howard's ladies-in-waiting. There could be something in the Book of Hours that corroborates the codex. This could be the proof we need. I must text Piper."

"NO!" Jenny shouted, her voice fraught. "Do not, under any circumstances discuss this over any of your electronic devices with Piper or using your old contact details. I've set up secure email addresses for the two of you on The Dairy computer. I've already sent Piper the information concerning her new accounts and how to access her messages via a secure portal. Would you please do the same if you're using your own laptop to contact her, rather than the computers in here. We use the portal when we're off-site and also for sending information to Jerusalem. It can be accessed safely from all over the world as long as you have these passwords."

"Why?"

"Please, Perdita, trust me, it's safer this way. There's also a secure face-to-face mode."

"OK," said Perdita, startled by the sudden sharpness in Jenny's voice and her ashen face.

"Thank you," Jenny whispered. "Now, it's all in there. Good luck." Jenny looked near to tears as she hurried back down the corridor and through the security door.

What was that all about? wondered Perdita. Then she drew her attention back to the room she had entered. Again, the décor was subtle and tasteful. It was also a direct copy of the office Perdita had adopted in the main research centre. *My grandmother was certainly a creature of habit*, she thought as she looked around.

Her laptop was on the desk which was over to one side of the room which offered views of the gardens and an ornate, gushing fountain, the water creating floating rainbows as it danced through the sparkling summer air.

Running along another wall was a conference table with chairs around it, and dominating this were three vast, foam wedges covered in smooth, lint-free cotton. The copy of the book she had been studying earlier lay at the end of the row of wedges. Dumping her bag on the large leather chair behind the desk, she walked to the table and began examining her treasure.

Resting on the first foam wedge was the book of local legends. Having already seen a more up-to-date version, Perdita was intrigued to examine the original. Pulling on some cotton gloves, she examined the stiff wooden cover. It showed only the title and the author's name. Perdita was disappointed, she had hoped for an illustration of the mermaid. She gently turned the vellum leaves and after checking the index, found the tale of the mermaid who was supposed to live in the lake in the grounds of Marquess House.

To her surprise, it was shorter than the version she had read earlier. Fetching her notebook from her computer bag, she made a few comments concerning the legend but, as it had not featured in her grandmother's work, only in the bibliography, she decided to ask Jenny to return it to its safe storage area for the present.

Next, she turned her attention to the second foam wedge, her excitement mounting as she stared down at the ancient document. Resting in the middle of the cushioned base was a dark brown book, its cover made from smooth polished wood. There was no lettering, no mark of any kind to suggest what secrets it held.

Gazing down at it, Perdita felt her breath catch in her throat. Being in the presence of such a precious artefact was something she found humbling, so she was not surprised when her fingers trembled as she lifted the document from its safe resting place in order to examine it more closely.

In the top left corner, there was a small hole running through the cover and pages, where it had originally been joined together. However, somewhere in its history, the codex had been bound in the form of a traditional book.

"What tales will you tell me?" murmured Perdita as, with great care, she replaced it on the wedge and opened the cover.

It was lined with faded lilac silk and the frontispiece held an intricate illumination featuring the same mermaid who swam around the walls of Marquess House. Above its head were the Latin words: *Iuncta Sanguine* and below, *Semper Sorores*. Perdita smiled to see her familiar face, wondering how it was linked to the codex. *Another mystery to solve*, she thought. She also made a note of the Latin, translating the two phrases in case they reoccurred throughout the codex or had some other significance.

"*Iuncta Sanguine,*" she murmured as she typed it on to a new document. "Joined in Blood and *Semper Sorores* — Sisters Always."

Opening it to the first page, the exquisite writing was revealed. It was tiny but meticulous with a curious swirling grace. After a few moments of staring at it, Perdita's eyes gradually attuned to the style and she was able to decipher the words. Like small angels holding hands, the letters began to give up their secrets, their story unfolding across the ancient vellum.

"*August 1540, Hampton Court Palace…*" she breathed. "No way!"

Checking the manuscript of her grandmother's abandoned book, she flicked through until she found what she was looking for: "*Catherine Howard was presented as queen in late August 1540; it is unclear why Henry delayed the introduction as contemporary records have them marrying on 28 July 1540 at Oatlands Palace, Surrey. The Bishop of London, Edward Bonner, officiated…*" Next to this were a multitude of references corroborating these facts.

Pulling up a chair, Perdita settled down to immerse herself in the ancient document when there was a tentative knock on the door. Swearing under her breath at the interruption she nevertheless called out, "Come in," as politely as she could manage. To her surprise, Kit stuck his head around the door.

"Hello," she smiled, beckoning him into the room. "I thought you had a meeting with your dad."

"Yeah, I did but it was strange."

"What happened?"

"He told me I had to work with you and Piper on these documents and I was to put all my other projects aside, he'd deal with them himself."

"Why?"

Kit shrugged. "He was in a really odd mood," he sighed, sprawling in a chair opposite Perdita. "He was even more jittery than the day he decided to tell me and Stuart the facts of life."

She laughed.

"What else did he say?"

"That, as his successor here, at some point, there are secrets he'll have to impart, things which it'll be vital I understand, but until he feels the time is right to tell me them, he insists you and I work together on the codex. He said we needed to draw our conclusions so we could decide on what action we'd like to take in order to 'safeguard our futures'."

Perdita stared at him, perplexed.

"Safeguard our futures? Is he talking financially, do you think?"

"No, we discuss finances every day so it can't be that. I really have no idea what he means, Perds, I'm sorry. If you'd rather continue your research alone, that's fine by me. I'll go back to Dad and tell him it's a no-go."

"When I came down here, Jenny behaved very strangely too, she was almost in tears," she said. "I assumed it was something personal but maybe it was something to do with your dad's instructions."

"It makes no sense, though," said Kit, clearly irritated.

"Look, why don't you hang out here with me this afternoon, then tomorrow we could talk to your dad together and ask him to explain. He might be a bit less jittery by then."

"He gave me this too and told me I had to read it as quickly as possible so I could be a help rather than a hindrance." As he spoke Kit pulled a bound copy of her grandmother's manuscript out of the battered Fred Perry sports holdall he used as a computer bag.

"Would you like me to talk you through the basics?"

"No, you're busy doing your thing with the codex," he said, walking around behind her, appraising the book with his expert eye. "Wow, this is in pristine condition. It's bound though; a codex is usually loose leaves joined in one corner."

"There are holes here, top left," she said, pointing, "so I think the binding is later than the contents, possibly done by a subsequent owner in order to preserve it."

Examining it, Kit nodded, "Definitely," he concurred. "How far have you got?"

"The frontispiece and the first line," said Perdita wryly. "Then I was interrupted."

"Blame Dad," replied Kit, unrepentant. He walked back to his chair, sat down and flicked through the manuscript then looked up at Perdita, "Go on, then," he said, beaming, "demonstrate your brilliant lecturing skills, give me the short version. Why, apart from what's contained in the codex, did your grandmother believe that there is an anomaly in the accepted historical representation of Catherine Howard, aka Henry VIII's fifth unfortunate bride?"

Sliding off her white gloves, Perdita picked up her own copy of the manuscript and moved away from the codex so she was sitting opposite Kit.

"For now, I'll give you the basics," she said, "but if we've got to work on it together, it'll probably be easier if you do read it."

"I promise," said Kit, with a mock boy scout salute.

"My grandmother has structured the manuscript in quite an unusual way," she began.

"How?" he asked, flicking noisily through the pages of his own copy. She raised her eyebrows at him and he desisted.

"Well, rather than follow the usual chronological order of most historical biographies, at the beginning, she lists all the anomalies which have arisen in her study of Catherine's reign, then proceeds to discuss them," replied Perdita, giving him a quizzical look. She did not know how seriously he was taking this and she was not in the mood to be teased.

"So, there were some before she found the codex?"

"Yes, if you were looking, but if you took the accepted version at face value, it would be possible to gloss over them as unimportant. It's only when you view her reign as a whole, you realise the accepted version is full of contradictions."

"Were there many?"

"More than I would have expected for such a well-discussed period of history," she replied. "The first point Granny makes is that there is doubt over the characters who are always associated with Catherine. A great deal of information about her still comes from a document called *The Chronicle of King Henry VIII of England*, usually known as *The Spanish Chronicle*. It tells the supposed 'love story' between Catherine and one of Henry's courtiers, Thomas Culpepper..."

"That's quite well known though, isn't it?" interrupted Kit.

"Do you want me to explain or not?" Kit nodded and Perdita continued: "Except, we should view this document with suspicion as the author is unknown and it was written at least ten years after Catherine was queen. All that is known is the document came from Spain. It's possible the author was never at Henry's court but was writing from gossip and hearsay."

"So, not a reliable source," said Kit.

"An extremely unreliable source," she agreed. "Not only that, there is no mention in its account of events of either Francis Dereham or Henry Manox, who were supposedly Catherine's lovers, or of Jane Boleyn, the infamous Lady Rochford, who was executed with Catherine, allegedly for helping to facilitate her affair with Culpepper. A lady-in-waiting called Jane is mentioned but there is no surname to identify her and Jane was a very common name in Tudor England. Yet, these are the names that have been linked to Catherine throughout history."

"There must be other chroniclers though, who mention them?"

"A few contemporary writers mention Dereham and Culpepper but references to Manox and Jane Boleyn are more limited," said Perdita. "In fact, some of the contemporary writers at Henry VIII's court barely mentioned Catherine."

"It's pretty thin."

"There's more. The next point Granny Mary raises is the question of whether or not Catherine Howard was actually illiterate. History tells us she could barely write her name."

"Why would that be a question?" asked Kit. "Many women were back then. It wasn't seen as important to educate girls."

"And yet, they were supposed to run vast estates with their husbands, so the majority of well-born and noble women were educated," countered Perdita. "Maybe not to the same level as men but certainly so they could read, write and keep accounts. Catherine was a member of the exalted Howard clan, a good marriage was expected for her, so it's probable she was given a basic education. Especially when it's well-documented that she had dancing and music lessons."

"Did she?"

"Yes, she was supposedly seduced by her music teacher Henry Manox when she was approximately thirteen years old."

Kit looked disgusted. "I agree, if her guardians were paying for music lessons, it would have been odd not to give her a rounded education by the standards of the day."

"Exactly," said Perdita. "So, if we take it that Catherine was literate, why are there no letters to or from her during the period of her reign? Why is it that the only letter she left behind was the one to Thomas Culpepper? Particularly as this was the document that incriminated her. And, if no one is sure what her handwriting looked like because there are no other corroborating documents, how do we know she even wrote it?"

For the first time since he had been forced into working with her, Kit sat up alertly, his interest finally captured. "And I take it this was a love letter?" he asked. Perdita nodded. "How very convenient! I'm beginning to understand; the only sources used to tell her story are those that unequivocally incriminate Catherine? Any other details which could give an alternate version of events seem to have disappeared."

"Unless, of course, you're looking for them," replied Perdita, gratified to see he was at last giving her his full attention. "However, back to the Culpepper letter. What makes it even more interesting is that it was written in two different styles of handwriting."

"Meaning two people wrote it?" asked an astounded Kit, and Perdita nodded again. "Yet this was the letter which began the scandal that condemned her to death?"

"Yes," said Perdita riffling through her copy of the manuscript until she found the photograph of the letter. She pushed it towards Kit to examine. "It's thought by her most recent biographer, in a note Mary added earlier this year, that Catherine only wrote the first sixteen words, the formal introductory sentence asking after Culpepper's health, something which would be a normal part of her queenly duties, but that the rest is written by someone else. Although, as there are no other known documents to corroborate her handwriting, it's possible she didn't even write the opening sentence."

"This is an incredibly long letter, though," said Kit looking up from the manuscript. "How do historians explain it?"

"That she asked someone else to write it for her, probably Jane Boleyn."

"But there must be examples of Jane Boleyn's writing," he said. "Surely that would clear things up?"

"You'd think, and yet no one in all the books you read about Catherine has ever suggested that simple test."

"No way!" exclaimed Kit.

"Which makes it possible that this could be a contemporary fake, created to incriminate her," said Perdita. "Even though it's supposedly signed by her."

A look of excitement suddenly suffused Kit's handsome face. "The codex — doesn't your grandmother suggest the bulk of it was written by Catherine Howard? So we have a comparison at last."

"Exactly," agreed Perdita, "but stick with me. There are a few other discrepancies before we start going through Granny Mary's theories."

Kit's earlier flippancy had now turned to enthusiasm. "What else did Mary suggest?"

"There are a number of things and one of the more recently dismissed myths is in here too," said Perdita.

"Which is?"

"When she went to the block, Catherine supposedly gave a speech saying she regarded herself as the wife of Thomas Culpepper."

"Even I know that's unlikely," laughed Kit. "The Tudors were obsessed with having a good death in order to send them on their way to heaven. If fear hadn't consumed her and she could speak at all by then, I suspect she would have followed the more traditional: 'Henry is a good and righteous prince, I deserve to die for my transgressions…' line that Anne Boleyn and pretty much everyone else took on the scaffold."

"Of course, it has been utterly dismissed and put down to Victorian romanticism, but there is another odd thing. One biographer has claimed that while other wives were known for certain things — Katherine of Aragon for her piety, Anne Boleyn for her interest in theology and music — Catherine Howard was renowned for her style and her love of fashion. If this was the case, why are there no records stating what she wore at her execution?"

"There must be records," Kit said.

"Nothing of any great detail, which is odd because even poor little Lady Jane Grey, who was queen for nine days, even less time than Catherine, is recorded as wearing a simple black dress at her execution. Doesn't it strike you as odd that when Catherine Howard, the Tudor trendsetter, went to the block, no one recorded what she was wearing? I know it sounds frivolous but when combined with the other anomalies, it can't be ignored."

"You're right, history is in the detail," mused Kit.

Encouraged by Kit's growing conviction, Perdita continued. "It isn't only Catherine that provokes questions, though. There's Jane Boleyn too."

"Who was she?"

"She was the wife of George Boleyn, who was the brother of Anne Boleyn," said Perdita.

"And she was executed with Catherine Howard?"

"Yes. The thing is, most historians have always been baffled by Jane's behaviour. Why would she put herself in such danger? Jane had survived the biggest political scandal of the Tudor age: the trial and execution of Anne Boleyn. Her husband, George Boleyn, who was by then Lord Rochford, was beheaded — accused of incest with his sister; Anne died in the same way. Jane survived this storm and was forgiven. She was even allowed to return to royal life and was given a position in Jane Seymour's court, the woman who replaced Anne Boleyn, which is possibly why some historians view her as heartless. I suspect she felt she had no choice; it was that or go back to her parents' home and live in poverty, as the king had confiscated all her and George's lands and manors.

"Anyway, this woman was a consummate survivor. So, why, five years after making it through the terror of Anne Boleyn's fall and having spent that time rebuilding her battered reputation, would she throw it all away to help Catherine Howard have an affair with Thomas Culpepper? She was a career courtier, her father was Henry Parker, 10th Baron Morley, and her mother was Alice St John, who was connected to the influential Beauchamp family, making Jane half-second cousin to Henry VIII. The family was wealthy, respected and, most importantly, respectable. As seasoned courtiers, they were adept at surviving the politics of court life by learning to move with its endless, dizzying ebb and flow. So, why did Jane become involved in such a dangerous game with Catherine? She must have known it would end in disaster."

Kit was silent as he considered this wealth of information.

"Is there more?" he asked, no longer joking. Perdita suspected he was beginning to understand the far-reaching consequences of their endeavour.

Perdita bit her lip and nodded, absorbing some of Kit's sudden unease.

"There is also the strange lack of portraits of Catherine," continued Perdita. "Even now, historians argue over a number of different unnamed women in paintings trying to decide which one might be Catherine Howard. For many years, there was one particular Hans Holbein miniature, Henry's favourite court painter, that was considered to be Catherine. It's in the Royal Collection at Windsor. However, doubt has now been passed over that assumption and it's been suggested it may actually be a portrait of the king's niece, Lady Margaret Douglas, who was the daughter of Henry's elder sister, Margaret Tudor.

"Likewise, another image painted by Hans Holbein that was considered to be the young queen has again been dismissed. It's now thought to be an image of one of Henry VIII's nieces: again, possibly Lady Margaret Douglas, or Lady Frances Brandon or Lady Eleanor Brandon. In fact, records show this portrait was originally identified as being Eleanor Brandon, countess of Cumberland. It's even been suggested it may have been a portrait of Henry's daughter, Mary. It isn't Catherine, though.

"There are portraits of the other five queens, including poor old Anne of Cleves who was on the throne for even less time than Catherine. If Catherine was a beauty and the absolute love of Henry's life, why didn't he commission her portrait? He kept images of Anne Boleyn, Thomas Cromwell and various other courtiers whom he had sent to the block, why would he behave so differently towards Catherine? Did he have her images destroyed? Or have they been removed from history by someone else?"

"Put like that, it is odd."

"A few more things, then you need to read the manuscript yourself," she said, and Kit nodded in agreement. "The first is the anomaly of the Bill of Attainder which was passed, stating that Catherine Howard and Jane Boleyn were guilty of treason. It's also colloquially referred to as her execution warrant."

"And there was one of these for everyone who was executed?" questioned Kit, but Perdita shook her head.

"No, in most cases, people stood trial and were found guilty or not, then they were sentenced — there are court transcripts going back hundreds and hundreds of years — and not everyone was condemned to death. Anne Boleyn was tried in a court — a kangaroo court of men who knew she must be found of guilty of every charge — but nevertheless, she was at least given a chance to defend herself. However, Henry didn't really like being questioned over his decisions to murder people, so when he really wanted someone killed, he would issue a Bill of Attainder. This bill would be presented to Parliament and would be passed, generally the first time it was read out, sentencing the person named in the bill to death, usually for treason. By charging people this way, it meant Henry neatly bypassed a trial of any kind."

"And were many people sentenced like this?"

"A few — years before Henry was king, George Plantagenet, 1st duke of Clarence, was executed this way. Then, during Henry's reign, Thomas Cromwell and Margaret Pole, countess of Salisbury," said Perdita. "Anyway, the bill for Catherine and Jane was first introduced to Parliament on 21 January 1542. However, a contemporary witness — who is unfortunately anonymous — claims there was: 'uncertainty among the judges'. It was read again on 28 January and postponed once more. Finally, on 11 February 1541, it 'received the king's assent given in absentia by letter patent under the great seal of England'. So, in other words, the vital document condemning Catherine to death was never signed by the king," she said. "It was issued under the Royal Seal in his absence. Apparently, this was so as not to cause the king further distress, but it seems remarkably convenient that he never actually signed the document."

"But that's bizarre!"

"Like so many other unfortunates, Catherine was said to have been buried in the chapel of St Peter ad Vincula within the walls of the Tower of London," she said. "However, when it was excavated in 1876, other bodies were found that could be matched to those known to have been beheaded, but Catherine Howard's skeleton was never found."

Perdita looked at Kit. His blue eyes were hard as he thought through everything she had explained, "There's something else too," she said. This time, though, her tone was tentative. "It's not something of Granny Mary's, it was something I noticed last night."

"Go on," said Kit.

"Remember that silly rhyme: divorced, beheaded, died…"

"Divorced, beheaded, survived," he finished. "What about it?"

"Have you ever thought about how perfect it is?" she asked. "Almost too symmetrical?"

"What do you mean?"

Perdita grabbed her notebook and drew a two-columned chart.

"In the first column, there's Katherine of Aragon who was a foreign princess. She was divorced and replaced by a Howard girl, the Boleyn family being part of the clan, who was beheaded and replaced by a Seymour girl. In column two, the pattern repeats itself: Anne of Cleves was a foreign princess whom Henry divorced, then he married Catherine Howard before beheading her and marrying Katheryn Parr, who was part of the extended Seymour family."

Kit stared down at Perdita's chart, examining her evidence. When he did not speak, she continued, "It's so balanced, it's almost as though someone created it afterwards."

"So, what do you and Mary conclude from all this information?" he asked, his body tense.

Perdita took a deep breath, "That Catherine Howard may never have been executed at all."

Kit sprang to his feet and began pacing the room.

"You told me there were extraordinary things in Mary's manuscript, Perds, but this is explosive. You never suggested that Catherine Howard might not have been executed."

Perdita was surprised by his outburst. He was usually so easy-going that to see him so agitated was disturbing.

"I wanted to see the codex first," she explained, confused at his reaction, "rather than drop such a massive bombshell. Now we're working together, it seems important you should know."

"Catherine Howard's execution is a fixed point in our national identity. If Mary has found information that proves she wasn't, it could have serious repercussions."

"Why?" asked Perdita.

"It changes our collective past," he continued. "If it transpires the story we've all been told about one of England's most infamous monarchs is untrue, what else have we got wrong?"

"But it isn't a question of getting things wrong," Perdita replied. "It's about the continual unravelling of our past, reinterpreting and rewriting it as we discover more information. This is a new chapter in the study of the Tudor monarchy. You of all people should understand that, you spend your time buying, authenticating and restoring ancient, lost or suspect documents. You know history is fluid, each new discovery adds another layer to the past. This is a huge and important discovery."

"So why didn't Mary publish it?"

Perdita shrugged. "Perhaps your father could tell us," she replied, irritated by his dramatic reaction. "Kit, it's a new discovery, it's exciting and academically interesting, but it isn't the end of the world."

"It feels wrong, Perds," he said, dropping back into his seat and putting his head in hands, burying his fingers in his dark, floppy curls.

"Why?"

"Because, when was the last time you heard of anything new being discovered that changes the story of Henry VIII and his wives?"

"Never?"

"This does, though. So why didn't your grandmother, a noted scholar and historian, publish her findings and receive the accolades it would have brought? I don't know, for some reason — call it instinct after years of chasing documents, this feels..." he hesitated as he searched for the right word, "dangerous."

Perdita considered him, then stood up and returned to the codex. She was unsure how to react to Kit's outburst. Once more, she slid on the white cotton gloves. Kit had not moved, his head still in his hands, so when he spoke, his voice was muffled.

"If Mary suggested Catherine wasn't executed, what did she say happened?"

"Read the manuscript," snapped Perdita. She could not bear any more histrionics and returned to the document, carefully turning the pages to see what else it contained.

Kit sat up, pushing his hair out of his piercing blue eyes. "Sorry," he said. "I don't know where all that came from, I overreacted. You're right, I should stop behaving like a brat and read Mary's manuscript."

"She does have a theory about what happened to Catherine, several, in fact, but it might be better if you read it as a whole, then perhaps they won't be so shocking."

Perdita continued to study the codex. Kit watched her for a while, then his eye fell on the other foam wedges.

"What are these?" he asked, walking over to examine them and drumming his fingers on the table. He picked up the ornate library book and, after shooting a look at Perdita, opened it. He laughed when he saw the painting of his family. "I was so cute," he smirked, holding the page up to the side of his face as a comparison.

"Are you being deliberately annoying?" replied Perdita in a bored sounding voice, not looking up from the intricate design she was studying in the codex.

Kit laughed. "Actually, yes. As the youngest of three, being the annoying little brother is what I do best."

Perdita tried to keep a straight face but a tiny giggle escaped her. Finally, she looked up. Kit gave her an elaborate wink and a lopsided grin.

"It's the book of local legends Granny listed in the bibliography but I'm not sure it has much relevance, she doesn't note any specific sections. The other is an, as yet, unexplored Book of Hours that Mary bought from her old friend, Lady Pamela Johnson. It's suggested it may have belonged to Lady Kathryn Knollys. Jenny said her team have dated the book and it's the right time frame. If you want to make yourself useful, use your document detecting skills and see if there's anything inside it that we might be able to use to corroborate Mary's manuscript."

"Aye aye, cap'n," he said, taking the seat next to her and reaching over for a pair of white cotton gloves. "A Book of Hours was a prayer book, wasn't it?"

"A book of illuminated devotions, but yes, if you like, a prayer book. They were usually owned by high-status women," confirmed Perdita, "and often had notes written in them: household staff, guests, shopping lists, births, marriages, deaths, that kind of thing. Jenny's team hasn't started transcribing it, so it's virgin territory."

"Leave it with me," he murmured, taking an A4 notebook and, to her surprise, an expensive fountain pen, out of his bag.

Out of the corner of her eye, Perdita watched as Kit began to study the small, leather-bound book. Within moments, he was absorbed in his task, the tip of his tongue protruding through his teeth as he concentrated. Perdita grinned, then returned her attention to the codex. For the rest of the afternoon, they worked in companionable silence, occasionally checking references or showing each other things they had discovered.

Beyond the reinforced glass of the windows and the air-conditioned interior of The Dairy, the summer afternoon blazed golden and inviting. After several hours, Perdita stretched and looked over at Kit, who was still deeply engrossed in his work. A shaft of sunlight fell across his dark hair, making it dance with red and gold highlights, and for a moment she appraised him as she would any other good-looking man. There was no doubting Kit was attractive, as well as funny, intelligent and considerate when he was not being annoying. *What the hell is wrong with me?* she thought sharply. *One row with Warren and I'm eyeing up the local talent. I need to pull myself together.*

She also knew her concentration had peaked for the day and, with the thought of Warren, all the fear and doubt of the morning's argument flooded through her again. Pulling her phone, which she had put on silent, out of her bag, she glanced at it, hoping to see a string of missed calls from Warren, but there was nothing, not even a text message or email. Feeling her heart could sink no further, she threw her phone back into her handbag and stood up. Kit looked over and smiled.

"Are you done?" he asked.

"For today — you were right, my concentration is limited, but at least I've seen the codex. Tomorrow, I can begin crosschecking Granny's references and try to work out why she abandoned the project. There must be a reason. How are you doing?"

"Pretty well, the Book of Hours is quite fragile so I haven't pulled it about too much, but from the dates written on what I assume are Lady Knollys's comments — although, I'm making an academic guess until we can corroborate the writing with other known examples of hers — it was something she owned for years because it starts with her signing herself as Kathryn Carey which was her maiden name, but goes on to list all her children.

"I think it's likely to have originated in Belgium or the Netherlands as they were the major centres of production around that time," he said, then beckoned Perdita over to look at one of the beautifully illuminated pages. "These borders are decorated with a design known as 'swirling acanthus leaves'; it was typical of the Ghent and Bruges style. It would also explain the stylised drawing of the figures, which again leans to the Dutch style. It's beautiful and an incredible find. I can't wait to really get to grips with the contents."

"Thank you, Kit," she said, suddenly realising how useful it would be to have someone with Kit's expertise helping her unravel the mystery of her grandmother's work.

"No sweat," he grinned. "And I promise, I'll read the manuscript."

She laughed and began to gather up her belongings. "How does it work here? Does Jenny put everything away?"

"It's usually Izabel Barnes who clears up after us at the end of the day," said Kit. "She's Jenny's assistant and, because we like to keep things in the family, her granddaughter, too."

"Really?" said Perdita, surprised. "Jenny doesn't look old enough. What does Izabel do?"

"Jenny's training her to take over the running of the library one day but, at the moment, Izabel's main function is co-ordinating research and working with myself and Dad on applications for research grants across both Jerusalem and Marquess House. She also liaises with the conservators and restorers in The Dairy, as well as assisting Jenny and, most importantly, returning all secure items every evening."

"She must have an extensive knowledge of the archive."

"Like Jenny, she's passionate about the work we do here, which is why we're not allowed to touch Jenny and Izabel's beloved manuscripts and books more than is necessary," he grinned. "I'll give her a buzz." He walked over to the phone and dialled an internal extension, while he waited for it to connect, he continued, "Then, do you fancy a drink on the terrace? It's one of the more civilised pastimes Mary introduced. All summer, the end of the working day would involve an array of drinks: soft, hot, cold or alcoholic for everyone to enjoy and use to wind down."

Perdita gave a sad smile, "What a marvellous idea," she sighed. "I wish I'd been able to have a drink with Granny."

Kit finished speaking to Izabel then returned to Perdita and for the second time that day wrapped his arms around her. "Let's have a drink to her then," he said gently. "It isn't the same but it's the best we can do."

Swallowing the unexpected lump in her throat, Perdita nodded. There was a knock on the door and Kit released her. Jenny came in smiling.

"Izabel said you're finished. As I was passing, I thought I'd put all these away," she said, "then drinks on the terrace?"

"We'll see you there! Come on, Perds."

They made their way through The Dairy complex, along the winding path to the side entrance of Marquess House, down a corridor, across the Tudor Hall and into the Lady Isabel room where the huge French doors that led to the terrace were thrown open. Outside they could hear the clink of glasses and the murmur of voices and laughter. Kit stepped through but Perdita hesitated. This was one more thing that everyone had known about except her. It made her feel like a stranger again, an interloper in the lives of all the people who had known her grandmother. It was her house now, hers and Piper's, but so much was still unknown. I'd give it all back if it meant being able to have a drink on the terrace with Granny Mary, she thought. Swallowing her unexpected wave of grief, she stepped through the doors into the sunshine.

"There you are, safe and sound," called Alistair. "Kit, fetch Perdita a drink. We're on gin and tonics but we have a varied bar."

"Gin and tonic would be lovely," said Perdita, as Kit arrived with a glass.

"To your grandmother," he said quietly, so only Perdita heard. He tilted his glass to hers.

"To Granny Mary," she said, then she reached up and kissed him on the cheek. "Thank you for today, Kit. You've been wonderful."

In the distance, Perdita heard the ancient bell at the front door ringing. "Will someone get that?" she whispered to Kit, still unused to being in such a huge house and not really understanding how it functioned. Kit nodded.

"Come and meet some more people," he said, taking her hand and leading her across the terrace. "Some of the artists are back; they'd like to meet you."

She had barely taken a step when she heard a voice that made her stop and, dropping Kit's hand, she spun around.

"Perdita, I'm so sorry," Warren said, striding across the terrace. Silence had fallen as all eyes turned to them. "If I hadn't already asked you to marry me, I'd do it now. I'm a fool. I'm so sorry I upset you this morning. Please, my darling, please forgive me, I love you so much."

Warren opened his arms and Perdita, not really knowing what else to do, stepped into them, raising her face automatically and feeling the familiarity of his lips on hers. But for the first time, her heart did not race. She did not want to forgive Warren yet, not without a proper discussion about his attitude towards her and his remaining emotional entanglement with his ex-wife. He had staged this so she would not be able to question him. Suddenly, she felt manipulated and a wave of anger washed through her.

Aware, however, of a huge cheer in response to Warren's dramatic arrival, she felt her only option was to smile. When they were alone in her rooms later, she would give him hell, she decided. Releasing her, Warren bashfully took a bow as though he had not realised the impact of his apology. Forcing a smile, Perdita glanced around at the laughing faces. It was only then she caught a glimpse of Kit, his father and Jenny.

All three looked furious.

Chapter Three

Perdita and Warren left hand-in-hand. Drinks had turned into an impromptu party with Perdita being introduced to the remaining members of the Marquess House staff and the artists who were once more inhabiting the workshops. Had she not felt the constant brooding presence of Warren, it would have been a wonderful evening. Once the crowd created by his dramatic arrival had dispersed, her chilly manner had made it clear to Warren that he was not forgiven. Unmoved, he had walked off, intent on charming the crowd instead. In the end, Perdita was so irritated she had sought Kit out.

"Is it me," she had muttered as she splashed liberal amounts of gin into their glasses, "or is he behaving as though he owns the place?"

Unable to help himself, Kit had grinned, delighted to see Perdita so angry with Warren. "A bit," he admitted, aware it might be dangerous to say much more.

"Pompous git," Perdita had scowled, making Kit snort with laughter. But as she mingled back among the crowd, she was aware that she must stop treating Kit as though he were a substitute for Piper. *He's so easy to talk to, though*, she mused. Then, seeing Warren heading in her direction, she made a beeline for Alistair Mackensie in order to avoid her fiancé.

Now, as Perdita collected her computer bag from where she had left it in the Lady Isabel room and slung it over her shoulder, she dropped Warren's hand.

"We need to talk," she said.

"Here?"

"No, in my rooms. The party is breaking up, we won't be missed."

A few people passed them, calling good night. They replied in kind, then Perdita led the way into the Tudor hall and up the huge staircase.

"This house is amazing," murmured Warren gazing around. "The art collection is staggering."

Perdita opened her door and he followed her in.

"Stunning," he said. "Is that original William Morris wallpaper in the corner? The piece covered in protective Perspex?"

"Yes, it is," replied Perdita, flicking on a few lamps. As she did, the light over the huge portrait came on. Warren turned to look at it and raised his eyebrows in surprise, looking from the painting to Perdita and back again.

"It's uncanny," he said, moving nearer to examine the picture in more detail. "The likeness between the two of you is startling."

Perdita was not in the mood for his saccharine charms. She stalked into the kitchen where she made two mugs of tea before returning to the sitting room. Warren had fished his glasses from his pocket and was still scrutinising the portrait.

"I think this could be a John de Critz painting," he said as she sat on the sofa, placing the mugs on the long, low table in front of her. "He was the Serjeant Painter for James I. The clothes are the right era and it's certainly his style. Who is she? Do you know where Mary bought it?"

"I have no idea who it is and no, there are no records of its provenance," she snapped. "What's going on, Warren?"

"What do you mean, darling?" he asked, joining her on the sofa and picking up a mug with a genial smile.

There was a time, thought Perdita, *when I would have played along with this, pretended there was nothing wrong so as not to upset him and risk him storming off, but things have changed.*

"You really have to ask?" she said. "You ring me this morning to tell me the holiday is off because you need to nursemaid your ex-wife and her mother. You *order* me to stay here before turning up, uninvited and declaring undying love to me in front of a group of complete strangers, who also happen to be my employees. You then proceed to work the crowd all night as though you own the place. That, however, is irrelevant. The real issue is, what's going on between you and Jacqui? Until you answer, Warren, there is no hope for us."

Perdita wondered if he would respond. Throughout their relationship, she had never challenged him, always allowing herself to be swayed by his charm and his ability to twist situations to his advantage. Now she had seen through his emotional manipulation, she was aware his usual tricks would no longer work. Warren, staring at her through narrowed eyes, seemed to have drawn the same conclusion. He placed his mug back on the table, then fixed her with a cold look.

"Jacqui and I are still married."

Perdita felt sick.

"So, why did you propose to me?"

"I fell in love with you and knew that when Jacqui and I were divorced, I wanted us to be together."

"Why did you lie to me?"

"Would you have gone out with me if you'd known I was still married?"

"As long as you were separated, yes," she replied, then seeing the expression on his face, she shook her head in dismay. "I'm such a fool. You weren't even separated. Are you now?"

Warren sprang to his feet and walked to the window, looking out towards the black wildness of Llyn Cel. Perdita's eyes followed him. She was beginning to realise their relationship was nothing more than a web of fantasy.

"Answer me, Warren," she demanded. "Are you and Jacqui separated?"

"No," he said, turning to face her. "We were for a while, then her mother became ill and, somehow, we drifted back together. I do love you, Perdita. If you can give me some time, I'm sure things will work themselves out."

"Work themselves out? How? Or are you asking me to be your mistress?" she said, cold, hard fury rising in her. "I don't understand. If you and Jacqui are back together, what was that performance of undying love about earlier?"

"Because I saw you holding hands with that smug Mackensie kid and I wanted to show him who you loved," he snarled.

"And you think that's you, do you?"

Warren was about to speak, then he checked himself. "Perdita, I'm sorry, this is a mess and it's my fault."

"You're right, it is your fault."

Turning away from him, she bit back her tears.

"Would you like me to leave?" he asked. "I'll do whatever is best for you."

"*Best for me?*" she repeated. "Don't you think being honest would have been for the best?"

"I'm sorry, Perds," he repeated. Perdita looked away in disgust.

"You can stay tonight," she said, her voice low, "but I'd like you to leave in the morning. I need some time to think about what's *best for me.*"

He blanched at her sarcasm, hanging his head.

"Where shall I sleep?" he asked.

"There's a guest room," she replied, nodding towards the door. She slid off her engagement ring and placed it on the table, then gathering her handbag and her laptop case, she walked slowly into her bedroom and shut the door, locking it behind her.

Flinging herself on to her bed, she managed to hold back her tears until her twin appeared on the screen, then she let her misery erupt.

Chapter Four

"Don't you ever sleep?"

Perdita looked up. Kit was standing in the doorway, smiling.

"I thought I'd have an early start."

"Things didn't go well with Warren last night, then," he said dumping his bag on a chair before perching on the desk and looking sympathetically at Perdita. It was a statement rather than a question.

"Nope, it turns out he and Jacqui are still married. They're not even separated."

"What?" Kit sounded furious. "For God's sake, Perds, you're engaged. How could he have got that wrong? It's quite a major oversight."

"You'd think, wouldn't you? Anyway, past tense now, 'were' engaged," she held up her ring-free left hand. In an attempt to hide her despair, she forced her voice to take a lighter note. "He doesn't like you much," she continued, knowing this would amuse Kit, who grinned, delighted.

"Really?"

"He said the reason he staged his dramatic entrance was because he wanted to put you in your place."

"What had I done?"

"He'd seen you take my hand and, even though he hasn't admitted it, he was jealous. He called you: 'that smug Mackensie kid'."

Kit burst out laughing. "Kid! Doesn't he know I'm older than you?"

Perdita shook her head. "I didn't bother to enlighten him. I thought I'd leave him to wallow in his seething envy. I also decided not to tell him that you have a girlfriend."

Kit's dancing eyes shadowed slightly. He retrieved his bag before settling in the chair opposite Perdita. "Actually, I don't."

"Don't what?"

"Have a girlfriend. Lydia and I decided to gracefully call it a day when we went to Di and Stephen's wedding."

"Oh. Why?"

"We realised we'd grown apart and, while we still cared about each other, it wasn't the same. I think it's been a long time coming but it was the best decision for us both."

"You didn't tell me," said Perdita, confused as to why this was upsetting her so much. "You could have confided in me, I'd have been able to support you like you've helped me."

"Perds, there was nothing to tell," he said, "it didn't seem important." She turned away from him, strangely delighted by his unexpected announcement. "Are you all right?" he asked.

"Yes," she replied, quashing the rising tide of joy and forcing her emotions back to her wrecked relationship with Warren. "I'm not too bad. Sad and a bit shell-shocked but deep down, I've always suspected he wasn't being honest. Our relationship often felt slightly unreal, as though he were playing the part of the perfect boyfriend. I knew there were problems but I'd had so much unhappiness, I couldn't bear the thought of examining it and maybe destroying it. Fool's gold was better than no gold for a while. Maybe it's like you and Lydia, I was hanging on to something because it was there rather than because it was doing me any good."

Kit seemed about to say something, then changed his mind and instead said: "Is he still here?"

"No idea. He slept in the guest room and the door was shut when I crept out. I haven't been around the front to check whether his car has gone."

Kit squeezed her shoulder in an affectionate gesture and she gave him a watery smile.

"You'll be pleased to know, I read the manuscript last night," he said, changing the subject and producing his now well-thumbed copy with a flourish.

"It's so long, you must have been up all night!" she said, but her relief that they were no longer discussing Warren was palpable.

"Speed reading," he replied. "It was a very useful skill I acquired at university."

Perdita raised her eyebrows, impressed.

"What did you think?"

"You're right, the claims Mary makes are quite astounding, but it does all hang on the codex," he replied. "I'm intrigued to know what conclusions she drew in the final chapter. It's a shame she removed it."

Perdita pushed a few sheets of paper towards him.

"It is but if we have to guess, then these are the updates she made. I found them in her boxes of research and a few of them do corroborate some of her theories. However, unless we can find something tangible, the codex is our only source and, as Jenny pointed out, it could be a fake. Following all logical reasons, this is probably the reason why Granny pulled the manuscript."

"But you don't think so, do you?" said Kit.

"No and, to be honest, I don't think Granny did either."

"No, nor do I," he said. "I spoke to Dad about it last night after you and Warren had left the party. He told me that if Mary ever had even the slightest doubt about an item, she

263

would send it to us at Jerusalem, and it was removed from the public domain. She would have done the same with this if she had even the tiniest misgiving about its authenticity. When we're given a document, there are loads of processes we put them through before they're accepted as genuine, but Dad said Mary didn't put the codex forward for anything other than dating evidence, which is our most basic test."

"Did your dad give you any more information?"

"Not about the codex, no," replied Kit. "He did explain some of Mary's working method, though. When Mary was researching and writing a new book, she usually pulled together a very rough first draft to see if there was enough evidence to make a viable publication, and if there was, she would then involve Jerusalem to authenticate and validate any new documents. While this was happening, she would find her secondary source material and gradually piece it all together. However, it seems that, at the point she was about to use our services, your mother died and Mary abandoned the manuscript."

There was silence and Perdita once more felt the swooping sadness of loss. No matter which direction she travelled, everything seemed to bring her back to her mother's terrible car accident. It had always been the point where her life had changed but until now, she had never realised the full implications of her mother's death on all the lives of those who had loved her.

But then, I didn't know about all these people until a month ago, she thought.

Kit watched her. Then, in one of his usual about-turns, normally designed to distract her from her sadness, said, "Do you want to brainstorm?"

"I beg your pardon?"

"I've always wanted to say that," Kit grinned.

"Why?"

"Most of my work is done alone, it's good to be able to discuss this with you. I thought if we talked through what Mary has already found, it might point us towards details she missed."

Perdita's instinct was to refuse. Like Kit, she often worked alone and was used to puzzling things out by herself but she felt it would be churlish to refuse his suggestion when he had gone to the effort of reading the manuscript overnight.

"It could be helpful," she said, but she was tentative.

"Good, I think it'll help us sort out some of Mary's reasoning because, no offence, some of it is a little confused."

Perdita was about to leap to her grandmother's defence but then she paused. Kit was right, there were a few strands of Mary's manuscript that were very obviously still unfinished. This was compounded by the fact there was no final chapter offering Mary's conclusions.

"OK, let's give it a try," she said. "Would you like me to begin?"

Kit's expansive grin and nod made her smile and, although working in this manner felt alien, she decided it could be an interesting way to spend a few hours. It would also stop her lapsing into brooding darkness over Warren and his betrayal.

"Having been studying the codex, the pages aren't chronological," she began. "Some are pages of a journal, while others are letters. However, Granny tried to sort them into a more logical order in her manuscript."

Kit held his copy up as though it were an exhibit. Perdita rolled her eyes at him and continued, "The dates that *are* legible cover the period of Henry VIII's reign when he was married to Catherine Howard, so I agree with Granny's assessment that the bulk of the content was probably written by her when she was queen. Although, only a few pages are signed with what looks like a 'C', a 'K' and even more rarely, 'Catherine'; there are a few signed 'Kitten' or 'Kitty', which can be a derivative of Catherine and may have been how she preferred to be known, hence Granny's reasoning that these and the other unsigned pages were written by Catherine Howard, fifth wife of Henry VIII.

"However, it isn't all written by the same person. Some letters are signed 'IB' — potentially Lady Isabel Baynton, Catherine's half-sister through her mother, Jocasta Culpepper, and one of her chief ladies-in-waiting. Another is 'MD' and bears a crest and what looks like the remains of a wax seal — Granny thinks that could be Lady Margaret Douglas, Henry VIII's niece. During this period, she was engaged to Charles Howard, Catherine's brother, so it's possible she was closer to Catherine Howard than most of her biographies suggest. There's also another series of letters which are signed 'Kathy Knollys'. Although, all the letters in the codex seem to be addressed to either 'K' or 'Kitten' or 'C', and if they aren't, they usually discuss some aspect of this person's life."

"I was surprised about Margaret Douglas and Charles Howard," admitted Kit. "Especially as he seems to vanish from the records with no explanation."

"Strange, isn't it? About a year after Catherine disappears or was executed, if you want to take the traditional view, her brothers Charles and George are no longer traceable."

"There are letters from another woman too," said Kit. "She's often referred to as 'Lady A' or 'Sweet Lady A' or simply 'A', and this is one point I'm not convinced about." Kit flicked through to the relevant page and read Mary's list of suggestions. "Anne Parr, Mrs Herbert; Alice Wilkes Restwold;

Margaret Howard, Lady Arundell; Anne Shelton; Anne Bassett or Anne Foliot. The only one I think could be 'A' is Margaret Howard because she was Catherine's sister. The others might have been part of her household but there are no family connections. So, in my view, they would have been loyal to themselves rather than supporting a queen who was no longer in favour."

"I agree," said Perdita. "Although, I have another theory. Having read most of the codex now and assuming the unsigned pages were written by Catherine, then her marriage to Henry VIII was no spectacular romp, as the usual biographies and books would have us believe — it was a time of terror for the poor girl."

"What do you mean?"

"It's odd actually that Granny didn't expand upon this because I think it's the most important information. Catherine writes that the king is mad, that he beats her, possibly even rapes her on a regular basis."

"That's horrendous," said Kit appalled. "Do you think your Granny doubted the validity of it? Or didn't want to cloud Henry's image?"

"I don't know," said Perdita. "She certainly wouldn't have omitted it to spare Henry VIII's reputation. You know what a feminist Granny was; you only have to read her other books and her essays to understand her very clear views on women's rights. It was something I always admired about her. From what I've read, Catherine was like many other abused women. She presented a happy front to the outside world, but behind closed doors, the king was a cruel and violent thug and she lived in fear. Obviously, there was no rape within marriage back then and men were allowed to beat their wives with impunity, but who else might have experienced such behaviour?" Kit shook his head so Perdita continued. "Henry had another ex-wife living — do you think 'A' could be Anne of Cleves? They were the only two women alive who had been through the ordeal of being married to Henry. Isn't it possible they turned to each other for support?"

Kit considered this, tapping his pen on the table as he thought.

"Surely they were rivals, not friends?" he suggested. "One queen removed to make way for the other. Would Anne really have written to the woman who had replaced her on the throne of England?"

"The joint experience of their abuse at Henry's hands could have helped them break down the conventional barriers, so they reached out to one another for support. Don't you think it's possible they were friends?"

She turned the codex around so Kit could see the page she had been studying when he arrived.

"Look at this. Actually, I'll read it for you, her writing is a bit of a challenge: '*My sweet Lady A left for Richmond Palace this morning, how I will miss her. It seems such a short time ago that our positions were reversed and I, a mere maid, was requested to teach her to dance. How we enjoyed our afternoons together...*' but that's all there is, the rest of the page is torn away. When Henry VIII divorced Anne of Cleves, she was removed to Richmond Palace, which remained her main residence for some years. She was certainly still there in March 1542 as she became ill and Henry sent his own physician to treat her. This piece is dated 22 December 1541. And, Catherine Howard had been one of Anne of Cleves' maids of honour."

"But dance lessons? Is it documented anywhere that Catherine Howard taught Anne of Cleves how to dance?"

"No, not in any references in other biographies, but that doesn't mean it isn't true. Catherine is noted as being an exceptionally good dancer in numerous biographies and wasn't she supposed to have said, although, I suspect its apocryphal: 'There is no more time to dance' when she was arrested. So many documents have vanished that it's difficult to know exactly what did or didn't happen between the women at Henry's court. Not only that, according to most biographies by December 1541, Catherine was under house arrest at Syon Abbey for adultery, so why was she writing a journal that suggests she had spent time with Anne of Cleves? There is no evidence in either Catherine or Anne's biographies to suggest Anne ever visited Catherine during her incarceration."

"Maybe this is what your grandmother discovered and she expanded upon on it in the missing chapter?" said Kit.

"Perhaps," said Perdita. "I've noticed a few other things, too, that suggest Granny was still working on certain sections and was searching for other evidence."

"Go on," said Kit.

"First, there's the absolute absence of any mention of Jane Boleyn," said Perdita. "She was supposedly executed alongside Catherine Howard, which would suggest they were reasonably close, otherwise why would Jane have risked her life to allegedly help Catherine have an affair with Thomas Culpepper? Yet, there is no mention of her anywhere in the codex. There are no letters to or from her, no comments in Catherine's journal entries, nothing. If Jane was close enough to Catherine to be killed with her, why is there no evidence of her beside Catherine during this period?"

"You're right, that's strange," said Kit. "Mary mentions Jane a few times, but that's one of her unfinished strands."

"Which is a bit frustrating," admitted Perdita. "There's also something else that recurs in the codex that Granny doesn't expand upon, but is obviously my area of expertise."

"What's that?"

"Jewellery! Most particularly, Catherine's own jewellery, rather than the adornments of her position as queen. Catherine mentions a ruby ring and a silver locket. The locket was, apparently, a present from Lady Isabel Baynton and her husband, Sir Edward, but the ring is the most interesting piece."

"Why?"

"Throughout her manuscript, Granny refers to the codes Catherine used to send letters. Well, the ring keeps cropping up, particularly when there is a coded letter or a mention of a code or 'Sweet Lady A'," said Perdita. "In fact, going with the suggestion, 'Sweet Lady A' is Anne of Cleves, I think it was she who gave Catherine the ring. What's more, they seem to have used them to pass messages. I don't fully understand why Granny hasn't expanded upon it because if this was the case and a few of the comments back up my hypothesis, then it would show there was a strong friendship between the two queens."

"It's an interesting idea, Perds, but how would they have used rings to pass messages?"

"If the rings were identical, they could swap them. Tudor jewellery was often quite cumbersome and I've come across many examples which open to reveal small cavities where powders or notes could be concealed. There's a very beautiful locket ring that once belonged to Elizabeth I that opens to reveal two miniatures, one of Elizabeth and the other of her mother, Anne Boleyn. It's very chunky and would have been uncomfortable to wear, but it was something the Tudors loved.

They were always giving each other jewellery containing hidden messages, sometimes with a physical secret but more often with the use of symbolism.

"In 1527, Anne Boleyn finally gave in to Henry VIII's persistent courting by sending him a gift confirming that her love for him was reciprocated. It was a symbolic jewel, a small pendant with a picture of a maiden in a boat being tossed upon the waves. The symbolism of the boat meant Anne was asking Henry to protect her from the storms of life. The best way for a man to do this was to marry her. Anne's jewel gave Henry the spur he needed, and over the next seven years, he turned the religions and laws of England upside down in order to make the woman he loved his wife. Why would it be so strange, a few years later, for Anne and Catherine to pass each other notes or the cipher to codes in custom-made rings?"

Kit pushed his hands into his curly hair and tipped his chair back, thinking about Perdita's suggestion.

"I know it seems weird to us but it was an accepted method of espionage and subterfuge in the Tudor court," concluded Perdita.

Kit righted his chair so all four feet were on the ground.

"Perhaps, like me, Mary wasn't aware of the significance of jewellery so she missed the connection," he said.

"It's possible."

They lapsed into silence, both lost in thought.

"So, what would you like us to do next?" asked Kit after a few moments.

"I intend to continue studying the codex. Granny used a great deal of it, but there is a lot more here and I want to see if there are any clues as to what happened to Catherine's jewellery."

"In that case, do you have Jenny's scans? I'd like to use them to confirm that the writing in the Book of Hours matches those samples you have in the codex that are signed by Kathy Knollys. While I'm at it, I'll see if there's anything in it that could corroborate the codex."

Perdita walked over to the long boardroom table and sorted through one of the piles of paper. She extracted the documents Kit required and passed them over to him.

"Could you also look out for references to Jane Boleyn, 'Sweet Lady A' and either ruby rings or a silver locket."

Kit made a short list then glanced at the faded pages Perdita had given him. He considered them for a few moments, then fished his phone out of his pocket and spent ten minutes photographing the codex. When he clicked send, the state-of-the-art printer in the corner of the room whirred into life, spewing out a pile of high quality colour images. Perdita tried not to be intimidated by the sheer volume of technology that was now hers.

"Perfect," grinned Kit and made himself comfortable in front of the Book of Hours, his notebook, pen, a series of pencils and different strength magnified glasses lined up in neat rows beside him.

They set to; both in their element as they studied the ancient documents, checking and crosschecking references. After an hour, Perdita saw Warren's car drive past the window of The Dairy before disappearing around the bend and out of Marquess House. She felt a slight pang, then returned her attention to the codex, knowing the best way to deal with her ruined relationship was to distract herself with work and allow herself space to recover.

A few hours had passed and she was studying one of the numerous letters that had been written in code, comparing it

272

with the translation that was alongside it, when Kit pushed his chair back from the desk and stretched.

"Found something?" asked Perdita, pleased for an excuse to look up from the tiny lettering of the codes.

"I think so. I may even manage a smug grin."

"And why is that, Mackensie kid?" laughed Perdita.

"Because I've just finished translating this French comment from Lady Kathryn Knollys and, if what she said is true — and why wouldn't it be, this is her private journal — then she and a number of other women from Catherine Howard's court accompanied the young queen on a journey, the progress of which was carefully followed by 'the Lady Cleves'."

"No way! A journey without the king?"

"Yes, without the king, possibly without his knowledge — and what makes it so surprising is the date," he pushed the book and his translation towards her. Perdita looked down and gasped.

"April 1542. But history claims Catherine Howard was executed at the Tower of London on 13 February 1542. So Granny was right!"

"She was," said Kit, "this corroborates her findings in the codex."

"But if that's the case and Catherine Howard wasn't executed," said Perdita, "where did she go and what happened to her?"

PART FOUR: Northamptonshire, 1541

Chapter One

The room was in darkness; the tapestries hanging across the windows blocked out the bright summer sun. Figures moved in the stifling gloom of the best bedroom at Grafton Regis in Northamptonshire, the home of the duke and duchess of Suffolk, guiding the way through the blackness with shaded candles. A discreet tap on the door and the entry of another woman brought a momentary relief of light into the oppressive atmosphere. The new admittance hurried over to the heavily curtained and ornate bed that dominated the chamber.

"Is there any change, Issy?" Margaret Douglas' usually lilting, laughing voice was low and sombre.

"No," sighed Isabel. "Did you bring the sleeping draught? She gets fitful without it. The physician said she's to be kept as still as possible or there could be even more internal damage."

"Even more? Oh, poor Kitty, what did that brute do to her?" Margaret's voice was thick with unshed tears. She handed Isabel a small jug containing the sleeping tincture.

"Hush, Margaret, you know we've been instructed to tell everyone that Catherine was injured when her horse was stung by a bee. It went wild, she fell and was trampled. The king has no memory of beating her so he believes the story."

Margaret turned away, revolted by Isabel's words. Her uncle, the king, the man who held them all in his palm, had done this. She had always known he had a temper but she had excused it as one of the burdens of bearing the weight of kingship. What he had done to Catherine, she had realised, was not the lashing out of a man under too much pressure, this had been vindictive, deliberate and horrific. To her, this was unforgivable.

"How is Tom Culpepper?" she asked, her voice still low and troubled.

"Jane, Lady Rochford, is caring for him. His recovery is slow," replied Isabel.

Tom Culpepper had arrived too late to save Catherine; all he could do was throw himself on top of her to stop the king whipping her. He now lay in agony at Jane's family home of Great Hallingbury in Essex, his wounds infected, slipping in and out of consciousness while his wife tended to his every need.

"Poor Jane, she has very little luck with husbands," murmured Margaret. "Her first husband, George Boleyn, was framed for incest with his sister and executed, now Tom is lying in bed, beaten black and blue."

The figure in the bed stirred minutely, Isabel and Margaret immediately turned towards her.

"Thirsty," she croaked through swollen lips.

Isabel took a fresh cloth and dipped it into a goblet of sweet wine, then gently put the dampened linen to Catherine's lips, squeezing it to allow small drops to moisten her mouth. After a few moments, Catherine turned her head away and drifted back into a fitful sleep. Isabel put the cloth in the bowl Margaret held up for it, then stood up.

"She's sleeping, let's get some air."

They glided silently to the door and let themselves into the outer chamber. Isabel blinked, her eyes adjusting to the sunlight. Margaret Howard, Lady Arundell, another Catherine and Isabel's sisters, hurried forward.

"I'll sit with her, Issy," she said and slid into Catherine's darkened bedchamber.

Margaret Douglas led Isabel to a soft chair near the fireplace, then turned to the table where the other women were arranging plates of food.

"Victuals for Lady Baynton and myself," she commanded, and one of the maids of honour hurried to load up two trenchers and pour them sweet wine.

"Eat, Issy," said Margaret. "You won't be able to help Catherine if you weaken yourself by not taking nourishment."

"I know, my dear, but it's so difficult while she hovers between life and death."

The two women were silent for a moment, picking at the food in front of them.

"Has the physician given any indication when we might be able to move Kitten?" asked Margaret, eventually.

"The day after tomorrow," said Isabel. "The king is eager to move on, this is his summer progress after all. He wants to show Kitten off to the world, his beautiful, young wife with her incredible sense of style…"

"…who is lying broken and beaten in bed, thanks to him," interrupted Margaret, tears in her bright brown eyes.

"Hush, now," said Isabel, nervous that someone would overhear Margaret's outburst.

"All my uncle cares about is travelling to York to have words with my brother, the Scottish king," whispered Lady Douglas. "Well, I hope James leaves Uncle Henry standing alone at the altar at York Minster. He deserves to be publicly humiliated after what he's done to Catherine and Tom."

"Say nothing more, my dear," warned Isabel, "or you may put us all in danger. We must remain strong and get Catherine through this. The king sent a gift today to show Catherine how much he misses her company."

"What was it?"

"A diamond pendant in the shape of a heart, encased in a gold filigree cage."

"And is my uncle finding comfort elsewhere?"

"The duke of Norfolk and my dear husband have found him a companion," said Isabel, her eyes and tone glacial.

The morning after Catherine had been beaten, Thomas Howard had fabricated the story of her riding accident and offered to send the king a comely maiden to walk with him in place of the queen while she recovered. Delighted, the king had accepted what he saw as a kind offer, so the duke of Norfolk had sent one of Catherine's maids of honour, Katherine Tilney, accompanied by Joan Bulmer and Mary Lascelles.

"At least, if he is going to bed another woman, we should make sure she is a member of the family," he had reasoned to Edward Baynton. As an afterthought, he had sent young Francis Dereham, another member of the extended Howard clan, freshly returned from Ireland and betrothed to Katherine Tilney, to act as a calming male presence should the king begin to display signs of violence again.

"Is Tilney still with the king?" asked Margaret.

Isabel nodded. "She seems to think she'll be the next queen if Kitten dies."

"The heartless little strumpet."

"Exactly," scowled Isabel. "Tilney lacks many of the abilities necessary in a queen."

"Such as?"

"The ability to keep her legs shut!"

Margaret raised her eyebrows and a sly smile played around her lips.

"Has she bedded the king already?"

"Among other things, according to Edward," said Isabel. "Apparently, she has quite exotic tastes and the king seems to be more than amused. For now, at least — you know how quickly he can start to believe someone who delights him is a traitorous witch and demand their head."

They finished their meal in silence then Isabel excused herself, wanting to visit her husband and children before once more closeting herself in Catherine's bedchamber. After instructing the maid to clear their table, Margaret returned to Catherine's bedside.

"Has there been any change?" she asked Lady Arundell.

"No, she sleeps. Occasionally she's restless, but she seems very far away."

"If only we were all a long way from here," said Margaret. "When we reach York and my brother, the King of Scotland, Charles and I may return with him to Holyrood."

"Margaret, you can't!"

"I'm a princess of Scotland, as well as England, we'll be safer there and James has promised Charles a place in the privy chamber."

"And you?"

"I will serve his wife, Queen Mary," she replied. "One court in exchange for another. But when I am there, it will be harder for my uncle, the king, to stop my marriage to Charles Howard. Then we can somehow get Catherine to the Scottish court too, and safety."

"It's a lovely dream, dear," she said and patted Margaret's hand. Then a soft voice distracted them.

"Margaret?" whispered Catherine.

"Yes," they both replied, leaning avidly over her pale face on the pillows.

"The child," she gasped. "Did I lose the child?"

The two women exchanged a horrified glance.

"Oh, Kitten," said Lady Douglas squeezing her hand. "I think you did."

Catherine said nothing; turning her head away as tears slid down into her hair.

Chapter Two

"She was with child?" the duke of Norfolk asked again. "She definitely said she was with child?"

"Yes, your grace," confirmed Isabel. "However, due to the king's beating, she is no longer carrying the second in line to the throne."

"But don't you see," beamed the duke, "this is marvellous news. We know Kitten is fertile and, more importantly, we know the king is still able to father children."

"Are you completely insane?" snapped Isabel, observing Thomas Howard with disgust. "She may never recover and, if she does, who knows what damage he may have done when he whipped and kicked the child out of her?"

The duke of Norfolk glared back at Isabel.

"Your words could be construed as treason, Lady Baynton," he said, his pale grey eyes harder than granite.

"Yes, and your words could be construed as heartless. It's been nearly two weeks and Catherine has barely spoken. She's still slipping in and out of consciousness and when Lady Douglas tried to read her the note the king had sent, Catherine began to weep. It was several hours before she stopped."

"What are you saying?"

"Catherine has been taking beatings for nearly a year, but we've always been able to conceal any injuries. This time, the king's madness has reached even greater heights. Something must be done to protect her."

"You know as well as I do, Isabel, a man is allowed to beat his wife," replied Norfolk, dismissively.

"But if he beats her to death, it will be another opportunity lost to place a Howard on the throne."

Isabel hated herself for saying it, but she knew the duke would respond to the potential loss of dynastic ambition rather than any form of sentiment. Her words, she was sickened to see, had impact. She did not care though — if it meant Catherine was protected, she would say anything. The duke considered for a moment.

"We need to discover if anything particular provoked this episode," said Norfolk. "Do you think she may have told him about the child?"

"Why would that send him into a rage? It's what he wants!"

The duke of Norfolk shrugged.

"Why does the king do any of the things he does? Is Katherine Tilney still keeping Henry amused?" Isabel nodded. "Good, let that silly girl run wild so the king remains interested, while I decide what can be done to protect Kitten. Incidentally, how's Tom Culpepper?"

"His wounds are not healing, Jane is becoming increasingly concerned."

"Keep me informed of his progress too," said Norfolk, dismissing her with a nod.

Isabel was relieved to leave the duke of Norfolk's oppressive rooms for the fresh air of the courtyard. She knew the king was eager to be away; his sights focused on his meeting with his nephew, James V, the Scottish king, in York. Even his wife's injuries would not halt Henry's desire to assert his dominance.

As she rounded the corner, Isabel's heart sank. Walking towards her was the dowager duchess of Norfolk, Agnes Tilney, accompanied by a smug-looking Katherine Tilney, the ever-present Francis Dereham and a slightly more pale-faced Joan Bulmer. Mary Lascelles was nowhere in sight. Isabel suppressed a shudder. Despite the many hours Katherine Tilney had spent with the king, she had obviously not yet seen his darker side. Although, on closer inspection, Isabel noticed a bruise on Bulmer's neck — perhaps she was the one who received the beatings while Tilney watched, or God forbid, maybe held her down with Dereham's help. There had always been a cruel streak in the Tilney girl.

"Lady Baynton," said the dowager duchess, nodding a greeting. Isabel replied in kind. As the small group passed by, she heard the duchess comment, "Not so grand now, is she?" Katherine Tilney giggled and Francis Dereham snorted; only Joan Bulmer remained tight-lipped and silent.

Isabel sighed. *They were welcome to their silly games,* she thought. Her only concern was keeping her younger sister safe and, while Tilney might have the dubious pleasure of bedding Henry, as his current mistress, no matter how much the Tilney-Howards crowed over their perceived success at bagging a king, it was still Catherine Howard who was the queen. *If she survives,* thought Isabel gloomily, but as she entered the queen's chambers her mood lifted. The women were smiling. Had a miracle occurred? Was Catherine awake at last?

"Issy, come quick!" gushed Kathryn Knollys. "Kitten's awake and sitting up…"

Lady Knollys dragged Isabel by the hand into the inner chamber. Her face still swollen and bruised, Catherine was propped up against a pillow and her sister, Lady Arundell, was gently spooning broth into her mouth. She managed a small smile when she saw Isabel. Margaret Douglas, sitting on the other side of the bed, nodded to Isabel, a look of relief on her face.

"Where's Jane?" whispered Catherine.

"She's nursing Tom," replied Margaret, squeezing Catherine's hand. "Tom saved your life but he took quite a beating too."

Catherine closed her eyes again and shook her head when Lady Arundell offered the spoon up to her lips again.

"And the king?" she gasped.

"Uncle Norfolk told him you fell from a horse after it was stung by a bee and went wild," said Isabel. "He said the horse was trampling you when Culpepper came to your rescue, hence the reason you were both so badly injured."

"Lies," Catherine hissed. "All lies. He did this to me when I told him I thought I was with child."

"What happened, Kitten?" asked Isabel, taking Margaret's hastily vacated position by the side of the bed.

"He summoned me to his room and wanted to bed me but I explained my suspicions. At first he was delighted, then suddenly he changed, said I was lying or it belonged to another man. He had a horse whip…"

Her voice tailed off and Catherine closed her eyes again. Isabel did not want to hear the rest. She gathered her sister into a gentle embrace.

"Tell Lady Anne, the former queen," whispered Catherine into Isabel's ear. "Use the code in my Bible, you'll find it in the book of Esther, chapter one, verse 17, 'For the queen's behaviour will become known to all women, so they will despise their husbands in their own eyes'."

Catherine sank back, exhausted, into her pillows, her face ghostly. Isabel stared down at her younger sister, then with a breaking heart that Catherine's life had become such a web of subterfuge, bustled off to find the Bible and fulfil the queen's request.

Chapter Three

The king's progress northwards was inexorable. Neither torrential rain and muddy roads, nor his wife's ill health, halted the march of Henry and his court. For some weeks, Catherine was carried in a curtained litter but as her bruises faded, the king once more insisted she take to her mare, Moonbeam, and ride at his side. Dressed in a cloth of silver riding habit to complement his impressive cloth of gold cloak, the moon to his sun, his celestial lover, he wanted all the world to see his beautiful young wife and marvel at his virility.

Catherine smiled sweetly, waving to the crowds that watched them pass. But every evening when they stopped, either at a nobleman or lord's house, or in one of the extravagant tents used to create the miniature city that accompanied the king, she was relieved that it was Katherine Tilney who was summoned to share the king's bed. Although, she suspected her reprieve from his violence would not last long. After all, she was the queen and had a job to do, to provide an heir, not only for the sake of her country but to further her uncle Norfolk's dynastic ambitions.

A short interview with him a few days earlier had made his position clear.

"Isabel has told me you were with child," he had begun without preamble. No longer shocked by the harshness at court, Catherine had nodded. "Good. It was unfortunate that this happened," he waved his hand vaguely towards her fading cuts and bruises, "but next time, tell *me* first, then I will be able to ensure this situation is not repeated. We need you pregnant and a Howard heir to take the throne. The Seymour boy will be no problem to relegate to second place once you have done your duty."

He had swept away, leaving Catherine to wonder exactly how her uncle intended to protect her from the king. She had always assumed it was a duty of a wife to tell her husband about a pregnancy first, but obviously when you were queen, the rules were different. The thought of succumbing to the king's rotting bulk again made her feel sick. Since his last terrible seizure and the ensuing violence, she also found herself terrified of every aspect of him. When he touched her, which he did as often as possible, even when they were in public, she had to force herself not to go rigid with terror.

Although, at a banquet the previous week, she was not the only one who had been shocked by the king's strange behaviour. He had been laughing with Charles Brandon who, like Henry, had a much younger and very beautiful wife, when the king had begun bragging about how much more nubile she was in comparison with the duchess of Suffolk. To her disgust and most of the nobles around them, Henry had pulled Catherine onto his lap and begun unlacing her dress in order to show her breasts to the duke. It was Brandon who had laughingly brought the episode to a halt and dispatched his wife with Catherine back to her ladies before Henry could strip her naked in front of the entire banquet.

Now, as Catherine led her ladies to their overnight rooms, she felt nothing but pity for the foolish, giggling Katherine Tilney as she swept off in the opposite direction, obviously summoned by the king. Rumour had it Katherine was wanton and the king enjoyed watching her perform various dances and acts, sometimes alone, sometimes not. Catherine shuddered at the thought and also felt guilty at the relief she felt now the king was momentarily distracted. She would not even have cared if he decided to replace her with Tilney, make that silly fool queen.

"Bad news, Kitten," said Isabel as Catherine sank onto her ornate bed. "The king has requested your presence this evening after banquet."

"Oh no," she sighed.

"I've spoken to your brother George. The room where the king is lodged has a secret exit. It's behind the panel by the window and leads to a doorway that opens out into a small courtyard. There's a corridor which can bring you safely back here, so we'll ensure it's unlocked in case you have to make a run for it," said Margaret Douglas, who was unpacking Catherine's things.

"Charles and my husband Francis will be outside the door," continued Kathryn Knollys as she helped Margaret to shake out one of Catherine's gowns. "Shout and they'll come in to subdue the king while you flee."

"This is ridiculous," sighed Catherine. "No doubt Uncle Norfolk is behind this new plan to keep me safe now he knows I'm fertile."

The silence that greeted this statement was all the answer she needed. Rolling over, she buried her face in her pillow. There was a time when she had thought her uncle had cared for her; was the father she had never had. Now, she realised he had been honing her potential as a future brood mare to lure the king. He had successfully wafted both Anne and Mary Boleyn in front of the king. Although, once Anne had been queen he had been furious at what he saw as the Boleyn defection, when he felt they had cut him out of their rise to power and wealth. He also had very little control over Elizabeth, Anne's daughter, and because of this, he was obviously determined to be in full control of any royal heirs Catherine might produce. Edward

Seymour, the earl of Hertford and eldest brother of the former queen, Jane, had done the same. Strategically positioning himself as potential regent should the king die before Prince Edward reached his majority.

"Men and their petty schemes," she muttered. "They would all come to nothing if it weren't for us women, yet do they ever understand this simple fact?"

"You are becoming as wise as Master Thomas More," said Isabel.

"And look what happened to him when he crossed my darling husband," she replied. She drew her finger across her throat. "Lost his head completely."

"Why, your grace, that's treason," said Margaret Douglas in mock horror.

"So chop off my head and be done," replied Catherine. "The bright sting of the executioner's axe would be a lot less painful than taking another beating from the king."

Isabel, Kathryn Knollys and Margaret Douglas exchanged a worried glance. They were Catherine's constant companions these days, along with Margaret Howard, Lady Arundell, another of Catherine and Isabel's many sisters. When Jane had returned home to nurse Tom Culpepper, Lady Arundell had taken Jane's place in the inner circle. She was also useful as a spy among Catherine's other ladies, so her visits, although welcomed by the others, were often fleeting. Such a visit had just ended, with Lady Arundell assuring them they were safe to speak freely with no unfriendly ears to hear.

"I have sent word to my half-brother, King James V of Scotland," murmured Margaret. Catherine had once more buried her face in the pillows, but gave the minutest nod to indicate she was listening. "He has said he will give safe passage to myself and Charles, and a position in his court. He said any members of my entourage would also be welcome."

The words were loaded with meaning and Catherine felt a small thrill of fear and anticipation. She had an escape route. But how far would she get before the king sent his best soldiers to track them down? While she did not care whether she lived or died, she did not want the blood of those she loved spilled for her sake.

"He said his queen, Mary of Guise, would welcome the presence of noble ladies into her court, especially now," Margaret continued.

They all knew there were problems at the Scottish court. Only a few months earlier, King James V had been in a wonderful position. He had an heir, James, Earl of Rothesay, a sturdy one year old, and the queen had given birth to another son, Robert Stewart — but to the horror of their royal parents, both boys had died on the same day, 21 April 1541. Little Robert had only been nine days old. In one terrible blow, the king had lost both his heirs and, with his own health not always robust, it was no wonder his uncle, Henry VIII, wished to meet him to discuss future relations between Scotland and England.

Imagine if she had been able to escape while she was still pregnant. Her child would have grown up in the Scottish court. *It could have been chosen as James' heir*, she thought. Then reality hit her and her heart twisted with pain. But my child is dead, beaten out of me by its father.

"And if I agree to this dream of escape to the wild north," she said, "what would happen to the members of my family who have been left behind?"

She sat up and looked at the three beloved but ashen faces.

"You are all wonderful to risk your safety even talking about such plans," she said, "but I can't play games with your lives. I will see the king tonight and whatever will be, will be. Just promise me, if he does kill me, you will get away from him before he has a chance to hurt any more of the people I love."

Chapter Four

"Keep your eyes shut, my sweetheart," boomed Henry, his hand sliding up her waist to stroke the underside of her breast. She was perched precariously on the front of his saddle as they approached his extravagant new home in the north. What had once been St Mary's Abbey was now a vast and ornately decorated palace and the king had insisted on blindfolding her so she would see it first from its best angle. "Now, my love, what do you think?"

The soft cloth was removed and Catherine gasped. The building before her was a miniature, and equally exquisite, version of Hampton Court Palace, a building that Catherine still considered to be a magical and enchanted place.

"It's beautiful, Henry."

"Good!" he laughed. "And in this palace, we will make my duke of York. Sweet Catherine, if you had given me a son, your coronation would have been held at York Minster this very day. You will try harder and we will have a son, or I will be angry."

Catherine felt herself tremble with fear. Henry's words may have been said calmly but she recognised the weight of his threat.

"Sir Edward will show you your quarters," announced the king as he passed her down to the gathered attendants, lifting her as though she weighed no more than a child. "They have been decorated especially for you — you like mermaids and flowers, don't you? It's what your ladies told me — so I hope they are to your taste. Now I must attend to the business of state."

The king swept away and, for a moment, Catherine was left pondering the contradictory nature of her husband. He would go to the effort of decorating her rooms with mythical creatures because she liked them but in the same sentence was the veiled threat over her failure to provide an heir. Despite the bustle around her, Catherine suddenly realised that, in that moment, she was alone. Her ladies were still half an hour behind her and in the chaos of the court's arrival, for once there was no one stuck to her side.

"I will walk in the gardens," she called to her brother George who was helping the other members of the privy chamber to organise the muddle of people, trunks, goods and animals.

"Alone? Are you mad, Kitty?" he shouted over the hubbub.

"Send Isabel when she arrives, I won't go far," she replied. Then, gathering up her skirts, she walked purposefully through the rose-covered archway towards what were clearly the newly designed gardens.

As the noise of the court receded, she slowed to a dawdle, enjoying the quiet of the garden. Breathing in the early autumn air, she allowed her shoulders to sag. If the king had not beaten her, if she had not lost her child, she would now be preparing for a coronation. She wondered, *would that have made her safe? It had not saved Anne Boleyn*, she thought. *Oh, to be free of this nightmare.*

Trailing her fingers along the hedgerows of yew and rosemary, adding their fragrance to the air as she bruised their delicate leaves, she ambled deeper into the lushly scented garden until she reached a small square with a fountain bubbling at its heart. Sinking onto a stone seat, she shut her eyes, reached for the silver locket around her neck and slowly slid it backwards and forwards along its chain. She found the movement soothing and, as she relaxed, she allowed her mind to wander. Tonight, she would be summoned again. The reprieve that had been Henry's affair with Katherine Tilney was over. It was now business as usual.

Once more, she considered the offer Margaret Douglas had made — to whisk them all away to her brother's court in Scotland. It was a dream, she realised. Henry would hunt and kill her if she attempted such an escape. She sighed, turning her thoughts to the arrival of King James V, Margaret's half-brother. *I wonder what he will be like*, she mused. *Will he be as attractive as his sister?* She laughed at herself: the girl who had once watched the boys shyly from the edges of the clamouring crowd at her step-grandmother's might have thought such a thing, but as queen, such dreams were lost to her forever.

Her mind went to the planned events of the next few weeks. This meeting of kings would be the grand ending to Henry's triumphant progress through his kingdom. A moment when he would negotiate a peace treaty with Scotland and his nephew, James. A thought suddenly struck Catherine: *I wager he won't come.* From where this came, she had no idea, but she knew it to be true. James would renege on the meeting and Henry would be furious.

A high-pitched giggle nearby disturbed her reverie. *Tilney*, she thought, shuddering. She felt nothing but sympathy for the poor girl who seemed to think she was soon to take Catherine's place next to Henry as queen consort. Tilney's constant companions, Joan Bulmer and Francis Dereham, seemed to believe this too; only Mary Lascelles had sensed the danger and recently asked to be dismissed from court claiming ill health. Granting Mary leave to go, the last Catherine had heard was that she was staying with her pious Protestant brother, John.

Out of the corner of her eye, Catherine saw Tilney, Joan Bulmer and Francis Dereham scurry into view. Adopting an imperious expression, she wondered idly how they would react when they discovered her on the stone bench. Tilney led the way, her thin face alight with excitement. She turned to say something to Joan, then saw Catherine and stopped abruptly. There was a suggestion of hesitation before all three sank to their knees. Catherine counted slowly to ten before she allowed them to rise. Even when they were girls at her step-grandmother's house in Lambeth, she had never liked Katherine Tilney. A manipulative bully, she had forced Joan Bulmer into many tricky situations and had once tried to ensnare Catherine into her circle of intriguers, but she had slid away from them and their often cruel antics.

"Your Majesty," said Katherine, her voice ringing with contempt, "we thought you would be inspecting your apartments."

"You were wrong," replied Catherine. "Did you want something, Katherine?"

"No, we were, we were…"

"Then, please, leave me in peace. Your help is probably required in arranging my rooms," she said, dismissing them and putting them in their place with one effortless glance. Greatly affronted, the trio departed.

"She might order me about now," hissed Katherine Tilney, unaware she was still within earshot, "but I will soon be queen. I shall tell the king I am carrying his child."

"It didn't work for Mary Boleyn," said Joan spitefully. "Her daughter was illegitimate, so was Bessie Blount's, and she had a son…"

"Shut up, Bulmer," snapped Katherine. "I'll tell him Catherine Howard had an affair with you, Francis. That should have her thrown in the Tower, then I can comfort Henry."

"And what about me?" snarled Dereham.

"I'll have you pardoned and blame stuck-up Catherine..." Their voices tailed off as they wandered away.

Stupid, stupid girl, thought Catherine. Waiting until the three intriguers had disappeared, Catherine rose from her seat and smoothed out her gown. With heavy feet, she retraced her steps. But before she reached the house, Isabel, Kathy and Margaret rushed towards her.

"Where have you been?" gasped Isabel. "Edward and Charles are convinced the Spanish have kidnapped you!"

Catherine laughed. "Alas no, I was walking in the garden where I met Tilney and her rabble."

As her women escorted her back to the house and her spectacular new rooms, she told them what she had overheard.

"I'll tell Edward at once," said Isabel. "They are empty threats, but he should know what the silly girl is saying. Has she no idea how dangerous it is to speak in such a manner?"

Catherine swept through her apartment, nodding to her ladies, and into her inner sanctum.

"Your correspondence," said Edward Baynton, who was bustling around Catherine's rooms. "This appears to have followed us from Richmond in Surrey," he said pushing a small, square envelope into her palm. She nodded and slid it into one of the hidden pockets in her capacious sleeves. It was from Anne of Cleves and Catherine could not wait to read it.

"Do you think we will be in York long?" asked Catherine. Edward shrugged.

"Who can say, Kitten?"

Catherine glanced at the other letters Edward had left on the small writing table. "This is from Great Hallingbury in Essex," she exclaimed. "It must be from Jane, perhaps there is good news of Tom."

But as her eyes raced across the small note, her face paled.

"Tom's dead," she whispered, sinking into a chair.

"No!" exclaimed Edward, taking the letter from Catherine's shaking hand.

"And Jane has lost her mind," continued Catherine. "This letter is from her father, Henry Parker, Baron Morley. She is being cared for at the family home but he wishes her illness to be kept private."

The women huddled together, tears welling in their eyes.

"Poor Jane," murmured Margaret Douglas. "To have survived so much and remained strong for so long, this was one thing too many."

Catherine walked to the vast mullioned window and stared out across the elaborate grounds, her heart pounding with fear and grief. All she could think was that Tom Culpepper's death and Jane's madness were bad omens, shadows of terror looming over their frightening and precarious lives, pushing them further into the darkness. *We are cursed*, she thought. *We exist in this world of jewels and jousting, banquets and masques, the sparkle and finery of endless enjoyment. Yet underneath this glossy veneer, we fight for breath each day as though we are drowning. Which of us will be next? Who will have their life snatched away by the whim of Fate?*

In the garden below her, she saw Katherine Tilney laughing and shuddered.

Chapter Five

They had been in York for three weeks when the storm of Henry's temper broke over their heads. So attuned was Catherine to her husband's violent outbursts, she could tell his mood from the thud of his uneven, limping footfalls as he approached her rooms. Even she, though, was unprepared for the sight of him as he came crashing into her rooms.

"Where is my niece?" screamed the king, his face puce, his eyes almost swallowed by the fleshiness of his face. "Did she know about this? The deceitful little whore…"

Horrified, Catherine leapt from her chair, resting her small white hand on Henry's arm, she whispered, "My good lord and husband, what ails you? Here sit, let me help you?"

She was shaking, terrified his arm would sweep out and knock her to the floor, but she was determined to protect her ladies, particularly the king's two daughters who had never seen their father in such a fury and were seated near her by the fire.

"Where is she?" he seethed. "Lady Douglas, daughter of my accursed slut of a sister. Where is she, wife? Don't hide her, it will be worse for you…"

Catherine turned helplessly to Isabel. "She is resting…" she began.

"Resting!" he screamed. "Fetch her now or you will pay the price…"

"I am here, Uncle," came a cold voice from the doorway behind the king that led to one of Catherine's inner rooms. He spun around to face Margaret, who stood tall and regal, her brown eyes fixed unwaveringly on her uncle's face. Catherine moved to stand between them but Isabel grabbed her arm, holding her still while the king advanced on his niece.

"Margaret, no," gasped Catherine struggling to free herself from Isabel's grip, fully aware of what Henry could do when he was in such a state.

"Did you know?" he asked, his voice low and menacing. "Was this a plan you concocted to embarrass and ridicule me? You and your vile Scottish half-brother?"

Catherine's heart was pounding so fast she could barely breathe. Even though they had waited patiently, it was clear the king of Scotland was not going to uphold his side of the bargain. It appeared he had never intended to treat with his uncle in York and, furious at being publicly humiliated, Henry wanted someone to blame. For a moment, Margaret contemplated her uncle, then she sank into a deep curtsey, her head bowed.

"Uncle, I would never conspire to hurt you," she said. "My brother sent word nine days ago that our mother, your sister Margaret, is ill. It shocks me that he has not written. Perhaps someone has deliberately kept his word from you in order to create discord within our family."

Catherine held her breath, waiting to see how Henry would respond. She glanced around and felt sick as she realised that Elizabeth was the nearest to her father. If he lashed out, she would be the one to receive the full force of his blow. Oh, please God, Catherine prayed, let him be calm, let him be calm, protect the innocent Lady Elizabeth.

The king was still staring down at Margaret, his teeth bared, but the colour in his face was receding and his stance was softening, his muscles relaxing.

"My sister is ill?" he muttered. "Why did no one inform me? Rise, Maggie, rise. Come, let us write to your mother and see if we can help with what ails her. I will write to your brother today to offer my help. His letter must indeed have gone astray. Catherine, we will be leaving shortly, it is time I returned to London. My son will be wondering where I am."

Henry leaned forward and raised Margaret to her feet, leading her from the room, his face now full of concern. His guard followed him and Catherine's heralds shut the doors with a defiant ringing slam. The silence in the room was tangible. No one dared to move. Catherine knew all eyes were upon her. Still trembling all over, now from the relief that they had all survived the king's rage unscathed, Catherine forced a tremulous smile to her face. The women were all staring at her in confusion; none of them had ever before witnessed the swiftness of mood change that could overtake the king. She knew it was her place to reassure them, convince them all was well with their monarch.

"My ladies," she said, trying to control the tremor in her voice, to make it sound warm and consoling, "the king was out of sorts. Let us all pray that his wisdom and kindness have now been restored. Lady Mary," she said turning to the king's eldest daughter, "perhaps you could lead the ladies in a prayer for the health and majesty of the king, your father."

Startled, Mary nodded. "Of course, Lady Stepmother."

"Lady Baynton, Lady Knollys, perhaps you would accompany me to my bedchamber so we can pray in private for my husband and good sovereign lord." She gave a small smile and, on shaking legs, led the way to her bedchamber.

Kathryn Knollys had barely shut the door when Catherine collapsed on to the bed. Tears sprang to her eyes.

"I thought he was going to hit Elizabeth," she gasped. "She was so near him. If he'd lashed out he would have killed her..."

Panic was rising, threatening to overwhelm her.

"Kitten, it's over," said Isabel gathering her younger sister into a hug. "He's calm again. Margaret will resolve this and now we can return to London."

Wiping her eyes, Catherine nodded. She knew Isabel did not truly understand the fear she felt whenever she was near the king. To beat her was Henry's prerogative as her husband: her status of queen did nothing to protect her from the law that stated she was his property and he could treat her as he saw fit. Yet, she feared him more each day. His constant mood swings left her increasingly terrified as she awaited each fresh attack on her person. Her ladies tried to protect her but, while they could heal her bruises, they could not heal the scars Henry left on her mind. Taking a shuddering breath, she tried to calm her frantically beating heart and focus on the news they would soon be returning to London.

"Yes, you're right, Issy," she said. "We must begin to pack. No doubt Henry will want to be on the move soon."

Three days later, the order was given for the court to return to London. The huge procession slowly wound its way from York, back down the length of the country, heading for the capital. As they wended their way, news came of the death of Margaret Tudor, Henry's elder sister and last remaining sibling. Although he had always been jealous of her status as queen of Scotland, at the news of her demise, Henry fell into a fit of melancholy, refusing to see anyone but the members of his privy chamber. Finally, on 26 October 1541, they arrived at Windsor Castle, only to be greeted with the alarming news that the king's son, Prince Edward, was seriously ill.

Catherine sat with the rest of the court in St George's chapel within the castle, praying for the recovery of the little prince:

the shining hope of the Tudor dynasty. She also prayed that she was with child. Not only would a child secure her position, but if she bore a son, he would be Edward's successor and, in such turbulent times, only this, she believed, could save her from Henry's wrath.

Finally, word came that Prince Edward was recovering and Henry decreed that special prayers should be said around the country for his son and his beautiful wife, Catherine, who had helped to pray his son back to health. Each day, Catherine waited to be summoned to Henry's bedchamber but no such request came. The king was barricaded in his private rooms with his most trusted advisors, and rumours that he was soon to dispose of Catherine in order to remarry Anne of Cleves crept through the corridors of power.

Catherine ignored them, but with no word from Henry, she was becoming increasingly nervous. One rainy afternoon, she sat beside the fire, her women all around her, listening while Margaret read to them from the Bible. Isabel and Kathryn Knollys were bent over their tapestry while Catherine's other sister, Margaret Arundell, wound the precious embroidery silks into skeins before slipping each one into its own protective cotton sleeve. Her other women were variously employed either on their sewing or writing, while others sat quietly, absorbing the story Margaret told in her beautiful lilting voice, when suddenly the peace of their afternoon was shattered by the tumult of marching boots and a threatening hammering on the door.

"Open up, in the name of the king!"

She nodded for her herald to throw open the doors and stood as Henry's personal guard in their distinctive Tudor-green livery, marched in.

"Your Grace," said their sergeant dropping to his knee as he addressed her. "We come on the word of the king."

"What is going on?" she asked, her voice shaking as she stared at the rows of guards, swords glittering at their waists, eyes averted and faces blank.

"We have a warrant of arrest," he announced. Catherine felt her stomach turn to ice — it was happening again — Henry had removed her cousin Anne Boleyn on trumped-up charges, now he was doing the same to her. But the guard continued, "For the woman known as Katherine Tilney and her accomplices Joan Bulmer and Francis Dereham."

From behind her, Catherine heard a scream of fear.

"No," she gasped. "No, they are under my protection. Let me speak to the king."

She had taken a few faltering steps when Charles Brandon, the duke of Suffolk, pushed his way through the guards to her side. He caught Catherine in his strong arms and held her still.

"There is nothing you can do," he whispered. "The king is convinced Tilney is a witch and that she cursed not only Prince Edward but also Margaret Tudor. He also thinks she has cursed you, which is why you are not yet with child. By removing her, he is convinced you will be protected from her evil ways."

"But…" stuttered Catherine, trying to make sense of events through her rising tide of panic.

"You have no choice, Kitten," said the duke urgently. "If you fight for Tilney, the king will believe you were part of the plot and it will be your head on the block. Let her go, Kitten, there's nothing you can do to save her, Bulmer or Dereham. Dereham is already in the Tower."

Blinking back tears of terror, she nodded and the duke released her. Hating herself, she stood aside and allowed the guards to take Katherine Tilney and Joan Bulmer, two young girls, white-faced and sobbing with terror. As the doors slammed shut behind them, the women wailed in shock and fear.

"Fetch my uncle Norfolk," whispered Catherine to Suffolk. "He has been closeted with the king these past days. This is his doing."

"Don't fight it, Kitten," warned Suffolk. "You cannot win."

Catherine glared up at him. "I've got to try," she replied and swept into her inner chamber, followed by her ladies.

Chapter Six

Thomas Howard, the duke of Norfolk, was beside himself with glee.

"In the Tower," he chortled. "Jumped up little madam. Why did she think she was anything other than a dispensable whore? Giving herself airs and graces, imagining she was going to be queen. You silly Howard girls are all the same, thinking you can outwit me. Madge Shelton took up her position on her back when Anne was carrying a child; Tilney was merely another body to keep the king satisfied. Better one of our family than someone else trying to usurp our place of power."

"Despite your plans, sir, it seemed Katherine Tilney was not entirely loyal to her family. She was spying for the Seymours too," said Edward Baynton, "and believed she could play you off against one another in order to gain a throne."

"Then she's an even bigger fool than I first thought — a Seymour help a Howard to power? Greed and lust, that's what drove the fornicating little goose, and now she is being suitably punished!"

Catherine, who had been sitting white-faced by the roaring fire, staring at the flames while her uncle crowed over Katherine Tilney's downfall, started at these words. She looked up, her blue eyes steely, ready to shout her uncle down, but her brother Charles caught her eye and gave a minute shake of his head. Tilney's arrest still horrified her. Admittedly, she had never liked the girl much, but she would not have wished this on her or anyone for that matter.

"I knew those letters to Cranmer would work!" chuckled the duke, rubbing his hands in delight.

"What letters?" asked Charles.

"I persuaded that pompous fool John Lascelles and his witless sister, Mary, to send a few of my suspicions to Thomas Cranmer, the Archbishop of Canterbury, claiming them as their own," he laughed.

"Mary? But she asked to be relieved of her court duties because of ill health, she wanted to return to her husband…" began Catherine. But the duke, still smirking, cut across her.

"No she didn't," he crowed in delight. "Well, she did, but on my orders. Mary Lascelles wasn't sick, she was in my pay. I needed her reunited with her idiot brother so I could feed them a few suggestions, but I couldn't be seen to be involved, hence my idea of her asking for leave from your court, Kitten."

"What sort of suggestions?" asked Catherine quietly, raging inside at her uncle's manipulation of all their lives.

"That Tilney was in league with the devil, you know, that sort of thing," said the duke dismissively. "I also suggested that Dereham had been her lover throughout her time with the king and that she might try to pass his bastard off as the king's child. Cranmer clearly felt there was enough evidence to warrant further investigation into the possibility of treason."

"Treason on what grounds?" said Catherine.

"Fornicating with other men while she was the king's concubine," responded her uncle.

"I thought that was only treason for a queen," she said.

"The king is easily persuaded if he thinks his royal personage is in danger."

"It would have been considerate if someone had informed me that my ladies and my secretary were about to be arrested. This affects me and my court directly. Why did you not tell me about your plans?"

"Inform you?" her uncle was incredulous. "What business is it of yours to meddle in court politics? I've never heard anything so ridiculous. You might be queen, but your duty is to open your pretty little legs and give the king an heir, not to become involved in men's work."

"Except, when I fulfilled that duty, my insane husband beat the child out of me," she said. "Now he intends to murder two women and one man under my care. Would you not say that I'm involved, Uncle?"

Catherine's voice had not risen above a quiet murmur, yet every word she uttered fell into the silent room with the impact of a cannon ball.

"You say we women are disposable — Mary and Anne Boleyn, Madge Shelton, even poor Jane Boleyn. Now it's Tilney and Bulmer. Who's next? Me, if I don't produce a child soon? You say you don't need us women, but without us you would have no heirs, no daughters to barter with in the marriage market. You cannot sit on the throne but, as a woman married to the king, I can. Take care, Uncle, you have made me queen. While he is sane, my husband does all he can to please me. You would be wise to remember that on occasion."

"Are you threatening me?" laughed the duke.

"No, just explaining that I might not always be on the end of the string when you wish to play puppet master with my life, and the lives of those under my care."

There was an uneasy silence; the duke was so stunned by Catherine's unexpected words that he did not have a response. Edward Baynton spoke, bringing the conversation back to the matter in hand.

"Have you implicated any of the Seymour men yet, your grace?" he asked, taking a step forward in order to block the duke's view of Catherine. "If you have, we need to remove any of their kinswomen from Catherine's court immediately."

Thomas Howard was still staring wonderingly at Catherine, but he turned his attention to Baynton.

"No, not yet, but that's not to say I won't at a later stage..."

An urgent knock on the door only added to the tension in the room. On the duke's shout of "Enter," Henry Howard, earl of Surrey, the duke's eldest son, thundered in and bowed. Surrey looked white-faced and strained as he handed a note with an official seal to his father.

"The dowager duchess of Norfolk has been arrested. She's being taken to the Tower. She's insisting you go to her," he said.

Even the duke was startled by this unexpected turn of events.

"My stepmother?" he asked.

"Yes, sir, Agnes Tilney, the dowager duchess," repeated Surrey.

There was a tense silence. Catherine felt her heart quicken. If the dowager had been arrested, who would be next? Would she be in danger? Or Isabel? Thomas Howard seemed to be thinking along similar lines.

"Catherine, return to your chambers and remain there. If the king sends for you this evening, make no mention of the arrests unless he does and then pretend you know nothing about them. Let him tell you everything, it would be interesting to hear his views on the situation."

He turned away, dismissing her with his gesture. Catherine was about to comment when Charles took her arm and pulled her to her feet.

"Don't say anything to him, we don't want him turning on us like he did with cousin Anne and the rest of the Boleyns," he whispered. "You need to make sure the king is utterly smitten with you, in case Uncle Norfolk decides things are getting too difficult for him and tries to makes you the scapegoat."

"Can he do that?"

"Anne didn't even see it coming, and she was shrewder than all of us put together."

Catherine nodded. She took her brother's arm and allowed herself to be led back to her chambers. As they entered, her women curtseyed and Catherine was aware of the many white and tear-stained faces. She realised that a number of people were absent, most noticeably Lady Cromwell, who by birth was Elizabeth Seymour, the sister of Henry's former queen, Jane Seymour. Margaret Morton, who had worked closely with Katherine Tilney and had been her friend, was also missing. So was Margaret Benet, a former friend of Joan Bulmer, a sly girl who would do anything to be the centre of attention. *Her absence did not bode well*, thought Catherine. She was tempted to sweep past and closet herself away with her favourites but she knew she should say something reassuring first.

Isabel, Margaret Douglas, Kathy Knollys and Margaret Arundell were waiting to one side. Catherine nodded to them, then turned to her ladies.

"This is a shocking and frightening time," she said, her blue eyes moving from one familiar face to the next. "But rest assured, I will use all my power to protect you. If anyone knows anything that could help either Katherine or Joan, then please know you can confide in me in complete confidence. Neither woman has committed the crimes of treason or witchcraft of which they have been accused and I will do the best I can to have them removed from the Tower at the first possible opportunity. Francis Dereham, likewise, is innocent of treason, and I will endeavour to secure his release too. In the meantime, we shall continue as normal."

She nodded regally, then swept into her private solar, followed by her two sisters, along with Margaret and Kathy.

"Kitten, what do you think you're doing?" snapped Margaret Douglas. "Your speech out there, it was treason. If we have any spies planted here by the king, you could be the next one in the Tower."

Catherine stared at her white-faced. "I wanted to offer some reassurance. Tilney and Bulmer are annoying, but they don't deserve this punishment," she said, unrepentantly. "If we have a spy in our midst, we'll soon know. In the meantime, is there anything we can do to save Tilney and Bulmer?"

"No," said Margaret Douglas. "You have no choice but to go along with this, Kitten."

"Very well," she said, but she seemed to be speaking to herself. She walked to the fireplace and, feeling along the ornate wooden frieze, stopped at a section of carved Tudor roses and acorns. Taking great care, she slowly slid out an entire section to reveal a cavity within which contained a packet of letters, spare writing parchment, ink and a quill.

"We must write to Lady Cleves immediately," she said removing the writing implements and carrying them to her small ornate writing table. "We must warn her to burn all our correspondence in case this situation becomes more troublesome."

Her ladies watched her in astonishment.

"While I write, would you all please bank up the fire and burn these letters one at a time, ensuring every scrap is destroyed," she said, handing them to Isabel. "Although Anne and I have always written in code, a spymaster could crack them."

"Kitten, when did you write these?" asked Isabel in amazement. Catherine smiled.

"At night or in the early morning, when you were sleeping. Anne and I are the only living women who know what it is to be married to the king. We have given each other great succour when times have been difficult. She is a true friend and I would hate for our letters to put her in danger."

Margaret Douglas could not help herself; she opened the top one and stared at it in surprise.

"This is a complex code, Kitten," she said, impressed. "I assume you've been changing the cipher word each time. How do you and Anne tell each other?"

In her state of paranoia, Catherine was surprised at this question and felt disinclined to answer it. Instead, she smiled, "We have our own way. Would you burn them please, Margaret?"

Realising what she had said, Margaret nodded.

"I'm sorry, Kitten," she said. "We shouldn't be discussing such things. I'll make sure they're all destroyed."

Lady Arundell joined her at the fireplace and they began placing each letter in the flames, watching and waiting to ensure no scrap of it remained before they added the next. At her writing desk, Catherine pulled her Bible towards her and flipped through to the book of Esther. She always used a key word from this book, while Anne used the story of Susanna. Following the lines with her finger she came across a suitable line of text and chose a key word, then quietly scribbled a series of numbers and letters on the corner of a scrap of parchment: *Est 7, 5, 7*. Later, she would conceal this in her ruby ring and send it with the letter so Anne would know how to decipher it.

She had just finished the short note when there was a flurry of activity in her outer chambers. Edward hurried in, accompanied by the princesses Mary and Elizabeth. He bowed low to the queen and the two young women curtseyed.

"The king has summoned you," he said, simply.

And Catherine felt fear grip her heart.

Chapter Seven

"The princesses have been instructed to help you dress," continued Edward. "Then you are all to be accompanied to the Great Hall by Henry's guard."

Catherine forced a smile to her numb lips. "How wonderful," she said. "A surprise from my husband, as well as time spent with his beautiful daughters."

The others took their lead from Catherine and immediately lightened their expressions, although it did not stop Edward's eyes from flickering around the room and taking in the scene. His eyes sought Isabel's, who swept forward, followed a heartbeat later by Kathy Knollys, both women aware of how to play the game of court politics.

"And what a treat to see you both," said Isabel raising Mary and Elizabeth from their curtseys, blocking their view of the fireplace. As Isabel and Kathy fussed around the princesses, Margaret Arundell slid the frieze back in place with one smooth, deft movement. "The queen was catching up on some correspondence, so you must excuse the mess, Edward. No lady likes to be interrupted unexpectedly."

Although her smile was warm, Isabel's eyes were fierce and Edward touched her elbow complicitly.

"And it is not for me to pry into the inner chambers of my queen," he said, but his next words were loaded with meaning. "However, the king expects you all in the Great Hall within the hour, so it would be best to have cleared away *all* your feminine fancies by then, dear wife."

"Thank you, sweet husband," she replied and gave a quick bob. As Edward closed the doors behind him, they heard him call: "The queen is not to be disturbed, no one enters without the permission of my wife, Lady Baynton."

There was a tense silence.

"I must finish this," said Catherine and returned to her coded letter. "Isabel, would you please organise things? Lady Douglas, please continue with the task I set you earlier. My dears," she turned to the princesses, "Lady Knollys will tend to you for a few moments as this letter cannot wait."

"Can Elizabeth or I be of any help, Lady Stepmother?" Mary asked. "We both have excellent penmanship."

"It's kind of you to offer, Mary, but it is nearly done," Catherine smiled.

"I can write in Latin and Greek and French and Italian," confirmed Elizabeth, standing on one leg for no particular reason.

"She's a very talented pupil," added Mary proudly.

"Now, ladies, let us leave the queen to finish her correspondence. Perhaps you could help me to select her jewels," said Kathy Knollys. The princesses followed her to the other side of the chamber. In the moment of respite, Catherine tore off the scrap of parchment on which she had written the coded numbers, folded it and slid it carefully into the secret chamber of the ruby ring Anne had given her. As she pushed the tiny door closed the ring gave a satisfying click, then she slid it onto her finger.

"I will be wearing the ruby the Lady of Cleves presented to me on my marriage to the king," she announced. "I'd like a gown and jewels to compliment it. Lady Arundell, perhaps you could clear my writing table."

In the flurry created by Isabel and Kathy Knollys preparing Catherine's clothes, the two Margarets managed to conceal and destroy any potential evidence that could be used against Catherine, too aware that Cranmer's men would be very thorough in their search of her rooms while she was in the Great Hall attending to the king and the court. Once done, Isabel summoned Catherine's other women and, in a whirl of tense, forced smiles, Catherine was once more primped and polished, ready to be delivered to the king. As Isabel fastened the final earring in place, Catherine murmured in her elder sister's ear: "I grow so tired of being the king's toy."

"Oh, Kitten," whispered Isabel, hugging her tightly.

"Perhaps the sting of the axe wouldn't be so bad," she sighed.

Isabel looked horrified but, before she could reply, Catherine's expression changed to one of pious delight. Giving Isabel a wide smile, she gathered her skirts in her hand and swept forward, her ladies falling into a train behind her, every inch the queen as she led the procession to the Great Hall where Henry awaited.

Although Catherine presented an appearance of outward calm, her mind was racing. Since Tilney's arrest, she had been filled with a growing sense of unease. Was this plot, which she now knew had been fabricated by her uncle, a ruse to remove her from Henry's side? While she did not mind that too much, she was scared about the effect it would have on those around her, particularly her immediate family. And, what of Anne, the Lady Cleves? Would she be implicated alongside Catherine if her uncle chose to oust her from the throne? And if he did, who would be his next Howard victim to be queen?

As Catherine entered the Great Hall, her name was announced and heralds played a triumphant fanfare. She was so frightened, convinced this was merely a prelude to public humiliation, that it was a few moments before she realised the gathering was being given in her honour. Her crest of a rose without a thorn was flying on enormous banners all around the room, accompanied by her motto: *No other will but his*. Henry waited on the dais, his face radiating excitement.

"My beautiful lady!" he exclaimed, taking her hand and leading her to an ornately decorated chair at his side. "Such is her sweet modesty that it was only by chance I discovered today is her birthday, the eleventh of November, a day we must always remember and celebrate, for this was the day my true and perfect love was born."

Catherine's cheeks flamed crimson as Henry led her to the seat of honour.

"Let the revels begin!" he commanded.

A cacophony of sound erupted as musicians and entertainers filled the hall and the unexpected masque unfurled like an exotic Turkish carpet.

"Henry, thank you," said Catherine. "This is a wonderful surprise."

He grinned, displaying a shadow of his once great good looks, now swallowed by age, excess and illness.

"My sweet wife, one doesn't have a sixteenth birthday every day," he smiled. "Tomorrow, I have decreed that all the churches in the land shall say a special prayer for you."

She smiled, yet still she did not feel reassured by his words. His mood could change in the flicker of a candle flame.

"And here is another surprise," exclaimed Henry, thoroughly enjoying himself. The crowd parted and the four-year-old Prince Edward walked forward, accompanied by Anne of

Cleves. The little boy bowed with great solemnity to his father and stepmother, then presented Anne.

"My Lady Aunt of Cleves," he said as Anne curtseyed and Henry beamed, saying: "What a family gathering this is!" as Mary and Elizabeth swept forward, curtsied, then took their places with the rest of the royal family.

Catherine stared around her at the glittering court, the laughing faces, the sumptuous clothing, the twinkle of thousands of pounds' worth of exquisite jewels — this was all for her: the beloved queen consort of a powerful monarch. Yet, she felt utterly detached, as though she were watching the spectacle of her own life through a window. All she could think of was Tilney in the Tower, of Anne Boleyn, of Katherine of Aragon, of the succession of royal and noble women whom Henry had brutalised, destroyed or murdered, while he sat beside her laughing, joking, calling for wine — the ever wise and bountiful ruler.

He beat my child out of me, she thought, as he toasted the duke of Suffolk, *I told him I was carrying his longed-for heir and he accused me of adultery then attacked me with a riding whip. He is mad but he is my husband, so I must succumb to him, no matter what.* She felt sick at the thought and a growing feeling of panic began to rise inside her.

"My dear, will you dance for me?" Henry's voice seemed to come from far away. "Perhaps with the Lady Anne?"

His eyes glinted with excitement and his smile became slightly too wide and knowing to be friendly, almost a grimace of lust. The expression passed in a moment but it was enough to make Catherine shudder and think of what had happened the last time Henry had watched her dance with Anne, of the poor girl he had murdered. She smiled, hiding her revulsion.

"Of course," she replied, watching as Henry beckoned to Anne. As the two women linked arms, walking sedately to the dance floor, Henry stood and announced in his booming voice: "My wife, Queen Catherine, and my beloved sister, the Lady Anne, will lead you all in the pavane."

The musicians struck up the stately refrain and other couples fell in behind Catherine and Anne. In the general mêlée, Catherine took her chance. Surreptitiously she loosened the ruby ring on her finger, relieved to see Anne was wearing its twin. Waiting for the cinque pas, when she and Anne would cross in front and around each other, she caught Anne's eye and winked quickly, moving her hand so Anne would see the ring. The other gave a tiny, complicit nod. Under the guise of a complicated hand movement, Catherine slid her ruby ring from her finger and palmed it, then as she passed back across Anne, pushed it into her hand. On the return pass, Anne mirrored Catherine's movements and by the end of the dance, the women were wearing rings again, with no one any the wiser of the swap.

As the dance ended, Catherine felt the strong, bony grip of her uncle, Thomas Howard, on her elbow.

"The king has granted that we should dance together, sweet niece," he said, his voice surprisingly soft.

"It would be an honour, Uncle," murmured Catherine and swept a curtsey as the faster rhythm of the almain flooded the hall. The swirling frantic dance floor was, she knew, one of the best places to exchange secrets unheard and she suspected her uncle was about to impart news. He had spent many hours closeted with the other members of the Privy Council trying to clear his stepmother, the dowager duchess of Norfolk, from all blame. He took Catherine's hand and led her into position.

They both smiled, respectively bowing and curtseying to the king, before the duke of Norfolk whirled Catherine into the crowd.

"What news?"

"Tilney is still claiming to be carrying the king's child," he whispered. "She's being moved to the priory at Syon Abbey where she'll be held to see whether nature takes its course."

"What of Joan Bulmer and Francis Dereham?"

"Joan is to accompany Katherine, as is my stepmother, Agnes Tilney; Lady Margaret Howard, my half-brother's wife and Lady Anne Parr," he said. "They are there partly to spy for Cranmer but also to tend Tilney. If she does indeed carry the king's bastard, she will probably be allowed to deliver the babe before she is sentenced. Dereham is to be executed."

"What?"

"Letters, genuine letters have been found between him and Tilney, in which she claims to love him and no other. They are dated during the time when she was Henry's mistress."

"So, the reason for your forged letters about treason was because you truly were worried she might be trying to pass Dereham's child off as Henry's, which could jeopardise all our positions, particularly if it is a boy?"

Her uncle nodded.

"We couldn't run the risk, Kitten," he said.

"It's a shame you didn't find the real letters earlier, you wouldn't have had to risk compromising yourself," she said, her voice laced with contempt.

"My thoughts exactly."

"And if she isn't with child?"

"She will probably be executed."

"And Joan?"

Her uncle did not reply but she knew the answer would be the same. The dance came to an end and Catherine curtseyed once more before the duke led her back to Henry, whose face was avid with lust as she approached.

"Bed him tonight," he hissed. "We need you pregnant."

"And if I refuse?"

"I will ensure your head is the next one on the block."

Chapter Eight

After the arrest of Katherine Tilney and Joan Bulmer, the mood in the palace became increasingly tense. Worse were the whispers telling of the torture of Francis Dereham in the Tower. The echoes of Anne Boleyn's fall from grace were unmistakable. Many of her ladies requested leave from her chambers and, understanding their fear, Catherine allowed them to return to their far-flung estates, envying them their escape from the oppressive terror of the court.

Henry had retired to his rooms in a storm of paranoia, closeting himself with the few powerful men he still regarded as trustworthy. Outside the large carved oak door to his chambers, the giant, handcrafted golden lock he used when he travelled was in position, guarding and protecting the monarch from both his real and imagined foes. Katherine Tilney, Joan Bulmer and their small entourage remained at Syon Abbey in Isleworth, Middlesex, while the queen tried to use her influence to obtain the best outcome possible: their removal to Holy Orders, rather than an early morning appointment with the executioner's axe.

On the surface, Catherine maintained the pretence that all was well, encouraging her ladies to practise their singing for the Christmas entertainments, to make gifts and to pray that the king would be well enough to enjoy the festive period. When the order came that Francis Dereham was to be hanged, drawn and quartered at Tyburn for treason on 10 December, Catherine wept at her inability to protect the people in her court, even if she had never been overfond of Dereham. Her mask of insouciance only slipped when she was alone with her confidants, and they planned how they might survive should her uncle, Thomas Howard, be true to his word and turn upon her as he had done her cousin, Anne Boleyn.

Her worries increased with each passing day. How could she conceive an heir when her husband no longer summoned her to share his bed? The duke of Norfolk would not count this as an acceptable excuse, he would blame her for no longer being able to arouse the king.

Now, as she sat in her presence chambers awaiting a visit from another Howard uncle, Lord William Howard, Henry's Scottish envoy, she wondered what news he had of the faraway court. Was this a possible escape route? Or merely a disaster waiting to happen? Such was the turmoil of her mind, she had no clear insight into whether this plan would save or damn her.

"Your grace," said a smooth voice, rousing Catherine from her thoughts.

"My lord uncle," she replied, holding out her hand for him to kiss. "How fare you? Was your journey from Scotland agreeable?"

At thirty-one, William Howard was a tall, imposing man with the piercing dark eyes of the Howards and the same charisma possessed by Catherine's brother Charles. Both men carried themselves with an indefinable quality that caused women to find them attractive and men to want to either befriend or destroy them. Arranging his cloak and crossing his legs to make himself comfortable, William smiled. "Thankfully, my dear, I was able to sail from Scotland to France on a small errand for the king, then return via Calais. A far more pleasant trip than facing the perilous roads from the north at this time of year."

"Far more agreeable," agreed Catherine. "How was the Scottish court?"

"There is much sadness: the loss of the two heirs has weighed heavily on the king and queen, but it is hoped Queen Mary will soon be with child again," he replied. "What news here, your grace?"

"We, too, hope for a happy announcement soon," she murmured, pushing aside the rush of fear this subject always created within her.

"It has also pleased me to be able to deliver some small tokens from King James to his half-sister, Lady Douglas," he continued. Catherine kept her face impassive while wondering if one was a message.

"Please leave them with Lady Knollys," she said, beckoning Kathy forward. "She will ensure they are delivered to Lady Douglas."

William Howard rose to his feet and bowed deeply. Once more he bent low and kissed the back of Catherine's hand. As he did, she felt a small sting as the edge of a tiny sealed note was pushed into her palm. "Good day, my queen."

A string of visitors followed and Catherine attended to each, until at last, Lady Knollys closed the main doors of the presence chamber, indicating that Catherine was retiring to her inner chambers to prepare for the main midday meal in the Great Hall. The moment they were alone, Catherine removed the note her uncle had given her from a small pocket in her sleeve and slit it open.

"It's from Lady Cleves," she whispered to Kathy, then hurried to her jewel chest where she found her ruby ring. Clicking it open, she extracted another small piece of parchment and read the letters and numbers written on it, then she pulled her Bible towards her and began translating the short note.

"How do you know what she's saying?" whispered Kathy, who was hovering behind Catherine, squinting down at the coded note.

"It's easy when you have the cipher," replied Catherine, indicating Lady Knollys to fetch a chair. "The other day, when we saw Lady Cleves, she and I swapped rings. Inside each is a chamber where we hide the key to our next letter. See…" she pushed the scrap of parchment towards Kathy. "The letter 'S' means the word Lady Anne has used to disguise her message is in the Bible in the history of Susanna, the number five indicates the fifth verse and the number nine indicates the word," she explained pointing to the word 'ancients', "then this final number, seven, means Anne has shifted this cipher seven letters to the right. So, I write out the alphabet, then on the line underneath, I count seven letters from the right, which is the letter 'G'. The key word is 'ancients', so this is where I begin my cipher. I place the word on the second row beginning under the letter G. If there is more than one of the same letter in the key word, I only use the first one. I then fill in the remaining letters of the alphabet in order. Do you see?"

Lady Knollys looked bemused, so Catherine hastily scribbled out the letters of the alphabet, slotting in the cipher word underneath before filling in the remainder of the alphabet in a neat row:

ABCDEFGHIJKLMNOPQRSTUVWXYZ
UVWXYZANCIETSBDFGHJKLMOPQR

"The Lady Anne has used this cipher. She would write her message normally, then use the code to hide its true meaning. For example, if I wanted to write 'Hello Kathy' using this code," continued Catherine. "I'd begin by finding the H on the top row and seeing which letter is underneath, it's an N. So, you would use the N in place of the H."

Seeing Kathy was still mystified, Catherine drew another chart and pushed it over towards Lady Knollys.

HELLOKATHY

NYTTDEUKNQ

"Look, 'Hello Kathy' would translate to: Nyttd Euknq. Then, because I have the cipher, I can do the reverse and translate it. Do you see now?"

Kathy was still unsure, so Catherine pointed to a word on the note: "Look at this one: wdlhkcyh. It means nothing written like that but if I translate it using Anne's information: I find the W on the bottom row, and above it is the letter it really represents, which is a C, the D is an O, the L is a U, and so on. Look, it spells COURTIER."

WDLHKCYH

COURTIER

Lady Knollys looked at her in awe.

"My goodness, Kitten," she whispered. "This is an extremely sophisticated code."

"What choice do I have, Kathy?" she said. "It may be our only chance of survival. While I don't care about myself, it would break my heart if any of you were punished in my stead."

"And it would break ours if anything happened to you, Kitten," said Kathy, her eyes wide with a determined fury.

"We may need the chance of a way out," Catherine murmured. "Not only for me, but for all of us. Margaret has written to her brother, King James of Scotland, and asked if his promise to give us safe passage through the mountains is still valid. With all the upheaval since York and with the arrests here, he may have changed his mind and we need to know. If escape to the Scottish court is no longer viable, my Culpepper relatives have property in Kent and I feel sure they would hide us until we could find safe passage to France…"

"Kitten, hush, what if someone hears," whispered Kathy Knollys frantically.

Catherine shrugged as though there was nothing to be done about it: this was life and they had to survive it or be crushed by the might of the Tudors.

There was a tentative knock on the door and both women jumped. Kathy stood in front of the small writing table as Catherine called, "Enter." Margaret Douglas swept in, followed by Charles Howard and Catherine and Charles's other sister, Margaret Arundell. Both Margarets dropped into a curtsey and Charles a bow.

"You summoned us?" asked Lady Douglas.

"Please get up, ladies," said Catherine, "and you, Charles. You don't need to bow and scrape in here."

"We were unsure who was with you," whispered Margaret Arundell, standing elegantly, aware the door was still ajar. "Lady Latimer is outside and she hinted you had company."

"Did she indeed?" muttered Kathy Knollys, bustling forward and throwing a furious glance at Lady Latimer before slamming the door shut.

"Kathy, would you please give Margaret the tokens from her brother, King James, and see if there is a note," ordered Catherine.

"Nothing," said Margaret a few moments later, "a small jewel but no note. He did say we would be welcome, though. Are you considering going, Kitty?"

"Events can make people nervous and cause them to change their minds," said Catherine. "It isn't for me I ask. It's in case you or Kathy or Issy, or any of you have to escape, I want to know you have a means to get safely away."

Throughout these exchanges, she had been diligently translating Anne's note. Now she read through the few short lines. "Oh my!" she gasped. "Charles, you'll need to find men we can trust."

"I'll speak to Uncle Norfolk..."

"No!" Catherine cut across him. "Do not under any circumstances speak to him."

"Kitten, what's happened? What does the note say?" this time it was Kathryn Knollys, her voice high-pitched with fear.

"Anne has heard rumours which confirm my suspicions," said Catherine. "She says there is a whisper that our uncle of Norfolk is preparing to create a new queen."

Everyone around her gasped.

"But, Kitten, why?"

"Because I'm not carrying the next Tudor heir!" she said. "Because Henry beat my child out of me but, as he is mad, we can't tell him he murdered his own progeny." There was a horrified silence, so Catherine continued. "Anne also said she has heard the duke fears the king's affair with Tilney could tarnish us all..."

"But he was the one who put Tilney in the king's bed," exploded Charles.

"Which has ended in her arrest," retorted Catherine, "and you know our uncle, the duke — he will always save himself first, so we must prepare for the worst."

"I'll fetch Isabel and Edward, they'll know what to do," said Lady Knollys.

"No, Kathy, leave them for now," said the queen. "They're spending a few days with their children. There will be time enough to tell them our plans. We are all family too: you, me, Charles, my Margarets. Then there are my other siblings who must also be protected: Joyce, John, Ralph, Henry, George, little Mary. We are all joined; blood and death, mixed at birth, bonds tightened by marriages. Sometimes we stand together, at others we serve up betrayal, such is life and love and family. We, our inner court, must stand fast together, we must protect each other during this storm, offer each other shelter — then, if God's willing, we will all survive."

The others listened in awe. Catherine was no longer the impressionable child who had arrived at court with the hope of frivolous fun and a good match. She was queen consort of England, the wife of one of the most powerful monarchs in Europe and, despite her youth, she had learned quickly the frightening game of court politics.

"Uncle Norfolk is not yet our enemy and may not become so," she said quietly. "These whispers are still rumours. However, as current events have shown, it is wise to remember how quickly rumours can be turned into brutal, verifiable fact, even if there is no shred of truth in their wicked lies. When cousin Anne was deemed to have become too troublesome, Uncle was quick to condemn her. He may yet do the same to us."

These words pained Catherine, even though she now understood that the favouritism he had shown her was because he was already planning to dangle her in front of the monarch. He had seen a spark, a small hint of potential and he had decided to groom her. Perhaps he had done the same with Tilney as she was family too, although more distantly related and without the allure of Catherine's noble Howard blood. It was possible Tilney had believed she was Norfolk's favourite girl, which could be why she was so foolishly deluded that the duke would intercede with the king and help her out of this plight.

Catherine shuddered. She still remembered huddling on the stairs with the other girls at her step-grandmother's house, listening in horror as Anne Boleyn's fate became public knowledge. They had heard the duke of Norfolk disowning her; he who had pushed so hard for both Anne and her sister Mary before her to grace Henry's bed. Now, Anne had become troublesome and Norfolk, the consummate politician, had not only distanced himself from his former protégée but had been the voice who condemned her. It seemed he might be planning to do the same with her.

Silence had greeted Catherine's words.

"We continue as normal but we put our plans into place so, if we are in danger, we can leave," she continued. "I trust everyone in this room and I will do whatever I can to keep you all safe if the worst happens."

She looked around at the gathered members of her inner circle: Kathryn Knollys, Margaret Douglas, Margaret Arundell and Charles Howard.

"Now, if this were a normal day, you would be getting me ready to preside over the midday meal. Let's continue as though this conversation has not taken place, but Margaret, if you feel you are able, please will you write to your brother again and confirm we are welcome at his court."

"I'll go now if you can spare me," she said and bobbed a curtsey.

"Of course," replied Catherine. Charles gave her a small bow, then took Margaret's arm and they left, their heads bowed together conspiratorially.

Catherine turned back to her cousin and her sister, holding out her arms for them to lace, pin and ravel her into the elaborate court gown her status demanded. She had never imagined she would ever be clothed in such finery. Although, none of it was hers. The king may have bestowed jewels, estates and elaborate gifts upon her, but he could take them back just as quickly.

Her sister Margaret, Lady Arundell, was fitting Catherine's elaborately jewelled headdress when there was a knock on the door and Eleanor Paston, the countess of Rutland, announced the arrival of Henry Howard, the earl of Surrey, whom the king had sent to accompany her into the banquet. Regally, she rose from her seat and allowed the earl to lead her into the clamouring noise of the banqueting hall, ready once more to play the part of the joyous queen, her serene smile belying her pounding heart and churning fear.

Chapter Nine

"Catherine, wake up," Isabel's urgent voice whispered through the darkness. "It's the king, he's demanding to see you."

"It's the middle of the night and the king is ill, why does he want me?"

As wakefulness crept over her, so did fear. Henry had never summoned her like this before — either he was seriously ill or in one of his rages. Neither prospect gave her any joy.

"Quickly, Catherine, get out of bed," her sister insisted and Catherine caught the tension in her voice.

Awake now, she struggled from beneath the heavy bedclothes, allowing Isabel to slip a fur-lined wrap around her. Margaret Arundell swept a brush through Catherine's hair and Isabel handed her sweet herbs to chew to freshen her breath. Lady Knollys appeared with the box of precious oils and sprinkled a few drops of sweet lemon over Catherine's hair.

"Lemons?"

"Yes, it'll help," whispered Lady Knollys. "He's delirious, talking about Spain."

"Spain? The old Queen Katherine?"

"Yes," said Isabel, her hands and voice both shaking with fear. "He runs mad, Kitten. He probably won't know you, but he is demanding the presence of the queen. Even your uncle of Norfolk is horrified. There will be a guard outside the door, shout any of our names and we will save you."

"Shout your names?" Catherine was aghast. "Isabel, he could kill me before you get into the room."

Her sister did not reply, instead she forced a pair of embroidered slippers on to Catherine's feet, trying to disguise her tears, then led her into the shadowy corridor. A troop of the king's guard was waiting, their green and white livery glimmering in the torchlight. Charles Brandon, the duke of Suffolk, was at their head, his handsome face pinched with worry.

"We must hurry," he said, taking her arm. "The king calls for you."

"For me?"

"He calls for Queen Katherine of Aragon," he admitted, "but as he thinks I am his elder brother Arthur, things have definitely gone awry with his mind this evening."

"But if you're Arthur and I'm the late queen, does he not think we are married?" whispered Catherine.

"Thankfully, no, that piece of information has fallen through the gaps in his memory," sighed Brandon.

As Catherine hurried to keep up with his long, determined stride, casting sideways glances at him, she could not help but notice that he seemed to have aged overnight.

"What has caused this?" she asked. "Is it a curse? The full moon? Witchcraft?"

"Any of those are possible," agreed the duke in a low voice. "However, it is more likely that he is in the grip of the poison of his condition."

They had arrived outside the king's chambers and Brandon turned to Catherine, his eyes glistening with unshed tears. "My dear, I know he has treated you roughly, but he is my friend, almost my brother. To see him this way is more than I can bear…" His voice petered out. Catherine stared at him in confusion, then Brandon continued, "The king has not seen you for several weeks due to the pain in his leg but we can only hope he will recognise you and his love for you might bring him out of his madness."

"His love…?" she spat.

"You may not believe or understand it, but in his way, he loves you," said Brandon. "We'll be outside the door." Then he knocked, turned the handle and led Catherine inside. "My lord, I bring Queen Catherine," he announced, then with a bow, he left the room, abandoning her to the shadowy darkness.

"Who is there?" came a voice from the floor. "Is that you? My wife, will you ever forgive me for the things I did?"

Catherine stood frozen, waiting for her eyes to adjust to the gloom, her heart racing, her palms sweating with fear. She could see the outline of the king curled in a ball by the flickering firelight. He was hugging something, but in the gloom she could not see what it was. Did he think she was the old queen? Or was he speaking to her?

Taking a deep breath, she whispered, "Yes, my love, I'm here," inflecting her voice to have a lilt, which could have been a hint of a Spanish accent.

"You *are* here," he gasped. "My wife, my true wife. Will you ever forgive me for the things I did to you, to our daughter?"

"I forgive you, my dear," she whispered. She had no idea what to do — she thought she had experienced every twist and turn of the king's mind, but this was new. She had never known him to mistake her for his previous wife.

"The full moon brings you back to me," he said. "Will Anne forgive me?"

"Anne?" said Catherine in a choked voice.

"The Lady Boleyn, my lady of the darkness. Her eyes, her hair, she drew me into her midnight web and I loved her, I loved her so much she drove me mad." He shifted slightly and in the glow of the firelight Catherine saw he held a pillow from his bed, cradling it in his arms as though it were a child. "I had to kill you, Annie," he continued speaking to the cushion, "I had to, you looked at me with such disappointment, such fury when our son died. Killing you was the only way I could sleep peacefully."

"Our son?" whispered Catherine, wondering what new madness was about to be revealed. With the exception of Princess Elizabeth, all Anne's other pregnancies had ended in stillbirths.

"Our son, William, I didn't mean to do it, he was so delicate and he died. Why did he die? We were happy. Katherine was dead. I had just forced Chapuys to bow to you. We were triumphant and I held him. Then you made me angry and he began to cry. I held him — tight, tighter, tighter — to make him feel safe. It was the only way he would stop crying. Then he stopped moving and no matter how hard I shook him, he wouldn't wake up. You were so angry, so sad. You had to die too or you would have told everyone the truth. I had no choice, which was why I agreed to the French swordsman, why I designed your scaffold myself, it was an act of love. I'm sorry, Annie, but I'm king. You threatened me and no one, not even you, can threaten a king. I'm so sorry, my darling. Cromwell made it happen, then he had to die too, once he had killed everyone who might have betrayed me."

Standing alone in the shadows Catherine thought she might vomit. *Was this true? Or were these the ramblings of a madman?*

"Then there was my other son, Henry Fitzroy, the bastard duke of Richmond and Somerset. Little Bessie Blount had been so warm and generous in bed. She gave me a healthy son, so I changed the law allowing me to choose my heir, but he turned against me too. He was plotting, like you all do. He wanted my throne, wasn't prepared to wait, so I had him poisoned, Annie. Told his father-in-law, your uncle, the duke

333

of Norfolk, to take him away, the worthless bastard son who nearly tricked me into making him my heir. As if a bastard could ever wear my crown! Only my angel will ever take my place: my Edward, named for my grandfather and sent to me by God himself, who appeared once I had purged the others in that glorious year of 1536…"

Catherine wanted to put the words down to madness, but they held an eerie ring of truth. Perhaps Cromwell had done as Henry had ordered and covered up the terrible truth, until one day, the king's paranoia had also led him to destroy his most loyal henchman. Unable to help herself, she stifled a sob of fear. The tiny noise seemed to bring the king from his delirium.

"Little Kitten, is that you?" Henry's voice was suddenly stronger, more balanced.

"Yes, my lord," she whispered. "I came to check you were well."

"Come to the fire, my sweet child," he said. "You must be cold. These February days bring the snows and ice, they could chill you to death in a moment and I have endured too much loss."

She hurried to him, her heart pounding in terror at this abrupt mood swing. He seemed to be the kind king again, the rambling monster of a few moments before had vanished as quickly as mist on the water. Now, he gathered her shaking body into his embrace, tucking a heavy blanket around them both, putting the pillow behind her back.

"I have had many strange dreams this night," he said. "My wives, Katherine and Anne, were both here. They forgave me."

"Oh, Henry, surely there was nothing to forgive?" she said nervously.

"You are too sweet, my child, too kind," he mused. "You don't understand the deviousness many will stoop to in order to try to gain my favour or push me from my throne. There are still those who would see me replaced by a Plantagenet usurper. I must be ever on my guard."

He sighed, running his hands possessively over her body, his face buried in her hair, as though breathing her in. She could feel his excitement and tried not to tense; any sign of resistance only made him angry and his mood was so wild, she could not predict what would happen next.

"Tomorrow," he whispered, lifting her long auburn hair and running his tongue down her neck. She shuddered in disgust but the king took it to be passion, "I must order the execution of your faithless little whore-maid, Tilney, and her devil-worshipping slut. Do you know what she used to do?" His voice was excited and disgusted at the same time. "She would take my manhood in her mouth and she would suck it. She would moan with greed as she swallowed my seed, consuming me with witchcraft. Then she would beat her maid, both of them naked, while I watched, before forcing me to bed the maid from behind, rutting like a dog, while she beat me with a whip. I am ashamed, Catherine, I am so ashamed but I was enchanted. Do you forgive me?"

"Yes," she whispered faintly, too horrified to say anything more.

"You will be with me when the axe falls?" he said, unlacing her gown and pushing it from her shoulders, before moaning with greed at her naked body.

"If you wish," replied Catherine, staring at the fire, too scared to disagree.

"As her life is snuffed out and witchcraft is eradicated from my realm, we will be together as a husband and wife and make new life," he whispered in her ear as though it was a prayer. His hands were moving more quickly over her body. She allowed herself to go limp, leaning back against him, pretending she was enjoying the roughness of his touch as he pawed at her breasts, pinching her nipples and making her wince in pain. "We will make new life and when the witch dies we will assert my superiority, maybe we will make twins."

She did not resist as he laid her out on the rug by the fire. His hands were eager on her thighs, forcing her legs open, his eyes avid as strings of drool escaped from his gaping, wet mouth.

"You're mine," he hissed, his fingers scrabbling with his stained nightshirt, tugging it to one side, his breath coming in short, excited pants. "As all my wives are mine to do with as I choose and if you are not with child by Easter, I will remove you as I did your cousin, to make way for another woman who will give me an heir."

As he forced himself upon her, Catherine made herself go numb, mentally removing herself from the grunting, heaving bulk that was her husband. It was only with his final brutal thrust that she screamed in pain and once more she prayed she was with child. If she were, then, she vowed, she would take it as far away from its father as possible.

Chapter Ten

By the window lay a crumpled cloak. The duke of Norfolk saw it as soon as he entered the king's privy chamber and was about to call one of the servants to demand why such a costly item had been left abandoned on the strewing herbs — then he saw it move. Not the skitter of a rat or one of the many toy dogs that scurried around the palace, but as though something underneath it were breathing. He edged closer, wary now of what he might discover. Glancing down, he felt his heart quicken as he saw a series of bloody footprints, then a long red smear on the wall, as though someone had slid down it, leaving a trail of gore in their wake.

For a moment, he recoiled as he was taken back to another time, another palace, and a young man, now deceased, scrubbing blood from the floor, removing all evidence of the king's violence. The warmth drained from the duke's body as he understood who was under the cloak. Catherine had been summoned to the king's chambers in the early hours of the morning. The king had wanted her there while he watched the execution of Katherine Tilney and Joan Bulmer. Had the king once more lost control and gone too far? Edging forward, he cautiously lifted one corner and peered underneath.

"Mary, Mother of God," he gasped, hastily dropping the cloak back in place and crossing himself. He hurried to the door and summoned one of his Howard guards: "Send for Lady Isabel Baynton immediately. Tell her to bring her husband, Lord Baynton, my nephew, Charles Howard and Lady Margaret Douglas. Speak to no one else and run all the way. Nobody but members of my family are to enter this room," he barked, then slamming the door, he hurried back to the crumpled cloak.

Skilled politician and courtly player though he was, in this situation he had no idea how to cope. He did the only thing he could think to do: he sat on the floor beside her, gathering the cloak carefully around her body. He did not dare pull her into his arms, scared he would inflict more terrible injury upon her. Instead, with tears pouring down his face, he gently stroked her hair, whispering repeatedly: "I'm so sorry, my sweet girl, I'm so sorry. I will make this right. You'll never have to endure this again."

This was his fault, he knew it and it sickened him. All those months ago, he had deliberately placed Catherine in front of the king, knowing she was everything the monarch would find attractive. He had ruthlessly used her, even though she was his favourite; now, she lay close to death because he had married her to a maniac. A sharp scratching in his throat caused him to gulp as hot tears spilled down his dry, lined cheeks. Echoes from the past rang in his ears as he sobbed — Anne's voice, pleading for his help; George hammering on his wooden prison door, begging him to intercede — but he had denounced them both, sending his niece and nephew, Anne and George Boleyn, to their deaths. He may as well have done the same to Catherine.

"Oh, my sweet Kitten," he murmured, kissing her matted auburn hair, "I would never have turned on you. Forget what I said, I didn't mean it. No matter whether you have a child or not, I will do all in my power to protect you."

Catherine remained inert, unconscious, barely breathing, unaware of his presence.

Hurried footsteps and the hushing of the herald alerted the duke to the arrival of the others but he did not move. A timid knock on the door followed and when he called out, Isabel entered. She stood for a moment taking in the scene, all colour draining from her face, then with an expression of total determination, she took control. Ushering Margaret, Edward and Charles inside, she began issuing commands.

"It appears the queen has been taken ill," she said calmly, though her hands shook, and the others choked back their disgust and horror at the carnage confronting them. They listened carefully to Isabel's instructions and following her lead, remained calm and quiet, determined to get Catherine to safety as quickly and efficiently as possible.

"Edward, Charles, please send for a litter to convey Kitten back to her own chambers where she'll be more comfortable? Call my physician to meet us there and ask Lady Knollys and Lady Arundell to prepare her bedchamber. Dismiss the other women, tell them the queen has a fever and must have complete rest." She turned to the duke. "Perhaps you should go with them, your grace?"

"No," he said, his voice hoarse. "I'll stay with her."

After her husband and Charles had hurried out, Isabel shut the door, turning the key in the lock.

"Please your grace, move aside," she said gently. Margaret stared down in transfixed horror and when Isabel drew back the cloak to reveal Catherine's pulped and bloody face, Margaret turned away, stifling a sob. "There will be time for crying later, Margaret," she said sharply. "For now, we have to help Kitten. Send the page for hot water and linen cloths, we need to clean away the blood as best we can before we move her. I don't want any more gossip than is necessary."

While they waited, Isabel took a pillow from the bed and placed it under Catherine's head, then covered her with a blanket. A discreet knock on the door brought the water and within minutes, Isabel and Margaret began tending Catherine's wounds. The duke of Norfolk watched as Isabel bathed the worst of Catherine's cuts. She asked him to turn away when she uncovered Catherine further, sending him to the corner of the room to find the embroidered nightgown and fur-lined wrap Catherine had been wearing when she had left her own bedchamber the previous night. The delicate lawn nightgown was in shreds but the heavy outer wrap was intact. With Margaret's help, Isabel used the nightdress to staunch the lessening flow of blood from between Catherine's legs before lifting her limp form into the outer gown.

When the litter arrived, Isabel would allow no one in but Edward and Charles. Together, with the duke's help, they carefully lifted Catherine onto the soft cushions before Isabel and Margaret tucked warm blankets around her.

"Draw the curtains, we don't want anyone to see her," commanded Isabel, then turned to the duke of Norfolk. "Your grace, would you please send a message to the king and the Privy Seal that the queen is unwell and has a serious fever. She will remain in her rooms until further notice."

"Of course," he stuttered, his face still ashen. Isabel called the pages to carry Catherine to her rooms. As she turned to leave, the duke touched her arm. "Before, when he beat her, was she this bad?"

"Yes," replied Isabel simply. "You didn't see her for several weeks and by then the swelling and bruises had gone down."

"No, I mean, the blood..." he broke off.

"Last time, the blood came later, when she lost the child. I think this time there is no child to lose — he was violent, forcing himself upon her," she looked sickened.

"Is there a chance she could be with child?"

Isabel turned on him in fury.

"It'll be a miracle if she makes it through the day!" she hissed. "And you dare to ask about a child. Is your political ambition so great that even now, while Catherine's life hangs in the balance, you are craven enough to want a Howard heir…"

"No, Isabel, you misunderstand me," said the duke cutting across her. "If she is with child, we must know so we can hide her from him. We must keep her safe. Not because of any heirs or claims to the throne," he added hastily when she opened her mouth to berate him again, "but so that I can formulate a plan to get her away from the king."

Isabel stared at him in confusion. "What?" she uttered. "You want to remove her from the king's side? How would we manage that? She's the queen. When he's in his right mind, he adores her. How can we possibly keep her safe?"

"I have done many dark things in my time, Isabel. Lying to a king is but a minnow to a whale in comparison with what I have had to justify to myself over the years. No more members of my family will die at that man's hand," he said, his dark brown eyes turning black with determined fury. "If it is my head on the block, then so be it, but I will keep her away from him, whether there is a child or not. Leave the king to me and later, we will talk, you, me, Edward, Charles and George. There is a house. It was part of Anne's dowry when Henry created her Marquess of Pembrokeshire. It is far, far from here and came to me upon Anne's death. The king will never find her there."

PART FIVE: Marquess House, 2018

Chapter One

Rocketing around the country lanes with her music blaring, Perdita felt her heart lighten. Much as she enjoyed Kit's company, this was the first time she had been out on her own for ages, and it was something of a relief. Naturally shy, she had found the past few months at Marquess House surrounded by new people, overwhelming. Living in a property that required such a huge number of personnel merely to make it function was not something she had come to terms with yet.

Today, though, she had decided to take a day off to explore the countryside. With Alistair Mackensie only recently returned from a trip to Andorra, where he and Susan had been helping their daughter Megan finalise the details of her approaching December wedding. Kit was spending the day with him to bring him up-to-date on, not only Jerusalem's newest acquisitions, but also the day-to-day running of Marquess House.

Slowing down, Perdita drove into the tiny village of Dale. Now the school holidays were over, everywhere was quiet once again. The sweeping natural harbour that had bulged with boats and crafts of all shapes and sizes during the summer months was nearly empty. The field where the dig had taken place was still fenced off, but the bulk of the area had been returned to its previous use. The only clue that there had been any underwater activity were the buoys positioned roughly where Perdita guessed the remains of the wreck lay on the sandy seabed. Olaf had emailed her a few days earlier, thanking her for the generous grant for restoring the golden cup and asking whether they could discuss the raising of the wreck. She was still staggered with the fact that she was in a position to help him fulfil his dream.

Perdita parked her car and wandered to the café that overlooked the bay. She ordered a coffee and continued to mull over the possibility of funding such a huge and important project. Choosing a seat in the sunshine, she stared out to sea, her mind wandering away from work and on to her conversation with Piper the previous night over their new secure devices.

"Why though?" Piper had asked and Perdita had shrugged.

"No idea," she replied, "but everyone here is very jumpy about security. Maybe they've had problems with things being stolen or plagiarised. Anyway, let's not complain, it's a much better connection! How are things with Jeremy?"

"Apparently, I'm hysterical and you're not to be trusted now you've taken up with the 'weirdos' at Marquess House," she had said, trying but failing to make light of the situation.

Perdita had been stunned. She had always classed Jeremy as one of her closest friends. To hear him making such scathing comments about them both was as unexpected as it was hurtful.

"And Kirstin?" Perdita had asked, refusing to rise to Jeremy's provocation.

"Oh yes, she's part of nearly every conversation we have these days. I might ask her to move in," Piper had replied, trying but failing to keep her voice flippant. Her eyes were wide with despair.

"Come home," Perdita had said as her anger flared. "At least here, with the weirdos at Marquess House, there are people who love and care about you. Please, Pipes, let me look after you and we'll get through this together."

"I'll think about it," she had agreed. "Any word from Warren?"

Perdita had shaken her head and also lifted her left hand to show her sister she was no longer wearing her engagement ring.

"It's over," she had said. "Even if he wanted to come back, how could I ever trust him again?"

Warren, she thought, pulling herself back to the present, *I was so sure of him, of our love.* It had been here he had broken the news of her grandmother's death, wrapping his arms around her, telling her things would be fine. Shaking her head, as though this would dislodge the thought of Warren, something struck her for the first time. In fact, she could not understand why she had not thought about it sooner but, she supposed, in the upheaval that had followed his announcement — their inheritance, the funeral, the discovery of her grandmother's unpublished manuscript — his unexpected arrival had seemed unimportant. Now, though, it bothered her in a way she could not explain.

How had Warren managed to get to her so quickly? As far as she had been aware, he had been in Peterborough giving a lecture on the morning her grandmother's body had been discovered — a journey of at least 280 miles. The only way he could have reached her was if he had flown but there were no commercial flights he could have taken and, as far as she was aware, he did not have any friends with aeroplanes or helicopters who could have whizzed him to her side. Not only that, he had his car with him, so he must have driven...

"Hi, it's Miss Rivers, isn't it?"

Startled, Perdita looked up. A tall man was standing in front of her, smiling. He had thick dark hair and was in his fifties. He looked vaguely familiar but she could not quite place him.

"No, Dr Rivers," she corrected him.

"Sorry," he said, gazing at her curiously before continuing. "I'm Stephen Haberfield, I attended your grandmother's funeral."

It came back to her in a flash; he had been with the elderly man in the wheelchair, the man who had been involved in the car crash that had killed her mother. Perdita stared at him in disbelief. She did not want to speak to him, she wanted nothing to do with either him or the other man. As she struggled to recall the name of his companion, unexpectedly, it rose to the surface of her mind like poison.

"Morton Keller," she said. "You were with him. Neither of you had any right to attend my grandmother's funeral. It was a private service for family and close friends only."

Haberfield gave her a searching look, as though he was appraising the strength of her reaction.

"My apologies, we meant no harm, we merely wanted to pay our respects," he said smoothly, but there was something about him that made Perdita uncomfortable. She drained her cup and, slipping her handbag onto her shoulder, she rose.

"Good day, Mr Haberfield," she said formally, then walked away as quickly as she could without breaking into a run.

Once back inside the safety of her Land Rover, she locked the doors, fired the engine and cursed. There was a one-way system in the village, one way in and one way out, which meant she would have to drive past the café where Haberfield might still be sitting. Edging out of the car park, she glanced to the right, scouring the café's tables. To her relief, there was no sign of him. Weaving her way carefully through Dale's narrow lanes, she circled the village and headed towards the coast road in the direction of the ancient and tiny city of St David's that was out to the west.

As she drove, she tried to make sense of Haberfield's sudden and unexpected appearance. Alistair had not told her the man was local, nor his connection to Morton Keller. He did not strike Perdita as someone who would work as a carer to such a frail old man. The most obvious answer was that Haberfield lived in Dale, which would explain why he had approached her while she was in the village. Telling herself she was overreacting, she decided she would ask Kit when she returned to Marquess House and pushed the encounter from her mind.

She swung the car down the narrow road leading to the cathedral. Squeezing into a parking space, she slung her leather rucksack over her shoulder and set out. She had read about this ancient monument but had never visited it before. Now as she walked through the stone archway at the end of the lane, the cathedral came into view for the first time and she gasped at its beauty.

It sat in a dip, its tower reaching into the brilliant September sky, every inch of it exuding serenity. Walking down the steps and the long slope that led to the entrance, Perdita's natural love of all things historical overwhelmed her and for the next few hours she was absorbed in a happy world of archaeology and ancient beliefs.

Returning to the autumn sunshine, she was looking for somewhere to have lunch when she heard a voice calling her name: "Perdita! Over here!"

Squinting into the sun, Perdita waved in surprise. "Briony!" she called, walking towards the smiling blonde girl. "How are the horses?"

Briony laughed. "They're as happy as happy can be!" she replied. "When are you coming down for a riding lesson? Your mum was a natural, so was your gran. It'll be in the genes."

"Perhaps," she said. Ever since Perdita had first visited the farm, once her childhood home, that housed all the animals in the Louisa Woodville Animal Sanctuary, Briony had been playfully trying to persuade her onto a horse. Having never ridden and naturally wary, Perdita had yet to succumb.

"How are the puppies?" Perdita asked instead.

"Gorgeous," replied Briony. "Would you like me to reserve you one?"

"Our dog died not long before Dad," said Perdita, "and I haven't had the heart to get a new one. Let me think about it."

The two women walked slowly up the hill together, pausing at the top where two coaches were negotiating the tight curve in the road. As the second vehicle moved, Perdita glanced up the road and her heart stood still. Only a short distance away was the man from earlier, Stephen Haberfield. He was staring at her, his expression cold and calculating.

"What's he doing here?" she said, surprised.

"Who?" asked Briony.

"That man, Stephen Haberfield. He came up to me earlier in Dale. How weird, do you think he followed me?"

She turned to look at Briony, who was white-faced. "He shouldn't be here," she said, her voice furious. "He knows the rules and he's in breach of them all."

"What are you talking about?" asked Perdita, bewildered by the sudden change in the usually cheerful Briony.

"Haberfield, he's not allowed anywhere near you! He knows that. He's pushing things because Alistair's been away."

Perdita looked back to where Haberfield had been standing, but he had disappeared.

"Briony, what are you talking about?"

"The Milford Haven Treaty."

Perdita looked blankly at Briony.

"The what?"

"You don't know about the Treaty?" Briony's hand had gone to her mouth in horror. "Oh my God, I forgot, you *don't* know."

"Tell me then, what's the Milford Haven Treaty, and what has it got to do with that man?"

Briony shook her head. Suddenly she was close to tears. "I can't, Perdita, you'll have to ask Alistair, I don't know the details. All I know is that man Haberfield shouldn't be anywhere near either you or Piper when you are under the protection of Marquess House."

"Under the protection...? Briony, what are you talking about?"

"You must tell Alistair that man has spoken to you," she insisted. "He'll know what to do, how to keep you safe."

"Safe from what?" snapped Perdita. Briony looked as though she was about to cry. "Safe from what, Briony?"

With great reluctance, Briony spoke in a choked and horrified voice, "From the men who murdered your mother!"

Chapter Two

Murder. It seemed impossible. Her mother had died in a car accident. It was tragic but Perdita wondered how it could have been construed as murder.

She drove back to Marquess House with these questions running around her mind, convincing herself with each mile that Briony must have been mistaken. Yet, even as she thought this, she felt doubt tingeing her reasoning. Briony was the granddaughter of Mary's best friend, Bethan Bridges, later Bethan Lacey after she had married her childhood sweetheart, Walter. Briony's mother Jane was Bethan's eldest daughter. The family had lived and worked in St Ishmael's all their lives and had been intertwined with the family at Marquess House. Jane's sister, Sarah, was now the housekeeper at Marquess House, and was married to Alan Eve. They were part of the tapestry of her grandmother's life, her mother's life. Briony had always struck her as an honest young woman with no agenda, other than saving and loving animals. Was it possible Briony had let something slip in error? Could the people at Marquess House still be colluding to keep secrets from her and Piper? And if so, why?

None of it made any sense and, as Perdita flung her trusty Land Rover around the tight bend leading up to the gates of Marquess House and sped towards the manor, she once more felt her temper rising. For most of their lives, she and Piper had been cut out of their grandmother's life. This had been achieved with the cooperation of the vast number of people at Marquess House. When her grandmother had been alive, this had been her directive, but Mary was dead and the house now belonged to her and Piper. *They have no right to keep anything from us any more*, thought Perdita, furiously. *If Mum was murdered, we need to know. It is not Alistair's decision to keep such vital information to himself.*

Skidding to a halt, the engine had barely cut out before she was marching towards the front door. She was only a few steps away from it when Kit walked out, his face starkly white, his blue eyes grim and determined.

"My mother…" began Perdita, her voice harder and higher than usual, but Kit held up his hand.

"Not here," he said, his voice was so low it was almost a growl. It halted Perdita in her tracks. "Not here," he repeated. "Come with me." And taking her arm, he led her down the winding path and through the ornamental garden to the sandy shore of Llyn Cel.

"Kit, what's going on?" she asked, hurrying to keep up with his determined stride. "What's happened?"

"My dad…"

"Is something wrong?"

"No, he's fine, but…" his voice faded away as he came to a halt on the sandy shore of Llyn Cel, where he stared out across the choppy water of the lake. "Remember, a few weeks ago, when Dad told me I had to work with you because 'there are secrets he'll have to impart, things which it'll be vital I understand', but not until he felt the time was right to tell me?"

"Yes, of course, it was when Warren and I split up…"

"Today," he interrupted her, sounding desperate, "Dad took me into his confidence and told me those secrets."

Perdita felt herself go cold. During her journey home, she had been ready to defend her corner and demand to know the truth, but it seemed Alistair had taken advantage of her absence to unload this burden onto his youngest son's shoulders. If this information had reduced the irrepressibly cheerful, indomitable Kit to this white-faced, wide-eyed state, she was suddenly afraid, unsure whether she did want to know what had really happened all those years ago.

"Perds, we need to sit down," he said, pulling a picnic blanket from his battered Fred Perry bag, which was slung over his shoulder, and throwing it on the ground.

"Why?" she muttered, stalling for time.

"There's a lot to tell you and we might as well be comfortable," he gave her a weaker version of his normally sunny grin.

Breathing in the scent of the water, hoping it would act as a soothing balm to her jagged nerves, she reluctantly stepped onto the rug. As the soft wool gave way slightly under her boot, she felt as though she had moved from the relative safety of her known world into the unsettling darkness of a strange new existence. Once this secret was told, she would never be able to return to her current state of unknowing. Once Kit had spoken, the curse was released. Taking a position opposite him, Perdita sat rigid in a cross-legged position, waiting.

"First," began Kit in a rush, not meeting her eye, "practical stuff: I spoke to Dr Dade. He's delighted with his grant for the restoration of the gold cup."

"Thank you," she murmured, relieved he was stalling, giving her a few more moments of blissful ignorance.

"I also organised the annual cleaning, mending and general restoration of the chapel," he continued. "I'm telling you this because, in future, Dad wants me to take more of a role liaising between Marquess House and Jerusalem, as he did with Mary, and his father, my grandfather, Kenneth, did before him."

"Should I be more involved with the day-to-day running of the manor?" asked Perdita.

"No, it's what we do. Dad always says the Mackensie family are the Lord Chamberlains for the women in Marquess House."

Perdita shook her head, slightly bemused.

"Lord Chamberlains?"

"Dad's words," said Kit. Perdita watched this new version of Kit with growing dismay. He still would not meet her gaze, instead fiddling with a small pile of stones he had unconsciously gathered while they were talking. As the silence grew between them, she decided to give him some breathing space and voice her own concerns.

"While I was in Dale today, I saw the man who was at my grandmother's funeral, Stephen Haberfield."

"What?" said Kit, jerking his head up and finally meeting her eye.

"Then after I'd been to the cathedral, I bumped into Briony. While we were chatting, we saw Haberfield again and she reacted extremely strongly, blurting out that my mother had been murdered and Haberfield was somehow involved. She was wrong though, wasn't she? My mother died in a car accident caused by Morton Keller. She also mentioned something called the Milford Haven Treaty. Do you know what that is?"

Her words were spoken quietly, but Kit reacted as though she had punched him. He winced and took her hand.

"Oh, Perds," he whispered, squeezing her fingers, his blue eyes dark with sorrow, "I wish you hadn't found out that way."

It was a moment before Perdita understood but as his meaning flooded her, she gasped, finding it difficult to breathe. Briony had been correct.

"What?" her voice was hoarse. "Why didn't you tell me?"

"I didn't know until today," he said. "Dad told me this morning."

Perdita stared at him, white noise filled her ears and for a moment the world blurred as the horror of his words sunk in.

"Oh, Perds, I'm so sorry, this isn't going to be easy to hear but there are things I must tell you," said Kit, lifting her hand to his cheek and cradling it there as though it were a baby bird. "Things you and Piper should have been told years ago. I was furious with Dad for keeping this to himself, but he said it was on Mary's instructions. Since her death, things have changed and he's realised you'll both be safer knowing the truth."

Perdita dropped her head so her hair fell forward, obscuring her face from Kit. *Safer*, she thought, *there it is again. Safe from what?* Whatever it was, she knew she was about to find out and she was ready. She needed to know, there could be no more hiding, no more secrets.

Throwing her hair back, she met Kit's tense blue gaze with calmness.

"Tell me," she said. "I want to know everything."

Taking a deep breath, Kit squeezed his eyes tight shut as though bracing himself, then opening them again, he gave a small smile and began to speak.

"Remember the photographs from your dad? The ones signed, 'Your loving son-in-law'?"

"Yes."

"It transpires James was in touch with Mary throughout his lifetime. They spoke several times a week and, from what Dad said, Mary would have loved to have had you both in her life."

"Why didn't she then?" asked Perdita, bemused.

"Because she was scared you would be murdered like Louisa was in 1993."

"But Mum died in a car crash. How can that be murder?"

"It was no accident," said Kit. "The brakes of the car had been tampered with, so when Morton Keller drove at her at sixty miles an hour, your mum slammed them on but nothing happened — instead, she swerved, lost control of the car on the muddy road, hit a stone wall and skidded over the cliff. Even worse, the seatbelt mechanism had been removed so she was flung through the windscreen. She died from a massive brain injury. Mary was horrified. It was her car, you see, but Louisa had borrowed it because hers had a flat battery."

Perdita stared at Kit in revulsion at the brutality of his words.

"But, if your father knew it was deliberate and that it was Morton Keller driving the other car, was he arrested?"

"He was questioned then released. The official verdict of Louisa's death was an accident," said Kit. "However, Mary knew differently. You see, Morton Keller is what your grandmother always referred to as a Watcher."

"What's a Watcher?"

"This is where things become a lot more complex," said Kit, "so, bear with me."

Perdita nodded, feeling there was no other option but to listen, even while she dreaded what was to come.

"Dad has always told me that Mary was a talented historian and a fearless teller of the truth, but we both know there is always more than one interpretation of any historical event. As hard as Mary fought to reveal her version of the truth, there were those who were determined to keep the 'accepted version of history' in the public domain, even if it meant suppressing new discoveries which might hint at anomalies…" began Kit.

"What do you mean 'accepted version of history'?" interrupted Perdita.

"I'm getting to it but I need to fill you in on the background first," explained Kit. "Please, Perds, I know it seems as though

I'm rambling, but this is all vitally important. You need to know this, you need to understand."

She saw the despair in his eyes and squeezed his hand.

"Sorry, I won't interrupt again, this must be difficult for you, too."

He shot her a grateful look and, taking a deep breath, continued: "In the early 1900s, my great-great-great grandfather, Douglas Mackensie, formed Jerusalem. He had originally been employed by a lesser-known section of the Secret Service and was tasked with buying and preserving historical documents from all over the world. After a while, he realised that many sensitive or controversial findings were being destroyed. Any documents that contained even slightly dubious content were permanently removed from the public domain and he began to feel increasingly compromised, so he left and set up a similar organisation."

"Why would the government want to destroy historical documents?" asked Perdita, unable to contain herself. "Were they trying to hide something? Sorry, sorry…"

"When Douglas Mackensie left the Secret Service, he decided to investigate this peculiar department," continued Kit. "It took him many years and his son, Edward, continued his work after Douglas retired. Through a huge amount of research, they discovered that, sometime in the seventeenth century, an order of guards called The King's Men was formed. This elite group was tasked with protecting someone called The Scribe. This person, who was working on direct orders from the king, altered contemporary documents."

"You mean deliberately rewriting events in order to cloud or even hide the truth?"

"Exactly. A precedent had already been set with Henry VII," continued Kit. "Three months after Henry Tudor had destroyed Richard III at the Battle of Bosworth and seized the crown of England, he had the statute book changed. He backdated his reign to beginning on 21 August 1485 — the day before the battle had taken place. By doing this, the royal records state that he was king when he fought, making Richard the usurper and his supporters the traitors. It was a clever way to bolster his shaky claim to the throne."

Perdita knew about Henry VII's deviousness but had assumed it was a unique event, she had never considered other documents could have been altered.

"And you're saying other official records were changed sometime around 1660?" clarified Perdita, and Kit nodded. "What were they hiding?"

"The King's Men and The Scribe did a very thorough job and we don't know," said Kit. "However, Mary was obviously beginning to uncover too many contentious documents, hence Louisa's murder."

"And what happened to The King's Men?" asked Perdita, floundering slightly with all this new and unexpected information.

"Dad and his predecessors at Jerusalem believe that once all the necessary documents had been recreated, they were executed so the secret and the subterfuge used to disguise it would remain hidden. However, two men escaped long enough to write a confession, which Douglas was lucky enough to buy before the Watchers knew about its existence. It reveals nothing about the secret that was being hidden but it was enough for Douglas to realise how high up this deception went. Further investigation proved that this elite force was once more established during the reign of Queen Victoria, this time named The Queen's Men, and the Watchers, or MI1 Elite, to give them their correct title, are the most recent incarnation of those first King's Men, sworn to protect the secret, whatever it may be. Dad suspects that MI1 don't have a clear idea either. Although, they probably have enough information to form a working hypothesis. They don't search for evidence, they're a preventative force, suppressing any information found by historians or researchers that they consider to be contentious."

Perdita stared at Kit, her eyes wide with disbelief.

"The reason Douglas bought Castle Jerusalem was because, back then, Andorra was almost impossible to access. He felt it was a good place to disappear to for a while. He put it about that he had retired and was simply an enthusiastic amateur collector of historical documents. In reality, he was far from amateur; he was determined to preserve any documents that revealed historical anomalies, as he believed that was where the truth about the past could be found. He named it Jerusalem after a William Blake poem: *Jerusalem – The Emanation of the Giant Albion*, which tells the story of the fall of Albion, Blake's embodiment of man. Dad thinks Douglas felt the destruction of our past by the Secret Service was akin to the fall of man."

"But, Kit, this is madness," gasped Perdita.

Kit, however, ploughed on. "I thought so at first, but Dad told me to remember that there are many who consider history is in the past so it has no power to hurt us. He said, 'Those of us with any wit or intelligence, realise this is simply not the case'."

Unable to help herself, Perdita smiled. She could imagine Alistair's stance would have become almost Churchillian while he delivered such a line to his youngest son.

"And, he's right," said Kit. "How we view ourselves as a nation comes from the way we regard our collective history. But what if it were wrong? What if the version of history we have all been taught, that academics have studied for centuries, is in fact nothing more than a huge fabrication? That we have all been duped into believing lies, and that it's all been done with the collusion of successive governments."

"But that would be impossible," said Perdita.

"Dad claims not. He even gave me a recent example of history changing."

"What?" gasped Perdita, startled.

"Richard III."

"Richard III? The last Plantagenet king."

"Correct and, until a few years ago, he was most famous as the wicked king who murdered his two royal nephews, the Princes in the Tower, in order to gain a throne," said Kit. "He was the archetypal villain."

An uneasy understanding bloomed across Perdita's face. "But now, he's being rehabilitated in the public domain and questions are being asked as to whether or not he actually did murder the princes. In fact, some historians are trying to shift the blame to the Tudors."

"Exactly," said Kit. "Something that was made even more mystifying when his bones were found in the car park in Leicester under a mysterious letter 'R' painted on the tarmac. Almost immediately, genealogists traced a descendant who could give DNA to prove whether this was the missing king or not. Richard's infamous hunchback was proved to be scoliosis of the spine and he was reinterred at Leicester cathedral, his crimes questioned but more or less forgiven. With this discovery, how we viewed this part of our collective consciousness was altered, history was rewritten."

"But with every archaeological dig, every new scrap of paper discovered, history is muddied again and again," retaliated Perdita.

"I know, but Dad seemed to think this was a major shift and it happened at a particular moment."

"What do you mean?"

"It was 2012, the year of the London Olympics and Queen Elizabeth II's Diamond Jubilee; all eyes were on us, so it was the perfect time to have a major historical discovery and to change our collective history."

"And there was an eclipse," murmured Perdita.

This time it was Kit who looked confused.

"Why is that relevant?"

"Five days before Richard III was interred at Leicester Cathedral, there was a solar eclipse in the UK. It tallies with the 'sun in splendour' legend," explained Perdita. "There is a story that claims a celestial event occurred while the York princes: the future Edward IV and the future Richard III, along with their brother George, duke of Clarence, awaited the cry to begin the battle of Mortimer's Cross. They saw the meteorological phenomenon of what appeared to be three suns shining in the sky, or the sun in splendour, as it's known colloquially. Edward saw it as a good omen of victory and, after they had won the battle, he used the emblem on his personal badge to represent the three sons of York, echoing the three suns in the sky. Two meteorological occurrences at pivotal moments in the lives of the York kings? It can't be a coincidence."

Perdita stared into Kit's eyes, they reflected her own reluctant realisation.

"Dad said this was the version of this period of history that had been universally accepted, even if the identity of who did kill the princes in the Tower has never been resolved," Kit continued. "It was a major event in the timeline of our country's zeitgeist; it had remained the same for centuries.

Then, almost overnight, it changed to a new version of events, one that alters our collective past, and this is the version we are told we should now believe. Forget what went before, this is the new story: Richard was not a villain, he was merely misunderstood. Everyone change their views and raise a cheer for good King Dick because it has been decided that this is what happened."

"Yet, the Tudor dynasty, despite being one of the most studied periods of history, has remained unchanged," said Perdita, her uneasiness growing. "There have been minor evaluations, yes, tiny deviations from the accepted norm but no major discoveries, which, given the amount of money and interest lavished upon it, is remarkable. Surely, the question is: why have there never been any new leads?"

"Because when any new discoveries are made, they're suppressed, unless they've been sanctioned by the government, of course," said Kit. "Mary was the last person to find something so startling; she had to be stopped."

Perdita was having difficulty taking it all in.

"As Dad pointed out, if there was a department of the Secret Service with Watchers in every university and scholarly institution entirely devoted to preserving the accepted version of history, while destroying anything and anyone who challenges this version of events, it would be possible," Kit paused and skimmed a pebble across the darkening water of Llyn Cel. "Then he said the most mind-scrambling thing, Perds."

"More mind-scrambling than the existence of Watchers?"

"He said, 'George Orwell had to get his inspiration from somewhere'."

"No," gasped Perdita. "Are you referring to the Ministry of Truth in his novel *1984?*"

Kit nodded.

"Apparently, Orwell had his suspicions and had hinted at this manipulation of the past with Winston Smith's job in a government department responsible for propaganda and historical revisionism. Did you also know that Orwell died the year after the book's publication?"

Perdita's eyes were wide with surprise.

"I did, but I'd never really given it much thought before," she stuttered. Suddenly, she understood why her father had chosen such an odd reading for his funeral service. Had it been a clue or a warning? One that Mary had repeated in her will.

"Kit, are you saying this is why my grandmother's car was tampered with all those years ago? She had found something that could challenge the accepted version of history?"

"Yes."

"But instead, it was my mother who was killed because she borrowed my grandmother's car."

"This is why Mary distanced herself from you and your father. The grief and guilt she suffered after your mother's death was apparently awful for everyone, Mary and James particularly. Mary blamed herself and she feared immediately for your lives. Your grandmother became convinced that the only way to protect you was to distance herself, so she made it known she was estranged from you and your father. Her theory was that, if the Watchers knew she had nothing to do with you, when she eventually died and you inherited her fortune and her home, you could do so safely because neither you nor Piper would know anything about her work or any secrets she had inadvertently uncovered. She didn't bargain on you becoming an historian and then going on to do a PhD in Archaeology. Trying to protect you both was also the reason she pulled *The Catherine Howard Anomaly* from publication. It was this book that was upsetting MI1 Elite."

"But now we've inherited Marquess House, what's to stop MI1 turning up here and pushing us all off a cliff?" asked Perdita, her voice unsteady.

"The Milford Haven Treaty," replied Kit, "and this is truly crazy."

She felt she must have gone into a state of shock. She was numb. Everything Kit had said seemed ludicrous, and yet her grandmother had been no fool. She had taken the terrible decision to distance herself from them, to sacrifice a life with them in order to ensure hers and Piper's lives were not cut tragically short as their mother's had been. It was this extreme action by Mary that stopped Perdita from dismissing Kit's words as nonsense.

"Go on," said Perdita in a strangled voice.

"Are you sure?"

Perdita nodded.

"The Milford Haven Treaty was drawn up in 1886 when The Queen's Men approached your ancestor, Lettice Lakeby. As a girl, Lettice had been told that Marquess House had once been in her family, so when it came up for sale, shortly after she had married her wealthy businessman husband, William Lakeby, he bought it for her. While it was being renovated, using Lettice's money as she was an heiress in her own right, she discovered a series of letters in the attic from a Penelope Fitzalan, which mentioned a ruby ring and a secret so dangerous that Penelope had been prepared to die to protect it.

"This secret was apparently hidden somewhere in the house, but it has never been found, despite Mary's extensive searching. Lettice, though, never took it particularly seriously and thought it was all rather charming and romantic. When she was approached by a representative of Queen Victoria's government concerning the house, she thought it was because it had once been part of Anne Boleyn's dowry when Henry VIII created her Marquess of Pembrokeshire, so she agreed to their terms and the Treaty was ratified in October 1886."

"And what does the Treaty say?" asked Perdita.

"It creates a sovereign state within Marquess House and its grounds, and it also states that those under the protection of the estate — that is, we who live here — cannot be arrested, approached or otherwise molested by members of MI1 Elite anywhere within a thirty-mile radius of the house. They have no jurisdiction over the house and its grounds. They are also not allowed to gather or use any intelligence that originates from the house. In other words, while you are here, you are safe from the Secret Service."

Perdita stared at Kit, shaking her head in disbelief.

"What unnerved Dad the most," continued Kit, "was seeing Keller and Haberfield at Mary's funeral and the fact they felt able to breach the Treaty. This has always been a sacrosanct agreement, so it makes him wonder if the new head of MI1 Elite is trying to change the rules."

"And who is that?"

"A man called Inigo Westbury. He took over the top position in February this year, and since then, there have been changes which suggest they are no longer prepared to wait quietly in the wings. They seem to be becoming increasingly militant again, as they were after the Second World War. Apparently, your mother's death shocked everyone back in the 1990s: it was known among all the agents that she was an innocent. Dad said she was also one of the kindest, gentlest women you could ever meet. The operatives at MI1 Elite were horrified by her death too, and it was the catalyst for a truce. However, Dad claims that Westbury is young, brash and wants to make his name in the Service. Until Mary's death, you and Piper weren't in any danger because the Watchers were still focused on Mary, but the moment she died and her will was released naming you two as her heirs, you became the new focus."

"Surely MI1 knew we would inherit the estate, though?" said Perdita. "We may not have known anything about it, but surely they were fully aware."

"Dad says not," he said. "Mary and your father had played their parts well and the Watchers truly believed Mary had cut you both from her life. MI1 was working on the assumption that Mary's nephew, Randolph Connors, as her next closest living relative, would inherit."

"Randolph Connors, he was Cecily's son, wasn't he?" she said. "Mary mentioned him in the notes she wrote all over her books."

"Yes, and he was convinced Marquess House would be his. He was furious when he was left nothing," said Kit. "He badgered Dad for weeks after you'd accepted your inheritance. He even said he might contest the will, but Dad sorted him out."

"Why didn't you tell me?"

"You had enough to deal with," said Kit. "Dad didn't think it was important. Randolph has always been a troublemaker."

"And what about this man, Inigo Westbury?"

"He's ex-military and saw action in Afghanistan then returned to a British posting and was approached by MI1 Elite. He's worked for them for six years, rocketing through the ranks until he was given the top job earlier this year. He's been divorced three times and is currently single. He has no children. There were suggestions that at least one of his wives cited mental cruelty as the reason for divorce but all access to his records is Top Secret so these are unconfirmed rumours. Whatever the reasons they had for leaving, his war record shows he's a man with no compassion and much ambition, which is never a good combination."

"He sounds charming," murmured Perdita. She stared out over Llyn Cel, trying to rationalise all she had been told, then a wave of panic hit her. "Piper," she exclaimed. "She's more than thirty miles away from Marquess House. She isn't protected by the Milford Haven Treaty. She has to come home. I have to talk to her."

"Dad said that MI1 has no extradition treaty with the US for anyone protected by privately signed documents."

"You mean there are others, we're not the only ones?"

"I don't know. I assume there must be."

"Nevertheless, she would be safer here…" Perdita could have bitten her tongue. Ever since she had arrived Alistair had been saying the word 'safe', now she was doing it too. "Things are going badly with Jeremy, so she's decided to go and visit her best friend Gemma in Italy, then she's going to fly here and stay while she decides what to do about her marriage. Can we guarantee her safety?"

Kit picked up a stone and skimmed it across the water. "I'll ask Dad to organise things."

"Thank you," she said. "Is there any more?"

"Isn't that enough?"

They sat in silence, the echoes of Kit's words floating across the obsidian water like ghosts, until Perdita spoke again in a soft, thoughtful tone, giving voice to her last desperate hope, "Do you think it's true?"

"Yes," sighed Kit, sadly. "It would be too much for Dad to make up. He has very little imagination and, anyway, why would he and Mary bother?"

While Kit had been speaking, the black night had risen around them. Stars twinkled in the inky sky, while the bright moon cast her eerie shadow across Llyn Cel. Perdita stiffened as Kit slipped his arm around her shoulders, then pulled her tightly into his side. After a moment, she relaxed, suddenly in need of human contact in this strange new world she had entered. Breathing in his scent, she listened to the lapping waves as she tried to make sense of his frightening revelations. Eventually, she could stand the silence no longer and pulled away from Kit's embrace.

"I'm cold," she said, standing up. "We should go back to the house."

Kit scrambled to his feet and she deftly folded the picnic rug, tucking it under her arm. "Don't suppose you brought a torch?" she asked, and he pulled one from his pocket.

"You get used to having a torch handy when you live in the countryside."

"Come on, then," she said and set out through the trees back to Marquess House.

Kit hurried after her, the powerful beam of yellow light guiding them. "Aren't you going to say anything?" he asked as he padded along by her side.

"What do you want me to say, Kit?" she asked. "You've just told me there's a government department whose sole aim is to kill me and my sister because of something my grandmother discovered. You've also told me this same department murdered my mother, even though they were aiming for my grandmother. It's because of this terrible accident that not only did I lose my mother but I also lost my grandmother because, after Mum's death, we never saw Mary again. How do I even begin to respond?"

Pushing her hair from her face, Perdita strode away from Kit, drawn now by the glimmers of the decorative lighting that brought the Marquess House gardens alive at night. In the distance, she could hear the fountains and a clanging from an artisan blacksmith working late in the artist's studios. An owl hooted in the distance and, as Perdita rounded the corner, she saw light spilling from the open kitchen door. Breaking into a run, she was inside within moments. Sarah looked up, startled, "What's the matter?" she asked, leaving the hob and its bubbling pots to gather Perdita into her arms in a maternal hug.

"Kit's told me what really happened to Mum," she said, gulping back a sob. "He said she was murdered…" her voice faltered and faded to nothing. She looked around, her eyes full of the distress and confusion that was now hitting her after Kit's startling revelations.

"Oh, sweetheart, come and sit down."

They were alone in the kitchen and Sarah pushed Perdita onto a chair at the long table that would soon be groaning with food.

"Your mother was my best friend," said Sarah, squeezing Perdita's hand before sliding a box of tissues along the scrubbed wooden surface and sitting beside her. "You may not know this, but I'm your and Piper's godmother."

"Are you?" gulped Perdita through her tears, surprise in her voice. "Dad said we'd never been christened."

"You were, here, in the chapel," sighed Sarah. "The reception was in the grounds, it was a lovely day."

Perdita hunched her shoulders, as though trying to shrug off everyone and everything she had seen or heard that day. When she did not speak, Sarah continued, "Even now, I find it difficult to speak about Lou's death. It was a shocking and tragic day. Louisa was one of the most caring, beautiful women in the world." Perdita had dropped her head into her hands, so Sarah kept speaking, "Everything Mary and James did was to protect you and Piper. Don't be angry with them. Giving you up was the darkest and most desperate moment of your grandmother's life. Remember, Perdita, those bastards are still sitting in their snug Whitehall office, thinking they've got you where they want you. Direct your anger and your rage at them, not at your grandmother and your father. Finish what Mary started, find the truth and tell as many people as possible what you've discovered in as many ways as you can."

Perdita looked up startled, this was the last thing she had imagined Sarah would say.

"Oh, don't worry, Sarah," she said, her voice suddenly steely. "I have no intention of hiding here. They stole our lives and, whatever Granny discovered, Piper and I will do our utmost to prove it's the truth. If we can't publish through traditional means, we have the internet, which wasn't available to my grandmother at the time she wrote the manuscript. I think it's time MI1 Elite realised they've got a fight on their hands and, no matter how dirty they play, we'll play dirtier and we will win."

Chapter Three

"So, what do we know?" asked Perdita, standing in front of the whiteboard in her office in The Dairy. Her hand was poised holding a purple marker pen, waiting to begin what she viewed as her 'war' with MI1 Elite.

It was four days since Alistair had revealed the existence of this frightening organisation and since then, Perdita had made many decisions. On the evening of Alistair's revelation, she and Piper had discussed it at length and agreed they needed to be together.

"But go to Gemma's first," Perdita had insisted. "Alistair said it would be safe, then you can come home."

Despite the fact that Alistair had insisted he arrange a discreet bodyguard to tail her during her time in Florence, and this was making Piper vacillate between hysterical laughter and silent fury, she had agreed.

"But you need to speak to Alistair," Piper had insisted before she vanished from the screen.

"Kit has told you then?" Alistair had said when Perdita had arrived unannounced in his office the following morning.

"Yes, Piper and I talked about it last night," she had said. "If we put Mary's manuscript back in the box and walked away, do you think it would stop MI1 targeting us? Dad and Granny Mary made huge sacrifices to keep us safe and, while I'd love to take on MI1 in a face-to-face battle, I don't want to let them down. By restarting the investigation into Mary's manuscript, I feel as though I am."

Alistair had gazed at her, gathering his thoughts before speaking: "Prior to your grandmother's death, I would have told you to stop," Alistair had said. "Your mother was killed because of what MI1 feared Mary had discovered, and my concern at losing any of you children would have been enough for me to refuse you access to her research or even allow you to consider delving back into the past. However, since Inigo Westbury has been in charge, things have changed. Much as it saddens me to admit this, I think even if you never looked at the research again, he would still come after you."

"Why?"

"He wants to make his name in the Secret Service," Alistair had said, and once again Perdita had the feeling he was not telling her the whole truth.

"Would continuing with the research and finding this incontrovertible truth that's supposed to exist somewhere, keep us safe? If we discovered this secret, would it give us leverage over MI1 Elite?" she had asked.

"I think it might be the only thing that will save you."

Perdita had left, once more making for the shore of Llyn Cel in order to organise the whirling, frightening thoughts that filled her mind.

After a few days of soul-searching and discussing things with both Piper and Kit, Perdita had made her decision. Confident in the knowledge that her sister was protected and would soon be by her side, she had decided to throw herself into uncovering and proving the truth that MI1 was so determined to keep shrouded in mystery. She would show them that she was a force to be reckoned with, even more so than her late grandmother. Now, she stood looking at Kit with anticipation.

"Traditional view first?" checked Kit, and Perdita nodded. He had barely left her side since the revelations, helping her to make copious notes which he began to read aloud. "No one knows exactly when or where Catherine Howard was born, but it's thought to have been somewhere between 1521 and 1524 — recent historians favour the later date — possibly in London."

Perdita wrote the two dates and the place on the board, underlining the second date, 1524, and putting the word: 'BIRTH?' next to it.

"Her mother was Jocasta Culpepper, spelt variously with a single or double 'p'. We've decided to use the double 'p'," Kit continued. "She died sometime around 1527-8 because, in 1528 Catherine's father, Edmund Howard, married a widow called Dorothy Uvedale."

Perdita wrote this underneath Catherine's possible birth date.

"But this marriage was short-lived because he married again a few years later, this time to another widow named Margaret Jennings, daughter of the Mundys of Markeaton Hall in Derbyshire."

Perdita added the new name and said: "And this was while Edmund held the position of Comptroller of Calais, which he was given in 1531 thanks to his niece's intervention. His niece being Anne Boleyn, the daughter of his elder sister, Elizabeth Howard who had married Thomas Boleyn. Edmund held this position until he died in 1539, but despite this, he was always in debt and scraping around to support his huge family."

"Exactly," said Kit. "Now, it's thought Catherine was 'put-out' to the Lambeth home of her step-grandmother, Agnes Tilney, the dowager duchess of Norfolk, sometime in 1531."

Perdita turned to the growing timeline. "Isn't the next definite date 1536?"

"Yes, this is when it's documented she received music lessons from Henry Manox, who was also said to have sexually assaulted her."

Scowling at this, Perdita wrote it on the board. She then added a few extra details, "This was also the year of Anne Boleyn's execution and Henry's marriage to Jane Seymour."

"The other odd thing here though, is the fact that Manox was never tried or punished for abusing Catherine," said Kit thoughtfully. "Francis Dereham, who was also accused of touching her when she was in Lambeth, was executed, but Manox escaped even though he was questioned too."

"Another anomaly in the life of Catherine Howard. Although, you have to remember this 'affair' wasn't highlighted until 1541, when Catherine was in trouble, so it's likely it was fabricated to make her seem even more flighty. It was Mary Lascelles who gave evidence about this," continued Perdita, "and according to the history books, it was also Mary Lascelles who blew the whistle on Catherine's former affair with Francis Dereham, and hinted at her supposed affair with Thomas Culpepper."

"So, not an entirely reliable source," Kit said.

"Exactly!" said Perdita. "What's next?"

"In 1537, the extremely arrogant Francis Dereham arrived at Lambeth. He was originally having a fling with Joan Bulmer, who, it seems, may or may not have been one of Catherine's ladies-in-waiting later on. Some historians think she was but a few believe she was never invited to court. Anyway, Francis soon transferred his affections to Catherine, allegedly calling her wife and insisting she call him husband. However, when the dowager duchess heard about it, Dereham was sent packing to Ireland."

"Now we have a bit of a blank for Catherine, don't we?" confirmed Perdita.

"Yes, she doesn't appear again in any records until 1539. By then, Henry had married Jane Seymour, who gave birth to

Prince Edward on 12 October 1537. She then died on 24 October 1537 and was buried in St George's chapel in Windsor Castle. Shortly after, Thomas Cromwell began scouting around for a new bride for Henry. However, because he'd already executed one of his wives, it took a while to find someone willing. Finally, Anne of Cleves was selected as the winner of the Henry lottery and she arrived in England on 27 December 1539.

"In the run up to this, though, Thomas Howard, the duke of Norfolk, arranged for his niece, Catherine Howard to be a maid of honour to the new queen. Catherine left Lambeth for the king's court in December 1539."

"Yes, Anne of Cleves married Henry VIII on 6 January 1540 but it's thought that by February 1540, the king was already involved with Catherine, although there are no records of how they actually met," said Perdita. "So, it's strange that, in March 1540, there were rumours suggesting Catherine was betrothed to her distant cousin, Thomas Culpepper."

"It's even stranger that, according to some sources, Francis Dereham challenged her about the rumours," added Kit.

"Especially as he was supposed to have been banished to Ireland, so therefore shouldn't have been at court, or know anything about it."

"Exactly."

Perdita's timeline was slowly taking shape. She had divided the board into three sections: the first she was filling with details of what else was happening in the court at pivotal dates, the second listed all the accepted events of Catherine's life, and the third column was currently blank. Perdita's intention was to write in here what she viewed as the real story of Catherine Howard, as discovered by her grandmother, and see how the events compared.

"Now things become more interesting," said Perdita. "Thomas Cromwell?"

"Oh, the lovely Cromwell," said Kit. "On 18 April 1540, Henry created him Earl of Essex and Grand Chamberlain of England."

"But his reign of power was short and probably not very sweet because, on 10 June 1540, barely eight weeks later, he was arrested for treason."

"And on 26 June 1540, Anne of Cleves and her household were moved to Richmond Palace. On 6 July, Anne agreed to an investigation of her marriage. Then, after the shortest inquiry in history, Henry gave her a document on 7 July agreeing to an annulment, which she signed. On 28 July 1540, Thomas Cromwell was executed, then on the same day, Henry married Catherine at Oatlands Palace in Surrey, officiated by Edward Bonner, the Bishop of London. What an old romantic," sighed Kit, and Perdita laughed.

"Catherine was his fifth queen," said Perdita, drawing a crown.

"And it's now that things become strange," continued Kit, surveying what they had already collated on the board.

"Let's keep going then," said Perdita. "On 8 August 1540, Henry presented Catherine as queen at Hampton Court Palace, then two weeks later, on 22 August, Henry and Catherine set off on a mini-progress taking in Windsor Castle and Reading before travelling to Ewelm, Rycott, Notley, Buckingham and Grafton. Then, in September, they travelled to Ampthill and then The Moor in Hertfordshire…"

"Which had once been the home of Cardinal Wolsey," interrupted Kit, and Perdita nodded. "There are also records in 1540 of Catherine interceding on behalf of a number of people and being a financial patron."

"All the time surrounded by rumours that she was pregnant," added Perdita. "Although, it seems that, despite her supposed many lovers, she was never caught out. But, rather than concluding she was barren as so many historians have, there could actually be a far simpler explanation."

"Which is…?"

"That perhaps she didn't have any lovers, therefore no babies. And, perhaps the reason she never conceived with Henry was because he wasn't capable."

"Why, Dr Rivers, that's treason!" exclaimed Kit.

"Off with my head," she laughed. "What's next?"

"On 3 January 1541, Anne of Cleves arrived at Hampton Court with two horses as a New Year present for Henry. This was the first time Anne and Catherine had seen each other since she became queen, and apparently Henry retired to bed and left the ladies to dance the night away."

"More evidence for those dancing lessons," said Perdita. "Next, in February 1541, Henry became seriously ill, and it has always been suggested that this was when Catherine might have begun her alleged relationship with Thomas Culpepper, although most of the detail about the so-called 'affair' conveniently came to light after Mary Lascelles's accusations about Catherine. As with Jane Boleyn, historians are bemused as to why Culpepper — another successful career courtier — would risk trying to seduce the queen."

"Meaning what?" asked Kit, looking up from their notes.

"Well, opinions are split," continued Perdita. "Some scholars — mostly male, mostly Victorian — believe Catherine and Thomas were two lustful individuals who couldn't control themselves; while modern historians believe that the relationship — if it happened at all — was never consummated. Although, it's suggested that Catherine and

Thomas were in love. Another recent feminist interpretation claims Culpepper blackmailed the queen into giving him sexual favours, or he threatened that he would tell Henry she hadn't been a virgin when she married him. And yet another version has Culpepper blackmailing Jane Boleyn in order to get close enough to the queen to seduce her.

"So, whether he was a thorough cad or a man indulging in some courtly flirting, I think that the inability of scholars to be able to find any evidence on which they can agree means that the 'affair' probably didn't happen. The fact both Jane and Thomas present such problems for historians even now, shows there was something suspicious about their representations in Catherine's story."

Kit nodded. "Well argued, Dr Rivers," he said with mock seriousness. She threw a marker pen at him and he ducked. "However, by March 1541, the king had recovered and still besotted, he threw a water pageant for his lovely new bride. In April, Catherine pleaded for the release of her half-brother John Leigh from the Tower of London. A few days later, she summoned Culpepper to her chambers to give him a gift of a velvet cap and a brooch, which was not an unusual thing to do in her position as queen."

"By June 1541, they were on progress with the queen rumoured to be unwell for some of it," continued Perdita. "By August things were going awry for Catherine. On the sixth, watchmen found a door unlocked and it has been suggested that this was how Catherine and Culpepper met for naughty night-time liaisons, then on 27 August, Francis Dereham was placed in Catherine's household as her secretary."

"Which is utterly bizarre," commented Kit. "If she really had been having some sort of relationship with him during her time at Lambeth, why would anyone in their right mind put him so near her again? Anyway, shortly after this on 29 August, Mary Lascelles approached Thomas Cranmer, the Archbishop of Canterbury, with information about the queen's 'lewd' behaviour."

"And now everything begins to unravel for Catherine," sighed Perdita. "By November, Cranmer had told Henry of the accusations and Catherine was confined to her quarters while there was an investigation."

"After Cranmer interviewed Catherine and she denied everything, her brother Charles Howard was banished from the king's privy chamber and on 11 November 1541, Catherine was removed to Syon Abbey in Isleworth with her half-sister, Isabel Baynton, and three other women."

"Interestingly, on 15 November 1541, there was a rumour that a son born to Henry and Anne of Cleves was being hidden in Anne's home. However, an investigation by the king and his council exonerated Anne and her household," said Perdita.

"On 22 November 1541, Catherine was stripped of her title as queen — she was now known simply as Lady Catherine Howard — and after this, her family was slowly rounded up and questioned, all of whom dropped the poor child in it even further."

"On first December 1541, Culpepper and Dereham — but not Manox — were found guilty of treason at the Guildhall in London. They were executed on 10 December 1541 at Tyburn. A number of Catherine's relatives and ladies-in-waiting were also found guilty of treason and forced to surrender their titles, land and goods, as well as being imprisoned for life. These included Agnes Tilney, the dowager duchess of Norfolk, Katherine Tilney, Joan Bulmer, Anne Howard, Margaret Benet and Alice Restwold. In January 1542, the Bill of Attainder — aka the execution warrant — against Catherine and Jane

Boleyn, who was supposed to have been her accomplice, was introduced to Parliament and, after a few attempts, was passed in absentia of dear old Henry," said Perdita. "In the eyes of the law and the king, they were already dead," she continued. "The reason they were condemned under a Parliamentary bill was because it avoided giving them a trial. Passing an attainder — which means 'tainted' — was an ancient way for the reigning monarch to do as he pleased without anyone else's interference — no jury, no trial, no possibility of anyone being acquitted. Culpepper and Dereham did not have 'execution warrants' because they had been tried in a court and found guilty.

"On the tenth of January 1542, the dukes of Suffolk and Southampton escorted Catherine and Jane to the Tower of London — Catherine was hysterical and Jane had supposedly gone mad — then on 11 February 1542, the Bill became law and, on the morning of 13 February, Catherine Howard and Jane Boleyn were executed and their remains buried in the Church of St Peter ad Vincula in the grounds of the Tower."

Next, they moved to the blank section and began filling in the details and anomalies flagged by Mary in her manuscript and other conclusions and discoveries they had made themselves until eventually, they had what Perdita described as a Map of Time.

Standing back to admire their work, Perdita turned to Kit with a satisfied smile, "When you lay it out like this," she said. "The 'accepted' version looks less and less robust."

"It's definitely shaky," he agreed. "The trouble is, even with the Book of Hours backing up a few bits from the codex, ours is largely conjecture. It's a great theory, but MI1 could refute every claim we've made."

"Yes, frustrating, isn't it?" replied Perdita. "Although, last night, I was going through the Book of Hours again…"

"When did you do that?" asked Kit in surprise.

"I haven't been sleeping well and I came down for an hour or so," she admitted. "Anyway, and you might dismiss this but, near the back is a tiny drawing," she put down her marker pen and walked to the foam wedges where the Book of Hours lay closed. Opening it carefully, she turned the pages until she found what she was looking for, then weighted the book open with ropes of heavy beads. "Look," she said, pointing to a small ink sketch, "do you think that could be Marquess House before all the extensions were built?"

Kit considered it.

"It certainly looks similar. There are original plans in the archive, we could check," he rummaged in his bag and removed an eyeglass before examining the small sketch.

Perdita watched him for a moment, then walked towards the window where she perched on the low sill, waiting for Kit to finish studying the image. One finger went to her hair and she began unconsciously curling a strand around it while she thought.

"Where are you going with this, Perds?" asked Kit, straightening up.

"I have a theory," she said, "and seeing all this laid out in front of us has helped me clarify a few thoughts."

Kit leaned against the table, giving Perdita his full attention.

"I knew you'd found something," he said. "Your brain is even sharper than Mary's and it was always fascinating to watch her work through her theories. Have you discovered something else or made a crazy connection?"

"A connection, I think. It was you and your dad who gave me the idea," she said. "When you told me about those letters from Penelope Fitzalan, the ones Lettice found when she first bought the house. They mention a ruby ring and a secret she was prepared to die to protect."

"Do you think they were real?" mused Kit. "I wondered if they were Victorian fakes."

"I asked your dad and he confirmed that Mary had them dated. They're seventeenth century, so they're the right period. Not only that, a Penelope Fitzalan is named as the author of *The Llyn Cel Mermaid and Other Local Legends*, so whoever this person was, she's definitely connected to Marquess House," said Perdita.

"Are you saying you think Penelope Fitzalan was somehow linked to Catherine Howard, and the ruby ring she mentions is the one referred to in the codex?" asked Kit. "Isn't that a bit of a leap?"

"On its own, yes, but remember what else your dad said, the secret Penelope was hiding was supposedly hidden somewhere in this house."

"But Mary searched and searched. She didn't find anything."

"You're missing my point. The treasure was supposed to be in Marquess House. The ring was with Penelope and she wrote about the lake attached to this house, and then there's this image, possibly of Marquess House in its early days, in a Book of Hours we're fairly certain belonged to Kathy Knollys."

Perdita could see from Kit's expression that he did not understand where she was heading with her theory; it was essential to convince him. Taking a deep breath, she delivered the crux of her new idea.

"From all we've discovered, I think this house is somehow linked to Catherine Howard's story."

"But, Perds, how? It's hundreds of miles from London. How would Catherine have ended up here?" said Kit before giving her a curious look. "Have you found something else?"

"No, but I think there is a way we could find out. Look, I admit some of this is gut instinct, but if you look at the broader picture, there is increasing evidence. Henry Tudor was born in Pembroke Castle which is only a few miles away, and when he came back to claim his throne, he landed at Mill Bay in Milford Haven. From there he marched inland and went on to win the Battle of Bosworth against Richard III, so this area is the Tudor heartland," said Perdita, glancing at Kit to read his expression to see if he was still listening. He looked bemused but the focus of his eyes encouraged her to continue.

"Not only that," she went on, "we know Marquess House was once part of Anne Boleyn's dowry from that book in the library *Marquess House: A History* by Arabella Talbot, which was written in the eighteenth century. Before he married her, Henry wanted to elevate Anne to the highest ranks of the aristocracy, so he created the title Marquess of Pembroke for her. It was the first hereditary peerage title granted to a woman, hence the reason she was a Marquess rather than the usual female title of Marchioness; it was where the house got its name. After her fall, the house and its lands were returned to the king, who gifted the estate to her uncle, Thomas Howard, the duke of Norfolk, as a reward for dealing so swiftly with the problem that Anne Boleyn had become. Thomas Howard was Catherine's uncle and Kathy Knollys, who, we know from her own account, went on a journey with Catherine, has drawn a sketch of a house that looks like the original part of the building. I think the ring was left behind by Catherine, and was evidence that she had lived here at some point. Penelope found it or acquired it and became determined to keep the secret of what really happened to Catherine Howard…"

"But we're back to the problem of proof!" exclaimed Kit.

"Do you know if there are any household records, accounts, laundry lists, from that era in the archive?"

"Yes, as far as I know. Why?" Then understanding bloomed on his face. "You think Catherine Howard might be mentioned in the household records?"

"Yes!" exclaimed Perdita. "So much of history is hidden in the everyday details of life. I might be completely wrong but don't you think it would be worth discovering who was in residence in this house at the time it states in Kathy Knollys' Book of Hours that Catherine and some of her ladies took their journey without the king's permission, especially as, at that date in the accepted version of events, Catherine Howard should have been dead? Catherine was the secret, Kit, I'm sure of it and the ruby ring is the final piece of the puzzle. It was her ring and it proves she was here after the date of her supposed death; that was the secret Penelope was prepared to die to keep."

Kit stared at her, awestruck.

"You're incredible," he said, then reached for the phone to call Jenny and ask her to find the household accounts for Marquess House during the 1540s.

Jenny and Izabel arrived with a trolley holding two storage boxes.

"I'm intrigued," Jenny said as they lifted them onto the boardroom table and began arranging the contents. "Two days before Mary died, she requested the same items: it's why we have them. These are among the original documents that Mary inherited with the house when she was twenty-one. Most of them are extremely fragile and are usually stored at Jerusalem, where they have an even greater capacity than we do and where their humidity controls are even more advanced than ours."

Perdita's eyes widened in surprise.

"Did Granny say why?" she asked.

"No, she merely requested they be brought out of deep storage as there were a few things she wanted to check," replied Izabel. "It's why we were able to access them so quickly for you, otherwise it would have taken a few weeks. We were already in the process of fetching them when Mary died, so when they arrived, we put them in our storage area until they could be returned." Izabel finished lining up the foam wedges with their ancient ledgers. "See you later," she said and disappeared back to the library.

Perdita and Kit were already walking along the row of books, eagerly examining the dusty volumes.

"They're in surprisingly good condition," said Jenny. "The housekeeper back then, Mrs Page, believed in buying quality ledgers, so these have survived. It isn't a complete set — we're missing January, February and December. If it's important, I can contact my counterpart, Dr Deborah Black, at the Jerusalem library to check whether they've been filed with another year in error. These will start you off though, Perdita. What are you looking for?"

"Names of guests," replied Perdita, pausing in front of the ledger labelled May 1542, "you're very welcome to help us." Then a thought struck her. "Are they in Welsh?" she knew it would not be an insurmountable problem but it would delay their quest while they had them translated. Jenny took the volume marked June 1542, then shook her head.

"No, they're in English. Mrs Helen Page took over as housekeeper in early 1541 and she was originally from London. Her husband Joshua accompanied her and worked as the chief steward," she replied. "We do have some in Welsh from other years after the Pages left."

"You know a lot about the Pages," commented Perdita.

"They're mentioned in one of the older books about Marquess House," she said. "Apparently, they moved here after their daughter Maud was murdered. They must have wanted a new start."

"How awful, the poor things."

Kit opened the book marked July 1542 and began running his finger down the endless lists of household orders.

"What am I looking for?" asked Jenny, making herself comfortable at one of the desks and perching her glasses on her nose.

"Any comments about female guests, particularly Lady Isabel Baynton, Lady Margaret Douglas, Lady Kathryn Knollys or Catherine Howard herself," replied Perdita.

Jenny stared at her agog. "You think they stayed here?"

"It's a theory we're working on," Perdita replied before turning her attention to the ancient ledger in front of her.

With her expert eye for detail, Perdita quickly learned to decipher the extravagantly swirled handwriting of Mrs Page, so she was soon scanning column after column, looking for clues. At first, all she could find were entries listing the usual household requirements: tallow candles, poppy seed, linen, beeswax, barley for Mr Evans, payments to local butchers, flour from the miller, coal for the blacksmith, but nothing about guests.

Maybe this is a wild goose chase, thought Perdita, but her instincts told her to keep searching, particularly now she knew her grandmother had requested the same items. Turning page after page, detail upon detail of how Marquess House was managed in May 1542 unfolded before her eyes, each instruction or order flowing across the ancient paper. A vision of the house began to form in her mind with such vividness, she could almost hear Mrs Page's voice echoing through the centuries. Her eye ran down another column near the end of the month.

"Oh!" she exclaimed.

"What?" asked Kit.

"'*Linen for Lady I Baynton*' and '*divers herbes for Lady Tudor*'," read Perdita, triumph in her voice. "Poor Lady Tudor, whoever she was, wasn't very well," she said and read the items out loud: "Aloe, lovage, comfrey, Solomon's seal, wood sage, carraway, chervil, as well as multiple visits from the apothecary, the barber surgeon and a local healer."

Kit pulled his laptop towards him and after a few moments said: "All those herbs were used for healing bruises, cuts, broken limbs and fevers," he looked up with an expression of revulsion. "Do you think Lady Tudor had been tortured?"

"I hope not," Perdita shuddered.

"Who's Lady Tudor, though?" asked Jenny.

Perdita shrugged. "Part of the entourage, maybe? Placing Lady Isabel Baynton here corroborates the comments from the Book of Hours. If Isabel was here, it's possible Catherine Howard was too."

Perdita turned back to her ledger and continued searching. Jenny and Kit followed suit.

"'*Paints for Lady Knollys*'," read Kit. "And," he could barely keep the excitement from his voice, "'*Ink for Lady Douglas*', Perds, you were right! They were here!"

"We still need a reference to Catherine herself," said Perdita, delighted that her hunch had been correct. "Keep looking!"

As Perdita and Kit searched the books for the name Catherine Howard, Jenny began logging the references made to her ladies-in-waiting.

"There's a Charles Howard listed here," said Kit after a long silence. "'*Riding boots and travelling cloaks*'. Maybe he was heading back to London."

"Charles Howard," Perdita murmured. "Catherine's elder brother."

"Yes," said Jenny, noting down Charles's name. "As you both know, he was engaged to Lady Margaret Douglas during his sister's reign as queen, although his fate is unknown. He disappeared from court records in 1542 and Lady Douglas married Matthew Stewart, the earl of Lennox in 1544."

"But, if Charles Howard was here…" Perdita began, then Kit cut across her. "'*Flemish wine for Thomas Howard, duke of Norfolk*'!" he exclaimed.

Perdita returned to the whiteboard, examining the information they had collated.

"They were all here," she said, quietly, "all the people we know were in Catherine's inner circle, all the people whose letters are either included in the codex or are referred to…"

And then, suddenly, she understood.

"Lady Tudor!" Perdita gasped. "What if Lady Tudor was Catherine Howard? Her identity disguised so Henry VIII wouldn't find her? We know from the codex that he had beaten her regularly throughout their marriage," her eyes widened. "Lady Tudor, she wasn't tortured, she was recovering from being brutalised by her husband. It has to be her, it has to be Catherine Howard!"

Jenny ran her eyes down the list of references, "You could be right, Perdita, the name Catherine Howard is conspicuous by its absence…"

"Which is all very well," cut in Kit, trying not to sound exasperated, "but if she isn't named, we can't prove it was truly Catherine Howard."

Perdita continued to stare at the timeline. "It must be her," she said. "Catherine Howard was at Marquess House, there isn't any other logical explanation. Although, if she escaped to Pembrokeshire, who was executed on 13 February 1542? Was anybody actually executed or was the Bill of Attainder a complete fabrication?"

She turned to look at Kit, her face wreathed with confusion. "We seem to be creating more problems than we're solving."

"Don't give up now, Perds," Kit said. "This is a massive step forward: we can prove Catherine's ladies, her brother and her uncle all visited this house in 1542. Somehow, somewhere, we'll find a way to prove whether or not Lady Tudor was Catherine Howard. Come on, there are two ledgers left to check, I'll take October, you take November."

Sitting down once more, Perdita's mind was whirring. Placing Catherine's half-sister, Lady Isabel Baynton; her brother, Charles Howard and her uncle, the duke of Norfolk at Marquess House was startling, but unless they had a record of her name, it proved nothing. Forcing herself to focus on the ledger in front of her, Perdita concentrated once more on Mrs Page's elaborate handwriting. Three pages in, she called out, her voice unexpectedly harsh and urgent. "Kit, Jenny: look!"

Her eyes were wide as she pushed the ancient book towards them. "Five lines down, '*A woollen shawl for Lady C Howard*', but it's been crossed out and replaced with the name Tudor. It was her. She was here!"

All three of them stared at each other in delight. Jenny seized the book and turned a few more pages: "*Linen for Lady Howard, ink for Mistress C Howard…*"

"But why suddenly use her real name?" interrupted Kit.

"Human error," suggested Perdita, "or maybe Henry was no longer looking for her. He married Katheryn Parr in 1543. Perhaps he was so enamoured with her, it was safe to use Catherine's real name again."

Kit still looked perplexed. "What?" asked Perdita.

"She was here, we can prove that, but what happened next? Where did she go afterwards?"

"I don't understand…"

"She was a young woman. If she was now free from the king," said Kit, "do you think she stayed here? Lived in Pembrokeshire for the rest of her life?"

"Let's keep looking," said Perdita, fired up with enthusiasm and energy now they had made this huge discovery. She returned to her ledger and continued to scour the pages.

Suddenly, she saw something that made her gasp in surprise.

"What?" asked Kit.

"I think I've found the real reason she was here," said Perdita, and pushed the ancient book towards Kit and Jenny. Both of them read the entry that had startled Perdita and looked at her, their eyes round with wonder.

"But that's impossible…" whispered Kit.

"Perhaps this is what MI1 wanted to stop Granny Mary telling the world," replied Perdita, gazing down at the ledger as the words reached out from another time, finally revealing this greatest of secrets. "While history might tell us that Catherine Howard was executed at the Tower of London on 13 February 1542, it seems she was actually alive and well, living in Pembrokeshire and preparing to give birth."

Chapter Four

Perdita came to understand the full power of Marquess House as a centre of research. Jenny and Alistair invited her into an official meeting and they explained how her grandmother had structured a process for cataloguing new information.

"Whenever Mary found documents she felt were important, our task force was activated so the information could be captured quickly and efficiently," Jenny had explained. "My team will translate and digitise the original documents so we have an immediate record, making the information more accessible for future research. I also wondered whether, with this discovery, you would like Izabel to head up a team to cross reference all the information in the ledgers with that in the codex so we can create a timeline of Catherine Howard and her entourage's movements from February 1542 onwards."

"Can we do that?" Perdita had asked. She was used to the slow wheels of academia, committees, steering groups, recommendations, the trickle of funding and endless pointless meetings before research could begin. This swift, efficient system was something of a shock.

"Oh yes, it's what we do best," Jenny had replied, her eyes sparkling.

Now, two weeks later, Perdita felt they could conclusively prove that Catherine Howard had taken refuge within the walls of Marquess House. They were still awaiting the arrival of the household accounts from 1543, 1544 and 1545, which were in deep storage in Castle Jerusalem. Dr Black had suggested it might be quicker for Perdita to pay them a visit in Andorra to view the documents if it was urgent, but as she was awaiting the arrival of Piper, she had decided to wait. At present, she had more than enough to be dealing with, processing the information from the 1542 books.

Letting herself into her apartment, she dropped her bags onto an armchair then wandered into her bedroom where she kicked off her boots and brushed her hair, pulling it up into a ponytail. It had been another hectic day and her mind was still teeming with all they had found. Kit had invited her to join him and his friends at the pub but she had refused, wanting to spend the evening writing up her notes. Time and research had taught her that, when she had this amount of information whirring through her mind, the only way she could deal with it was to write it down, then her brain would relax enough for her to focus on other things, like sleep.

Returning to her sitting room, she grabbed her laptop, wandered into the kitchen where she poured herself a glass of red wine, then settled herself on her sofa, her computer on a cushion on her lap, and proceeded to type. An hour later, she was finished. Sipping her wine, she read back through her notes, correcting the occasional word, clarifying certain sections, until she was satisfied with what she had written. She put the laptop on the coffee table in front of her and closed her eyes, happier now her observations and ideas were out of her head and safely on paper.

If only Granny were here, she thought. *She would have been so excited to see what we've discovered. I wonder if this was what she had concluded in her final chapter...*

Suddenly, she sat up. Her eyes alert, why hadn't it occurred to her before? Mary must have had a computer, whether it was her own laptop or a dedicated unit in her office. If the missing chapter was anywhere, it would surely be there. Glancing at her watch, she saw it was still reasonably early. Assured neither

Alistair or Susan would mind this small intrusion into their evening, she dialled their number.

Ten minutes later, Perdita was letting herself into her grandmother's suite. It was the first time she had been in there since she and Piper had explored it before Mary's funeral. When she had offered to return the keys to Alistair, he had smiled and folded her fingers around them.

"They're yours," he had said. "Everything belongs to you and Piper. Everything."

The room was spotlessly clean. Obviously, Sarah's team had continued to keep Mary's room pristine. Perdita had a sudden pang of guilt. She had been so engrossed with her research, she had not given any thought to Mary's belongings and what to do with them. Eventually, she and Piper would have to make these decisions, it would be peculiar to leave the room exactly as Mary had kept it in life, but then, *she kept our rooms ready*, thought Perdita. Shaking her head, she pushed these thoughts away. There would be time to decide when Piper arrived, for now she had other things on her mind.

The layout of Mary's room was the same as hers, so without hesitation Perdita hurried across the room and opened the door to Mary's office. For the first time, she caught a waft of Mary's scent — Chanel No. 5 — and she breathed it in hungrily. It felt like a good sign, as though Mary were watching over her. Apart from being kept clean, the office had not been touched; it looked as though Mary had left it moments before. Swallowing the unexpected lump that rose in her throat, Perdita seated herself at her grandmother's laptop and turned it on. Following Alistair's instructions, she unlocked the top drawer of the desk, where he had left an envelope containing her grandmother's passwords.

"As executor to her will, she insisted on always leaving me with her passwords," he had explained. "In the immediate aftermath of Mary's death, we did commandeer her laptop as there was some information on it we needed to access, but we've finished with it now. I returned it and the passwords to her rooms a few days ago. The laptop and its contents are yours now, Perdita."

"Mine," she breathed. "Mine and Piper's."

She felt a certain amount of trepidation wondering what she might discover as the laptop blinked into life. Like everything else, it was laid out with precision and it did not take Perdita long to find Mary's archive of work. Scrolling through, she resisted the urge to check every file, but focused instead on searching for the missing chapter. But, twenty minutes and many searches later, she was slightly flummoxed. If the missing chapter wasn't here, where could it be? Finally, she braved the folder marked 'Family Stuff'. Bracing herself, she looked at the contents, there were two documents, one named Perdita and one named Piper.

"Oh shit," she murmured but she clicked them open, one after the other, expecting a letter. She was rather startled instead to see a familiar Bible quotation. It was the passage from Susanna that she had read at both her father's and Mary's funeral. Glancing at Piper's message, it was the brief paragraph from George Orwell's *1984* that she had read.

To her right was a long oak bookcase and on the top shelf was a leather-bound Apocrypha. On the shelf below, immediately underneath this, was a copy of *1984*. *It's too much of coincidence*, she thought, *Granny must be pointing us toward something*. Perdita sprang to her feet and pulled both books off the shelf. Hidden within the pages of the Apocrypha was an envelope addressed to her, in *1984* was one for Piper.

"Oh Granny, what are you up to?" said Perdita, but she ripped open the letter and unfolded the single page of heavy lilac writing paper.

Mary's elegant handwriting filled the page but what caught Perdita's eye was the date. Her grandmother had written this letter three months before her death. Sitting back at the desk, Perdita spread the paper out in front of her and began to read:

My darling Perdita, if you are reading this, then Marquess House must now be in the possession of you and Piper. This will mean I have missed my chance of my dreamed of reunion with you, my beautiful girls. My words here must suffice instead: please know this, I love you. I have always loved you and I will never stop loving you. I distanced myself from you both to keep you safe and, I hope, as time goes on, you will understand my motivations and you will forgive me.

You did not know, but I was never far away. Your father kept me informed of your life and I witnessed many key moments. My favourite was the day I saw you receive your doctorate. A moment of such pride, I nearly broke my own rule and approached you to offer my congratulations. However, your safety was more important, so I resisted.

Now, I must impart vital information. If Alistair Mackensie has not yet told you about the Watchers, I implore you speak to him immediately, telling him I give my express permission for you to know everything, but if these words do make sense to you, then perhaps the following lines will too. If not, then again, Alistair will explain.

The missing chapter and the additional information I discovered for my unpublished manuscript The Catherine Howard Anomaly *is in my safe. The code is your and Piper's birth date. I did not publish this book as I always felt it was the cause of your mother's death. This is the same for my other unpublished work. However, today I received news that has made me realise things have changed and secrecy will no longer keep you safe. You must solve the mystery I inadvertently began to unravel all those years ago. I feel sure it is the only thing now that will save you both.*

Good luck, my beautiful princess.

I will watch over you always.

Granny Mary xxx

Perdita was on her feet and across the room. Her safe was hidden behind a very beautiful but extremely old tapestry of a mermaid. In the same position on Mary's wall was one of her father's swirling abstract paintings. Pulling the corner, it swung forward, revealing the safe door. Keying in her birth date, she heard a click and wrenched it open. A box file filled most of the space. Perdita pulled it out and the label on the top read: *The Catherine Howard Anomaly.* Placing it on the floor, she searched to see what other treasures her grandmother had stowed in the safe, but there was nothing else.

I wonder if she put it in there every night, thought Perdita, slamming the door and returning her father's painting to its correct place. *I suppose at eighty-six years old, you never take a sunrise for granted.*

Gathering the box file, the letter and Mary's laptop, Perdita returned to her own room, unable to bear being among her grandmother's possessions any longer. Everywhere she turned was heartache and loss caused by this secret. Her grandmother may have spent years protecting them from it but, in her own words, she had told her granddaughter things had changed. Quite what had prompted this unexpected turnaround was not clear, and Perdita intended to question Alistair as soon as possible.

Now she had a purpose and, more strikingly, her grandmother's permission to finish the manuscript that Mary had begun all those years ago. It was not something she needed, but she was glad to be working with her grandmother rather than being haunted by the constant feeling she might be letting her down by returning to her abandoned research.

Back in her own room, Perdita took up her position on the sofa again and reread her grandmother's letter. The only line that jarred was the last one. She had not expected her grandmother to use the pet-name 'princess'. *I obviously don't know her as well as I think*, mused Perdita. Then, carefully placing the letter on the table where she could see her grandmother's writing, she opened the box file.

It was full to the top and the first item in the pile was a plastic wallet containing the missing chapter of her grandmother's manuscript. Perdita glanced at the documents below but they were mostly earlier drafts and photocopies from books. Quickly, realising they were the references for the final chapter, she put them to one side and pulled the missing chapter out of its protective wallet. She noted the date was the day before her grandmother had died, and she began to read.

Chapter 26: Life Beyond Death

This work has so far concentrated on the life and anomalies of Catherine Howard and her loyal court of ladies: Lady Isabel Baynton, Lady Margaret Arundell, Lady Margaret Douglas and Lady Kathy Knollys. There have been references to Catherine's predecessor in Henry VIII's bed, Anne of Cleves, and discussion of the baffling Jane Boleyn, Lady Rochford. However, now, to bring their tale to a conclusion, I must take you briefly down another path.

In 1953, at the age of twenty-one, I inherited Marquess House from my mother, Eleanor Fitzroy. My mother had died shortly after the birth of my younger sister, Cecily, in 1940. Her estate had been left to me as the eldest, with a sizeable trust fund for Cecily. Staggered to be the owner of such a vast property, I began to sort through the massive archive which I now owned, along with the house. Expecting to find nothing of interest, I was surprised when I discovered, what has become known to me and my team at Marquess House as The Catherine Howard Codex and which has provided the bulk of the primary source material for this book.

It had been put into storage with the household accounts and, at first, I paid it no attention. My interest became piqued after the visit of my friend, Lady Pamela Johnson, who had inherited her title and estate when her brother, her only living relative, had died. She knew I was interested in documents from the Tudor era, and had some she wanted to sell in order to pay the heavy death duties. I agreed, again not expecting to find anything of interest but because I was in a position to be able to help her. It was she who first began to read the codex and it was her brilliance that connected it to some letters she had discovered in her own family home.

She recognised one particular piece of handwriting, the delicate hand of Lady Isabel Baynton, half-sister through their mother, Jocasta or Joyce Culpepper, to Henry VIII's fifth queen, Catherine Howard. Lady Pamela was descended from Isabel's husband's family and had seen letters written by Lady Isabel before. Surprised, I began studying the codex and discovered not only letters from Isabel but also from Lady Kathryn Knollys, Lady Margaret Douglas, Lady Margaret Arundell and another woman who signed herself in a number of different ways: 'C', 'K', 'Kitty', 'Kitten' and on a few occasions 'Catherine'. It was this woman who intrigued me.

After piecing together the information available, I created a workable hypothesis that this unnamed woman could be Catherine Howard. Although, if this was the case, then I had discovered a bigger mystery than I had ever expected. If the dates on the letters were to be believed, Catherine Howard was still alive in May 1542. My initial thought was, it must be another noble woman with the same name as the unfortunate fifth bride of Henry VIII, because Queen Catherine was supposed to have been executed three months earlier on 13 February 1542.

397

Once more, Lady Pamela's remarkable archive shed light on this perplexing puzzle. In among this batch of letters — the first of many caches of Tudor and Stuart documents that she sold me over the years — was one from a friend of Joan Bulmer's, lamenting her loss. Joan Bulmer was a contemporary of Catherine Howard's and as young girls, they had both been boarded out at Lambeth House, the property owned by Agnes Tilney, the dowager duchess of Norfolk. Historical legend tells us that Bulmer and Howard shared a lover, Francis Dereham. He was first introduced to the house while he was involved with Joan, then rapidly turned his attention to Catherine who, with her Howard blood, was a far better catch.

When Catherine became queen, Joan wrote to her offering advice and, it has been assumed by some historians, requesting a place in Catherine's household. However, there are no official records placing Joan in the queen's court. Yet, this letter claimed Joan had indeed been at court during Catherine's reign and that she had been executed. In it, the writer begged the recipient (whose name unfortunately has been lost to time and mice) not to think badly of Joan but to feel pity. It was dated the 24 February 1542.

Intrigued, I spoke to a friend who worked at the Tower of London and asked about their execution records, but upon checking the dates, explained there was no record of the execution of Joan Bulmer, only Jane Boleyn.

It was a revelation. Jane Boleyn has always been one of the unexplained characters in the tale of Catherine Howard and her rapid downfall. Historians have never been able to fully explain what would have motivated this previously canny survivor to throw in her lot with the young queen, risking everything to supposedly facilitate the queen's affair with the courtier Thomas Culpepper. Now I had been presented with this new information, I couldn't help looking at the two names and noticing their similarity. I wondered if this could explain the mystery of Jane Boleyn's supposed execution:

JOAN BULMER
JANE BOLEYN

It would not take much to alter one to the other, they were the same length, the same initials and similar in the letter span. I began to wonder, had Joan Bulmer been executed instead of Jane Boleyn? If so, why? What had happened to Jane Boleyn? And why had the names been changed?

After a great deal of painstaking research, I was able to procure Jane's family Bible, that of the Parker's of Great Hallingbury, Essex, and discovered something curious, but which gave me confidence in my theory. In the front was the usual list of births, marriages and deaths. Jane's triumphant marriage to George Boleyn and her rise to become Viscountess Rochford as his wife were detailed.

Surprisingly, so was a second marriage in February 1541, to Thomas Culpepper, a member of the king's privy chamber. Most interesting, however, was the entry of later in 1541, recording the deaths of first Thomas Culpepper on 29 August 1541, followed by Lady Jane Culpepper two months later and the details of their joint tomb in the Parker family vault. If Jane Boleyn, now Lady Culpepper, died in October 1541, how could she possibly have been executed alongside Catherine Howard on 13 February 1542?

Similarly, if Catherine Howard was, as the letter I had discovered suggested, still alive in May 1542, who was executed in her stead? Was this the reason why the Bill of Attainder that sentenced both Catherine and her lady-in-waiting, Jane Boleyn, to death was never signed by the king but by using his dry seal, because it was never theirs in the first place?

Feeling certain this was the case for Jane Boleyn, further investigation revealed a possible candidate who may have been executed instead of Queen Catherine: Katherine Tilney. She was another member of the extended Howard family and many historical documents place her in the vicinity of Joan Bulmer. She and Joan both disappear from official records at the same time. Again, the similarity in name length struck me. The same first name, which could be spelled in a number of variations, followed by six letters in the surname.

KATHERINE TILNEY
CATHERINE HOWARD

But, if my hypothesis was correct, it begged the questions: why were Tilney and Bulmer executed? And who altered their death warrant, the Bill of Attainder that had been presented to Parliament?

There is also the question of Thomas Culpepper. Like Jane Boleyn, Culpepper is another person in the tale of Catherine Howard who mystifies historians. As Jane was a career courtier, so was Culpepper. He had risen through the ranks of the Henrician court to hold a trusted position in the king's privy chamber. Would he really throw away his life's work to bed the queen?

As I have discussed here, there is evidence he was married to Jane Boleyn. If this was the case, how is it possible that he stood trial at the Guildhall in London and was convicted of treason in December 1541? History tells us he, along with Francis Dereham, was executed on 10 December 1541. Yet, according to the Parker family Bible, Culpepper had died in August of that year.

I would suggest that if a Thomas Culpepper did stand trial, it was not the man who had been in the privy chamber. It is well documented that there were two Thomas Culpeppers in the same family. The elder was a violent rapist, the younger a career courtier. If the Bill of Attainder for Tilney and Bulmer was altered, could it be that the transcript of the trial for a man named Thomas Culpepper was altered in order to implicate a different Culpepper? One who bore the same name but who would have been of a high enough rank to seduce a queen, thus causing the downfall of Catherine Howard?

My suggestion is that Jane died, possibly as the result of a nervous collapse following the death of her second husband, Thomas Culpepper. However, for reasons I cannot explain, forever afterwards, Culpepper has been linked romantically to Catherine rather than Jane.

While this offered a workable hypotheses for Jane Boleyn and Thomas Culpepper, what of Catherine Howard? If she was not executed on that fateful day, where did she go? On 12 July 1543, Henry VIII married Katheryn Parr, so his fifth bride had certainly disappeared from his life.

It was as I puzzled over this, studying the details of the codex, that I began to notice something I had previously dismissed as trivial, but I now began to wonder if the answer had been hidden in plain sight all along. The intriguing woman signing herself Kitty, seemed to have adopted a motto: Spe et nereidum — *hope and mermaids — something that reminded me of my arrival at Marquess House as a child of seven.*

In January 1940, my mother, Eleanor Fitzroy, had removed us from our London residence to take refuge for the duration of the Second World War in her family's home in Pembrokeshire. I had been unimpressed until I had caught my first glimpse of our new home, Marquess House. With its tower and crenellations, it was bigger than any property I had ever seen and, as it twinkled in the winter sun, I thought we had come to live in a fairy tale castle.

Marquess House, it transpired, was a paradise of freedom and fun, especially once I had made friends with Bethan Bridges, whose family managed our estate's farm. We were inseparable and, as the dark days of winter gave way to a golden spring, we investigated Marquess House and the surrounding area, usually with our gang of friends. One of our favourite places was the mysterious island that sat in the middle of our lake, Llyn Cel, and this was largely due to Bethan's grandmother.

She was known to all as Old Mrs B and was a source of endless local tales. Our favourite was the story of the Llyn Cel mermaid.

On stormy nights, the Llyn Cel mermaid, a beautiful and terrible creature, was supposed to leave her watery home, discard her tail and walk on land searching for her lost love. The tale dated back to the sixteenth century, when it was said a noble lady, who had fled her cruel husband and their violent marriage, had taken refuge with the nuns at the tiny priory on the island, where she gave birth to twins, a girl and a boy. The

401

children were taken from her and raised by other families who did not know their true identities in order to keep them all safe from her powerful husband.

In time, the woman fell in love with a local fisherman but, because she was still legally married, they could not be together. Both were devastated as they were deeply in love. Then one day, news came that the woman's husband had died and the pair planned to marry. They agreed to meet in the porch of the church that night but, while he was out fishing on the stormy lake, the fisherman was washed overboard and drowned. The legend says the woman waited and waited, until eventually the priest told her the sad news. She was so distraught, she threw herself into the water determined to find her lover. As soon as the waves closed over her head, the onlookers swore they saw her legs turn into a tail and she vanished beneath the water.

However, a few days later, at the full moon, there was another storm. Late that night, when the priest left his church, he thought he saw a woman waiting in the porch, but as he approached her, she vanished. The next morning, villagers discussed the shadowy figure of a woman who had walked the streets singing a haunting lament. Soon, the legend grew that, on stormy nights, the mermaid rose from the waves and walked the village singing her song of love and loss. It was said that, should any man hear her, he would be bewitched and would follow her to a watery grave. So, the women would leave trinkets for the mermaid, hoping she would take these and leave their husbands safely at home.

Bethan and I were determined to find out more by exploring the ruins of the Llyn Cel priory, where the tale claimed the woman had lived before she became a mermaid. We also, secretly, hoped we might catch a glimpse of her shimmering tail and flowing red hair.

The night before our adventure, I headed to my favourite part of the house — the library — in search of a book of local legends and, to my astonishment, I found one. It was entitled The Llyn Cel Mermaid and Other Local Legends by Penelope Fitzalan, and contained a detailed account of the mermaid. From reading this version, I learned her name was Catherine and her lover was Owain. Another layer of romance had been added too, with the mermaid leaving trinkets to her children so they would be able to prove their identities when they were adults. It was also a way for the mermaid to recognise her beloved, lost offspring.

Even better, there was a map showing a passageway leading from the Marquess House chapel to the tower on the island, which was all that remained of the ancient priory. As our chapel had been locked up for the duration of the war, our only hope of discovering whether or not this tunnel existed was to visit the island. It added an entirely new layer of excitement to our adventure, particularly as there were sketches of the tunnel and one room in particular, that was described as being 'Catherine's room'.

We found the tunnel behind a brick marked with a crude depiction of a mermaid and the Latin motto — Spe et nereidum. When this was pushed, a door opened to reveal the entrance. In later years, I discovered its twin in my chapel, pushing the stone above it opened the door from this end. As children, Bethan and I used the tunnel as our hideout. We swore a blood oath to keep its location a secret. I took this very much to heart and refused to even tell my younger sister, Cecily, where the entrance to the tunnel lay hidden. We did find a room that we decided was 'Catherine's room' as the fireplace seemed to match the sketch in the book but, despite extensive searching for the trinkets left by the Llyn Cel mermaid or, even better, the treasures she had supposedly bequeathed to her children, we were unsuccessful. I forgot about our childhood searches until I read the codex.

It is a well-known academic trope that myths and legends have their basis in fact and I propose this: the legend of the Llyn Cel mermaid was based on the true story of what happened to Catherine Howard, the fifth bride of Henry VIII. I have found sufficient evidence to suggest she was removed from Henry VIII's court and was never mentioned in official records after 13 February 1542. Yet, these letters, dated after this, suggest the woman signing herself by that name had knowledge of the court and the king. Could it be another woman bearing the same name? An *anomaly that was not unusual in Tudor time. Or, had the former queen consort, Catherine Howard, been spirited away for another reason?*

If the legend is to be believed, Catherine was pregnant, something possibly corroborated by a short snippet in the codex, 'my clothes are so tight, I feel I shall burst…' *In which case, surely, she should have been at court revelling in her triumph as she carried a legitimate Tudor heir? My only other theory is that Catherine was pregnant by another man and, perhaps it was from here the legend of her promiscuity grew. However, if she was, would her family have risked all to hide her from the king? I suspect not.*

The codex also suggests Catherine had suffered intense violence at the hands of her husband. Perhaps this was the reason she was removed from his side; her family keeping her and the child safe until its birth. The fact that history tells us Henry VIII married Katheryn Parr in 12 July 1543 suggests Catherine and her offspring may not have survived…

But, to Perdita's frustration, the chapter finished mid-sentence.

"Oh, Granny, don't leave me hanging like this," she exclaimed. "Surely there must be more…"

And she turned the page over. Her eye widened in surprise. On the back of the typed sheets, dated the day before she died, her grandmother had written: *'The Penelope Fitzalan letters! The fireplace sketch in the last letter is the same as the sketch in the book. But who was PF? And who was she in relation to CH? Could the 'token' mentioned in the PF letter be the ring mentioned in the Llyn Cel story? Passageway? Will ask Kit to explore the tunnel with me in the morning. Fireplace!!!'*

Perdita put her hand over her mouth in shock. Had her grandmother finally discovered the key to the secret?

PART SIX: Marquess House, 1542

Chapter One

Catherine stared out of the window at the bright spring sunshine. Wildflowers were pushing through the grass and spreading across the lawn, weaving themselves into a living tapestry. It reminded Catherine of the beautifully patterned tiles in the entrance hall. Cascades of primroses, varying in colour from buttercup yellow to the pale and delicate Pembroke pink, festooned the shallow grassy bank that surrounded the gardens to the side of the house. The simple beauty made her smile.

A proper smile, she marvelled. *When was the last time I smiled for no reason?* Her expression faltered and she moved closer to the fire, hugging her arms around herself, as though shielding her body from attack. She was allowed to be happy. Her sisters Isabel and Margaret both said she was free and could do as she pleased now, but she still could not fully believe them. Even her uncle, who wrote regularly, implored her to forgive him his part in her misery. He asked her to remember the happy girl she had been when she was in the care of her step-grandmother at the house in Lambeth.

It seemed a lifetime ago: those crowded rooms, the constant noise of the busy, bustling house by the river. It was all so innocent back then, the mild flirtations, the silly intrigues, the ridiculous dramas they created, fooling themselves into thinking they were dying from love. She shuddered. She *had* nearly died, although not from love, but from a vicious beating from her husband, the king, immediately after what should have been a sacred act of love between husband and wife. The brutality of their last coupling still made Catherine shake with fear.

Her memory of events was hazy. Henry had summoned her in the early hours of the morning, excited by the prospect of the double execution of Katherine Tilney and Joan Bulmer, the two women he was convinced were witches. Such was his terrible fear of what they might say or do, he had forbidden anyone but a few witnesses to be at the execution. He, however, wanted to watch as these two women had their lives swiftly extinguished.

"The Devil may fight for them," he had whispered hoarsely in her ear. "They are His handmaidens and He sent them to seduce me. They did terrible things, they forced me to enjoy their base entertainments, their unholy couplings. They used their forked tongues on my most sacred places. These creatures must die because they are not women, they are she-demons."

All Catherine had seen as Henry commanded her to look out of the window at the scaffold, were two scared, young girls trying not to cry. Two innocents who had been used by the men around them. Fed on lies and false promises, they had believed their manipulators and played their parts to the hilt, hoping for riches, glory and power, but instead, they had been served betrayal, degradation and death.

She had been startled when Henry's fumbling hands had flung aside her wrap and ripped her beautiful lawn nightgown from her shoulders, and even more revolted as he stood behind her, fondling her breasts while the girls were prepared for their executions. His excitement had mounted as, first, Tilney had spoken, praising Henry as a sweet and gentle prince before kneeling and placing her head on the block. Catherine had felt his hardness against her as the axe fell and blood flooded from the stump that had been her lady-in-waiting's neck only a few seconds earlier.

"Now," he had hissed into her ear and had pushed her forward against the wall, entering her from behind, crushing her against the folded wood panelling, his thrusts becoming even more frantic as he saw Bulmer slip in Tilney's blood and begin to cry. "Cry you little whore," he snarled and Catherine was unsure to whom he was speaking, herself or poor Joan. "Cry and beg for mercy," he roared, pounding into Catherine. She remembered a blow to the back of her head, the feeling of something warm between her thighs, whether her own blood or the king's seed, she had no idea; intense physical pain and fear as the king roared again and again until she felt he would rip her in two. Then, his hands were around her throat and he was screaming incoherently before blackness descended.

Isabel had told her the rest, how their uncle of Norfolk had discovered her, barely alive, under a cloak on the floor in Henry's private chamber. Henry must have beaten her after she had lost consciousness as her face had been so swollen and battered, her uncle confessed he had not recognised her at first. It was possible Henry had raped her again while she was unconscious; she had no recollection. The next thing she remembered was the swaying movement of the litter as she travelled through the darkness, swaddled in furs and blankets, cradled in her sister's arms. Then nothing more until she had woken one morning with the early spring sunshine on her face and a view from a window she did not recognise.

Her body had ached and her face had still been sore and marked. She was horrified to find one of her back teeth was missing. Had he hit her so hard he had dislodged it? Red marks, fading bruises and cuts covered her skin. When she moved, her ribs protested, and around her neck there were still lesions from Henry's fingers. But she was alive and, from the silence around her, she had realised she was no longer at court.

"We're at a house in Pembrokeshire in Wales," Isabel had told her.

"Wales? Where's that?" she had asked.

"A long way from the court," Lady Kathryn Knollys had answered.

"But won't the king want to know where I am?" she had said, her heart quaking with fear even mentioning his name.

"Uncle Norfolk has told the king you are seriously ill and for his majesty's safety, you have been removed to a house where you can be nursed and he will not catch your illness," said Isabel.

"What if he discovers we're lying?"

"He won't," Margaret Douglas had said darkly as she offered Catherine a sip of watered wine. "He will never find you again."

It had been some weeks since then and Catherine was finally beginning to believe she was safely away from the violence of the king. She had also realised something else. At first, terror had engulfed her as she feared her uncle would insist she return to London, but now she wondered if she truly would be safe to confide her secret and that she would be able to stay hundreds and hundreds of leagues away from her insane husband.

"You're looking very thoughtful, Kitten," said Isabel as she swept in with a trug full of wild flowers.

"Issy, can I tell you a secret?" she asked tentatively.

"Of course, my darling girl, you can tell me anything."

"Even if it could put us both in danger?"

"If that's the case, you must definitely tell me," Isabel replied, her face paling. "What it is, Kitten?"

"I think I'm with child. The king's child."

"What makes you think this?"

"The morning of Tilney's execution, he forced himself upon me. I think more than once," she said, her voice tinged with disgust.

"You think?"

"Once while Tilney and Bulmer were executed but then perhaps afterwards too, when I was unconscious. He had boasted of doing that to other women and the girl he'd killed first..." her voice trailed away. Isabel looked appalled. "But, since we've been here, my monthly courses have stopped and today I noticed this." She took Isabel's hands and placed it on her small rounded belly. "You're a mother, Isabel. Does this feel like a child?"

"Oh, Kitten," there were tears in Isabel's eyes. She could foresee only more trouble if Catherine was indeed carrying Henry's longed-for heir but she could also see the hope shining in her younger sister's eyes. "It might be, we'll have to wait a little longer to be certain. But, Kitten, we should keep this to ourselves until we're sure."

Catherine nodded.

"If I am, would I have to go back?"

"No, sweet girl," said Isabel. "You're never going back."

Isabel was unsure what the duke of Norfolk was planning but he had assured her that Catherine would never return to court or be at the mercy of the king. However, if Catherine was carrying a Tudor heir, this might weaken his resolve, particularly if the queen delivered a healthy boy. Despite the fact the duke seemed to have aged years since he had discovered Catherine's bloody and bruised body, would the chance to put a male Howard heir in line to the throne be too much for him to resist?

Catherine's voice cut through Isabel's fearful thoughts.

"Truly?" asked Catherine, her face radiant. "I never have to go back to court?"

"Your uncle has told the king you're too ill," she replied. "Kitten, don't mention the possibility of a child to anyone yet; we need to be sure."

Humming to herself, Catherine settled near the fire and began to work on a new piece of tapestry, a delicate and beautiful mermaid. Isabel watched her for a few moments, then with a frown, began arranging the flowers from her trug into a tall vase. They worked in silence until hurrying footsteps caused them to exchange a curious glance. The door was flung open and Margaret Douglas burst in, her face flushed with excitement.

"You'll never guess what?" she gasped.

"Tell us then," said Catherine, a spark of her former laughter and *joie de vivre* in her face.

"A letter from my brother, the Scottish king," she said. "His wife, the queen, the lady Mary of Guise, is pregnant. They will have a new heir to replace the poor boys who died last April. This is such good news for us."

"Why?" asked Isabel.

"It's the perfect reason for me to travel to Scotland," she said. "And all of you will be hidden in my entourage. It gets us safely away from Uncle Henry with no hint of suspicion."

"But…" Catherine began, then stopped.

"But what?" asked Margaret.

"Nothing, I was only thinking it's such a long way. When would we have to leave? I'm not sure I'm strong enough yet."

"We won't have to go for a while, Kitten, you'll be fit to travel by then," Margaret assured her, whirling back out of the door. "I must find Charles."

Isabel and Catherine exchanged a glance.

"Let's wait and see, Kitten," sighed Isabel. But as she turned back to her flowers, once more, fear rose in her heart.

Chapter Two

"But what will we do?" Edward Baynton's voice was tense. It was the question they had all been struggling with ever since Catherine's condition had become apparent.

"We'll have to tell the duke," said Charles.

The small and loyal core who had fled the court with Catherine during the February snows stood in the sunny solar of Marquess House, the manor they had made their home ever since. Sir Francis and Lady Knollys, Isabel and Edward Baynton, Charles Howard, Margaret Douglas and Margaret Arundell, exchanged uncertain glances.

"Why should we tell the duke?" asked Margaret Douglas.

"He's the head of our family," replied Charles.

"He is many leagues away. He need never know that Kitten is having the king's child," she continued. "Catherine could be delivered of the baby and arrangements made for its adoption without him ever knowing."

"The baby is of royal blood," said Sir Francis, taking his wife's hand. "You of all people understand what danger and responsibility that brings, Margaret."

"If it's a boy, it would be second in line to the throne of England behind Prince Edward," insisted Charles.

"But, if you tell the duke, he might demand Catherine returns to court," Isabel's voice was waspish with concern. "If she does, it's unlikely the king will believe the child is his and he could well try to beat her to death again as he did the last time she told him there was an issue. Have you forgotten?"

"Of course not," snapped Charles. "She's my sister too, but we're talking about a Howard heir, a claimant to the throne of England. A strong, healthy boy…"

"And you'd sacrifice Catherine for the sake of being uncle to the second in line to the throne?" asked Lady Arundell.

"You're twisting my words!" retorted Charles. "It sickened me to see what the king did to her, but if the child is a boy and healthy…"

"Exactly, *if*?" interrupted Isabel.

"You're forgetting the laws of nature, Charles," said Lady Arundell. "Kitten is young and strong but we've all witnessed many birthings and there is no way of knowing whether the child or mother will survive. Although, as you all seem to be forgetting, this child might be a girl, in which case, she would be further down the line of succession and there would be fewer problems."

"Which brings us back to the point in hand," said Edward before the Howard siblings could begin bickering again. "We need to make a decision as to what we are going to do."

"I favour Margaret's plan," said Kathy Knollys, speaking for the first time. "Keep Catherine here until the child is born, then arrange for its placement with people we can trust. The Devereux family is not far from here at Lamphey. I'm sure they could be persuaded to help. Then, if there comes a moment when we have to reveal the child's identity and claim the throne, so be it."

Sir Francis gave his wife a warm smile. There was silence as they all contemplated their difficult decision. Eventually, Edward, with his years of experience at the Henrician court, spoke, his words delivered in a reasonable tone but with a certain finality.

"We must make plans for all eventualities," he began. "And whether we like it or not, we must inform the duke of Norfolk." He held up his hand to quell the flow of interruptions and protests the others began to muster, continuing: "If the child is a boy, we must protect him and the duke is one of the most powerful men in the country, we will need his influence. If it's a girl, she will need to be found suitable care too. She would also be a legitimate Tudor heir, and at present, many would consider her claim greater than that of the princesses Mary and Elizabeth. An Act of Parliament has declared them both bastards, so a princess of legitimate birth would also be second in line to the throne. Whether male or female, this child is in danger."

"And Catherine? After she's given birth? What about her safety?" asked Isabel. "She is aware of the danger she'll be in if anyone ever finds out she's still alive."

"But how will they?" said Charles.

"If we reveal there is a Tudor heir, we would need to prove its legitimacy. At some point, this would mean Catherine appearing in public," retorted Isabel.

"No," said Margaret Douglas. "We can always say she died in childbed. Who would question it? Then she could stay safely hidden for the rest of her life."

They were silent as they considered this possibility.

"If the king wanted to marry again, it would be bigamy," pointed out Francis.

Isabel shrugged. "No one would ever know."

Charles dropped his head in his hands. "If we were ever discovered, we would be executed for treason."

"It's either that or hand Catherine back and stand by to watch her be murdered…" began Lady Arundell, but Edward cut across her.

"When is the child likely to arrive, Isabel?"

"In the winter, before the Yuletide celebrations," she replied.

"Then there is time to make decisions," he said wearily.

"We still have safe passage to Scotland and my brother's court," Lady Douglas reminded them. "But if we were to travel there, then the sooner the better for Kitten's sake. She's already quite large even though there are still many months to go."

It was becoming difficult to disguise Catherine's condition, even with looser, more flowing summer clothes. She was growing far more quickly than Isabel had imagined.

"It's because she is so small," said Lady Arundell. "It looks as though she is carrying heavily."

"Unless, of course, she bears more than one child," suggested Francis. They all looked at him, startled. "Although it's rare, we all know these things happen. Men of science and learning are discovering extraordinary things every year, and for a woman to have more than one child in a single pregnancy is unusual but it can happen. Perhaps that is why Kitten has bloomed so quickly."

"In that case," said Charles, "we should definitely tell the duke. One Tudor heir we could disguise, two could cause a new war."

"And you would be uncle to two heirs to the throne instead of one, which would improve your status considerably," snapped Margaret Douglas. "Do you work for your own ends, Charles, or to protect us from the wrath of the king?"

"I work to protect us all from being attainted for treason," he shouted, his fear finally breaking free.

There was a tense silence. Edward and Francis, the two most senior courtiers, exchanged a glance.

"Charles, contact your uncle," said Edward, "but be circumspect. Nature often resolves these issues for us and we would be fools to put anything incriminating in writing."

He allowed the significance of his words to be absorbed before taking Isabel's arm and leaving the room, followed by Sir Francis and Lady Kathy and Lady Margaret Arundell.

Charles turned to Margaret Douglas, reaching out, his eyes beseeching, but her fury was apparent,

"I would never hurt Kitten," he implored but her eyes were narrowed in anger.

"You have seen the cruelty my uncle is capable of," she hissed. "I do not care if it his legal right to beat his wife, his humanity should have stopped him from these terrible crimes long before now. So know this, Charles, if the duke attempts to return Catherine to the king, then I will remove her and you'll never see either of us again."

And Margaret swept from the room.

Chapter Three

The duke of Norfolk stood by the fireplace, thinking hard as he watched the letter burn away to ash and embers, its dangerous message disappearing to the skies, piece by piece. What should he do next? There were several options and he was dimly aware that a few short months ago, he would have acted upon the one that most benefited himself and his family name without a moment's consideration for anyone else. Now, things were different.

He stared at the fiercely burning logs and shuddered. He would never recover from the horror of finding Catherine bleeding and broken on the floor of the king's chamber; discarded under a cloak like a forgotten piece of rubbish. Somehow, when it had been the remains of a nameless wench, he had been able to wash away the image, leaving himself with a conscience as clean as an angel's wing. Yet, since his niece's beating, he had finally understood the grief he had inflicted upon another family; on how the loss of an innocent could destroy the lives of those around them.

Looking down at his hands, he saw they were trembling. Balling them into fists, he dragged his mind away from the vivid images of brutality that haunted his every waking hour and back to the contents of Charles's letter. Catherine was carrying the king's child. It was all he had prayed for, a legitimate Howard heir. But now his prayers had been answered, he no longer knew how to proceed. The most obvious course of action was to return the queen to court in triumph. However, by doing this he would be placing her in terrible danger.

He threw the last fragment of Charles's letter onto the flames and, satisfied that every scrap of it had been destroyed, he walked across his richly decorated rooms to stare out of the window at the endlessly rolling waves of the River Thames. As he watched the hypnotic flow and listened to the calls of the boatmen, he pondered, wondering whether it would be possible to return his niece safely to Henry's court.

As long as he ensured enough people witnessed her arrival and saw her obvious condition, perhaps that would be enough? He could install a court of senior ladies around her and place his own household guard there as extra protection. However, if Henry decided the child she was carrying was not his, then imprisonment for treason would follow swiftly and brutally. Even if she were allowed to give birth to the child, there was a chance Henry would still have her executed afterwards and the child banished and declared a bastard. The duke was repulsed at the thought. He had already sent one niece and a nephew to their deaths, he could not bear to be responsible for the death of another Howard girl.

The other option was to take up the suggestion of Lady Margaret Douglas and remove Catherine and her small entourage to Scotland. The legitimate Tudor heir would be raised as a ward to the Scottish king. James V was, after all, part Tudor himself, the son of Henry's sister, Margaret. The child, male or female, would be an ideal companion for the future heir whom the Scottish queen was currently expecting. He mulled the merit of this idea for a while and despite his misgivings, he could not entirely dismiss it.

His main concern, though, was that a legitimate claimant to the throne of England would present a focal point for rebellions. The country had endured decades of war as the descendants of the sons of Edward III battled for the right to rule. Pushing another Tudor heir to the fore, especially if it was a boy, could do untold damage to the nation.

Grimacing in frustration, he knew that whichever course he chose there would always be danger, but, as Isabel had pithily pointed out in a separate note, until they actually held a healthy child in their arms, there was very little to worry about. Even then, the child was not guaranteed to reach maturity.

With Isabel's words dancing around his mind, the duke made his decision. He would leave Catherine where she was until the child was born, then he would consider moving her. One or both of them might die: it was heartless but it was true. If there was no child, there was no need to endanger Catherine further by forcing her to travel to Scotland, she could remain in the sanctuary of Marquess House. If Catherine were to die, then there was no proof of whom the child's parents really were and he could hide it in a Howard household. If it ever became necessary to reveal its birthright, then he would deal with that issue when it arose.

He settled at his desk to write a response to Charles. Isabel had stated the child would be born in late November or early December, so they had time to make their plans. There was also the matter of maintaining contact with the Scottish king, something that Lady Margaret Douglas had already begun, and he felt he should continue to manage.

He had never condoned the engagement between his nephew and the Scottish princess, fearing her flighty and unreliable. Now, though, he was impressed at how she had shown herself to have an unexpected mettle. She was no longer the wilful girl who fell in love at the turn of a card, but an astute young woman who could hold her own in the harsh politics of courtly life. *A true Tudor princess*, he thought and grimaced: *there were too many of them for comfort and not enough Tudor princes.*

While he was organising his correspondence, he added a suggestion to Charles to make themselves known to the priory on the island of Llyn Cel. It was a remote house and one that had so far escaped the excesses of Henry and the late Thomas Cromwell's purges.

"They may be of use later," he wrote, knowing Charles would take the full weight of his meaning to heart.

His nephew was a sensible boy under all his bravado, and he, like Lady Douglas, was proving to the duke that he was capable of standing firm in the fluctuating and dangerous tides of Henry's court. It pleased him to know that the years he had spent on training the next generation of Howards had not been wasted. He made another mental note, George Howard, another of Catherine's brothers, was still serving in Henry's privy chamber. *It was time he was removed too*, thought the duke. He did not want any members of Catherine's immediate family at court. *Yes*, he thought, *George would need to go abroad, perhaps to France, while the duke tied up the loose ends of this intrigue.*

Once the note to Charles had been sent by his most trusted messenger, the duke prepared himself to take the air. Not only did he need to find George Howard to tell him he must leave as soon as possible, he wanted to judge the atmosphere at court and ascertain whether the rumours that had reached him about the king's sudden infatuation with the widow of Lord Latimer, the beautiful and twice widowed Katheryn Parr, were true.

If they were, then he knew he would have to tread carefully as she was a member of the extended Seymour family, not to mention the niece of Thomas Cranmer, the Archbishop of Canterbury. Rumour also had it that, before the king had

421

shown an interest in her, the Lady Latimer had allowed herself to be courted by Tom Seymour, the younger brother of the former Queen Jane. It seemed that Henry had forgotten he was married. *Although*, thought the wily duke, *perhaps we can turn that to our advantage.*

There was an unexpected spring in his step and a look of smug satisfaction on Thomas Howard's face as he entered the hustle and bustle of the king's outer chamber. New strewing herbs had been laid and the smell of lavender and rosemary disguised the usual pungency of the massed members of the court. As the heralds announced him, all faces turned in his direction. But, instead, of the usual deference and the occasional flash of fear, there was curiosity and a few obvious sneers.

Very well, he thought as he made his way through the colourful crowd of courtiers, nodding to his allies, and ignoring those who had ever shown even the faintest whiff of disloyalty, *the tide is turning but for once I have no intention of trying to stem the flow. Let the flood of the Seymours' ambition wash over me; they might think they're dragging me down in the storm of their success, but it could solve many of my difficulties.* He came to a halt beside Charles Brandon, the duke of Suffolk.

"Your grace," Suffolk greeted him, "we have been concerned by your absence." Then he lowered his voice, glancing furtively over his shoulder to ensure they would not be overheard. "How fares the queen?"

"How would it best serve me for the queen to be — bonny and on her way to recovery or on the point of death?"

"The king has a new infatuation," was all Brandon replied.

"In that case, the queen's health fails a little more each day," Thomas Howard responded.

"This is a sad piece of news," replied Suffolk.

"And does the king enquire after the queen?"

"The king forgets he is married," said Suffolk, the strain of the situation showing in the deeply etched worry lines around his eyes and mouth.

"He is worse then?"

"He runs mad," replied Suffolk shortly. "He thinks his last wife was Queen Katherine of Aragon and that she died but a few months past. It is the mystery of his reaction to Thomas Cromwell all over again. We both know that in the months following Cromwell's execution, the king asked for him repeatedly. He had forgotten he had sent the man to the scaffold. I had no choice but to fabricate the story the king now believes: that Cromwell went to Italy, became ill and died." He paused, his handsome face troubled, "How is Catherine, really?"

"Catherine is healthy and bears the king's child," he said, speaking softly so no one would overhear.

The duke of Suffolk's face froze, all colour draining from it until he was as white as a corpse. "No, no, this cannot be, not now."

"It is so. The child will arrive in the winter. A legitimate Tudor heir conceived in wedlock," Thomas Howard continued. Suffolk swayed and for a moment, Norfolk wondered if the man was about to faint. Brandon breathed deeply then took charge of himself and gave a curt nod.

"I see," he murmured. "You are making plans?"

Thomas Howard nodded, then continued in the same low tone, "What does the court make of the queen's absence?"

"Most people believe Henry has tired of her and put her aside," said Brandon. "The word is that he can't be seen to execute another wife, so she has been sent to a nunnery and the marriage annulled. When the French ambassador asked after Queen Catherine, the king assumed he meant his first queen. I spoke your Catherine's full name in Henry's presence and he had no recollection of her," he paused, glancing over Thomas Howard's shoulder. "Edward Seymour approaches, we must be cautious."

The duke of Norfolk inclined his head in response, then with a contemptuous expression, turned to greet Seymour.

"Gentlemen, you are engrossed in a secret conversation, tell me, what intrigue do you spin?" sniggered Edward Seymour, earl of Hertford, as he drew level. His usually pinched and miserly features were, for once, expansive as he gloated over the two dukes, a sardonic smile playing on his pouty, wet lips, his entire demeanour exuding pomposity.

"We were discussing the health of Queen Catherine, my niece," replied the duke of Norfolk, his voice icy with disdain.

"Ah yes," said Hertford, "the little queen. How does she fare? Such a shame the king has put her aside. I don't imagine there were many suitable nunneries left to place her, not since Henry and his bully boy Cromwell destroyed them all."

"You are too seasoned a courtier to believe the gossip of the court, Hertford," sneered Norfolk. "The queen has not been banished, she is ill but with God's good grace we are still hopeful of a full recovery."

"And if she rallies, will she return to court?"

Norfolk did not deign to reply, he merely nodded at Suffolk before throwing a glance of utter contempt at Hertford, then turned on his heel and marched from the room. While he had no intention of returning Catherine to court, he would not allow any member of the Seymour family to try to take a position of superiority over him. As he arrived back at his rooms, he wondered whether Katheryn Parr would be a suitable consort. She was older and childless, so had Henry given up on the idea of another heir? Perhaps. Another Seymour to replace a Howard: even he had to smile at the irony.

We are so entwined, he thought. The two families who already have heirs — our Howard girl, Princess Elizabeth, and the Seymour boy, Prince Edward — both our families so determined to see their blood on the throne of England. But at what cost? He suddenly saw himself in his true light. A life of scheming and plotting, of lying and cheating and yes, he was a wealthy and powerful man but, if the king chose, it could all vanish in an instant. Suffolk's words came back to him — that the court believed Henry had put Catherine aside, that he could not be seen to execute another wife.

An idea suddenly struck him and, taking a small piece of parchment, he wrote out two names, one underneath the other, then smiled. *Perhaps*, he thought, *it could work. Catherine Howard. Katherine Tilney — the same number of letters.* He wrote another name: Joan Bulmer and paused, then inspiration struck and he carefully formed the letters "Jane Boleyn". *Why not?* he thought. She was of a high enough rank to accompany a queen to the scaffold, and poor Jane and her family would never know what he had done. She herself would never be able to complain as she had died some months earlier.

Thomas Howard stared at the names, wondering if such an audacious plan could succeed. The longer he thought about it, the more convinced he became that this was the solution. *It's not as though this will be the first time official documents have been changed to hide the truth*, he thought.

It was widely known that Henry's father, Henry VII, the first Tudor monarch, had altered documents to serve his own purposes. The most famous being the back-dating of his reign to beginning on the 21 August 1485, the day *before* the Battle of

Bosworth. *A cunning move*, thought the duke. If he were already king, all those who backed Richard would have been considered traitors, so it was easier to confiscate their lands and wealth, as well as stripping them of their titles. *Henry VII had used this power to control people and stop them questioning his right to the throne*, thought Norfolk. *Perhaps I can change the records to protect Catherine.*

If he did this, she would be safe forever. Granted, the Howard family name would once again carry the taint of treason but he would know the truth and any potential dishonour in the eyes of posterity would be worth it in order to keep Catherine away from the king. After all, he reasoned, who will ever look again at the Bill of Attainder that was passed to execute Katherine Tilney and Joan Bulmer? It had passed through Parliament without a murmur. *It's possible no one will ever discover my subterfuge; the scribes and monks will keep it somewhere until the mice eat it.* The king had not even signed it, the document had been passed by the Lord Privy Seal, William Fitzwilliam, earl of Southampton using Henry's dry stamp. Yet, for him, it would serve a purpose and it would remove any possible threat to Catherine if the king thought she was dead.

If his madness ever lifted and he remembered his young queen, he could show the king the document and assure him he was free to marry again. Charles Brandon, the duke of Suffolk, would support him and between them, they would pull the remaining nobles into line; they were the most powerful dukes in the country, they would be able to persuade or, if necessary, threaten and blackmail the nobles into supporting this alternate version of events. Even the Archbishop of Canterbury, Thomas Cranmer, would gain status if the king decided to marry Katheryn Parr. She was, after all, his niece. Thomas Howard nodded, he saw no problem persuading Cranmer to collude in their lie either.

He summoned his servant and sent a message to the Lord Privy Seal, William Fitzwilliam, the earl of Southampton. He had always known it would be useful to have one of the most powerful men in the court indebted to him. He would promise to write off Southampton's gambling debts if he helped him in this scheme.

Afterwards, the duke decided, *I can retire from court, knowing I have gone some small way to repair the damage my long history of scheming and plotting to advance my family has created.* He smiled: this was the solution. Not only would they all be safe, but he rather enjoyed the strange symmetry it created in the way Henry had chosen his wives: a foreign princess divorced, a Howard girl executed, a Seymour girl died, then repeat. Although, of course, he had no way of knowing how Katheryn Parr would fare if she did become Henry's sixth queen.

For the first time in months, he felt a soothing sense of peace. He could not physically change the past but he could do this, and in so doing, perhaps protect future generations of Howards and atone for his failures with their parents.

Chapter Four

Catherine was uncomfortable. No matter how she arranged herself at the writing desk she could not ease her discomfort. She was only small and this baby was so huge it seemed to have taken over her body. She tugged fruitlessly at her gown. It was loosened to its fullest extent but it was still too tight. Reaching forward, she dipped her quill in the inkwell and leaned awkwardly towards the parchment on the desk. Isabel had warned her that the child was near and, while she had persuaded her sister not to lock her away in confinement as was usual with noble women, her sisters and other companions had warned her things would happen soon whether she was in confinement or not.

However, she was determined in her endeavours, for the letter she had to write was too important to leave to chance. She wanted to ensure it was despatched and that Isabel had her instructions, in case the worst happened. Shifting again, she considered the best way to address the situation. She trusted Isabel implicitly but she also knew that Isabel only had so much power, which was why she had decided to turn to the Lady Anne of Cleves for help. She was too tired for codes, this letter would only be despatched upon her death and if she wrote carefully enough, it would look like nothing more than a final bequest from one former bride of Henry's to another. She had to ensure her ring and locket were safely passed on and that her child knew its true parentage, even if neither of its parents were alive or able to acknowledge it.

My dearest friend, she wrote, the days grow dark once more, but with the coming of the Yuletide celebrations, I give you this gift, a letter to keep in trust until the day comes when it may be needed, along with the tokens which I have enclosed. It is a story I have written and tells of great adventures, yet every word is true. Should ever it need to be told, I ask with all my heart that you will pass on my sacred words to those who should hear it. If God is willing, we will meet again soon. Take care, my dearest friend, my love will always protect you.

She would place the ring and locket with the letter so that Anne would know it was from her. Anne would also ensure that, when the time was right, her jewellery would be passed on to her child. The other item of importance she would include was the story she had written, *The Legend of the Llyn Cel Mermaid*, telling the tale of a woman with royal blood who was forced into hiding in order to keep her child safe. To disguise herself, she had created a love story, including the birth of twins to the woman.

The tale ended with the woman becoming a mysterious mermaid who would return to land whenever there was a storm and search for her lost love. It was based on a local legend told to them by the housekeeper Mrs Page, but Catherine had altered it to include her story. Lady Cleves would understand the meaning, that Catherine was the mermaid whose children had been taken away. She felt giving the woman twins somehow included the other child she had lost through its father's brutality. *Although*, she thought, *the size I am, it feels as though I'm truly carrying more than one child. Perhaps my tale will prove to be prophetic.*

As for Mrs Page, she knew she had her utmost loyalty, as she was the woman for whose life Catherine had begged when she had not long been queen. Her uncle had arranged for the Pages to come to Marquess House shortly after Catherine had saved the woman's life. *Perhaps*, thought Catherine, *he finally felt the pangs of guilt for the sacrifice of their poor murdered daughter, Maud, and had given the Pages a new and better life away from the horrors of London.*

Sealing the letter, Catherine stretched and moved closer to the fire. The relief of deciding to send Anne the story and the instructions of where her two pieces of jewellery should go if she did not survive the birth, was huge and she felt herself relax. Holding her hands out to warm near the blazing logs, she wondered whether her uncle, the duke of Norfolk, would arrive this day, as Isabel had said he would. He claimed he wished to ensure Catherine's safety during the birth and the protection of both her and her child afterwards. She hoped she could trust him to carry out the plans they had discussed and agreed upon, especially if the worst happened.

Warm now, Catherine waddled to the window seat which offered views of Llyn Cel, the huge, grey expanse of water that dominated the west side of the estate. Her thoughts turned to her loyal band of ladies. Their prolonged absence was beginning to cause a stir at court and, as no one wished to raise suspicions or inadvertently lead anyone to Catherine's hiding place, there was no choice but for them to resume their old lives after the birth.

Catherine knew Margaret Douglas was eager to escape to Scotland, preferably with Charles, although her plans were being hampered by the current unrest as Henry had sent an army to meet James V at Solway Moss. The duke of Suffolk was leading it, even though Norfolk was supposed to have taken charge. He had claimed ill health in order to join Catherine in Pembrokeshire. The court assumed he was at his own country seat of Framlingham in Suffolk. With every passing day, Margaret waited anxiously for news from her half-brother on how the battle was advancing and also for news of the pregnancy of the Scottish queen, Mary of Guise. The arrival of a strong, healthy heir was now of the utmost importance.

Isabel would soon have to return to court. Her husband Edward had been forced back to London on her uncle's insistence. Henry was wooing Katheryn Parr, and as previous Vice Chancellor to all Henry's other wives, it would look odd if the reliable Sir Edward Baynton were absent. His loyal and respected wife could also not be seen to be missing for much longer. The thought of Isabel leaving caused Catherine such intense sadness, she could not allow her mind to dwell on the prospect for long.

Kathy Knollys was also eager to return. She was a creature of the court and found the isolation of Marquess House a trial on her nerves. It was her devotion to Catherine that had kept her there for so long. Only Catherine's other, older sister, Margaret Arundell, would remain to care for Catherine and her child. Catherine also hoped that, in time, their younger sister Mary Howard could join them in Pembrokeshire too, along with some of their Leigh half-sisters.

Catherine sighed. She ached all over and wanted the confinement and the birth to be over so she could cradle her child in her arms.

"Have you finished, Kitten?" Isabel had walked quietly into the room.

"Oh yes," replied Catherine. "This is a letter for the Lady Anne of Cleves," she paused and took a deep swallow, taking control of her wavering voice. "If I should die in childbed, will you please ensure this is delivered to the former Queen Anne."

"Of course, my darling," said Isabel. She was too seasoned in the birthing chamber to make any false promises. "And now, if you're ready, we must leave for the priory. It's snowing again, so Margaret and I have decided it would be safer to walk through the passage."

"Very well," said Catherine taking a final glance around her solar. It was a warm and comforting room, one that she had adopted for her daytime use. She took a long last look at the lake before struggling to her feet. "I didn't see the mermaid," she said as Isabel fastened the fur-lined travelling cloak around Catherine's shoulders.

"The mermaid?" her sister said laughing. "What nonsense is this, Kitten?"

"Did you not hear Mrs Page's tale?" asked Catherine. Isabel shook her head. "According to local legend, there's a mermaid in the lake."

"Really?" said Isabel, smiling at Catherine's whimsical nature. "I thought they were creatures of the sea, not lakes."

"Where's your sense of romance, Issy?" smiled Catherine. "There might be such wondrous creatures as mermaids living in any stretch of water. Wonderful and amazing things happen. After all, whoever thought I'd escape the cruelties of my marriage? But I did. We're here. There's always hope, Issy, always hope and mermaids."

She smiled with such radiant beauty that a lump rose in her sister's throat.

"You're right, Kitten," said Isabel, gathering Catherine into her arms and hugging her tightly. "There is always hope and mermaids."

"Come then, my sweet sister, let us go to the nuns and pray with them for a swift and safe delivery of my child," said Catherine.

She held out her hand and the sisters walked towards the beautiful entrance hall where Catherine's new and unusual motto: *Fide, sed cui vide* — Trust, but be careful in whom — was emblazoned over the doors. They walked out into the gathering twilight of the November afternoon and followed the path to the small chapel. The other women: Lady Margaret Douglas, Lady Kathryn Knollys and Lady Margaret Arundell, were waiting. Together they processed up the aisle to a small door that led them down a winding staircase to a long, torch-lit tunnel, taking them to the priory on Llyn Cel island.

As they emerged into the cloister of the small convent, Catherine turned and looked across the lake towards Marquess House, nodding her thanks to the building that had given her refuge during her darkest hour. She prayed she would soon be back inside its warm embrace with her child safely in her arms.

Looking down at the choppy grey water of the lake, her eyes scanned the surface, hope lighting them as she searched for a glimpse of the magical mermaid. As the snow thickened, falling in white drifts of purity and innocence, Catherine was momentarily dazzled by the brightness and as she blinked, she thought she saw a shadow travelling smooth and fast below the surface of the lake: a long, fish-shaped tail but also human arms and flowing hair, shimmering red, but she blinked again and it was gone.

Behind her, the Prioress was beckoning and Isabel was calling her name. Catherine Howard tore her eyes away from the waves and allowed herself to be led away to her destiny.

PART SEVEN: Marquess House, 2018

Chapter One

Perdita stared down at her grandmother's notes. Here were the answers. The final secrets revealed. It was as she had hoped, Catherine was the secret and this ruby ring, wherever it was, would prove it. Her grandmother had reached the same conclusions as she had herself.

Reaching for her computer bag, she removed her now battered and annotated copy of her grandmother's manuscript and began mentally ticking off the discoveries and theories in her head as she assessed each chapter heading. If this was what had happened to Catherine Howard, and she was almost certain it was, why had history been rewritten and by whom? Was this the work of The Scribe who Alistair had told them about?

Holding the manuscript like a talisman, Perdita allowed her mind to wander. It was something she did when she was looking for connections to prove a hypothesis. She found if her brain was relaxed, forgotten nuggets of information often floated forward to reveal important links. Her grandmother believed, as she did, that Catherine had escaped from her violent marriage. The codex, the Book of Hours and the account books had proved she had travelled to Marquess House, a property owned by her uncle, Thomas Howard, 3rd duke of Norfolk. These documents had also proved she had been pregnant. The question was, if Catherine Howard had given birth to a child, what had happened to it? Had it survived? Equally as important, had Catherine?

Suddenly, and for reasons she could not fully explain to herself, it became a matter of paramount importance to Perdita to discover whether Catherine and her child had lived. All the records they had led up to November 1542 but, at present, they had nothing transcribed that could tell them the end of the tale. *If only we had the next set of account books here*, she thought. They might tell us something, but they're in Andorra while I sit here in a house full of history.

A house full of history. Then she remembered: the Tudor graffiti.

Alistair had mentioned it on her first visit. Perdita had, of course, examined it, but then it had meant nothing. Now, though, as she recalled the words carved into the wall, her heart began to race. Was this graffiti the answer to the question? The truth hidden in plain sight all along, just as her grandmother suggested? And the ring mentioned by Penelope Fitzalan in her letters, who must surely be the same person who had compiled the book of legends. To have drawn the same image in both the letter and the book of legends had to be significant. Had her grandmother and Bethan Bridges discovered the fireplace when they were children? Was there a secret cavity within it?

Placing the manuscript and the missing chapter back in the box file, she stowed it in the safe behind the ancient framed tapestry of a mermaid. Collecting her phone and a notebook, Perdita hurried out of her apartment and down to the library.

Throwing open the double doors, she flicked on the main lights and hurried to the far end of the room where the magnificent stained glass windows dominated one wall. The five panels each depicted a woman, the imagery all taken from Greek mythology. Perdita, however, for once did not pause to admire its beauty. Instead, she headed for the central window and the Perspex sheet situated beneath it. This protective covering shielded the last remaining section of original Tudor panelling where there was the priceless example of sixteenth century graffiti.

Using her phone as a torch, Perdita examined the carvings, before taking a series of photographs. Then, balancing the notebook on her leg, she sketched the graffiti. Carved into the ancient wood were the letters *CH* and the date: *1542*. Next to this, faintly scratched, were the names: *Elizabeth* and *Nicholas*.

Perdita traced her finger over the covering, following the letters: *CH*. Catherine Howard. *It has to be the real Catherine Howard*, thought Perdita, her heart pounding, *especially as 1542 was the date they could irrevocably place her at Marquess House thanks to the household accounts.*

Adrenalin pumped through her as the enormity of her discovery hit home. Her eyes scanned down to the final part of the carving, the names *Elizabeth and Nicholas*. Both Tudor names, although Nicholas was not used often. *Elizabeth and Nicholas. Elizabeth and Nicholas.* Why those two names? She stared at it for a moment, then realisation hit her with the full force of a tsunami.

Shit, she thought, rocking back on to her heels so she was kneeling; her eyes level with the ancient letters. Tracing her finger across the names, she finally allowed herself to think this most unbelievable thought: *Catherine Howard had twins, a girl and a boy, and their names were Elizabeth and Nicholas.*

This was more than Perdita had ever imagined. When they had been searching the household accounts, they had discovered costs for a wet nurse, a birthing chair, swaddling bands and herbs associated with easing the pains of childbirth: wood betony, columbines, mallow and peony. There had also been an order for a cradle, all for Lady Tudor. They had assumed Catherine had given birth to one child, but here, written on the wall were two names — a girl and a boy, a princess and a prince. This was backed up again by the legend of the Llyn Cel mermaid: the woman in the story, Catherine, gave birth to twins who were brought up by other families, unaware of their true heritage. The coincidence was too great to dismiss. The story also said she had left them trinkets so they could identify themselves and she would recognise them: was this a reference to her own jewellery, the rings and the locket?

Hardly able to breathe, she dialled Kit's number. When it went to voicemail, she swore but left a short message for him to call her urgently. *If only Piper were here*, she thought. *This is a huge moment, I wish we could do this together, but Piper was still in Italy and would not be leaving for Marquess House until the following day. I can't wait until tomorrow*, she thought.

Perdita moved to one of the window seats and continued to contemplate the graffiti. Yet, she still could not make sense of their discovery. If Catherine Howard had given birth to two children, one of them the longed-for second male heir, why had this legitimate Tudor prince been written from history?

She sank back on to the cushions and began trying to rationalise her findings, but no matter how hard she tried to bring her analytical powers to the fore, all she kept thinking was: *Catherine Howard gave birth to Henry VIII's twins. Catherine Howard had twins.* The words revolved around her mind, chasing each other in circles as she battled to grasp the enormity of this discovery. Two more Tudor heirs. Legitimate heirs. So, why had Catherine's family hidden her in Pembrokeshire rather than revelling in her triumph at court?

Maybe the babies weren't Henry's? thought Perdita, following her grandmother's line of reasoning. However, she quickly dismissed this: if Catherine had been unfaithful to the king and was trying to pass another man's bastards off as Henry's children, the senior members of her family would not have stood by her, particularly, Catherine's uncle, Thomas Howard, the duke of Norfolk. Yet, the household records showed he had stayed at Marquess House when Catherine had been in residence. Perdita shook her head. *No,* she thought, *the children must have been Henry's offspring. But what happened to them? Did they survive or did they die young?*

Toying with these questions, she forced herself to abandon the emotion of the discovery and reason it out in a calm academic manner. The most likely explanation was that the children had died, possibly Catherine too, but it still did not explain why there were no official records of this pregnancy or why history stated Catherine Howard had been executed in February 1542. Perdita thought for a while, working out dates from the information they had gathered from the household accounts. Catherine gave birth sometime in November, so she would have conceived in February 1542, the point where she disappeared from the official version of history.

This is it, thought Perdita, *this is what MI1 doesn't want us to know.* Catherine Howard wasn't executed, she escaped from her violent marriage and gave birth to Henry's heirs. For some reason, two of her ladies-in-waiting were beheaded and their death warrant was changed to implicate Henry's fifth queen and her companion, Jane Boleyn, even though Jane had actually died a few months earlier. Why, though?

Raking her fingers through her hair in frustration, she forced herself to concentrate and then it came to her. Catherine's children must have survived, she reasoned, or it would not have mattered. Catherine would have been remembered as the queen who died tragically in childbirth, like Jane Seymour, and her children would be recorded in perpetuity. There would have been no need to hide the truth if they had died. If they had survived, however, then there might have been more of a problem.

Suddenly, Perdita had a moment of clarity. Not only had the children survived, she realised, they must have reached maturity, then tried and failed to claim their birthright, which was why they had been written out of history. *Who were they?* wondered Perdita. *Who were these Tudor heirs? And what did they do that caused a later generation to wipe away all trace of them?* Even more confusing, where did the mysterious Penelope Fitzalan fit in? The dates of her letters were from the 1660s, so she could not have been Catherine's daughter, yet she claimed to have Catherine's ruby ring.

The revelations of the night flowed around her mind, splashing against the sides of her brain like an angry tide until, like a piece of flotsam, an idea bobbed to the surface and her mind calmed. She knew what she had to do next.

But as she stood up, her phone buzzed.

"Kit!" she exclaimed in relief. "Where are you?"

"Walking up to the house," he replied. "What's happened?"

"I've found it, all of it, the secret MI1 doesn't want us to know. I'm in the library, I'll meet you in the Tudor hall. We need a torch. We're going to the chapel to see if we can find Catherine."

Perdita heard the key turning in the huge front doors and Kit was in front of her. He had two jackets slung over one arm and a torch in his right hand.

"What's going on?" he asked. "You look completely wired."

"The graffiti," she replied. "*CH, 1542* and two names: *Elizabeth* and *Nicholas*."

"Yes, I've seen it, many times."

"And?" urged Perdita. "CH — Catherine Howard, two names, Tudor names. We know she was pregnant, the household accounts show that. What if she had twins?"

She waited for his response but there was silence.

"Catherine Howard had twins," repeated Perdita. "She came here because she was pregnant and she had twins, a girl called Elizabeth and a boy called Nicholas."

"But, Perds, if she did," began Kit, his tone hesitant, "they were legitimate Tudor heirs. Henry would have claimed his son, even if he didn't bother acknowledging another daughter."

"How could he if he didn't know they existed?"

"It's hard to believe someone as ambitious as Thomas Howard, the duke of Norfolk, wouldn't have shoved his male Howard heir into Henry's arms himself."

"We have a record of things being ordered for Thomas Howard while Catherine was in residence at Marquess House. He came to visit but it doesn't seem that he came to remove her. If he had helped to hide her from the court — and it would have needed someone very powerful to smooth over her disappearance — why would he then put her and her children in danger?"

"But a male Tudor heir? A duke of York? Do you think Norfolk could have resisted a Howard prince, potentially a Howard king?"

"It seems he did," said Perdita.

"Maybe the baby died," reasoned Kit. "The daughter might have survived and was hidden for her own safety, but perhaps the reason there was no record of a Prince Nicholas was because the little boy died."

"Possibly, but I don't think so," persisted Perdita. "My instinct tells me they both survived. The secret that MI1, or The King's Men or The Queen's Men, or whoever they were originally, was created to protect is obviously huge and this is enormous. I suspect Catherine's children grew up and someone for some reason at some point further on, decided it was better to remove them from history, so things were altered and the 'official' version was created. Don't you see, Kit, this is big enough to warrant being hidden and using an entire government department to do so. Something massive happened that the establishment wanted to suppress and I'm certain it began with Catherine Howard and her children."

Kit had a pained expression on his face, as though he did not want to destroy Perdita's theory or the hope in her eyes, but reason could not let him believe her version of events.

"Or the children could both have died and that's why there's no record of them," he said, unable to help himself.

"But that wouldn't make sense," said Perdita, frustrated with his inability to see what seemed so obvious to her. "MI1 Elite is so determined to stop us revealing something that they tried to murder my grandmother. Unfortunately, it was my mother who became the victim of their evil desperation. Anyway, Granny Mary agreed with the hypothesis that Catherine was pregnant, something we have now proved with the household accounts. She also thought there was a link between those old letters from Penelope Fitzalan, the Llyn Cel mermaid legend and the words: *Spe et nereidum.*"

"What?"

"I found the missing chapter," explained Perdita. "Granny wrote me a letter and hid it in her Apocrypha. She told me where the final chapter was hidden and she said, because of a change in circumstances, she no longer thinks dwelling in secrecy will keep us safe, she wants us to finish her work and find the truth."

"Us? You and Piper?"

"No, you too. She wrote a note the night before she died saying she wanted you to explore the tunnel with her."

"But that's a legend…"

"No, it isn't," interrupted Perdita. "Granny discovered the tunnel when she was a child. She and Bethan Bridges used it as their secret hideout and she thinks the ring might be hidden there. I think they may have found something when they were children, a fireplace, perhaps with a secret cavity."

For a moment, they stared at each other.

"Perds, this is crazy!" Kit exclaimed, but this time his voice rang with excitement rather than scepticism.

"I also have a theory."

"Which is?"

"If Catherine gave birth to her children here, if she or they died, they might be in the chapel. If they're not, then we must assume they survived, for a while at least."

Their conversation had taken them through the house and down the passage to the kitchen.

"What do you want to do first? Grave or tunnel?" asked Kit when they reached the back door.

"Grave," said Perdita. "Unfortunately, Granny didn't give details for the entrance to the tunnel, although she did give a clue as to where it comes out on the island, so we might have to take a boat over there tomorrow."

"OK, grave it is then," he said. "I brought you a coat, it's pouring with rain."

Pulling on a far-too-large waterproof jacket, she found a woolly hat in the pocket. Tucking her hair inside it, she led the way out into the stormy night. Following the winding path, they ran through the rhododendron grove, past the mermaid fountain and down the footpath to the kissing gate. Sheltering for a moment under its roof, they paused, then sprinted to the chapel's porch and threw themselves into its dry interior. Pulling off her hat and shaking the worst of the rain from it, Perdita looked around for a light switch.

"Here," said Kit reaching into a shadowy corner and flooding them with light, "the main light board is inside." He opened the solid mediaeval door and after a few clicks, the chapel was bathed in a warm golden glow. Perdita followed Kit inside and started.

"I'd forgotten it was being cleaned," she said, looking in dismay at the two scaffold towers positioned at either end of the aisle and the ghost-like draperies of the dust sheets. Kit had set off towards the chaplaincy at the far end.

"It shouldn't matter," he called. "The burial records are in the safe out the back. If Catherine and her children are buried here, the records will say where, so we won't have to search every single centimetre by hand."

"What, burial records that go back to 1542?" asked Perdita.

"Perds, it's a family chapel, the number of burials is quite limited," echoed Kit's voice from the transept as he disappeared around the corner.

Perdita pulled a face at Kit's retreating back but her excitement was building, she was convinced Catherine would be here somewhere. She gazed about her, it was the first time she had been inside since her grandmother's funeral, and she had forgotten its true magnificence. As she admired the blue ceiling sprinkled with golden stars, a thought struck her: *the mermaid that marked the beginning of the tunnel was also in here, although Mary had not given the location. But then, why would she need to*, mused Perdita, *she had thought she would be able to show Kit.* Looking upwards, she searched the ceiling, although, sense told her the carved mermaid ceiling bosses were not the key to the secret entrance.

Mermaids again, she thought. There are mermaids on the walls around the house, a tapestry of a mermaid, the Llyn Cel mermaid, even a mermaid marking the entrance to the passage. Did Catherine Howard put them here or was it subsequent generations? *Have other women known this secret and passed it down from mother to daughter for centuries?* she wondered.

Her eyes shifted to the beautiful carvings of the women on the central bosses and it was then that Perdita noticed it: there were only four faces. Moving further into the light, she looked from one serene image to the next. Four women whose faces were endlessly repeated throughout the chapel. All thoughts of the mermaid vanished as this new anomaly presented itself. There was still no sign of Kit, so Perdita threw off her jacket and approached one of the scaffold towers. Checking it was securely anchored, she began to climb.

Within moments, she was at the top, only inches from the delicate carvings. She examined each one, taking in the different appearances and the various styles of headdress, suggesting they were all from different eras. Pulling her phone out of her jeans' pocket, she took a series of pictures of each face. *If only you could speak*, Perdita thought, gazing into the dark eyes of one of the women.

"You, Madam," she said addressing one boss, "look familiar and, I would suggest, you might be a depiction of Anne Boleyn, particularly as this was once your house."

Searching in her rigorous, academic way for more identifying clues, it took only seconds for her to discover the tiny initials at the base of the carving: *A.B.* Surprised, she moved to the next image of another younger woman, and there in the same position at the base were the letters *C.H.* She felt a chill run down her spine. Moving swiftly to the remaining faces Perdita found two more sets of initials: *A.S.* and *P.F.* — Penelope

Fitzalan. Taking a series of pictures of the initials, her mind began whirring once again.

"Anne Boleyn," she whispered, "Catherine Howard, Penelope Fitzalan and another woman who was linked to this house…"

"Perdita, what the fuck…?"

Kit was standing by the altar looking up at her in horror. He had reappeared from the back rooms and was holding a large leather-bound book but his eyes were on Perdita.

"It's Anne Boleyn," said Perdita pointing at the carving, "and I think this is Catherine Howard and this could be Penelope Fitzalan who compiled the book of legends but this one, I'm not sure yet…"

"Get down, now!" he shouted, his voice tense. "Those towers aren't the safest pieces of equipment we own."

"OK, OK," said Perdita and began her descent. A moment later she was by his side. "Are you scared of heights?" she asked, wondering if this would explain his rather violent reaction.

"I don't love them," he admitted. Perdita could not contain the laugh that rose to her lips. Kit pulled a face. "I thought we were looking for graves," he muttered.

"You're right, we are," said Perdita. She slid into a pew and Kit followed. They placed the book of burial records between them and began searching the early entries.

"First one is 1536," said Kit, giving her a satisfied smirk.

"Nothing for 1542 or even early 1543," she said, her voice disappointed.

"Maybe they weren't buried here," suggested Kit.

"Maybe they didn't die until much later," replied Perdita running her finger down the page. The burials listed were names she had never heard before and were mostly in Welsh.

"Wild goose chase?" asked Kit, making to close the book.

"Looks like it, although…" she said taking it from him, wondering if the initials *A.S.* would correspond with any of the names in the records or whether a Penelope Fitzalan appeared. She turned another page and ran her eye down the list, nothing, nothing… Then she gasped.

"Lady C Howard, March 1552."

Kit leant over. "But how can it be?" he murmured staring at the faded writing.

"What do you mean?"

"Don't jump down my throat, I'm on your side, but if this really is Catherine Howard someone would have found this grave before now?" He looked at Perdita, an apprehensive expression on his face. Perdita, however, was calm, considering his doubts.

"True," she said, "but remember, history tells us Catherine was executed at the Tower of London in February 1542. No one but us and Mary have discovered she wasn't or that Catherine came to Marquess House to have her children. No one would have been looking."

"Agreed," said Kit, "but what about over the intervening centuries? You're telling me no one ever noticed her grave?"

"It could be unmarked…" suggested Perdita.

"Great," muttered Kit under his breath.

"Or," continued Perdita, ignoring him, "people assumed it was another Catherine Howard?"

"Another Catherine Howard?" asked Kit, incredulous.

"It was quite common in Tudor times to find duplicate names in the same family," she said. "There were several Thomas Howards, a few of whom were dukes of Norfolk, which can be confusing when you're studying them, at least two Thomas Culpeppers, who were thought to be brothers —

447

Granny has a theory about them which I need to tell you later — at least two Jane Seymours... Put Catherine Howard's name into any internet search engine and you'll see what I mean. At the time our Catherine was around, and in the ten years after, I discovered a number of other Catherine Howards too."

"What? Who were they?"

"There was Katherine Howard, countess of Nottingham who went on to be a lady-in-waiting to Elizabeth I, and was related to Mary Boleyn. Then there was Catherine Howard, countess of Suffolk; Katherine Howard, countess of Bridgewater and later on, there was another Catherine Howard, this time she was countess of Derby. So, even if someone discovered a grave marked 'Catherine Howard' in a far-flung place like this, it was never going to be connected with Henry's fifth queen. It would have been nothing more than an interesting anomaly. Unless, of course, you've discovered what we have."

Kit stared at her in wonder. "You're incredible," he said, then reached for the book. "Does it give the location?"

"There's something faded under her name..." she replied, suppressing the smile that was threatening to appear all over her face after Kit's compliment.

"Altar," said Kit. "She's buried under the altar."

He was on his feet and down the aisle before Perdita had even closed the burial book.

"Can you see anything?" she called, hurrying after Kit who was now on his knees, the torch in his hand, crawling across the ancient slate slabs leading up to the altar table. Perdita joined him, flicking on the torch on her phone, going from stone to stone, finally hoisting up the corner of the altar cloth.

Although the chapel was in the process of restoration, repair and cleaning, the area under the altar table was thick with dust.

The air current caused by her lifting the corner created small eddies and whirls making Perdita sneeze.

"Bless you," called Kit.

Perdita smiled but did not reply, instead she shone the thin beam of light from her phone across the floor. She was about to drop the cloth back into place when a glimmer directly below the golden cross on the altar above caught her eye. Perdita edged towards the glittering surface. As she drew closer, she realised one stone square was slightly lower than the rest of the floor and it was etched with gold. Cursing the fact she had none of her usual dig equipment with her, she reached into her pocket for a tissue to try and wipe away the dirt, but to her frustration it ripped within moments.

"Kit!" she called from her prone position. "Have you got a handkerchief?"

"Yes, here," he replied appearing at her side. "What have you found?"

"Not sure yet, maybe nothing," she said, taking the purple and white striped handkerchief and beginning to wipe away the layers of grime and dust. With Kit shining his powerful torch, Perdita painstakingly revealed a square of soft green local slate. Neither of them spoke, but as she worked, Kit altered the angle of the beam, keeping the light on the engraving that was rising to the surface after centuries in the darkness.

Finally, Perdita sat back and Kit shone the light on to the newly revealed grave marker:

Lady Catherine Howard, 1525 – 1552.
Rhosyn heb drain.

Underneath was an engraving of the odd pattern that proliferated around the walls of Marquess House, two interlinked rings with an oval between them, surrounded by tiny swimming mermaids.

"She's here!" whispered Perdita looking at Kit, her eyes shining with tears. "Catherine is here and she was even younger than we thought."

She could not explain why she was so relieved that Catherine had survived the birth of her children. It was visceral, primal, the relief at the survival of a woman of whom it had always been thought had suffered a violent end. Yet, here she was, hundreds of miles from the site of her supposed execution, in a grave that had been created with love and care.

"She's here, Kit, she's here."

They sat together gazing down at the green stone.

"What does the inscription mean?" he asked.

"It's Welsh, I think," replied Perdita, wiping her eyes on her sleeve, before tapping it into a translate app on her phone. "Oh my goodness, look!" She held up the screen for Kit to see and they both stared at each other in amazement. "Rose without a thorn. It was what Henry VIII called her, his rose without a thorn. It's definitely her."

Once more they stared at the stone in an awed silence. Then Kit spoke: "You realise this proves Henry VIII's marriage to Katheryn Parr was bigamy. He married her in July 1543, didn't he?"

Perdita nodded, then unable to help herself, she reached forward and traced her finger along the name.

"If she was a 'rose without a thorn', why isn't there a rose here?" asked Kit. "Why is there this strange emblem and more mermaids?"

He shone the torch on Perdita's fingers as they caressed the stone. She stared down at the headstone and suddenly, as though a voice had whispered in her ear, she understood.

"It's the two ruby rings," she gasped. "The jewels Anne of Cleves had made so they could safely pass messages."

"And the oval between them?"

"Her silver locket," she said. "The mermaids, though, Kit, we were right."

"They're not simply decorative then?"

"No, they're Catherine," she whispered. "According to the book of legends and the final chapter of Granny's manuscript, the name of the mermaid was Catherine. *She* was the woman who inspired the myth, she was the Llyn Cel mermaid. This was Catherine's emblem. She was the secret and now we've found her. She's been safely here all along."

Perdita's fingers snagged on more lettering, almost worn away with time. Using Kit's handkerchief, she dabbed at the small indentations until three more words were revealed: *Spe et nereidum.*

"It's Latin," said Kit. "It means hope and mermaids."

"Hope and mermaids," said Perdita. "It's written throughout the codex."

"It's on the carving in the Great Hall opposite the rose window too," said Kit, although his voice sounded tense.

"Which can also be known as a 'Catherine window'," said Perdita, her excitement growing. "Kit, it places her here even more convincingly. The mermaids all over the house, the legend of the Llyn Cel mermaid: they were all down to Catherine Howard. It's her, Kit, she came here after she'd escaped from her marriage to Henry and she gave birth to twins on the island. It all fits. All we need to discover now is what happened to her children. Why were they written out of history? And why was Catherine forever more portrayed as a good-time girl who had an affair?"

Sitting back, she gazed down at the grave, wondering about all they had discovered. *Oh, Granny*, she thought, *I wish you were here, you'd know what to do next.*

"We should tell Dad about this," said Kit, breaking into her thoughts.

"Good idea," she murmured. "Do you think he knew about the grave?"

"I doubt it. If your grandmother had never made the connection, Dad wouldn't have known either," he sounded nervous. "We should tell him though, this is a huge discovery."

She nodded. Kit stood and was already turning back towards the aisle, eager to return to the house to inform Alistair. Perdita was more reluctant to leave, she felt connected to the grave, to Catherine. She was not sure if she was ready to share the information immediately. Her instinct was to tell Piper first. Picking up her phone, she took a series of pictures of their discovery so she could send them to her twin. Then, because Kit was hovering at the beginning of the aisle, she turned to rearrange the altar cloth so it looked untouched.

It was as she crouched down untucking and straightening the folded hem, the image caught her eye. On the panel to the immediate right of the altar was the engraving of another mermaid. It was faint but it matched the mermaids on Catherine's gravestone. Staring at it, Perdita felt her heart thud, partly with nerves but also with a conviction that this discreet carving must be the mermaid Mary had mentioned in the last chapter of her manuscript. It was obscured by the brick that jutted out of the wall above it, casting it in shadow. If she hadn't been kneeling down, she would never have noticed it. Was this the entrance to the tunnel to Llyn Cel island?

"Kit, wait!" she called, her voice urgent.

"What have you found now?" he asked.

"A mermaid," she said, and glancing over, saw him roll his eyes.

"Another one?"

"I think it could be the entrance to the tunnel."

"Oh, Perds, try not to get your hopes up," he said, hurrying back to where she had squatted next to the carving. "Meggie, Stu and I spent most of our summers searching. We pushed every panel and carving in here and the house. It's a myth."

"No, it isn't," snapped Perdita. "Granny and Bethan Bridges discovered it when they were young. They used it as their secret hide out. The two girls swore a blood oath about keeping it a secret. Granny didn't even tell her younger sister, Cecily, where to find the entrance they took their bond so seriously."

"But she told you?"

"No, not exactly, it was in the final chapter of her manuscript. There were notes too. They were the last thing she ever wrote," said Perdita, her voice quivering. Turning to Kit, she looked up into his blue eyes. "The night before she died, she made a connection between the Penelope Fitzalan letters and a fireplace sketch that was drawn in one of them. It's the same as an image in the book Penelope Fitzalan wrote. Granny still isn't sure how Penelope is involved but she wrote: 'Passageway? Will ask Kit to explore the tunnel with me in the morning. Fireplace!!!'. Kit, she planned to show you where the tunnel entrance was hidden. She wanted you to help her retrieve a 'token'. I think she and Bethan found something hidden down there when they were children and I suspect it was the ring."

"But, Perds, if that's the case, why did Mary never retrieve it before?"

"I've no idea, Kit. Perhaps she'd forgotten all about it. Perhaps while she was writing, her memory was jogged and she wanted to see it again in case it was connected to her research," spluttered Perdita, frustration bubbling inside her. "I know she trusted you though, she wanted to let you in on the secret, and I think this might be the way in." Perdita pointed to the faint carving. "Have you ever tried pushing this image?"

Kit bent down beside her and a look of excitement spread across his face as he shook his head.

"No," he admitted. "This one eluded us. Unbelievable, I thought we'd covered every inch of this place. It must be because the protruding stone above throws it into shadow."

"I only saw it because I was at ground level straightening the altar cloth," admitted Perdita.

"Did Mary leave instructions on how to open it?"

"You push the stone above the mermaid," replied Perdita. Kit raised his eyebrows and she grinned. Then taking a deep breath, she placed her hand on the jutting brick. Closing her eyes and sending up a small prayer to her grandmother, she pushed with all her might. To her amazement, there was a click and the panel next to her moved inwards. She pushed again and it opened fully. It was a small doorway and it revealed a stone staircase that led downwards.

Kit was staring at the entrance in amazement. Getting to her feet, Perdita took the torch from his hand.

"Let's see what other secrets Granny's been keeping," she said and stepped through the door into the darkness.

Perdita flooded the spiral staircase with light.

"It's a long way down," she said as she hurried down, Kit fast on her heels. "Will you tell Meggie and Stu?"

Kit laughed.

"I'm not sure," he said. "You found the tunnel, it's your secret to tell, not mine. Do you think you'll tell Piper?"

"Of course. I think Meg and Stu should know too," she said and voiced something that had long been on her mind. "If Mum had never died, we'd have all been brought up together. The quest for the tunnel would have belonged to us all…"

"Unless Mary had told you," interrupted Kit.

"I don't think she'd have spoiled our fun," replied Perdita, certain this would have been the case. "She and Bethan discovered the tunnel alone, she would have left us to work it out for ourselves. We would all have been running about tapping panels and pushing bricks. It seems only fitting that all five of us should know because we should have been able to look for it when we were children. Together. Instead, Piper and I missed out on our childhood here."

They had reached the bottom of the tight, winding staircase. Kit touched her arm before she set off along the tunnel.

"If it helps," he said, "the three of us used to pretend you and Piper were here."

"Really?" she whispered, astounded.

"Yes, poor Meggie, she always used to say that if the two of you were here, it would have been me and Stu who were outnumbered. You may not have been at Marquess House or even known we existed, but we knew about you and talked about you all the time. It's why it was so peculiar when you finally moved in and you didn't have a clue who any of us were. We felt we'd known you all your lives."

Perdita was surprised at the sadness that clouded his face.

"We're here now," she said and he smiled, before she continued. "Come on, let's see what else we can discover. We need to finish what Granny started."

They were standing at the beginning of an arched passageway. It was cool and dry. The air was fresh, indicating it had been properly constructed with some form of ventilation. On the walls were brackets that had once held torches. Periodically, there were shadowy alcoves and small rooms leading off the central footpath.

"What do you think it was used for?" asked Kit as Perdita flashed the torch into the shadows.

"It must have been part of the priory," she replied, her eyes sweeping the ancient walls, looking for mermaids or for the motto: *spe et nereidum*. "The rooms look as though they could have been the nun's cells. Maybe it wasn't secret then, it was a normal conduit. I wonder why it was closed up?"

"Probably when the priory was dissolved," suggested Kit. "What are we looking for?"

"A mermaid symbol like the one at the entrance to the tunnel or the three-ringed design from Marquess House or the words *spe et nereidum*," said Perdita. "Granny thinks it might be in or near a fireplace. There was supposedly a sketch of it but I haven't seen a copy of it."

"Let's start checking all the rooms with fireplaces, then," said Kit, and together they set off down the ancient subterranean space.

The first room was tiny, a former nun's cell, and in the corner was a small fireplace. It was barely more than a hole in the wall with a flue to take away the smoke. There was no surround, no mantelpiece. Nevertheless, Perdita flashed her torch around the pitiful space, sweeping the beam from side to side, then knelt on the floor to examine the hearth itself and the chimney. The opening was so narrow, it took only moments to search.

"Nothing," she called.

"Nothing here, either," said Kit, who had been scanning the walls above it.

"It's grim, isn't it?" said Perdita, taking in the bare walls, the earth floor and the minute dimensions of the cell. "There's hardly room to lay down."

She shuddered.

"Let's try the next one," said Kit and headed back to the passageway to continue the search. But, by the seventh room, with no luck, Perdita could tell Kit was having serious doubts. Yet, somehow, the fact they were being made to search so comprehensively for their prize was bolstering Perdita, making her even more convinced they would soon find the 'token', which she knew would be the ruby ring.

"Eighth time lucky," called Kit from the doorway of the final room. Perdita smiled and followed him in.

A sixth sense told her immediately that this was it. The room was larger and more luxuriously appointed with the remains of wooden panelling on the walls. A dust-covered table stood in one corner with a crumbling chair leaning drunkenly against it, and in the centre of the back wall was a proper fireplace with a mantelpiece. Fireplace. This must have been the one her grandmother meant.

Her heart pounding, Perdita fought to control the sudden tremble of excitement that ran through her hands. Moving swiftly, she focused her attention on the fireplace and its surround. Beginning on the left-hand side, she swept her torch across it looking for any of the telltale markers. Nothing down the left side. She scanned the area around the mantelpiece — nothing — then switched the angle of her beam and illuminated the right side of the fireplace.

"Here!" she shouted, her voice unexpectedly loud in the tense silence. Kit turned.

"What is it?"

"A mermaid, give me some light while I see if this brick moves."

Carved on the jamb to the side of the mantel was the faintly traced but familiar figure of the mermaid. Pushing it, as she had the entrance to the tunnel, the brick remained immoveable, so it was not a mechanism. Kit moved forward to help.

Perdita felt around the edges of the brick, using her fingertips she wiggled it.

"It's been moved before," Kit said, pointing at the crumbling mortar surrounding it. Perdita reached forward and brushed away the crumbling cement.

"We need to be careful," she said. "We don't want to damage anything. Damn, I wish had some tools."

Kit fished around in his jacket pocket and handed her a Swiss Army penknife.

"Perfect," she said and, selecting a tool, began to chip away at the edges of the brick, until she had created a space large enough for her fingers to grip.

Wiggling and tugging, taking as much care as she could, it gradually began to move. Finally, with one last tug, the brick gave and fell out into Perdita's hand. Handing it to Kit, she shone the beam of the torch into the dark cavity.

"Oh my…" she gasped, reaching in and removing an aged, mottled wooden box.

"On the table," said Kit, unwinding the scarf from his neck and laying it across the dust begrimed top, his voice full of excitement.

"Let's see what the mysterious Penelope Fitzalan hid in the tunnel four centuries ago," grinned Perdita, placing their treasure on the centre of Kit's scarf.

"Do you really think the ruby ring is in there?" asked Kit, leaning forward, his voice eager.

"I hope so," said Perdita.

"Ready?" she whispered, and Kit, his eyes wide, nodded.

The box was approximately the size of a greeting card and roughly ten centimetres in depth. It was dark with age but its storage place had been dry and there were no speckles of damp, only the marks of centuries of dust and grime. It was hinged down one of the long sides and there was a clasp, delicately engraved and shaped like wings but it had been rusted to powdery verdigris.

Perdita searched through the tools on Kit's knife until she found a long, slim screwdriver. She would have preferred to have had her roll of jewellery maker's tools that she found invaluable when examining finds, but this would have to do instead. With great care, she lifted the clasp and opened the box.

Perdita's breath quickened as she looked inside, gazing upon what was unmistakably a faded, mottled, dark green leather jewellery case. Suddenly, she hesitated, aware that, like Pandora's Box, this could release more evil into the world, endangering herself, her sister and the Mackensies, whom she was fast beginning to view as the family she had never had. The tale of the Greek myth returned to her and the knowledge that when Pandora opened the box, not only were all the miseries of the world unleashed, but so was hope. It was hope she needed now. Hope of a resolution to this search, of a way to prove her grandmother had been correct, hope that they would continue to stay one step ahead of MI1.

Kit reached over and squeezed her hand, offering reassurance.

"Go on," he murmured as her hesitation became more prolonged.

"What if it's empty?" she said.

"Then we keep looking," he replied. "But I don't think it is, do you?"

"No," she breathed.

Bracing herself, she swallowed, attempting to calm her nerves, then she gently removed the leather case from its wooden tomb, laying the two boxes side by side. With the utmost care, she opened the ancient lid revealing its secret for the first time in nearly 400 years.

"Oh my goodness…"

Kit gaped in stunned amazement.

Inside was a soft padded lining of what had once been white velvet. Now the fabric was stained and crumbling. In one corner, nestled into a neat slot, was a heavy red ruby ring.

"Catherine's ring," said Perdita but she did not touch it. Instead her eyes took in the other mysteries within the box. Adjacent to the ring was another slot, and below, an oval indentation. "The other ring and the locket are missing."

"Do you think they were stolen?" asked Kit.

"But why leave this ring behind?"

Kit shrugged. However, it did not matter. They had been looking for Catherine's ring and their mission had been successful. The ruby ring, created in the sixteenth century, now presented itself to a new owner, one who had yet to discover its secrets.

Desperate to examine it further but nervous about touching such a rare and ancient artefact without protective gloves, Perdita wiped her hands on her jeans, then carefully lifted the ring from its velvet lining and began turning it over in her hands.

The setting was old and cumbersome compared with modern-day jewellery, but there was no denying the beauty of the ruby at its centre. It was oval-shaped with a deep, dark hue, and was encased in a delicate golden filigree cage. This was set on a wide golden band, slightly worn now, and studded with tiny diamonds, five on either side, although only a few of the delicate rose-cut stones remained.

As Perdita ran her fingers gently over the ring, they snagged on something underneath. Turning it over, she saw a small lever set with an emerald, which once would have sat smoothly in the channel at the side of the filigree cage, but with time and use, it had become twisted and now protruded slightly.

"A mechanism," she said, turning the ring so Kit could see the pinprick of green on the golden lever.

"To reveal the inner cavity that was used for passing messages," said Kit. "You were right, Perds. Oh my God, you were right. They used the rings to communicate secrets to each other. This is more proof it was Catherine's ring."

Once more, using the narrow metal screwdriver, Perdita lifted the lever, hoping it would release a catch and not simply sheer away from the body of the ring. Gently increasing the pressure, there was a minute click and, to her amazement, the underside of the ring opened. Barely able to breathe now, such was her excitement, she placed the ring on the soft scarf covering the table and with the greatest of care, pushed open the hinged section of the ring. Kit passed her the torch. Flicking its powerful beam onto the cavity, she looked inside.

For a moment, she felt she might faint. Her hands were shaking and she had to take deep breaths to steady herself.

"There's writing engraved in the lid," she whispered.

"Is it *Spe et nereidum*?" asked Kit.

"No," said Perdita, her voice faintly surprised. "Although, it's equally as significant: it says — *Iuncta Sanguine. Joined in blood.*"

"What?" said Kit, peering in to examine their find.

"Look," she angled the ring so he could see.

"Joined in blood," he echoed. "Do you think Catherine put it there?"

"No idea, but it was obviously important because it's one of the phrases on the frontispiece of *The Catherine Howard Codex*. Perhaps Penelope Fitzalan put it there to prove the ring and the codex were connected. We've done it, Kit," she said, her voice full of excitement. "We've found the proof we needed, this ring places Catherine Howard at Marquess House, we know what really happened to her and she wasn't executed. Instead, she escaped her loveless and violent marriage and lived the remainder of her life in Pembrokeshire on the banks of Llyn Cel. *Her* story is complete. Her children, well, that's a tale still to be told."

They stared at each other, beaming. Delight was coursing through Perdita. Mary had led them to the proof they needed.

"Come on," said Kit, running his hands through his hair, bemused by all they had discovered. "Let's get back up to the house and tell Dad. He's going to be amazed."

"Piper, too!" exclaimed Perdita. "This is unbelievable."

With great care, she returned the ring to its bed in the leather case before stowing it inside the box. Kit wrapped his scarf around it, then handed it to Perdita, who tucked it under her arm.

"Let's go and change history," she laughed and they clattered back up the corridor, unable to contain their excitement.

Chapter Two

Still discussing their discovery, Perdita and Kit hurried back to the chapel. As they clicked the door back into place, Kit's phone rang.

"Better take it, it's Dad and there are, my god, twenty-six missed calls."

He moved away and after a short conversation, he hung up, looking uncharacteristically serious.

"We need to go inside," he said.

"Why? What's happened?"

"Not sure, but Dad checked you were with me then insisted we meet him in the Lady Isabel Room as soon as possible."

Perdita felt a cold shiver travel down her spine. Running through the rain, they were back inside Marquess House within a few minutes. But as they burst into the Lady Isabel room, they came to an abrupt halt. Kit's parents, the Eve family, Jenny Procter and Izabel, all turned to look at them, their faces pinched with worry.

"Where have you been?" gasped Susan.

"In the chapel..." began Kit, but Perdita spoke over him.

"What is it? What's happened?" she asked.

Alistair moved forward, ashen-faced.

"You must leave now, both of you, or I can't guarantee safety."

"What?" gasped Perdita.

"Dad?"

Perdita stared at Kit, then back to Alistair and Susan.

"A warrant for your arrest has been issued under the authority of The White List, as reinstated by Inigo Westbury,

Head of MI1 Elite, three days ago," he said, his voice crisp, tight, fighting back emotion. "Under the terms of the Milford Haven Treaty, I will be able to halt this action, but I will have to go through the proper channels and that could take time. A minimum of a few days but, at worst, a month, maybe more."

"What are we supposed to have done?" asked Perdita, not quite able to comprehend the situation.

Alistair hesitated.

"They claim treason," he said, and Perdita gasped. "It's a trumped-up charge, created by Inigo Westbury in order to interrogate you…"

"The White List?" Kit's voice was so horrified. If Perdita had not seen him speak the words she would not have believed such a tremulous noise could have come from his mouth.

"What's The White List?" she asked, fear growing with each second.

"It's an assassination register," said Susan, gravely.

"What…?" began Perdita, but Alistair cut across her.

"Nevertheless, it is illegal under the terms of the Milford Haven Treaty and I will be able to revoke it," he snapped. "But I need you two away from here until it is done. I will not risk your lives."

Perdita was struggling to come down from her high of discovering Catherine Howard's grave, the tunnel and the ring but as the seriousness of the situation hit her, she found another layer of worry erupting within in her heart.

"What about Piper?" she asked. The distance between herself and her twin had never felt so vast.

"She is already en route to Castle Jerusalem in Andorra," said Susan. "Alistair contacted her immediately because she had planned to hire a car and drive across Italy and France before returning here, but we can't allow this. Charlie has chartered a private jet to fly her there this evening. Megan will call the moment Piper is safe."

"A private jet?" said Perdita, trying to keep the surprise from her voice.

Their wealth was still new to her, but from the way Susan spoke, this seemed to be an ordinary occurrence. For the first time, she wondered about the true scale and worth of Jerusalem and Marquess House. Since her inheritance, her focus had been on the Marquess House estate and its constant surprises. There had been little room left in her head to wonder about the organisation owned and administered by the Mackensies. Now her curiosity was piqued.

"...and that is how you and Kit will be reaching Andorra too," continued Alistair, bringing Perdita back to the moment. "We have a plane at Withybush Airfield near Haverfordwest. It's only a few miles away. I've spoken to the pilot and he's readying the aircraft as we speak. You two need to pack a few essential items and leave before Inigo can find a way to arrest you. Once he has you, retrieving you will be immensely difficult."

"Alistair, this is insane!" exclaimed Perdita. "Why now? Why is he doing this?"

Out of the corner of her eye, she was aware that Susan was hurrying everyone out of the room until it was only her, Kit and Alistair.

"Perdita, there is no easy way to explain this and, please believe me when I say it had never been my intention to break this news to you in such a blunt and unfeeling manner."

"What...?" she began.

"I believe the warrant has been issued now because the known Watcher who has been tailing you for the past few years has made his final report."

"Who?" said Perdita. "A Watcher, you mean, one of MI1 Elite has been following me. Alistair, it's ludicrous."

She looked to Kit for some reassurance, for him to turn this farcical situation into something that made sense. Kit, however, was looking at Alistair, who gave him a sharp nod, then turned away.

Taking a deep breath, Kit spoke, "Warren works for MI1 Elite, he's a Watcher. He targeted you deliberately…"

"NO!" the force of her response forced Kit to take a step away from her. "No, you're lying…"

"He isn't," Alistair's stern voice cut across Perdita's shriek. He was beside Kit. "Look at this first," he said forcing the brown folder into her hand. "Read it, Perdita. Kit is telling the truth. Warren is a Watcher."

Perdita stared at him as though he were speaking a foreign language. Her panic was making it impossible for her to grasp his words. As the blood thundered in her ears, she felt the world tilt, then she forced herself to take deep, calming breaths. Panicking would not help. Instead, she looked at the brown folder that was trembling in her shaking hands and, after glaring at both Alistair and Kit, tore it open and began scanning through the documents Alistair had so painstakingly gathered during Perdita's relationship with Warren.

Shaking her head, she shut her eyes as though trying to deny the evidence.

"No," she whispered. "No, he was a lecturer, we met through work, he loved me."

"I think he did fall in love with you, Perdita," said Alistair, trying to soften the blow, "but it didn't begin that way. You were targeted in order to try and discover whether or not you were in touch with your grandmother. Warren, however, is human and I believe his feelings for you, which began as an act, became real."

Perdita sank into an armchair, the folder on her lap, the photo of Warren staring up at her like an accusation.

"There's something else," continued Alistair, "and this is only a suspicion, but you need to know."

"Go on," muttered Perdita, not looking either man in the eye but continuing to stare down at the photo of her former fiancé.

"We think your grandmother was murdered…"

"No," moaned Perdita, shaking her head, dreading the words to come.

"Warren was in the vicinity the night your grandmother died. We didn't tell you at the time, but a window had been forced at the back of the house. It's possible he got in there, waited until the house was quiet and made his way to your grandmother's room…"

"STOP!" shouted Perdita, unable to listen to the details. "Why didn't you call the police? Why hasn't he been arrested?"

"For the same reason your mother's death was classed as a tragic accident, we have no proof. And even if we tried to find some, we would be blocked at every turn," replied Alistair, fear making his tone sharp and brutal.

"It would explain how he reached me so quickly to break the news. He was supposed to have been giving a lecture in Peterborough," she said. Then, with a swift, sharp movement, she slammed the folder shut and thrust it back at Alistair. "What do you think was in his report that has triggered off this chain of events?"

"The key fact is probably that, not only have you re-opened Mary's research, you have progressed," said Alistair.

"But you said continuing with Granny Mary's work was the only way to keep us safe," hissed Perdita. "When I asked you if

467

we should put it back in the boxes and lock it away, you were the one who said discovering the truth was our only chance at survival."

Perdita's fury was so intense, Kit stepped between her and his father. She had forgotten that her grandmother had issued identical instructions. Her fear was making her irrational and she wanted someone to blame.

"Perdita, I still believe that is the case," replied Alistair. "Westbury would have found another excuse to issue this warrant, even if you had never even discovered the unpublished manuscript. He is determined to make his name in the Secret Service and he has become obsessed with Mary Fitzroy and, by extension, yourself and Piper."

"Why though?" she asked, astounded.

"Unfortunately, I'm unable to answer your question because I don't know," sighed Alistair. "However, I do know he is acting in breach of the Milford Haven Treaty and, as I said earlier, I will be able to stop him. The trouble is, if he has already arrested you and spirited you away, then…"

He turned away from Perdita and his son, unable to finish the sentence.

Perdita and Kit exchanged a glance.

"Give me ten minutes," said Perdita.

"Me too, Dad," said Kit and, hurrying over, hugged his father tightly.

As they fled from the room, neither of them saw the terror on Alistair Mackensie's face.

Perdita raced around her rooms, gathering basic items and shoving them haphazardly into a rucksack. First, into a hidden inside pocket, she placed the recovered box containing the ruby ring, still cocooned in Kit's scarf, followed by her laptop that fitted into a slot at the back and the wallet containing the memory sticks that held her grandmother's entire collection of work. She felt sure there were probably copies at Castle Jerusalem, but she could not take the risk that they might not be there. In an outside pocket, she pushed the leather roll of jewellery making tools that she used when on digs or examining finds. No matter where she went, she carried it with her, and to leave it behind would have felt wrong.

Doing a final mental check that she had all she would need to get her through this emergency, she hurried over to the mermaid tapestry that hid the safe. Despite the urgency, she could not help but pause and search the intricate facial details for similarities to the ceiling boss in the chapel. Her scholars eye picked out face and brow shape as well as the colour of the hair. *They were there, possibly not identical but close enough.* Pushing this thought from her mind, she slid the tapestry aside and opened the safe, pulling out her passport and the final chapter of her grandmother's book. She slammed the safe shut and repositioned the tapestry.

With one last sweeping glance, she ran out of the room, slamming the door behind her, and raced along the corridor. It was only when she reached the top of the enormous, ornately decorated staircase that she halted. Directly opposite her was the carved wooden relief that echoed the beautiful stained glass rose window opposite. For the first time, she noticed the writing carved around the edge. The top of the image was hidden in shadow and for a moment she hesitated, wondering if she had time to dash along the Minstrel's gallery and take a closer look, then she heard Kit running up behind her.

"We'll look at the carving another day," he said grabbing her hand and pulling her down the stairs. "I don't know what's going on but I've never seen Dad so scared. For his sake, we have to do as he asks."

Perdita glanced at his profile. Kit's mouth was in a rigid line and his tone had been part apologetic, part entreaty.

"Of course," she said, squeezing his hand. "If your dad says we should leave, we'll leave."

Once more they hurried into the Lady Isabel room, where Alistair and Susan were talking to Sarah Eve. All three looked relieved to see them.

"Billy and Larry will drive you to the airfield," said Alistair. "The pilot's name is Elliot, as soon as you arrive…"

But he got no further, there was the thunder of footsteps and a shout, the door was flung open and Alan Eve hurtled through it, closely followed by his two burly sons.

"What?" said Perdita, her nerves becoming increasingly ragged. "What's happened?"

"All the exits are blocked," gasped Alan, clutching the stitch in his side. "There are unmarked cars by every gate and at strategic points all around the estate's boundaries. Worse, there are two black vans blocking the lane leading to the main gates."

Perdita felt sick. They were surrounded. Were they about to be murdered like her mother and grandmother? She turned to Alistair and true fear gripped her heart because he seemed as stunned as the rest of them.

"They've blocked the lane?" he repeated. "If they're on the boundaries too, we have no way out."

Alistair turned to Kit and, for the first time, he looked every one of his sixty-nine years. Susan, too, was ashen, gripping the back of an armchair for support.

"Kit, I've failed you…" he said, his voice a hoarse whisper.

"The tunnel," said Perdita, suddenly. "The secret tunnel to Llyn Cel island, we can get out that way."

"Perdita, it's a legend," said Susan.

"No, Mum, it isn't," replied Kit. "Mary left clues for Perdita to find and we discovered it this evening. It's where we've been, it's why I didn't get your calls. The tunnel is real and we found something else…"

Alistair's eyes cleared as Perdita's suggestion rallied him.

"And isn't it supposed to lead to the island?" interrupted Alistair, not taking in his son's words in his relief at this new way out of Marquess House.

"Yes," said Perdita. "Granny and Bethan first discovered it through the entrance in the old tower on Llyn Cel island, the only part of the priory that's still standing."

"The bay on the far side is hidden from the house," Alistair continued, thinking aloud as he formulated a new escape route. "I'll call Mark at Home Farm. He can row out to the far shore of the island and collect you. If they've positioned cars all around the boundary, you won't be able to use the roads. Briony can bring the horses and then you can take the bridle path across Trewarren Farm, through the wood and around the back way to the airfield. MI1 won't be expecting it. Billy, Larry, I need you to go too, in case Perdita and Kit need protection."

Billy and Larry Eve were the cousins of Briony, who ran the animal sanctuary, and her elder brother, Mark, who worked as a restorer in The Dairy. The Eve brothers nodded, already moving towards the door.

"What about you and Mum?" asked Kit.

"They don't want us, they want you. We'll be safe, but I'm not risking your lives," said Alistair, his voice returned to full strength. He hugged his son, then Perdita. "You must hurry. Call me when you're with Megan. I'll call Mark and Briony."

Susan stepped forward and, after giving them both a swift, strong hug, pushed Perdita and Kit towards the door.

"Now go," she said. "We'll join you all in Andorra as soon as we're able."

Perdita and Kit raced from the room, the burly Eve brothers leading the way.

They ran through the quiet house, not speaking, their pounding footsteps the only sound. Once outside the back door, their target was the chapel. Keeping low, the four of them skirted through the shadows, unsure whether the perimeter of the estate had been breached, taking no chances.

Perdita could feel panic rising. *What if the other end of the tunnel was blocked? They had not gone all the way through. Would they be arrested or would the Treaty protect them? Worse, would they be executed?*

The thought was so terrifying she felt momentarily faint. She understood now why her father and grandmother had behaved as they did all those years ago; this visceral fear, this seemingly unstoppable force that answered to no one but themselves was what they had been trying to protect them from. Now, Mary and James were both dead, and she wondered how long it would be before she and Kit joined them.

They skidded to a halt under the kissing gate, waiting while Billy and Larry flitted silently ahead, checking their path was clear. A moment later, Billy signalled for them to run. Slipping inside the old building, they closed the heavy door behind them and felt their way down the aisle past the shadowy scaffold towers and ghost-like dust sheets. Perdita pushed away the thoughts of her last visit here and all that she and Kit had discovered. It felt like a different lifetime, before the true terror of MI1 Elite had been unleashed.

"Where's the entrance?" came Larry Eve's gruff voice through the gloom.

"This way," said Perdita. Picking her way carefully to the altar, she knelt down. "I need some light," she whispered.

Billy handed her a torch, "Short bursts," he said. She nodded and crawled further along looking for the faint carving. On her third flash of the torch she located it.

"There!" she said. "The corner of the second panel, I see a mermaid."

Billy and Larry exchanged a sceptical glance but Perdita was bending down, pushing the brick and releasing the narrow door. The Eve brothers made noises of approval, impressed by this unexpected escape route.

"Come on," muttered Larry. "We need to get you away as fast as possible in case they're in the grounds. We'll use the torches the minute that door is shut. I don't want any overspill to give away our position."

Larry went first, feeling his way into the dark. Perdita followed, with Kit behind her, and finally Billy, who discovered a handle on the inside of the panel which he used to push and click the narrow door back into place. The darkness became impenetrable. Perdita was aware of Kit's closeness, his breath in her hair, his hand holding hers. She glanced up and saw the faintest outline of his face close to hers. He looked down, his eyes reflecting her own unease, then they were flooded with light.

"Come on," said Larry, flashing his powerful torch around the enclosed space. "Let's see where this tunnel leads."

They ran down the spiral staircase and into the arched passageway.

"What is this place?" asked Billy, astounded, pausing as he looked around.

"We think it was once part of the priory," replied Perdita. "It was probably closed off when the nuns left."

"We need to keep moving," urged Larry, glaring at his brother.

Picking up speed, they ran. Perdita kept glancing behind her, half expecting armed MI1 Elite agents to bloom out of the darkness like a curse but, as they chased through the shadows, the only footsteps were their own.

The tunnel was straight but long, and with each step, Perdita worried the exit might be blocked. All she could do was hold on to the memory that her grandmother had found the tunnel in the 1940s. With luck, Mary had continued to monitor it and keep the entrances open, even if she did not tell anyone else where these were. If this was the case then, with luck, their way out would be clear.

Finally, they reached a stone staircase identical to the one at the entrance. The Eves switched off their torches and Perdita and Kit followed suit.

"We'll go up first. If Alistair wasn't able to get hold of Mark, we might have to think of another way to get across the lake to the far bank," said Billy. "Stay here until we come back for you."

They fell silent, merging into the darkness, barely breathing as they waited. Once again, Perdita was intensely aware of Kit's physical closeness. She reached out, searching for his hand, craving reassurance. When she found it, he squeezed back in response to her touch and moved fractionally closer. She could feel his breath, the heat of his body, the force of his presence…

"The boat's here," came Billy's voice from halfway down the staircase breaking the unexpected tension between them, "but when we get outside, keep low, just a precaution."

Perdita went first and as she felt the cool night air on her face, the brief encounter with Kit vanished like an autumn mist as the terror of what they were dealing with flooded her once more, obliterating all other emotions. They emerged into the ruins of the tower where Larry hovered in the shadows, his eyes endlessly scanning the surrounding woodland. He pointed towards a clump of trees and began to move. Perdita ran, crouched and silent, behind the burly backs of the Eve brothers. Kit came last, constantly checking behind them.

The island was small and it did not take them long to reach the tiny hidden bay. The ancient trees that fringed the beach soon gave way to soft pale sand. A rowing boat was pulled up on the shore and a tall, dark-haired man in his late twenties was waiting.

The water of Llyn Cel remained black and silken, the only noise the lap of the waves and the nervous breathing of the fugitives. It seemed MI1 had followed some of the directives laid down in the Milford Haven Treaty and had not yet breached the boundaries of Marquess House, but Perdita knew this was still a terrifying possibility. *And what happens when we're outside the boundary?* she thought, then pushed the images of arrest and torture from her mind.

"Mark!" hissed Larry. Mark squinted through the darkness.

"It's all clear," he whispered. Billy beckoned Perdita and Kit towards the boat.

"There isn't room for us all," said Mark, speaking quickly. He threw two small canvas bags to the Eve brothers before taking Perdita and Kit's rucksacks and stowing them in the prow.

"Tents and food," he explained to Billy. "You two are going to have to stay here until the coast is clear. I'll come back for you then. Alistair said you mustn't go back through the tunnel. If there are Watchers in Marquess House, we don't want to give away its location." Billy and Larry nodded. "You two," he continued to Perdita and Kit, "get under the tarpaulin and try not to move around much. I'm going to drape fishing rods across you as extra camouflage, so if anyone spots me, it'll look like I'm night fishing."

Perdita turned to the Eve brothers, "Thank you," she said. "Take care of everyone for us."

Billy nodded, then Larry gave her a gentle push towards the boat. "Thank us another night, you need to go."

Perdita gave them both a swift hug, then hurried towards Mark. Kit paused to have a brief discussion with Larry but before she clambered into the boat, Perdita craned her neck across the black waters of Llyn Cel for a final, farewell glimpse of Marquess House. It happened in the briefest of moments, in the space between breaths but she was certain of what she saw: a long shadow with a fish-shaped tail but also human arms and flowing hair glimmering below the surface of the lake. She blinked and with a soft splash, the vision was gone.

Kit was by her side, taking her hand, helping her into the cramped space.

"Sorry," he whispered, squeezing in beside her, forced to bend his long legs across her. Then he glanced at her pale face. "What's the matter?"

"Nothing," she whispered. "Nothing, I thought I saw… It doesn't matter."

Mark pulled the heavy tarpaulin over them, tucking it in, ensuring they were hidden, then positioned a number of rods across them. Perdita wrinkled her nose and looked over at Kit, who rolled his eyes.

"Nothing wrong with the smell of fish," he murmured, but he moved slightly and slipped his arm around her shoulders, pulling her more tightly into his side. Perdita tensed briefly, then relaxed into the comfort of his closeness. A moment later,

Mark climbed aboard and the Eve brothers shoved the boat into the water. Perdita closed her eyes, willing them safely to the far shore, trying to ignore the terrible feeling of doom that was closing in around her.

There was a gentle bump as Mark grounded the boat, a splash followed as he leapt out and pulled the vessel onto the beach where he usually moored it.

"The coast's clear," he whispered. Perdita felt relief as the weight of the fishing rods was lifted off her legs. Then the tarpaulin was folded back and they scrambled out. "Briony was supposed to be meeting you with the horses," he continued, handing them their rucksacks, "but Alistair is concerned that if our house is being watched, it would look too suspicious if she saddled up three horses at this time of night."

"What does Dad suggest?" hissed Kit. "It's too far to walk."

"You're going to have to take Briony's moped," he whispered. "She's supposed to have parked it at the end of the lane. You can use the old bridle path, the one we always used for scrambling on our bikes when we were kids. It takes you to the far side of the airfield and the hangars. Ordinarily, you'd go through customs like a normal airport but tonight you're going to have to stow away."

"But what if we're caught?" whispered Perdita.

"Let's hope it doesn't come to that," replied Mark dourly. "The pilot you're looking for is called Elliot and he'll be in hangar five. Give him the password, Blake."

Perdita threw Kit a glance. She was nervous about these impromptu plans but, she supposed, caught unawares as they were, this was the best they could expect at such short notice.

"Can you ride a moped?" she whispered to Kit.

"Yes, don't worry about that," he replied. "I'm more concerned about the noise we'll make."

"It's that or walk, mate," said Mark, leading the way along a steep, sandy path. "Leave the keys under the wheel arch and I'll bring Briony down tomorrow to fetch it."

They crested the hill and saw the black moped parked in the shadow of the hedge, with two crash helmets hanging on the handlebars. Kit strapped his bag on to the carrier in front of him. Perdita realised she would have to wear hers.

"Thanks, Mark," said Kit, turning to shake his hand. "We appreciate all you've done tonight. You'd better make yourself scarce before I start the engine."

Perdita hugged him.

"Thanks," she echoed, then pulling on the crash helmet and fastening it under her chin, she climbed on the moped behind Kit and slid her arms around his waist. Mark melted away into the shadows, leaving them alone in the darkness.

"If we get away with this, I'll be amazed," said Kit, surprising Perdita with this sudden flash of pessimism. "Ready?"

"Ready."

He turned the key and the engine sprang into life. It sounded deafening in the quiet country lane and with the smallest amount of acceleration as he could manage, Kit pulled away.

It was the bumpiest ride of her life. The bridle path was old, mostly unused and littered with potholes. When things became unusually perilous, Kit would flick on the dipped headlight, but for most of the journey he drove in darkness. Perdita's mind flitted fast and nervously over events: the discovery of Catherine's grave, the ring, their escape, and the terror of MI1 Elite lurking in the depths of the shadows, forcing them to flee for their lives.

And suddenly, anger burst into her heart.

She had lost so much of her past to the darkness of time; so many people had been stolen from her by MI1 Elite. This evil organisation — acting with impunity thanks to government protection — had murdered her mother and forced her grandmother to step away from her and Piper in order to keep them safe. Her father had been left with no choice but to collude with her grandmother's plans, such was his fear that he might also lose his daughters. Now, MI1 had murdered her grandmother too and had forced her and Piper to flee for their lives: she through the cold, dark Welsh night and Piper across Europe to a castle carved into a mountainside.

Surely this could not only be because of something they or her grandmother had discovered during their historical research? What possible grounds did Westbury have to charge them with treason? *There must be something more*, she thought, although, at present she could not work out what that might be. *Any historical discovery we make could easily be covered up*, she thought. *It would not be difficult to dismiss our work and discredit our careers. Yet, MI1 seems intent on destroying us.* It made no sense.

Perdita knew these thoughts were the way of madness and, with huge determination, forced herself to calm down, to focus on the present. Alistair claimed he would be able to deal with this mess, that they would soon be able to return to Marquess House, the place she realised she now thought of as home. This was her small ray of hope and she clung to it with all her might.

She cast her mind to the wooden box they had discovered in the tunnel. Was this truly Catherine Howard's missing ruby ring? It seemed so unlikely and yet, the items she had seen recovered from archaeological digs throughout her career were often older than the Tudor period and were still intact. Despite the present danger, the thrill of discovery rippled through her. *Oh, Granny*, she thought, *what have you led me to?*

Suddenly, Kit slowed the moped, idling the engine as he peered into the darkness.

"What's wrong?" she whispered.

"There's a black van parked up ahead," he replied.

Perdita felt her hands go clammy.

"Do you think it's the Watchers?"

"Could be. This is where the bridle path crosses a road. It would be an ideal point to keep watch," he hissed. "Any suggestions?"

"Is it possible to go across county?" she replied, looking at the surrounding fields.

"I suppose but we'd be more vulnerable in the open."

They sat, paralysed with indecision.

"It might not be them," murmured Perdita. "Wait here, I'll go and look."

"No, you stay here," replied Kit. "I know more people, I'll be able to tell if they're strangers. Keep the engine running and if I shout your name, turn it around and head back to Home Farm. We might have to trust to the Milford Haven Treaty to save you if I'm caught."

"Kit, no…" she began, but he was already heaving himself off the moped, forcing her to concentrate on moving forwards so it would not topple over.

Realising she had no choice, and also agreeing with the wisdom of Kit's words, she manoeuvred the moped into the shadows, allowing herself space to turn around if she needed to flee. But throughout, her eyes never left the shape that was Kit creeping through the shadows.

He was within a few metres of the van when he stood on a branch and it cracked, sounding like a gunshot in the silence.

Perdita stifled a gasp and Kit froze. To her horror, angry voices rumbled from the other side of the van and Kit was flooded in the light of a torch. Perdita sat transfixed on the moped as two men walked towards Kit. Her instinct was to ride straight at them and grab Kit, but she knew this would be foolish. If nothing else, she had only ever driven a moped twice in her life and was less than confident that she would be able to pull off such a rescue. Instead, she waited, watching, fury rising in her. She could not lose Kit too. The Watchers were not going to take another person from her.

Determined to help, she took a deep breath, working up the courage to move. But as she revved the engine, she looked over at Kit and realised he was laughing. Seconds later, he was running towards her.

"Come on," he said. "They're going to take us to the airfield."

"What?" said Perdita bemused. "Who are they?"

"Jason and Nathan, old mates of mine," he said, removing the keys from the moped and turning it towards the van where the doors were already open.

"But won't we be safer on the bridle path, away from the road?" she asked, refusing to move out of the shadows.

"No," Kit whispered. "The reason they stopped is because they saw a van they didn't recognise blocking the far end of this path. They've also seen a couple of others and a group of men spreading out across the fields. They figured something was up. They thought it was a sheep rustling ring, but I bet it's MI1. They were about to call the police. If we carry on along here, the Watchers will get us. This is our only chance."

Perdita bit her lip, nervously.

"And we can trust these two?"

"Yes," he replied. "No question."

481

Perdita threw a glance at the two men who were waiting by the van, then gave a short nod. Kit grinned in relief and began wheeling the moped towards the waiting vehicle. Moments later, the two men had helped him lift it inside.

"Come on," Kit whispered, beckoning to her. Perdita, knowing she had to trust Kit's judgement, ran along the bridle path where he hauled her into the back of the van.

"Sit on the floor and keep out of sight," said the taller of the two men, before slamming the door and plunging them into darkness.

Perdita dropped her head into hands. The night was pushing her to the limit of her nerves. There was a roar as the engine started and they lurched out on to the road. The unexpected movement unbalanced her and she tumbled into Kit who was sitting beside her.

"Don't worry, Perds," he sat, helping her to sit up again. "We're safer here than out in the open, especially if MI1 are patrolling the fields. They probably know about the jet and are trying to stop us getting to the airport."

"They're doing a good job," replied Perdita. More than anything, she wanted this journey over.

In what felt like no time at all, the van crunched onto gravel and came to a halt. The back doors opened and Perdita could see lights in the distance.

"Kit, you need to be careful, there are people everywhere," whispered the tall man.

"Thanks, Jason," Kit replied. "Can you take Briony's moped back?"

"Yeah, no worries, it was coming in to me for a service next week anyway," he muttered. Perdita climbed out, her eyes on the perimeter fence.

"Thanks," she whispered to Jason.

"My pleasure, now get going."

Hulking buildings loomed in the night, their shapes blacker than the autumn sky as they ran through the shadows looking for number five.

"There," she said as they rounded a final corner. "The last one, there's a gate."

They edged forward, making it through to the relative safety of the shadows. The hangar doors were wide open and light spilled out on to the wet grass that edged the tarmac runway. Then Perdita saw something that made bile rise in her stomach and panic fill her head. Striding into the hangar were three men in black uniforms. In their arms they cradled guns that glinted menacingly in the dim light. One marched up to the waiting jet, where a tall slim man with a beard gave them a cautious nod.

"Shit, now what?" whispered Kit.

"If we go back, they might see us."

"But if we stay here, they'll definitely find us," he hissed. Laughter suddenly filled the air, pulling their attention back to the hangar. The three armed men said something to the pilot then vanished back inside the airport offices.

"Now," said Perdita, and ran forward.

"Blake," she whispered the password to the startled pilot, Elliot.

"Sam, they're here," he hissed and a woman with long brown hair, dressed in black, emerged from the jet. She hurried down the short flight of steps leading to the only door in the side of the jet and took Perdita's rucksack.

"Quick," she whispered, "those men are Watchers, they could be back at any moment. Lie on the floor."

Perdita ran up the short staircase, relieved that the plane had been parked in such a way that the side door they were all scurrying through was obscured from the office windows.

"Stay out of sight," instructed Elliot, who had followed them on board. "We don't have much time."

Perdita squashed herself into the small aisle between the seats. Kit squeezed in behind her. Sam leaned out of the plane, pushing away the steps before slamming the door. The engines roared and the small jet rumbled forward. Elliot spoke into his headset and they were given clearance for take-off.

Taxiing to the runway, the plane began to build up speed. As it did, the three armed men streaked into the night, running flat out towards the jet, shouting and firing rounds above their heads, their voices filling the air with violence. But the plane's nose was lifting. They were rising, rising, rising; the men were becoming smaller, smaller and they were up, flying free through the starry sky.

Chapter Three

The next month passed in a blur for Perdita. On arrival at Castle Jerusalem after their traumatic journey, she and Piper had fallen on each other, before finally collapsing into bed and sleeping almost around the clock. It was a few days later when Kit had shown her around properly, and she had realised the clue was in the name of the Mackensie's home.

"I know you've always said it was called Castle Jerusalem," she said, gazing up at the thick stone walls and the arched doorway that seemed to grow out of the austere mountainside, "but I didn't think it was a real castle."

"It's not much," laughed Kit, "but it's home."

It was a terrible joke and Perdita had looked at Kit in amusement. Megan had insisted on taking charge and showing the twins around the tiny nation of Andorra, while Kit had dragged them out to meet his friends and enjoy the night life, persuading them both they needed a holiday and a chance to relax. To her surprise, Perdita had found the fear of their escape subsiding as they settled into the Mackensie's home. Occasionally, a nightmare dragged her from sleep, but in the land surrounded by mountains, she felt safe.

After showing Piper the ring and examining it more thoroughly, Perdita had asked Megan to place it in the strong room. Until she knew what was happening in London, and when they would be allowed to return to Marquess House, she was reluctant to begin work on the ring and all the possibilities its continuing existence presented. Throughout her career, she had handled ancient jewels, assessing their meaning, their value and their significance, but she was hesitant of spending too much time in the company of the ruby ring. Deep within her, she knew that, once she began exploring its secrets, she would not be able to rest until she had discovered the truth and, at present, the task seemed overwhelming.

At last, Alistair and Susan had sent word they would be arriving in Andorra the following day.

"Do you think we'll be able to go home?" Piper had asked that evening as they sat in the two-bedroomed apartment where they were staying. It was located in one of the towers and offered spectacular mountain views.

"I hope so," Perdita had replied. "It would be great to be home for Christmas."

Now, they stood on the stairs leading to the Grande Hall, hesitating as raised voices reached them.

"Is that Kit and Alistair arguing?" asked Perdita.

"It sounds like it," replied Piper. "Should we interrupt?"

Alistair and Susan had arrived earlier in the afternoon. The greetings then had been effusive. Delighted though Alistair and Susan had been to see everyone, Alistair had refused to update them immediately.

"We need to sort out the luggage," he had said, pointing to the pile of boxes and suitcases stacked near the entrance hall, "and settle into our rooms. I suggest we meet for drinks in the Grande Hall at 6 p.m., then I can update you and we can follow our discussion with dinner. It's rather complicated."

"We're safe though," Perdita had whispered to him when he had hugged her.

"Yes, my dear, you're safe," he had reassured her.

Perdita and Piper hesitated, not wishing to interrupt the father and son altercation, but as Perdita turned to her sister to suggest they head to the other less formal sitting room for a few minutes to allow the discussion to subside, the door was flung open and Kit marched out, looking flustered. When he saw them hovering on the wide staircase, he halted.

Alistair appeared in the door way. He, too, looked less sanguine than usual, until he saw them, then his face split into a broad and delighted smile.

"Perdita! Piper!" he exclaimed, walking up to hug them fiercely, one after the other. "Come in, my dears. You both look ravishing."

Kit, after a moment of hesitation, followed.

A bowl of glühwein was warming on top of a small stove, Alistair ladled out two large glassfuls and handed them one each. Piper took hers and retreated to a wing-back armchair beside the roaring fire. Alistair followed, leaving Perdita and Kit alone.

"Is everything all right between you and your dad?" she asked.

"It's nothing," replied Kit. "We often disagree about things. You've just never heard us shouting at one another. Dad isn't always the calm, serene Dumbledore character you know. He has a real temper when roused."

Perdita laughed.

"Are you the same?" she asked.

"What, do I have a temper?"

"Yes. I certainly do. It's a long fuse, but when I blow up, which isn't often, it can be spectacular. Piper, on the other hand, will very quickly let you know when she's irritated."

"It's her red hair," he smiled. "But, yes, a bit like you, it's a long fuse but incandescent when I blow. Today, with Dad, well, it was more professional differences. We bicker a lot in our day-to-day work, this was overspill. Is Piper OK?" Kit asked, nodding towards where she was speaking intently to Alistair.

487

"Yes," said Perdita. "Although, we're both having the occasional nightmare about being chased, which is chilling."

"Same here," admitted Kit.

"We wouldn't be human if we didn't react," she replied, giving him a reassuring smile. However, before he could answer, the door opened to admit Susan, Megan and, her fiancé, Pablo, in a flurry of noise and wedding discussions. After helping themselves to drinks, they too grouped themselves around the fire, the conversation about the table plan coming to a natural end. Perdita settled on the two-seater sofa beside Piper's chair.

All eyes turned to Alistair who, after taking a sip of wine, began: "Last week, I had a meeting with the Home Secretary…"

"What?" exclaimed Perdita.

"It's not as strange as it sounds, my dear," chuckled Alistair. "He and I were at Cambridge together and we've remained good friends. I rarely use the connection professionally, preferring to keep our business and personal lives separate. This time I felt we needed to flex some political muscle."

"And what did you discuss?" asked Piper. Perdita noticed her sister's voice sounded strangely high-pitched and nervous.

"The situation with MI1 Elite, Inigo Westbury, the Milford Haven Treaty and the arrest warrants issued under the auspices of The White List."

Kit slid into the seat beside her. Perdita could not help but feel relieved; his presence was always comforting.

"And?" prompted Perdita.

"When I questioned him, the Home Secretary declared The White List to be a fabrication, a myth, I think were his actual words. However, I doubt his sincerity on this particular matter." Kit leaned forward as though he were about to speak, but Alistair gave a small shake of his head and Kit subsided. Alistair continued, "He did declare that the Milford Haven Treaty was valid and, if Westbury had issued such warrants, his actions would have been a violation of his position as head of MI1 Elite. However, as the men Westbury had placed around Marquess House, thankfully, failed to capture you, there is very little that can be done to prove these documents ever existed. Westbury has been questioned and denied all knowledge of either the warrants or despatching a guard to Marquess House. His office and computer have been searched and, at present, there is no trace of anything incriminating."

"But we have CCTV footage of the guard outside the gates…" interrupted Kit.

"And as I was saying to you earlier, the vans were all unmarked, the men were wearing dark clothing and the number plates of the vans were obscured, in other words, MI1 can disassociate themselves entirely."

"What about the men in the fields and blocking the bridle path? And the ones at the airport with guns?" asked Perdita. "They fired them into the sky when we were taking off."

"Again, these men were in dark, unmarked uniforms and, although I doubt you'll be surprised to hear this, there was a fault on the CCTV cameras at Withybush Airport that night, allegedly. Therefore, there is no footage or proof that those men were ever there. The local constabulary claim any loud explosions or noises were probably fireworks."

Perdita stared at Alistair, trying to stem the unease his words brought. Once again, she realised the sheer might of the force they were battling.

"However, despite the Home Secretary's assurances that Westbury will not cross our paths again, and Marquess House remains a sovereign state, he has agreed to an enquiry into

Westbury's behaviour and methodology. His appointment to the head of MI1 Elite was always a surprise and he does not appear to be making a success of it. In other words, the power is going to his head and he is beginning to believe he is above the law. The man is unpredictable, cruel and has no conscience, so until his superiors have decided what action to take concerning Westbury, Susan and I believe it would be safest for us all to remain here."

Perdita turned away, disappointment washing through her. Until hearing these words, she had not realised how much she had been hoping they would soon be on their way home to Marquess House. Now it seemed Castle Jerusalem would be their base for a while longer.

"You and Mum too?" asked Megan, trying to keep the relief from her voice.

"We can all work as well from here as at Marquess House. There is the secure portal for transference of files. I've been assured these are all still active and untapped by the Watchers, as agreed by the Treaty. Stuart will be coming here for Megan and Pablo's wedding and his plan was to stay until Christmas, but I will insist he remains until things have cooled down."

"What about the people at Marquess House?" asked Perdita. "Sarah and Alan, Billy, Larry, Jenny, Mark, Briony? Everyone else? Will they be safe from the Watchers? Marquess House belongs to Piper and me, we have responsibility for the people who live there, who rely on us."

"Once again, the Home Secretary has given us his word that the Treaty will be properly enforced and they are in no danger."

Perdita stared at Alistair, her temper rising.

"The Watchers threatened our lives then chased us out of the country, and we have to remain fugitives. It doesn't seem fair, Alistair," she snapped.

"And it isn't fair, Perdita," he agreed, "but we are a few steps ahead of MI1 at present and I would like us to remain so in our quest for the truth."

"What do you mean, Dad?" asked Kit.

"The two of you are able to categorically prove that Catherine Howard wasn't executed, but died peacefully at Marquess House. You have uncovered evidence to show she gave birth to twins. Perdita, you have proved Mary's theories and created new ones of your own. You and Kit, with Mary's help, have located the first of the three missing pieces of jewellery, which are supposedly the key to this mystery. We know there are two more that we need to find to ensure our safety. Whether they still exist or not, we have no idea, but we must keep looking. The first story is told but the next one is about to begin."

"Catherine's children," said Perdita, her fury subsiding, and Alistair nodded.

"Exactly, my dear. You have told the mother's tale, now you must discover what happened next. Indeed, if there is anything to tell."

There was silence as everyone considered Alistair's words. Perdita's eyes met Piper's and her sister smiled, ever defiant and encouraging. Beside her, she felt Kit's blue gaze, the electricity of his presence and his constant support. It was then she realised, for most of her life, she had been looking backwards, dwelling on her losses, on what might have been, on people she had never known and places she would never visit, but it was time to move forward. To continue along the path begun by her grandmother but which would now be finished by herself, Piper and Kit.

"Catherine's children," she repeated, as a small ray of hope teased at the edges of her heart. "We need to bring them home too."

"And you can do it, Perds," said Piper.

"You're probably the only one who can," added Kit.

"Yes," said Perdita. "No matter how impossible the task may seem, we must remember what Catherine always believed."

"What was that?" asked Megan.

"Things may be difficult but there is always hope and mermaids," said Perdita.

Her excitement was building and suddenly, a smile of such radiance burst across her face, it was as though she were a different person. The worries, the fear, the loneliness that had plagued her for years fell away as she stared around at the people she loved best. It was as though her grandmother was finally sitting beside her, smiling her approval.

She was with Piper and they were safe and sound at last.

Safe.

Just like Catherine, who had been right, there would always be hope and mermaids.

Epilogue: 1542

The woman cautiously approached the heavy wooden gate leading to the undercroft of the castle, the baby sleeping silently in her arms. She paused, her eyes adjusting to the intense blackness, then a candle bloomed in the distance and flickered slowly towards her through the velvet night.

"Who's there?" called a soft, heavily-accented female voice.

"It is I, Lady Margaret Douglas," the woman replied, throwing back the hood of her cloak to show her striking auburn hair.

"Oh, my dear," the woman hurried forward and made to embrace her, but Margaret opened her cloak to reveal the baby.

"May I present Princess Elizabeth Howard," she whispered.

The woman looked at the baby and her eyes filled with tears.

"She's beautiful, but we cannot call her this. We shall choose another name; more suitable."

"Whatever you wish," Lady Douglas murmured. "How fares your daughter?"

"She is weak," said the woman, tears welling in her eyes. "And her father is dead, yet this child…" her voice tailed off.

"…will solve many of your problems," said Margaret. She handed the sleeping baby to the woman. For a moment, the woman tensed as the weight of the infant filled her arms, then her face softened and she bent to kiss the child's soft downy cheek, tears of grief and despair dropping like promises on to the baby's skin.

"We will keep her safe," she whispered. "She will be loved."

"There is this too," said Lady Margaret Douglas, handing her a small leather pouch. "A gift from her mother, so she will know her later on."

"What is this?" asked the woman, startled. "You said no one should know. This will identify her."

"No, it is a ring, that is all. It is unremarkable, apart from the cavity within. Keep it safe and give it to the child if you ever have to tell her the truth."

With a certain reluctance, the woman weighed the small pouch in her hand, then tucked it into her sleeve, shaking her head worriedly.

Lady Douglas curtseyed, dropping her eyes as the woman and child merged back into the gloom. When their outlines had been swallowed by the shadows, she rose, staring at the point in the blackness where they had vanished, then she turned, hurrying back to where Charles Howard was waiting to escort her safely away. Once saddled, she gave the forbidding stone building one final glance and whispered:

"Good luck, my sweet child, may you always have hope and mermaids."

Raising her gloved hand to her lips she blew a kiss towards the castle, then gathering her reins, she dug her heels into the side of her glossy chestnut mare and they galloped away, disappearing into the depths of the winter night.

A NOTE TO THE READER

Dear Reader,

Thank you for taking the time to read my novel. I hope you enjoyed joining Perdita as she unravelled the historical mysteries buried in Marquess House.

I have always loved history and the idea for this story came to me when I wondered what would happen if new information was found that changed everything we thought we knew about our collective past. How would it affect the wider world? And, would radically different versions of events be ridiculed and repressed, possibly seen as subversive or studied and placed into historical context.

At the time, I was researching my own genealogy and it was as I discovered unexpected secrets in my own family history, I began to think: *what if?* And, as a writer, once you've had that thought, you have no choice but to follow your characters into the adventure.

Perdita and Piper arrived in my mind during my commute into London one morning and it was after this, having abandoned a previous character who had never been quite right, I began writing the story in notebooks on my way to work, typing it up either during my lunch-hour or when I arrived home in the evening. Mary had been with me even longer, as had Alistair and Kit. The rest of the gang arrived as I wandered around Marquess House with Perdita, slowly getting to know who was who and who you could trust or not.

This is a work of fiction. The conspiracy theory I have built around Catherine Howard is entirely my own creation. However, I have researched this period extensively and as far as it has been possible, I have tried to use verifiable historical fact for the rest of the story.

My version of Catherine Howard is quite different to the usual interpretation but I have tried to imagine myself into the Tudor period when women had so little power over their own lives, especially if they came from a wealthy and powerful family. The version of history with which we are most familiar is largely told through the voices of men, yet there were women at the heart of events too, and it is their voices, alongside Catherine's, that I have tried to use to give a new perspective on events.

All the characters surrounding Catherine are real people, even the servant Cox who receives one brief mention when Catherine arrives at court, is real. Most notable though, are her siblings and half-siblings, who all enjoyed elevated status during her time as queen consort but are strangely missing from many biographies.

Her half-sister, Lady Isabel Baynton, is one particular case. She is named as being in attendance on the disgraced queen at Syon Abbey during Catherine's incarceration and is also listed as one of her ladies-in-waiting. Isabel's husband, Sir Edward Baynton, was vice-chamberlain to Catherine. He also held this position for Anne Boleyn and Anne of Cleves. During Jane Seymour's reign, he was her Master of the Horse and Isabel was one of the women who walked in Jane's funeral procession. They attended the christening of Edward VI and were briefly guardians to the princesses, Mary and Elizabeth. Yet this Tudor power-couple are difficult to find in any biographies.

Mrs Helen Page is also a real person and Catherine did plead for clemency for her. The story concerning Helen's daughter,